RAMS HEAD

For Aandrea Carter,

my beloved sister-friend

and the inspiration behind this story.

You are a wonder.

APRIL 1919

CHAPTER ONE

In two days' time, I will be on Shelter Island. Rest assured, between William and me, we will get everything started. I can do this.

Your aunt's piano has been delivered and so has Lucille's gilt-framed mirror. Can you imagine how top-drawer the place will be? I can see it now – all sorts of society people arriving with their many trunks, taking in the serenity of the water views, dining on the veranda, playing chess in the lounge, maybe enjoying a game of croquet on the lawn —apparently a favorite among the upper crust. We must learn how to play. I am having some new dresses made, as I need to fit into this beautiful picture. You'll need a suit at the very least. And let's not forget the border collie you promised. I was thinking of calling him Mike – is that crazy? He will round up the sheep we plan to have. We will plant a garden right away to be self-sufficient as possible. Given how remote the inn is, we'll need to be.

Davidson, I know you're on your way back. That nothing could keep you away. I keep reliving our last night in bed, talking, making love, planning,
making love again, envisioning our inn. You held me and said as long as you have breath in your body, you would come back. I knew it then, and I know it now. I just wonder how long it will be.

"Do you like spontaneous?" Davidson had asked Carter that first night they met. They were walking home from a dinner party at a mutual friend's Manhattan townhouse. It was a warm, early June evening in 1917, almost three years after she arrived in New York.

"Absolutely!" Carter answered, because it was true.

"Are you free tomorrow?"

She made her own hours as a suffragist organizer, so yes, she was free.

"I'll collect you at 9 am."

"To do what?"

"You said you like spontaneous. I assume that includes surprises." He wore a mischievous smile.

"Yes, but do I pack a bathing costume or a dance dress?"

"Both."

Any other woman would have turned him down. It wasn't proper to be alone with a man, much less follow him to parts unknown. Carter was not any other woman, however. She was game for most anything and was guided by her gut about people. She trusted Davidson the minute she met him in her friend Bertha's parlor. He had a familiar look about him, as if she had known him forever. His hooded eyes seemed to have a light in them, bemused, as he looked at her, and she liked that he wore his dark brown hair longer than the fashion and somewhat unkempt at that. His suit was a bit worn, but clean. It all added up to a rugged man too busy to indulge in vanity. A man's man, like the kind she grew up with in Iowa. New York City men were typically too preened for her taste.

At 9 am the next morning, Davidson had arrived at her door, flashing a smile that sent a charge through her. He held a picnic basket and urged her not to ask questions. So she didn't, much as she burned with curiosity. She carried a valise with a bathing costume and a change of dress.

After a brief yellow taxi ride to New York Harbor, she found herself on a small, one-cabin boat, the name *Spinnaker* painted on its side. "My pleasure boat," Davidson explained. They set sail up the Hudson River. It was her first time on a boat of any size, a fact she hadn't mentioned. At first, she was unsteady on her feet, but soon she became swept up in the excitement of the day and the glorious breeze that caressed her face and lifted her fine hair. The freedom felt exhilarating. Life was to be lived, she told herself.

Until the motor sputtered and stopped. And there was no more breeze.

"Davidson? Are we going to sink? Should we swim to shore?"

"No," he said with a laugh. "Just give me a minute, I'll figure it out." It took far more than a minute. He called her over to help, asking her to hand him this or that tool or gadget. Every time he thought he solved the problem, he would retest the motor. But nothing,

"Davidson, I'm a great swimmer if need be."

"I've built these motors from scratch. They're not complicated and don't just die. I am not the kind of man who gives up." Sweat beaded his brow, and he kept at it, until finally, maybe 45 minutes later, the motor started again, a steady mechanical hum filling the air. He rinsed his greasy hands in the river and dried them with a tattered towel. "I had to jerry-rig a connection, so let's bring her back if you don't mind. We'll have our picnic on the island of Manhattan instead."

So that's what they did. It was one of those June days that went on forever. They settled on an old plaid blanket in Battery Park, not far from the harbor.

"Is this where you take all the girls? Carter asked.

"Just you," he said without smiling. "It's one of my favorite spots, and it feels good to share it with someone special."

"How can I be special? You don't know me."

"That's where you're wrong. I know special when I see it."

Flushed, Carter asked what was in the basket, and Davidson took out their lunch, as purchased and wrapped from a favorite sandwich shop by his apartment. He also produced a bottle of white wine and two glasses.

"This wine may soon be contraband if some states have their way," Carter said, watching him pour and hand her a glass.

"For now it's legal. I'd never ask you to do something illegal on our first date. Fourth maybe..."

"I reserve the right to slap you in that case," she laughed.

"Ouch!" He playfully fell down on the blanket. He then sat up, his expression serious. "You'd just have to say no, darling. I honor boundaries."

The kindness in his eyes made her feel safe. She prided herself on reading people. This was a man she could trust.

They talked long into the afternoon, until the sun was beginning to lower in the sky, casting long shadows on them long most of the other picnic groups had packed up and left. Like Carter, Davidson was on his own, with only an aunt and sister who lived in Michigan whom he didn't see that often. Also, like Carter, he had no plans to marry, at least not any time soon. At 29, he was traveling too much, he explained. Fine with Carter, who loved her independence and who had signed up for suffrage work, not only because the vote was essential, but because of the promise of traveling. She loved the camaraderie, as well as the sense of purpose. It enraged her to think how little power women had in this world.

She had grown up *Priscilla* Carter, an only child outside Des Moines, Iowa. Her father had been a respected lawyer, before he died in a carriage accident when she was a toddler. Her mother MaryLynn, a sunny and independent spirit, had no interest in marrying again. "You only get one great love in a lifetime, and I've had mine," she told Priscilla. "You'll have yours, too. Just wait."

To make ends meet after her husband's death, MaryLynn worked as a bookkeeper for Malcolm Roach, the town's only accountant. Mr. Roach had been a friend of Priscilla's father and was generous with MaryLynn. The only problem was he liked to drink at lunch and became verbally abusive when he returned to the office. This behavior increased over the ten years MaryLynn worked for him. She would come home early after what she called his "incidents." He always apologized the next day.

"The liquor that makes him act that way," MaryLynn said. Then one day, she suddenly quit and refused to say what led to her decision.

"The time had come, that's all," her mother offered by way of explanation. "I feel sorry for Mr. Roach. May God look out for him." Priscilla suspected the verbal abuse had turned physical. Religious in the best sense, her mother forgave everyone who crossed her, a trait Priscilla had trouble with. Soon after leaving Mr. Roach's employ, MaryLynn landed a bookkeeping position at the local infirmary, which suited her far more than being alone in an office. The only problem was the many germs circulating in the air.

At twelve, Priscilla's was unusually tall for her age – 5 feet, 7 inches already — causing people to think she was older than her years. Her icy blond hair and blue eyes made men all too happy to believe it. She was hired for an after-school job at a local grocery store, first in the stock room, then as a cashier. One evening, the owner cornered her menacingly in one of the back aisles. She grabbed a jar of tomato paste off the shelf and hit him with it, not waiting to see the mess it made as it crashed and splattered on the floor. She ran out of the store, never to return, not even to collect her weekly wage.

Priscilla moved onto similar jobs to contribute to the household. It seemed there were always handsy men about, so her defenses were constantly up. The two Carters made just enough to keep their small family going. The house they lived in had been fully paid for before Priscilla's father died, but they owned little else. Despite the financial hardship, Priscilla learned from her mother never to feel sorry for herself.

"If Father hadn't died, everything would have been so different," Priscilla said wistfully one night after a familiar dinner of eggs and beans.

"I don't see it that way," her mother answered. "If I hadn't met Father, I would never have known such wonderful love, his or yours. I thank God for that and feel fortunate your father lived at all."

Priscilla shared her mother's positive disposition, but she wasn't nearly as accepting of her fate. She was a fighter. She wanted the easy, breezy life she imagined other girls living – one with enough money and autonomy to shape her future. Priscilla felt like the perennial outsider looking in, waiting to be tapped on the shoulder and invited to the party.

Then she found her own party. One Saturday morning, Priscilla attended a local suffrage meeting. The group had been posting flyers all around Des Moines looking for volunteers. The connection was immediate. She soon learned that Iowa was a heated battleground for the women's vote. Priscilla loved the passion of the women she met. Iowan suffragists were creative in getting the word out – stamps, songs, entertainment, whatever it took.

"The women seem angry to me," her mother said, after going to a local meeting to see what Priscilla was involved in. "How will they ever meet husbands if they're always ranting at everyone? Men like to be in charge. They are better suited for it."

"Or so they've told us," Priscilla said, rolling her eyes. "We're just asking for the vote, to have a say in our lives. Surely you agree with that."

"Yes, but not with such hostility. It's unfeminine."

Priscilla saved her money and took her first out-of-state trip to Washington DC to march with the Iowan Chapter of the Woman's Suffrage Procession. For maximum impact, the rally was scheduled for the day before Woodrow Wilson's 1913 inauguration. Approximately 8000 women marched and over half a million came to watch. Violence was directed against the marchers, but the police did not intervene. Yet the message was heard: women would not be ignored. Priscilla returned to Iowa invigorated; she was determined to help on the national front in any way possible.

Shortly before Christmas the following year, however, MaryLynn became sick with a flu she brought home from the infirmary, one she could not shake. After a tortuous month, MaryLynn finally succumbed. By then Priscilla was nineteen years old, and for the first time, felt truly alone.

It was at another suffragist rally that she heard a speech by Carrie Chapman Catt, a native Iowan and the president of the National American Woman Suffrage Association.

"Service to a just cause rewards the worker with more real happiness and satisfaction than any other venture of life," Catt said. This appeal renewed Priscilla's commitment. She soon became known as P. Carter, prompted in part by the sale of her parents' home. The broker said it would be easier to get her price if the out-of-town buyers thought the seller was a man as opposed to a single woman. She hated the name Priscilla anyway. After the sale, she dropped the P and moved to New York, where Catt believed the focus of the suffrage fight to be vital.

Carter traveled all over the state, though she kept a room in a Madison Avenue boarding house in Manhattan. One of Catt's strategies was to recruit wealthy members of the woman's club movement, born of social and literary gatherings – a mutually beneficial marriage of those in the trenches and those with money and influence. Carter was intrigued by this world of fine china and beautiful clothes. It wasn't the wealth that seduced her, per se, but the quiet power and independence that came with it.

An affluent socialite, Bertha Krantz, introduced her to Davidson. "Come to dinner, it will be fun! You'll meet new people," Bertha had said. Evidenced by her magenta short hair, Bertha was a bit outrageous — a true bohemian, known for her eclectic salon gatherings. Carter looked up to Bertha.

Meeting Davidson changed everything for Carter. That first picnic date never really ended, their connection immediate and strong. That bond hadn't wavered in the year they were together. She could be herself, never worrying about whether she was using the proper fork or finding the right word to express herself. He was smart and engaging, and it was a relief as much as challenge to be with him. This was her one great love, and she knew it.

After seeing an advertisement for inexpensive property on Shelter Island, Carter came up with the idea of opening an inn. She thought it a clever way to keep Davidson on land, though still near the sea he adored. He loved the idea and immediately set to planning and building. A small island nestled between the north and south forks of eastern Long Island, Shelter Island was a port as well as a popular summer destination for wealthy New Yorkers. The inn business, it would seem, was ready made.

However, 1917 was proving to be a bittersweet year. On November 6th, New York women won the right to vote which brought joyous celebration, both on the streets and in fancy drawing rooms across the city. Carter felt that everything was going right in her life—winning the vote, Davidson's enthusiasm about the inn. He was determined to build it as quickly as possible because the United States was quickly deploying troops to Europe for the Great War, and he feared it was only a matter of time before he was called to duty.

"We should marry right away," he said to Carter, caressing her face in bed after a night of passion.

"I want to get married at our inn, after you return," she told him. She did not want the threat of war to be the motivation for their nuptials. He reluctantly agreed but insisted on putting the deed to the inn in her name, as well as designating her a co-signer on his bank account. "Just in case," he had said. Fortunately, he managed to spend the rest of the year without being called into service.

In 1918, however, the Spanish Flu spread yet another kind of fear. After watching her mother die of influenza, this new virulent strain scared her, and she felt extremely protective toward Davidson.

"I am not kidding. We need to protect ourselves," she said to him, as they walked through Madison Square Park in the evening. She badgered Davidson to adhere to all the recommended precautions – covering one's nose and mouth, not using utensils that haven't been boiled clean, avoiding public transportation and crowds of any sort, and seeking fresh air when and where possible. To her, that made moving to the fresh air of Shelter Island all the more urgent.

"We'll have sheep and get a border collie to round them up," she said, excitedly imagining their pastoral future.

He laughed. "If that's what you want, that's what we'll have."

But Davidson was drafted into the Navy in May of 1918. He returned when the war ended six months later. Their reunion was joyful but brief; after the start of the new year, he set sail on a commercial voyage to Barbados to earn money for the inn. He hadn't been heard from since.

CHAPTER TWO

"What kind of name is Carter?" Lucille Nesbit inquired when they were first introduced in her Fifth Avenue home. It was 1916, and Lucille was hosting a gathering of fellow members of a prominent New York women's club and a leading group of national suffragists. Lucille's drawing room was crowded, but Carter stood out above the rest with her pale hair and notable stature.

"A far superior one to Priscilla, my given name," Carter said. "When I was young, people would shorten it to Cilly or, even worse, Prissy."

"Fair enough. But Carter sounds like a man – and you only use the one name?"

"Yes. It's served me well in correspondence, especially when making introductions before I meet people."

"They must be dumbstruck when they see you," Lucille said. "And maybe even upset they were deceived?"

"It gets cleared up quickly – *after* I have my foot in the door."

Lucille laughed. "I like you, Miss Carter. You are quite the character. I do hope we can become friends." She extended her hand.

In three years' time, the two blondes became an unlikely duo: Lucille, the strawberry blonde of the two, was a soft-spoken and possessed a fine-boned beauty, whereas Carter was fearless as she was tall, with her bootstraps permanently pulled up. Opposite as could be, the two women formed a friendship so heartfelt they called each other sister-friend – an homage to the fact neither had an actual sister, or a brother for that matter. They had another thing in common: both lived contrary to convention for their day. At 26, Lucille was married but childless, and Carter, at 25, was single.

Lucille thought Carter was provocative, even scandalous at times. Carter constantly challenged the suffragists' New York chapter with outrageous ideas, like organizing a protest outside the townhouse of the governor's girlfriend when he was visiting Manhattan. Lucille envied Carter's willingness to push boundaries.

But now, opening an inn on her own on an isolated island? That was a whole other level of audaciousness.

"No, no, no, I must be misunderstanding," Lucille said to her dear friend. "Carter, you can't mean to move to Shelter Island by yourself."

"That's exactly what I'm doing." Carter answered, calmly placing her teacup on its saucer. They were in their favorite dress salon, Blanc Couture, waiting for Carter's turn to be measured. Given her six-foot height, Carter's custom-made dresses were less a luxury than a necessity. "The war is over, and people are picking up the pieces of their lives. Families will be looking for a respite in the warm months ahead. The inn is already built. Why not take advantage of it?"

Before Lucille could object further, Carter continued, "I don't have a lot of options, do I? I must get the inn up and running before the summer. I need to make money while I wait for Davidson."

It was a delicate subject. As far as Lucille was concerned—and most others as well—Davidson Surrey was never coming back. The merchant captain's ship had capsized two and a half months earlier, three miles off the northwestern coast of Barbados. Cargo, debris, and a number of bodies washed ashore, leaving little doubt of the ship's fate and that of the twelve men aboard. A memorial took place a month later for the New York members of the crew. Carter initially refused to go but relented out of respect for the lost souls who'd been identified. Yet without his remains, she would not allow Davidson's name to be recited at the memorial or eulogized in any way. Carter chose not to contact his aunt and sister in Michigan as she felt she had nothing solid to report, and they did not keep up with his travels in any event.

But Lucille knew Carter was running out of money, despite her access to Davidson's bank account. The inn's final construction costs were much higher than budgeted, and retaining her room at the women's boarding house in Manhattan was draining what savings she had.

"You're the one who keeps telling me I need to plan for a life without Davidson," Carter said, her eyes welling up. "Consider this a first step."

Lucille exhaled. "What can I do to help? I'm all yours – for the next three months, anyway."

"Right, that's when Mr. Perfect returns. I'm still not sure how you got out of joining him." Henry Nesbit left for London the previous weekend with his young associate Vance Broder. Now that the war was over, Henry was looking to expand his family's steel business overseas, where there had already been a great deal of interest before the war.

"I just said no, and remarkably it worked. Henry knows I don't fare well on ships. And I didn't care to isolate myself in a London hotel for long stretches of time. Instead, I'm here with you. I thought we would be having fun in New York City, but apparently, I will be heading to Shelter Island to help you open an inn."

"Hooray!" Carter stood up clapping, not caring who heard. "Think of the adventure we'll have!"

Carter left the dressmaker's shop an hour after Lucille, having ordered three Laurent Blanc dresses, while purchasing hats, a couple of shawls and a pair of gloves. It was an indulgent purchase, but Carter was determined to look the part of the elegant proprietress. Confident as she sounded to Lucille, answering Madame Blanc's many questions pierced through her bravado.

Genevieve Blanc, a petite brunette with piercing green eyes, was the couturier's wife, the expert seamstress of the shop. Carter always sensed there was more of a story to her than just a woman who pinned you into an elegant bespoke dress. All she knew about Genevieve was that she was born in Paris and raised by a single mother, also a seamstress, who imparted her expertise to her daughter. After her mother died, Genevieve married the couturier Laurent Blanc, and the two came to America to open his shop, Blanc Couture. Her English was excellent, and all the women adored her, including Carter and Lucille.

"Do you have a caretaker? Do you have employees?" Madame Blanc asked.

"Oh yes. Davidson hired this terrific man, a Mr. William Smythe, as Rams Head's general manager. He oversaw the construction and is staying on to run the place. He's a local and knows the island inside and out."

"It is just the two of you at this inn?"

"He is honorable, if that's what you mean. A gentleman." The truth was, she knew little about William, other than he kept to himself, but Davidson said he was extremely trustworthy.

"Thank goodness, but I was not thinking about that. No, I mean will just the two of you be the only workers on this property? Who will cook? Who will serve? Who will clean? Do you have a bartender? Waiters? Housekeepers? Repairmen? What happens when a shipload of people arrive all at once? Can you employ good people on an island? Where will they live?" The questions went on in an endless stream.

Madame Blanc was a shrewd one. Carter admittedly hadn't thought it all through. She'd been to the island several times with Davidson throughout the planning and much of the construction before he left for the war and again when he returned. She knew his plans and dreams for the inn, but assumed he had all the practical considerations mapped out as well. He was like that – smart, deliberate, practical, always thinking ahead. As a sea captain, he had to have his boat meticulously prepared before setting sail. It was its own little village, he once said to her. One had to foresee every emergency that could crop up on a personnel level as well as a navigational one. He would have run the inn brilliantly. No, he *will* run it brilliantly, Carter corrected herself. She just needed to get it operational enough until he could take over.

Blanc Couture packages in hand, Carter walked to the boarding house on Madison Avenue, determined as ever. Carter refused to believe she would lose Davidson after losing her father and then her mother. God couldn't be that cruel. Davidson would survive any shipwreck. This is something she knew.

In the meantime, she would put all her energy into Rams Head. Davidson had named the inn after Ram Island, where it was sited. Before he left, he had reviewed everything with her in detail – the business plans, the many reasons it would do well. He planned to build them a house adjacent to the inn, sharing the same shoreline.

In the couple of months or so since the news of the shipwreck, Carter had visited Rams Head twice. The last time was for a week, and William Smythe made sure she was treated well, despite the inevitable construction mess. Adam Smythe, William's brother, was the cook for the construction crew and took care of her meals, which were exceptionally good. Could he stay on? His wife and daughters helped with post-construction cleaning, so maybe they too could remain. Or perhaps she should be hiring employees from New York City and housing them in the small staff rooms on the top floor.

Carter had already thrown herself into decorating the inn, which currently was being painted and the floors finished. It had nothing by way of furniture, so she arranged for a shipping container of furnishings and accessories she had stored from her mother's house to arrive roughly when she did, including lamps, clocks, bed frames and nightstands. She ordered new tables and chairs for the restaurant as well as linens, tableware, stemware, silverware, and a long list of other items. Nothing fancy, but suitable. All the shopping, sourcing, and ordering had taken up so much of her time she hadn't focused on staffing in any significant way.

Carter also hadn't focused on the finances — and she was burning through money by the day. The proceeds from the sale of her parents' house were nearly gone. Davidson gave her access to what seemed like a small fortune, but that disappeared rapidly in completing the inn.

He had fully expected to return with a windfall from the Barbados voyage.

When pressed for answers to Madame Blanc's many questions, she answered, "I am heading out to Rams Head presently, and either problems will solve themselves, or I will solve them in a clever way. That is what we women do. We figure it out."

Brave words, but not heartfelt ones. Despite Lucille's promise to accompany her, Carter, once again, felt completely on her own — and, if she were honest with herself, fearful of what lay ahead.

CHAPTER THREE

Carter and Lucille sat facing one another on the Long Island Railroad train, their trunks in another car. While there were steam ferries that ran directly from New York City to the island, they ran infrequently this time of year. Instead, the friends had a long land journey, which included changing trains at Bridgehampton to head north to Sag Harbor. From there, a 30 to 45-minute boat ride to the eastern side of Shelter Island, or more precisely Ram Island, where the inn was.

Ram Island and its neighboring Little Ram Island were separated from Shelter Island during high tide to become distinct land masses. During low tide, a causeway connected the three islands, with Coecles Harbor on one side, Gardiner's Bay on the other. Local legend had it that when the tides allowed, farmers walked their rams and sheep to the smaller "Ram" islands to protect them from predators that inhabited the larger one. It's this lore that prompted Carter's desire for sheep, to bring them back to the island in homage of the past.

"Can you believe this?" Carter said. "I no longer live in Manhattan. Just Shelter Island."

"You'll always have a place with us, you know that. Henry adores you."

The girlfriends were their usual study in contrasts: Carter wore a fuchsia linen shirtdress with a lime-green satin sash at the waist; Lucille, a taupe raw silk tucked-and-pleated traveling suit. Margaret O'Reilly, Lucille's personal maid sat behind them, dressed in a tailored navy dress. Lucille had debated whether to bring Margaret along, but Margaret had begged to come. Besides, it would be useful to have an extra pair of hands at the inn.

"I feel like I've taken a major step to my life with Davidson." Carter smiled, not waiting for Lucille's polite, but sad "hmmmm."

"You'll love this place, Lucille. It has lots of property and its very own beach. The view alone!"

"I know nothing about Shelter Island." Lucille was from Chicago and had only lived in New York for five years. She and Henry had visited Southampton once or twice, but she knew little about other parts of Long Island.

"There's not a lot to know," Carter said. "It's small and not many people live there — under a thousand – though that's changing with more summer cottages sprouting up."

The 8,000-acre Shelter Island was originally a grant from King Charles and was eventually sold to to Nathaniel Sylvester, an English sugar merchant in 1652. West Indies and indigenous Indian slaves worked his plantation and made oak barrels for sugar cane operations in Barbados. His son's family sold the Ram Islands in 1728 to the Tuthill family. The small islands remained fairly undeveloped and wild, even as Shelter Island's overall population was growing.

"Sounds a little backwater, no?"

"Not at all. Shelter Island was a hopping place for nearly half a century. There was a grand hotel, Manhansett House, built in the 1870s, named after the island's original tribe. It had a golf course, tennis courts and a dance hall. People still talk about the place. It even had its own port; J.P. Morgan's yacht was a regular fixture there."

"Was?"

"Yes, the hotel was struck by lightning ten years ago and burned to the ground. But it introduced Shelter Island to New York high society. You and Henry would have stayed there for sure."

"We are not high society." Lucille playfully hit her friend.

"Far more than Davidson and I are," Carter smiled. "We're hoping to bring back high society to the inn — on a much smaller scale, of course."

Carter didn't know anyone who lived on the island. She'd heard of a number of prominent families who each own hundreds of acres, such as the Sylvesters, the island's founding family, as well as Francis Marion Smith, who made his fortune from mining, and Artemas Ward, who pioneered mass advertising. Oh, and Colonel Randall Perry, a railroad magnate. Davidson assured her the island was also an active port for various agricultural industries, so there would be restaurant and inn traffic for sure.

"Shelter Island sounds magical. I cannot wait to see it," Lucille said.

"I love your enthusiasm. I promise we will enjoy ourselves – no parents, no men. We make the rules."

Lucille smiled. "Make sure you stockpile the spirits – Henry says everywhere, New York included, will be dry in less than a year."

On January 16th, just three months earlier, the 18th Amendment had been approved by 36 states out of 48 states, the requisite number for ratification. The amendment expressly stated that it would become affective one year after ratification, which gave the government time to put enforcement in place.

Carter had met with members of the Woman's Christian Temperance Union and came to see their point about alcohol: so many men drink away their earnings and then come home and beat their wives and children. Women will never be able to rise if they are under attack in their own homes.

"I never thought it would happen," Carter said. "But still, this feels extreme; it didn't have to be an all-out assault on alcohol. Davidson has been transporting spirits on his ship for as long as he's owned it."

"Imagine the government coming into your home and telling you what you can drink. Or what you may serve at your inn."

"They won't come into your home, but they will make it impossible to buy alcohol once you've used up what you have. The inn won't be able to serve it in any event."

"Drats. I'm accustomed to having wine with dinner," Lucille said.

"And you will here too, I promise. I'm sure Davidson has made sure we're well stocked, if only for you and me."

The two friends laughed. Lucille hoped Margaret wasn't listening, as she tried to keep up appearances, especially with her staff.

Once they arrived at Sag Harbor station, Carter flagged down a porter who helped them with their trunks. He brought them to Captain Graham, a local who regularly ferried people and supplies between the mainland and Shelter Island. His *Swisher* was a private hire, as opposed to the main South Ferry, which had specific hours of operation and did not go to individual docks.

Carter was grateful the water was smooth that day, given Lucille's propensity for nausea at sea. Still, thirty or so minutes later, Lucille was grateful to have arrived at the dock of the inn. The were met by William Smythe, who had with him two men to help carry the ladies' trunks. Carter brought as much as she could on this trip, since she was moving here to stay. Lucille never traveled without a large amount of clothes, books and personal items. And of course, Margaret had her own valise.

As the men loaded the trunks onto trolleys, the three women drank in the site of the stately new inn — a long, mostly two-story building, shingled in cedar and accented with white window frames and doors. The third floor, which did not span the whole building, was centered over the structure with dormer windows overlooking the grounds — those smaller rooms were reserved for staff, Carter said. A long veranda fronted most of the inn for waterside dining and was crowned with a marine blue-and-white striped awning for shade.

The inn was situated atop a grassy hill, which gave it a grand feeling, causing the dockside and beach viewer to look up at it. Most of the property's four and half acres, Carter explained was waterside. Enormous oak trees dotted the lawn, offering shade to the many groupings of generously proportioned white Adirondack chairs.

"William, I'm impressed," Carter said. "The chairs have arrived! And so much has been done since I was last here. I love the awning — so nautical in feeling."

"It's coming along, Miss Carter," he said between grunts as he helped place trunks onto the cart. "We still have a way to go. We need to speak privately once you get settled in."

A trim dark-haired man in his early thirties, William was all business in his demeanor, which made him difficult to read. His stoic gaze traveled slowly from the men to Lucille and Margaret, giving nothing away. Davidson was grateful to have William, as he was efficient and on top of every detail. He was a Shelter Island native, another huge plus.

"I'm sure there's still much to be done," she said to William. "As you said, let us get settled in. For now, I want to focus on all that *has* been done."

The three women left the men to the trunks, as they climbed the steep grassy incline to the inn.

"Oh, it's marvelous, Carter," Lucille said, hand on her chest.

Margaret nodded vigorously as Lucille continued. "What you've done in such a short time is remarkable."

"You mean what Davidson's done.

He organized most of it before he left."

"Yes. But please give yourself credit for carrying it through."

"We'll, it's all according to his plan. I can't wait for him to see how well this is turning out."

Lucille smiled, clearly not wanting to pursue the Davidson discussion, which was fine with Carter.

The interior of Rams Head was one delight after another: the fireplace in the foyer, the multi-paneled glass doors that led to the veranda, the enormous dining room, flanked by fireplaces at both ends. Then there was the cozy lounge that housed the long mahogany bar, a room which Carter and Lucille agreed should be thought of as a small dining room in light of the impending alcohol ban. Just off the lounge, there was a stone-floored "Garden Room," which had three windowed walls that looked out over the inn's greenery.

The rooms were empty except for Davidson's gleaming baby grand piano in the dining room. It had been in his family, and he had it shipped in from Michigan to New York via the Erie Canal. Carter smiled at the sight of it. She saw Lucille's concern at the empty rooms.

"The furniture comes this week, so this will all make better sense," Carter said.

"What about our rooms? Are there beds?" Lucille's panic was evident in the question.

"Lucille, you said you were up for an adventure."

Even Margaret had to suppress a smile at the idea of Mrs. Nesbit sleeping on the floor.

Two and a half weeks later, much had been accomplished — the inn was up and running, albeit with a long checklist of items to complete. The main furniture shipment had arrived, and Carter was able to furnish the seventeen guest rooms, with the promise of finer, more detailed decorating to come. Carter and Lucille agreed they'd keep the downstairs blue and white to simplify the décor, as the blues would echo the luminous sky and water view surrounding the inn. Blue was also known to repel mosquitos, which was helpful for the months ahead. Every day brought small and big problems to solve. But word was out that the inn was open, and there was a small, but steady stream of people coming in and out, though many were just curious to meet the striking new owner.

Meanwhile, Carter and Lucille were delighting in observing their new guests. Given that it was the breakfast hour, those present must have stayed overnight. There were three men at one table, all casually but finely dressed. "Sea captains or business owners," the two agreed. A sweet-looking young couple sat at another table. "Bet they're building a summer house here," Carter said.

"Oh look, Carter, it's that stylish woman Miss Langley," Lucille said. "It appears she's checking out. Even her tapestry traveling case is elegant." The two friends observed the woman from the bar lounge where a breakfast buffet served the handful of guests staying at the inn.

"Isn't it though? She is just the kind of clientele we want here. This has all come together so smoothly, hasn't it?"

Chef Adam turned out to be a resourceful cook and was able to create a daily menu of offerings using whatever was available by land or sea. That he happened to be William's brother was yet another plus. Moreover, Carter discovered William was a beekeeper, the fresh honey from which he regularly donated to the inn. As hoped, Miriam, Adam's wife, agreed to come on as the receptionist and dining room manager, and their two teenage daughters, Cora and Dorothy, worked as chambermaids. Cora just needed to give notice to the family she was currently serving as a housekeeper in Oyster Bay, further up Long Island. Given how concerned Carter was about staffing, she was grateful to have this trusted family on board. She couldn't help but think Davidson was somehow behind her good fortune, if only in spirit.

Margaret was also willing to help out as much as she could. Since Lucille didn't require a personal maid or dresser at Rams Head, Margaret offered to do any and everything to insure she wouldn't be sent back to Manhattan. With her infectious smile and open demeanor, Margaret had already made a number of friends on Shelter Island during her various runs to the general store in town, including that of a handsome police officer she had crossed paths with twice. Seeing him again was more motivation to stay on the island. Margaret got along well with the Smythe brothers, as well as with Adam's wife Miriam and their daughters. The young women formed a first-rate serving and cleaning team, so Margaret's place here was assured – at least for a while.

Regarding the inn's finances, Carter reviewed the ledgers with William, which admittedly were disheartening. An unexpected tax bill was due immediately, which Carter paid out of her own savings, shrinking her reserve even further. William tended toward worry, which Carter appreciated. Someone had to keep a close watch on the numbers.

Fortunately, however, the restaurant and bar were starting to fill up for lunch and dinner with an interesting mix: locals, seaman living on their ships, traveling merchants, and a handful of people building summer homes nearby. A few stayed at the inn as well. It helped that the two nearest hotels, the upscale Empire House and the smaller Mayfair, were closed until Memorial Day.

Lucille and Carter noted that this stunning woman in the lobby was in a class all her own; they couldn't quite pin her down. In her early twenties, stylishly dressed and with golden blond hair, she was as poised as anyone who had ever entered Lucille's ballroom. She had been at the inn for two nights. But she was traveling alone, which was unusual for such a lady. Carter had introduced herself to Miss Langley the afternoon she had arrived. In response to Carter's few polite questions, Miss Langley's smile and curt answers made clear she was not there to make friends – at least not with Carter or Lucille. Lucille speculated that Miss Langley had left her husband and was hiding out at Rams Head, perhaps having an affair with the man she had met both evenings for dinner. Carter laughed that Lucille had been reading too many novels.

"I'm going to say goodbye to her," Carter said. Before she could stand, Miss Langley was heading over to their table as her trunk was being wheeled down to the dock.

"Miss Carter," Miss Langley greeted, also tilting her head at Lucille. "I've so enjoyed my stay, thank you." The young woman extended her hand, which Carter readily accepted. She felt something in the handshake.

"You're most welcome," Carter said, confused. "Didn't you settle up at the front desk?"

"Yes, but this is for you," Miss Langley spoke in a measured voice. "Again, thank you. I look forward to my return and hope to bring some friends next time."

"Oh, please do," Carter answered. "We would warmly welcome any of your friends. We're a new establishment and our only advertisement is through word of mouth."

"Naturally." Miss Langley nodded at both women and swiftly left before anything else could be said.

"We didn't learn her story," Lucille frowned. "I assume she left you her calling card?"

Carter opened her palm to a small envelope. Inside was a crisp ten-dollar bill.

"It's cash!" Lucille gasped. "Why would she give you money? Do people usually tip innkeepers?"

"I don't know," Carter said. "But what a lovely gesture. Especially since she knows I'm a new owner."

"That must be it," Lucille agreed. Without speaking, they both went to the window to watch Miss Langley make her way to the dock to where a private boat awaited.

CHAPTER FOUR

Just a few mornings later, another glamorous, yet unexpected guest arrived: Madame Blanc. Carter stood from her seat she had by the fireplace. "Hello! To what do we owe this honor?"

"I have come with your finished dresses!" Madame Blanc announced heartily, removing her wide brim feathered hat, as she stepped into the lounge.

Carter was alone, as Lucille was writing in her room, as she often did after their morning coffee.

"What a delight! Come sit down, Madame Blanc. Let us get you some tea," Carter said with a quick nod to Miriam as she led the Frenchwoman to the Garden Room just beyond the lounge. The sunny, intimate chamber was proving the ideal place to have private conversations. Reflecting the ample sunlight of its three windowed walls, the fourth wall now held an enormous gilt-framed mirror, that Lucille had gifted to the inn from her own home and had shipped over. The room's glass-paneled door separated it from the lounge, lending a modicum of privacy, while not being confining. The two women sat in tufted blue and white chairs that faced one another.

"Oh Miss Carter, this place is more beautiful than I imagined." Madame Blanc's hand swept the air. "The walk from the dock alone!"

"I'll give you a full tour in a moment, but first you need to tell me why you personally brought the dresses. You never leave the shop."

The petite woman bit her lip. "First, please call me Genevieve."

"If you call me Carter."

The dressmaker nodded. "I left more than the shop. I left Monsieur Blanc, Laurent, too." She exhaled. "I did not know where to go. I will do anything you need here – I sew, I keep books, I cook..."

"Goodness. Are you sure it's not just a disagreement that will pass?"

"No. I will not go back to him, *ever.*" She said the last word so fiercely that Carter knew not to press.

"I'm glad you came." Carter touched Genevieve's hand. "We have the room, and many ways you can pitch in. Mrs. Nesbit will be thrilled as I am to see you."

"Thank you," Genevieve said, giving way to tears. She looked away when Miriam entered the room and set down the tea between them.

"Please close the door behind you, Mrs. Smythe," Carter said quietly. "Thank you."

Carter poured the tea and waited for Genevieve to speak.

"My marriage has been a horror from the start. As soon as Laurent learned of my design and sewing skills, he invented himself. His name is Larry White from New Jersey. He is not French."

37

"Oh." Carter tried to keep the shock from her face.

"He was an American tourist when we met. He told me lies about his life in New York. My mother had just died. I was innocent and young and fell for him — and I believed the stories he told me."

"He can be charming, I know. He has that way about him," Carter said.

Genevieve let out a sharp laugh. "When he wants something, yes. As soon as we married, Laurent revealed himself. He waited until we were sailing to New York when he first lifted his hand to me. He told me I was his property — and his ticket to a new life. He would be a couturier, and I would create the clothes."

Carter shook her head, still finding it hard to believe. And yet believable, too. She never cared for Laurent, as there was always something stagey about his demeanor. Now she knew she wasn't imagining it. "You could have left him sooner, years ago. Everyone loves you."

"And go where? With what money? My English was not good then." She looked away, her lip trembling. "The only job I could get is factory work. Laurent loved to tease me about that. I picked up fabric and other bits at those factories. I saw the life they offer women. I always came back grateful for the home I had." She straightened and looked directly at Carter. "But now I have left him. I am here."

"You are," Carter smiled. "And he has no power on Ram Island, I can promise you that." Carter's smile quickly

38

left her face. "If there's one thing I despise, it's a bully of a man. I've met too many of them in my brief years on earth. You can imagine the ugly bruisers who showed up at the suffrage marches. I've been jeered at, pushed around, threatened – and worse. I know how to handle the likes of Laurent Blanc."

"Oh, he knows that. Laurent is scared of you."

"Is he? Well, that's good to hear."

"Yes. You are not like the other women we meet in the shop. You are fearless."

"That's kind, but all women have that strength within them. Look at Mrs. Nesbit. She seems reserved on the surface, but there's a spine of steel in there."

"Maybe, but she has Mr. Nesbit and her wealth to protect her. You are on your own. You led so many protests..."

"I was never alone in my work. We traveled in numbers for safety."

"But not all wore flaming red dresses like you. Not many women come to the shop looking for the brightest pinks, purples and reds. Plus, you are very tall – taller than Laurent, and most men."

"Well, not taller than my Davidson. He's six-foot-four—the only man I've ever looked up to," Carter said with a laugh. She then shook her head and heard his voice. *Nothing could keep me away now that I've found you.*

"I wish I had met him."

"Oh, you will," Carter said. "Now let's show you around and get you settled in. I'm anxious to see the new dresses. It's important I look like the kind of guests I want to attract."

After Genevieve had been settled in a room, Carter set out to the dock to see which deliveries had made the day's shipment. She hoped not all of them, as she was short on cash until she could get to her bank in Sag Harbor. She was fortunate there was a branch so close that held both her and Davidson's accounts, but it still entailed a half day's trip to get there and back. Fortunately, Captain Graham, a friend of Davidson's, knew of her budget woes and helped her juggle payments and deliveries as best he could. The expenses were overwhelming. It seemed every day William came to her with yet new and unanticipated bills that needed to be paid at once, as she had no credit and hadn't time to build up good will. Add to that, she had a bevy of neighbors who — resenting the daily water and motor traffic — were looking for ways to shut her down, and they just might succeed if her dwindling bank account didn't beat them to it. She felt everything everything conspiring against her. Even Lucille!

Just the night before when she was affixing the pink lantern to the dock – her signal to Davidson she was there — Lucille accompanied her and gently asked, "Carter let's say Davidson did survive, and I agree there's no certainty he didn't, he may be sick or injured and not in any position to come back and run the inn. And he might have lost his wealth at sea, which was supposed to finance the rest of the inn's construction. Shouldn't you think of what you will do as an alternative? It's not too late to sell this place and stop depleting what savings you have left."

"I'm not selling the inn," Carter said. "It is not mine to sell. It is mine and Davidson's."

"But he put it in your name for your security. He wouldn't want it to be a burden."

Carter clenched her jaw. "*I am not selling our inn,*" she said. Seeing Lucille's hurt expression, she softened. "I know you mean well, Lucille, but I need you to have faith in me. I can do this. *We* can do this."

"But the expenses…"

Carter put up her hand. "I know all about the expenses. I also know something will come to me. I'm sure of it."

Carter now waved to Graham who was waiting for her on the dock. She had insisted he and his teenage sons – his only crew – take their lunch at the bar, while she and Genevieve met. But now he wanted to settle up with Carter before heading back to Sag Harbor.

Carter counted five large crates on the dock. They had already brought up two to the inn. Five more seemed like too many, but then she remembered Genevieve said she brought clothes and presumably other possessions with her. Could that be the difference?

"Miss Carter," Graham said, tipping his hat, as he approached her. A tall, lanky man, he had a weathered face, though she was certain he wasn't all that old. "Thank you for lunch."

"Graham, I wasn't expecting more than two crates today. I'm scared to ask the tally."

"There is no tally."

"Excuse me?"

He stepped closer and spoke softly. "Your account is settled. You just need to hold these crates in your basement."

"I'm not understanding. Whose crates are they?"

"A Mr. Benjamin Goodwin's. He introduced himself at the dock a couple of weeks ago. I spent some time with him. Struck me as a trustworthy fellow — he worked with Davidson. I think they met during the war. I'm not sure. But they were good enough friends for Davidson to confide in him his plans."

"The plans for Rams Head?

"Yes, but also for storing liquor, which is what I reckon is in those extra crates. They're starting to crack down on any kind of large alcohol shipments – the damn government and its laws. When they came to ask about my load, I said it was supplies for your inn, which they knew about."

"What do I say if they come here looking to inspect the crates?"

"No one is coming here. You're above reproach. This is a legitimate business, and every day I'm bringing you more and more supplies, as I did for Davidson. Mr. Goodwin is happy to settle your daily shipment expenses in return for storing his cargo."

Carter bit her lip. This was too easy, and nothing in her life had ever come easily.

Graham continued, his voice reassuring. "Davidson had a special place outfitted in the basement for just this kind of thing."

"He did?"

"Yes. For *his* shipments. Ask William. Seems crazy to waste the space, especially now as the laws are tightening up."

Carter's head spun. She knew Davidson brought back rum and whisky from Barbados – he told her so — but she didn't think the inn was any part of that. Yet Graham was now saying otherwise. That a secret space had been mapped out for it. And that William knew as well. But these crates weren't Davidson's.

"Shouldn't I meet this Mr. Goodwin at the very least?"

"I'm sure he'll want to discuss all this with you. I told you he's a good chap. For now, just take the crates and accept his gift of paying for your deliveries. Come, I'll have my boys bring them to the basement and show you where they're going. We've got to be careful, though. The fewer people who know about this, the better, for all our sakes."

CHAPTER FIVE

That evening, Carter paused and straightened her shoulders in her new violet cotton brocade dress as she descended the main staircase to meet Lucille for dinner. Genevieve would join them later, after she played a few sets at the inn's piano. Genevieve's mother had taught her to play as a child, and Carter insisted on paying her a small sum, and a discreet dish was placed on the piano for tips.

Before joining Lucille at their usual table, Carter surveyed the dining room. She appreciated it was the most crowded to date thanks to a ship that had arrived earlier that day at South Ferry Harbor. The crowd proved that people knew the restaurant was open for business and would only get busier in late spring when the bigger hotels were in full swing. Carter prayed to her parents they wouldn't run out of food this evening. Fortunately, Chef Adam always seemed on top of things– everything to him was simply a shrug, something she adored about him.

Carter noticed a couple by the entrance, waiting to be seated. They were distinctively male, as both were broadly built with angular masculine features — except one of them wore a dress and an old-fashioned lace snood. Carter approached them.

"Good evening, I'm Miss Carter, the proprietress of the inn." They smiled, clearly relieved to see her.

"Good evening to you," the one without the snood said. He spoke with the trace of an accent, one Carter couldn't identify. "I am Alfred Schnedeker, and this is my wife, Edwina Schnedeker. We have been waiting to be seated for perhaps a half an hour or more. I should add that others have been seated who arrived after us."

"My apologies." Carter said. This was an unusual couple to say the least. She heard about men who liked men, but here one was masquerading as a woman – and posing as a wife. No doubt Miriam, who was hostessing that evening, sought to discourage them from dining at the inn. Carter wished to do the same, but having them standing in the lobby, practically greeting people as they entered, wasn't a good alternative. "Please, follow me. I will find you a table."

She led them to a table in the far corner, near the kitchen, and held out the chair facing the wall for *Mrs.* Schnedeker.

Mr. Schnedeker visibly flinched. "Surely you know a lady should be seated to face the room."

Carter was flustered. "My apologies. I am new to owning a restaurant and am not familiar with all the protocols."

"You're a lady, aren't you? I am sure *you've* been seated correctly in the past."

"I'm sure I have. But I'm also sure I hadn't noticed. Please switch seats then, and I'll send a waiter over right away." Normally she would offer a glass of champagne to smooth any ruffled feathers, but she did not want to

45

encourage this couple to linger, much less, return. What would her other patrons think?

Carter instructed George, one of the evening waiters, to please attend to the couple as swiftly as possible. George looked at them and widened his eyes at the prospect, which Carter chose to ignore. "Thank you," she said abruptly.

Exhaling as she moved on, Carter was relieved to see Lucille seated at their usual table, exuding the nonchalant and stately air of a John Singer Sargent portrait. She gleamed in a gold silk dress, the table's small candelabra softly illuminating her fine features as she read a book.

"I've ordered you some white wine and that beef pot pie you love so much," Lucille said, marking her place in the book before setting it down. Carter glanced and saw the title: *Sons and Lovers*.

"Thank you. That's a new new book you're reading, isn't it?" Carter asked, as she sat down. "I love the name." She knew Lucille was trying to read more modern books.

"Oh, it's marvelous, Carter." She glanced down. "D.H. Lawrence. A friend recommended. He's considered scandalous, and even banned in many places! I just finished another book she gave me, *Dubliners* by James Joyce, also new. Irish. Would you like me to lend it to you?"

"Sure, when I have some extra time on my hands." Carter's eyes wandered toward the eccentric couple that George was just now approaching for their order. She noticed a few diners looking at the pair. They must get that everywhere they go, she thought.

Lucille was oblivious to the couple or their plight. "Carter, I just remembered how much blue-and-white Spode china I have in storage, a gift from Henry's mother. She used to throw elaborate dinner parties for dozens of people, which I never will. So, I'm happy to contribute it to the cause. In fact, the more I think about it, I have so much I can give you once I go through our cellar."

The cellar! "That reminds me Lucille, I need to tell you something." She leaned in and lowered her voice. "I'm still trying to make sense of it and what, if anything, I should do." In hushed tones, Carter brought Lucille up to date about Graham, the friend of Davidson's and the crates in her basement.

Lucille was instantly wary. "But you don't know this Mr. Goodwin, do you? How can you trust him?"

"He and Davidson must have been close because he was aware of this secret storage – something even I didn't even know about. You must come and see it."

"This makes me nervous."

"There's more. Apparently, Davidson has been storing his own crates down there. I opened one, and sure enough, it's filled with rum, whiskey, brandy, among other spirits. Davidson knew what was coming. He was always one step ahead."

"Is this legal?" Lucille whispered. "You could get shut down, or worse, if anyone discovers what's there."

"I thought about that. But then, what if this is Davidson's way of taking care of me? I just have to figure out how to turn it into money to help run the inn."

"Let's not mention this to *anyone*," Lucille emphasized.

"You mean I shouldn't share it at the next town meeting?" Carter laughed and Lucille joined in.

Just then, a handsome, dark-haired gentleman appeared at their table.

"Mrs. Nesbit, I thought that was you," he said with a slight bow.

"Goodness, Mr. Bennett, hello." Lucille's expression was one of pleasant surprise. "This is my dear friend Miss Carter, the owner of this beautiful inn."

"Together with my fiancé, Davidson Surrey," Carter corrected, her hand outstretched. "How do you do, Mr. Bennett?" Carter did not want anyone – any man, in particular – to think she was here on her own. She feared it would make her seem vulnerable.

"Mr. Bennett is a friend of Henry's," Lucille explained. "They attended Princeton together."

He and Carter exchanged smiles. "Congratulations on this fine establishment. It's quite impressive, and much needed here on Shelter Island. I'm glad I can stay here should I not have time to return to the city after my ships have been unloaded. I intend to recommend your inn to my associates."

"Thank you so much," Carter said. "Referrals are everything at this stage of our business."

Turning to Lucille, he asked. "Mrs. Nesbit, what brings you here? Is Mr. Nesbit with you?"

"No. Mr. Nesbit is in London on business. I'm fortunate to be spending time here helping my friend as she gets started with this inn." Her smile then fell with concern. "How is your dear wife faring, Mr. Bennett?"

"Not well, I'm afraid. But she is at home in good hands with her caretakers."

"Sadly, Mrs. Bennett has been quite ill for a while," Lucille explained to Carter. To Mr. Bennett, "if there's anything I can do, please let me know. I still have staff at my house while I'm away. I would be all too happy to have them assist your household if needed."

"How kind, thank you." He then asked, "Are you staying here?"

"For a time, yes."

"Fantastic." He bowed his head. "I hope to see more of the two of you."

Lucille held her smile until he was out of earshot.

"Ugh. I didn't count on running into any of Henry's friends."

"Will Henry be upset you're staying here?"

"No, he's pleased I have my time with you while he's away. It's just that I'm enjoying not being a dutiful wife while I'm here. I am my own person."

"Do you not feel that way when Henry's in town?"

"I do when I'm alone with him. But there are social expectations: dinner parties, places we should be, people we should be with, clothes I should wear, boring women I need to befriend. This is just so liberating. And fun!" She let slip a girlish chuckle.

"Speaking of fun," Carter said, "guess who is now seated closest to Genevieve's piano, staring intently at her? Your Mr. Bennett."

Lucille discreetly glanced over.

"Hmmm. His wife Rebecca has long been suffering from a mental infirmity — though no one speaks of it. Of course, if it was he who was sick, Rebecca would be home caring for him every minute of the day. Instead, he's here making eyes at Genevieve. I can't help but wonder why he even needs to be here to greet his ships – surely, he has a crew. My guess is he prefers *not* being with Rebecca. Not that I should judge."

"Oh, judge away. Men have all the advantages. Where to be, whom to be with. Especially men of Henry's station."

Lucille smiled. "That's one worry I don't have. Our relationship is too tender and passionate for another to threaten it in any serious manner."

"That sounds ideal."

"It is, that side of it at least. But Henry wants a proper wife, a woman who loves hosting, who will be content at his side. He has been indulgent of my quiet ways, my love of reading for hours on end. Yet his ambitions require a more socially confident wife. I know that and have promised him I will oblige. Far more than that, however, he wants children. I'm viewing this as the last time I'll be on my own."

Before Carter could respond, the women noticed Mr. Bennett and Genevieve leaving the bar together, heading into the Garden Room.

"Goodness!" Lucille said.

"Goodness is right!" Carter agreed, laughing at Lucille's wide eyes.

Then Carter stopped laughing. First the crates of alcohol. Then that odd couple. Now a runaway wife with someone else's husband. This was far from an auspicious beginning.

CHAPTER SIX

A week later, a bright pink velvet wing chair was sitting in the foyer next to the fireplace. "Carter, what is this?" Lucille asked her friend who waited as she descended the stairs for breakfast. "I thought we agreed to keep everything blue and white on this floor."

"I know, but I needed to see some pink. It was the last thing I custom-ordered before I left the city."

"You have pink light bulbs everywhere outside – wasting valuable energy I might add."

"You know that's for Davidson. He'll see I'm here."

"I worry it makes the inn look like a brothel. Bad enough we have liquor underfoot."

"Do brothels hang pink lights?" Carter asked.

"How would I know?"

"Precisely."

Moments after the two sat down, Cora appeared with their coffee.

"Good morning," Carter greeted. "Cora, we are so happy you're here. And so are your parents."

"And I'm happy to be here after the place I worked."

"Your mother said the family wasn't particularly nice," Lucille said with a wince.

"No, they weren't."

The sweet, brown-haired Cora was seventeen and the daughter of Adam and Miriam. She had left her job as a domestic on the mainland to work full time at Rams Head.

Carter couldn't be more grateful. Miriam was too, as she didn't like Cora being away during the week.

"I head back to the city with Margaret in a few days," Lucille said as Cora took her leave. "I am excited to organize the many furnishings I plan to donate to the inn. Now that I've been here, I know what to look for."

"Anything you bring here will only elevate the décor. You have the best taste."

"*We* have the best taste, I agree. Though I do question that bright pink chair..." Lucille trailed off, as Carter smirked.

Genevieve entered the room. She wore a smoky gray dress with a delicate multi-colored bird appliqué on the shoulder. She waved, while heading straight over to the coffee service. Cup and saucer in hand, she joined Carter and Lucille at their table.

"Late night Genevieve?" Carter teased. It hadn't gone unnoticed that Mr. Bennett had all but been living at the inn. He sat with Genevieve at every meal and stood sentinel at the piano when she played each night.

"Mr. Bennett went back to the city early this morning, if that is what you are asking."

"I wasn't asking. It's just nice to see you so content."

And it was. Genevieve glowed from the attention. Carter found Stuart Bennett to be a gracious gentleman in their limited interactions. True he was married, but so was Genevieve.

"Thank you. It is nice to feel appreciated," Genevieve said. "I cannot tell you what being here means to me. At some point, I must deal with Laurent, but for now, I am very happy. I want to pay you – to give you rent when I can."

"Genevieve, just keep playing the piano, and maybe help dress some of our staff members. These are poor working girls, and I'd love to have them look a bit more polished, both on the job and off."

Lucille interjected. "Let me bring back some old dresses from my house. They are barely worn. Genevieve, maybe you can tailor them for the girls."

"Of course. But I also have a little money." She slid some bills into Carter's hand.

"Where did you get money from?" Silence. "Genevieve, answer me."

"Stuart. He wants to pay my room and board here, but I told him no. He left some money instead."

"And you want me to take it?"

"Yes. It is not all the money he gave me, but I would like to contribute something to my stay here. You are just starting out with this business, you cannot afford to be giving away lodgings."

"I know, but...."

"I insist," Genevieve said.

"Take it," Lucille advised. "We're here to help one another. Genevieve has a home for as long as she needs it. Stuart has money – lots of it from what I hear. If he stops giving, you can stop collecting. It's not like she's earning money on the street."

Carter looked doubtful. "Something feels wrong about it."

"Laurent stealing my talent and skills for himself, knocking me around when he was drunk and doing it all in the name of respectability — *that* was wrong."

"Yes, however…"

"Take it!" both women insisted at once.

Carter reluctantly agreed. Lucille and Genevieve fell into an animated discussion on the dresses Lucille would provide and how Genevieve might alter them for the staff women. Carter's eyes drifted around the room, and she noticed Cora filling a plate of food from the breakfast buffet, which would soon be cleared. Holding the plate, Cora then walked out of the room and headed to the staircase. Cora didn't live in the inn; she lived down the road with her family.

Carter stood. "Excuse me ladies."

She slowly climbed the staircase, only to see Cora continue from the second floor to the third. Why would Cora be feeding someone on the staff floor? Did she have a boyfriend? Carter followed as quietly as she could.

Cora took a left and softly knocked on one of the doors and slipped in with the food. Carter then walked to the very same door and knocked, fully expecting to find a boy. Cora opened the door and Carter saw a young girl behind her of maybe fifteen or sixteen.

"What is going on? Who is this young lady?" Carter sternly asked of Cora.

The girl started to cry. She was beautiful — long curly red hair tied back with tendrils framing her face. Her pale skin reddened as she stood there crying. Carter sighed. "Someone please say something."

Cora said, "She's my friend. She's run away from home."

"And you brought her *here?* What were you thinking?" Carter then turned to the girl. "Surely, your parents must be worried."

The girl spoke, her tears drying a bit. "I don't have parents."

"You have no family?"

"They don't want me," the girl said looking at the floor. "I'm with child. Cora offered to help me until I figure out where to go."

"Maybe your family is upset, but I'm certain they care. You must return to them."

"No, I won't! You can't make me. I will leave here right this minute." She started frantically stuffing things into a valise. "Cora, thank you for trying to help, but I must go."

"Go where?" Carter said. "I will bring you home myself and talk with your mother."

"NO!!!" The tears now dropped freely. "You can't possibly understand. I cannot go back to that house. No!"

Startled by the outburst, Carter took the few steps between them and put her arms around the shaking girl.

"It's fine. You're safe, I promise." Carter pulled back and kept her voice soft. "Please finish your breakfast in peace. What is your name?"

She paused. "Isabelle."

"Isabelle, I promise I will not do anything without speaking to you first, and together we will decide what to do. In return, can I trust you not to leave this room?"

"Yes." She whispered obediently.

"Thank you." She turned and, in a clipped voice, said, "Cora, come with me."

"Cora?" Isabelle looked at her pleadingly. Cora nodded in response.

Lucille listened while Carter recounted the story. They were in Carter's room, sitting on her two cherry-colored damask chairs.

"Oh dear." Lucille paused and shook her head. "I want to thrash that boy, whoever he is."

"Let's hope it was a boy and not an employer. I suspect Isabelle comes from the house where Cora worked on Long Island.

"Ah, yes. My mother once had a maid who was in the family way. The poor girl tried to hide it until she couldn't."

"What happened to her?"

"My mother fired her at once."

Carter asked, "Where did the maid go?"

"I have no idea," Lucille shrugged. "My mother was not going to entertain that in her home."

The two friends were quiet for a long moment.

"I have an idea," Lucille said. "I head to the city tomorrow with Margaret. Let me offer to take this Isabelle with us. I can pay her to help us at the very least. It will be good to have another pair of hands to assist us sort through the furnishings I plan to bring back. I can take her to my doctor and see if she is well or if he has ideas about what to do with her and the baby."

"Aren't we getting more involved if we do that?"

"Maybe. But at least she will be safe. I will use my most persuasive charms to get her to tell us more, so we can steer her where she needs to go. If she's from out of town, it's far easier to get on a bus or train from the city than out here."

Carter agreed that it was a sound plan, and she would ask for Cora's help in convincing the girl to accompany Lucille and Margaret back to New York City.

That same day after lunch, the elegant Miss Langley returned to Rams Head. This time she was with two women friends, both pretty and well dressed in harmonious, understated colors. Like Miss Langley, they appeared to be in their early twenties. Carter welcomed the trio while they checked in. Lucille, sitting by the fireplace with her writing notebook and tea, looked on.

"I don't have a good feeling about them, Carter," she said when her friend returned. "Miss Langley was one thing, but three?"

"We know nothing about them. They could be three old school friends having a retreat together."

"Unlikely. We agreed it was odd how Miss Langley came here and met with a man."

"Maybe it was a date."

"Carter, surely you don't think me that naïve."

"Fine. Let's say for the sake of argument they are meeting men here for that purpose. Unless they are a problem, they are not a problem. They certainly look good, don't they? Like the kind of people we want here."

"I could care less what they look like. It's what they do that concerns me."

"You're just looking for trouble. That imagination of yours. Let's wait and see."

"So, we just do nothing while Rams Head becomes a brothel? As my mother said, once you have a reputation, that's your reputation. Impossible to reverse. The same holds true for Rams Head."

Carter brushed off her concern. "I'm not going to worry about this. They look like proper young women to me."

"I'd bet my book collection those women are not the marrying kind, at least not to the men they are meeting."

"Maybe they will meet nice men, just like Genevieve did," Carter said. "You didn't have a problem with that."

Miriam appeared with more hot water for their tea. They both thanked her before resuming their talk in low tones.

"This is very different. Genevieve wasn't looking to meet anyone. It just happened."

"Honestly, Lucille, how different is it? Let's see. If the other two are anything like Miss Langley, we're fine. I have traveled near and far as a single woman with other women. Would you have thought me wayward too?"

"Lordy, I can't believe we're having this conversation."

"Neither can I. Let's not look for trouble where it does not exist. Their rooms are on the far side of the landing, away from ours or anyone else's for that matter. If I sense one whiff of drama, they're out. Okay?"

"And who will escort them out? Not you or me. William? Chef Adam? And what if there's a knife involved, or God forbid a gun?"

"Oh, stop."

"No, I won't stop. I am getting worried. We're hiding an unidentified pregnant teenager upstairs, more bottles of spirits than we can count downstairs. Now we have put out welcome mats for – whatever those women are pretending to be."

"Lucille, I thought I knew you better than that. You had no issue when I told you about the strange Schnedekers. You even felt I should have been more welcoming."

"Again, that was different. They are adults answering to themselves, not us."

"Yes, but they're dining in *my* restaurant, which *I* took issue with, given their appearances. These women are ladies. Real ones. I don't understand where you're drawing the line."

"You're drawing the line at what people look like! I'm drawing the line at outside trouble and the inn's reputation." Lucille crossed her arms.

Carter exhaled and then softened her tone. "Look, we just agreed on helping Isabelle to the extent we can."

"Yes, and I'm heartened she is willing to join me."

"Me too," Carter said. "Then the alcohol, well, we agreed on that, too."

"But these women, Carter…."

"You sound judgmental, which is the last thing I'd ever think of you."

"There are some things you must judge, and harshly. Exchanging intimate relations…" she leaned in, lowering her voice even further, "for money is one of them."

"Maybe so, but judge the men who pay them, not the women who need the money," Carter felt herself getting heated with emotion and she wasn't sure why. "God blessed them with beauty, which in this world is something to sell, like it or not. Don't judge them for using what resources they have to get by. Not every woman was born into a family like yours, looking the way you do, meeting a man like Henry and the future he guaranteed. Even if you didn't meet Henry, you would have been fine as an old maid living in your rich parents' fancy house."

"You've never seen my parents' house."

"Please. You had your own governess, for goodness' sake. I'm sure you didn't live in a hovel."

Lucille refolded her arms in annoyance.

Carter continued. "The point is, for most women even landing an ungainly, poor husband is good luck. At least they have a roof over their heads. Even if they get knocked around once in a while when their husband is drunk. Better than working in one of those factories or as a caretaker to someone's bratty children and being treated worse than the family dog. I had a single mother. Life was very, very hard – and she was a trained bookkeeper, a so-called respectable job that paid very little. My babysitter was a latched door. How can you possibly understand other women's plights?"

Carter was unable to stop the torrent of words. "Your life is perfect, Lucille. Picture perfect, in fact. You get to make all sorts of decisions – when to have children, whether to travel on a luxury liner or join your crazy friend for a frivolous adventure. The rest of us have to make our futures when the fairy godmothers of our dreams don't come through. It's a cruel world for women. I didn't join the suffrage movement because I was a rich, bored wife looking to fill my days. I wanted to help women."

Carter regretted the words the moment they left her lips. She had gone too far and knew it.

Lucille stood and said, "You want to help women by prostituting them – assuming they look good? Marvelous. I wish you luck with that." She gathered her purse and shawl and readied to leave.

"Go ahead and be righteous. I'm just a rich, bored housewife looking to fill my days. As to that, it's time to pack up my perfect life and head back to the city."

In an hour's time, Lucille left on the morning boat, with Margaret and Isabelle. Carter did not come out to bid her good-bye.

CHAPTER SEVEN

My Beloved Henry,

I miss you so. I had no idea how much I would. I had harsh words with Carter yesterday, and I'm not sure what I think any more. She thinks me provincial, which I am. She thinks me sheltered, which I am, too. But she thinks me judgmental – and of that I'm not so sure. Maybe anyone of privilege has the luxury of judging. We haven't been tested.

A dear, sweet girl of sixteen, Isabelle (she refuses to tell us her last name), ran away from home and wound up at the inn. She's in a family way, and it's clear she was abused on some level and is quite frightened and mistrustful. I brought her into the city to see my doctor, and Carter and I are trying to determine the best path forward for this girl's future. I tried to convince her to reveal her family name, which she would not even give to Dr. Jenkins. She visibly shakes when her family is mentioned.

Back to my question about judging. The world is a complex place, is it not? Who am I — a woman in love with my husband, with my life — able to question other people's choices? I accept far more human frailty in literature than I do in real life – what does that say about me?

All is well at home, Henry. I spend my days reading and writing away, both here in the city and at Carter's inn. I've been keeping a daily journal and have recently tried my hand at short stories, which I would love you to read when you return. I dream of you and eagerly await your next batch of letters. I live for your words; they make me feel we're together as only we can be. You and Vance are learning so much, and it all sounds so exciting. I love your descriptions of London, of your new friends, of your many delicious dinners. No detail is too small. You will laugh at how many I incorporate into my stories. You are my eyes, my ears, and even my tastebuds to a whole new world.

I love you, Henry. I miss lying in your arms, where all is right. At least in my little world.
Your loving Squirrel

Lucille sealed the envelope, knowing full well she should have included much more. As it was, Henry might be scandalized that she was assisting an expectant, runaway girl. Yet that was nothing compared to being party to a massive hoarding of alcohol, never mind staying in a house of wayward women. No, that would never do. Henry was indulgent when it came to his wife, but he was proper as the day was long.

Lucille thought about their relationship, and why it worked for her, despite the suffrage concern of women being dominated by the men in their lives. But theirs was a marriage born of love, and she never once thought of herself as being dominated in any way.

They had met as children in Chicago, where their parents socialized in the same circles. Yet they had only said hello on occasion; Lucille was shy, her nose always in a book, steadfastly avoiding any chance of conversation outside her two best friends Hannah and Rachel. Whereas Henry, a year older than Lucille, was outgoing, always in the center of any gathering. Everyone knew and loved him. He was handsome with dark wavy hair and a wide, easy smile. For Henry, talking was effortless, which made Lucille even shyer when he was in the room. Lucille had a wild crush on Henry; all the girls did. But she deliberately chose not to speak to him for fear she'd be awkward or say something ill considered. Her fear of misspeaking was why she wrote so fluidly in private.

When she was sixteen, Henry startled her one day after school. He came up from behind at the entrance of the building while she waited for Mildred, her governess, to escort her home.

"Finally, I find you without your friends on either side. Or your stern-faced governess, for that matter."

She recognized his voice immediately, and slowly turned around, unable to muster a word. He gallantly filled in the silence. "You're Lucille Kraft, aren't you? I'm Henry Nesbit. I've been trying to get your attention for some time now, but you are a squirrelly one."

"A squirrelly one?"

"Yes, those little guys who have a talent for running away. Well, Miss Kraft, you have met your match."

"I —"

"Squirrel away, because I don't give up. Ever. Something tells me we are to become important to one another, if I can get you to look up at me." He waited until she did. "Ahh, that wasn't so hard, was it? Your eyes are even bluer than I thought." He had a look of wonder as he stared at her.

She could see Mildred walking toward them. She pointed in Mildred's direction. "I —"

"Yes, yes, I see her too. I will be quick. May I call on you? Chaperoned, of course. Perhaps we could walk in the park."

Lucille managed a nod.

"Splendid," he said, smiling. "Absolutely splendid."

Mildred arrived and looked at him quizzically —and disapprovingly.

"Hello, my name is Henry Nesbit. And I will soon be calling on Miss Kraft. Our parents are friends, so no cause for worry. Good day to you both." He tipped his hat, and then looked at Lucille one more time. "Who knew squirrels could have such blue eyes – or such red cheeks?" He winked.

In a way, that first interaction set the tone for their courtship. It took her by surprise, and Henry filled in the blanks of her life – a quiet upbringing with a stoic mother, an often-absent father and myriad servants. With Henry's confident manner and determination, he quickly charmed her parents as well as Mildred. It didn't hurt that Henry was accepted to attend Princeton the following fall. His passion for Lucille was breathtaking, and his outward affection for her was like nothing she had ever experienced. He told her they were destined to be a couple, and that was that. Lucille was the envy of all the girls she knew.

Lucille was also deeply in love. Everything about him delighted her, from his strong, capable shoulders that assured her he could carry her over any threshold they encountered in life, to his astonishing aptitude for numbers and natural comprehension in all matters, be it cultural or economic.

Moreover, Henry's devotion gave Lucille the confidence she was otherwise lacking. At best, her mother nodded her approval of Lucille, not for anything she did or said, but that she fulfilled all the requirements of a well-raised socialite. Lucille was an only child and was expected to act a certain way, and she dutifully complied. Novels were her escape, giving her a worldly view and excitement that her real life lacked – *Wuthering Heights, Sense and Sensibility, Jane Eyre, Moll Flanders, Portrait of a Lady,* to name some of her favorites. Yet if someone as smart and dashing as Henry Nesbit could find her fascinating, even clever, surely she should hold her head high and not shrink from conversing with strangers.

Five years after they met, once Henry received his business degree from Princeton, they had an elaborate wedding at her parents' Gold Coast estate before setting up house in New York City's booming Upper East Side. Henry was to oversee a European expansion of his father's business. New York, with its international harbor, would afford them opportunities Chicago could not. Henry and Lucille had been in New York for five years, including during the war, when Henry's business turned to the war effort, supplying steel for military planes, weapons, and vehicles. His essential role in arms production had the significant advantage of keeping Henry from fighting abroad. He was needed here.

When the war ended, Henry and his father were eager to resume their goal of international growth, and Henry pursued opportunities through some of his wartime contacts. One English firm in particular was interested in partnering with Nesbit Enterprises. Its president had traveled to Chicago and New York to observe its operations, and now it was Henry's turn to return the visit, hence this voyage. The trip was originally planned to include Lucille and Henry's junior associate, Vance Broder. Lucille made it clear, however, that she didn't want to go.

"I just don't want to, Henry. Am I allowed to say that? Am I allowed to have a moment in my life when I say no, I'd rather not? Or must I forever obey what is asked of me by everyone, including you? Is that what you love about me?"

He was startled by her assertiveness, as he was used to cajoling and bending her to his will. But he could see the resoluteness of her gaze. Maybe it was his relentless talk of children, but Lucille had been feeling trapped and in want of a respite from Henry and their parents' expectations. Amazingly Henry agreed, but not without a warning. "Squirrel, I feel I indulge you in everything thing you ask. So yes, I will give you this time. When I return, however, we will finally start a family. No delay, no excuses."

She was so relieved and readily agreed, throwing her arms around his shoulders and kissing him. "Yes, yes. A boy and a girl, no question. Right in a row."

Henry, seduced by her kiss, said, "I leave in a week. Let's start saying goodbye now."

A few days after Lucille had left, Carter sat on a bench along the dock, waiting for Graham to arrive for his usual noon drop off. She forced herself to breathe in the cool air and appreciate the sunny skies above and rippling water below. She missed Lucille these past days. She regretted having words with her dear friend and knew she had been unduly harsh.

Still, Carter did not have the luxury of forgoing the extra income Miss Langley and her two friends brought in, both from their room rents and their elaborate dinners that always included plenty of top shelf spirits. Or that of Mr. Goodwin, who delivered another ten crates of alcohol, and picked up the tab for all her outdoor tables and chairs. While Rams Head's lunches, high teas and dinners were proving to be a robust business, she needed to lay out money for food and supplies. She also had a growing staff that had to get paid weekly. She couldn't put on airs about where her money came from if it was discreet. It was accepting the income or closing the inn until Davidson came home, if not forever.

Davidson. You need to send me a sign, otherwise I'll surely lose my mind. Where are you? I'm keeping the faith. I am. But it's not easy.

Carter wiped her eyes, feeling vulnerable and dejected all at once. And then she felt a drop on her shoulder. She looked. A bird dropping. Not exactly the sign she was hoping for. Just then, the *Swisher* rounded the bend into Coecles Harbor, and she stood and waved to Graham. He waved back. Then something caught her eye from behind. On a lower branch of one of the massive oak trees a cardinal was regarding her.

Could that be you, Davidson? It eyed her a beat longer, before flying off. She shook her head, laughing that she thought a bird could be the sign she was looking for. Then she remembered: before Davidson left for the war, she drenched one of her favorite lace-edged handkerchiefs in her perfume. "I am with you, always," she had whispered, while slipping it into his pocket. He returned from the war with her handkerchief, saying it had to be the most touched and kissed handkerchief in history. Before he left this last time, she had washed the handkerchief and dabbed it anew with her scent. Wherever he was now, it was in his pocket. Red as could be.

Call it another sign of good luck, but as Graham's steamer neared, Carter could make out not just the captain waving back at her, but Lucille, Margaret and Isabelle as well. Carter started to cry in relief.

71

She realized how important it was to have Lucille by her side — and not only for her emotional support and trusted companionship. Lucille, with her high-born style and kindly manners, helped to elevate Rams Head. It was Lucille who patiently taught the waiters how to set the table, how to fold the napkins, how to greet guests. Carter called her "fork smart," which made Lucille laugh. It could never be a house of ill repute as long as Lucille Nesbit graced its doors.

As the boat reached the dock and the women disembarked, Carter folded Lucille into a tight embrace. "You came back, dear sister-friend," Carter said, not letting her go.

"Oh, come on, my sister-friend," Lucille said, as she dabbed away her own tears. "I'm the penny who keeps showing up."

"My good luck penny!"

"And look at our sweet Isabelle. She was so helpful, you have no idea."

Isabelle smiled shyly, looking especially fresh in a new green-floral dress, which Carter assumed had been Lucille's. She even stood taller, Carter noted. Three days with Lucille would inspire any young woman's confidence.

"We thoroughly raided my basement and can't wait to turn over my dresses to Genevieve. Not to mention all the other items I found for the inn."

Margaret was especially enthusiastic. "Yes, we brought many of the smaller things with us, but we have a good deal of furnishings on their way – end tables, lamps. Such pretty wall tapestries, and paintings too!"

Lucille laughed. "I even brought some portraits of especially stern-looking men, though I have no idea who they are. They'll keep everyone honest out of sheer fright, like mean schoolmasters."

As they walked up the hill toward Rams Head, Carter whispered, "Did you have any luck finding out who Isabelle's people are?"

"None at all. We need to discuss the options — later, of course."

Carter nodded. She admittedly worried about the young girl staying at the inn but decided to just be grateful Lucille was back and work out the rest later. "With all that space you made in your basement, maybe we can store some alcohol there if we get too full."

"I don't see why not – in fact, what a great place to supplement what we have here. Who would ever suspect me? Certainly not Henry."

"Especially not Henry!" The two chortled like schoolgirls.

After the trunks were unloaded and the smaller furnishings distributed in various guest rooms, Carter and Lucille sat outside, despite the late April chill. For now, Isabelle had been situated in the staff room Cora originally put her in.

"She's such a sweet girl, Carter. Willing to do anything that's asked of her. I'm sure she could be useful here."

"I'm stunned you, of all people, would consider it."

"I will not dismiss her out of hand; I am not my mother. If you'd prefer, I can bring her back to the city and she can be part of my staff until we decide out what to do. I just thought she would be more useful here."

Carter pursed her lips. "What can she do here with a bulging stomach in everyone's view?"

"Her stomach isn't *that* bulging at this point. Anyway, I've thought this out. Chambermaids are rarely seen, right? Why not let her clean the rooms in between guests? Insofar as her appearance, surely Genevieve can help. She needs better fitting garments."

"Even if I agree, how long will that last? I see us stuck with a baby at some point."

Lucille's brow wrinkled at the thought. "You're getting ahead of ourselves. By then she will have figured out a solution. Or we will."

Carter rubbed her face with both hands. "I never envisioned such problems."

"You can only control what you can control. May Isabelle be the worst of our problems."

CHAPTER EIGHT

"As this is your third visit here, we thought it would be nice to get to know one another," Carter began, as Lucille quietly sipped a cup of tea next to her.

Carter had requested a meeting with Miss Langley and her two friends Miss Quince and Miss McFee, who had arrived late that morning by a chartered boat. According to Graham that seemed to be their mode of travel. On each of their last two visits, in addition to paying for three rooms at the front desk, Miss Langley had discreetly handed Carter another envelope as they checked out, as she did after her first stay. Carter accepted it with some unease. She felt a word was needed and invited the women for high tea in the Garden Room. Lucille insisted on joining them, and asked Margaret to serve the group, as they could count on her for discretion.

Miss Langley began. "We so enjoy staying here Miss Carter. You've created a beautiful inn."

"Why thank you. It certainly has been an experience, but we're very pleased how it's turned out. My fiancée, Mr. Davidson Surrey, is due most of the credit – this inn is a testament to his imagination and planning. Speaking of gentlemen, I noticed you seem to be joined by friends in the evening."

"Yes, we are. But our gentlemen friends require utmost privacy, so there is no need to worry that our friendships will reflect on your inn in any way."

"I appreciate that. I just want to have a better understanding of things."

"What is you you would better like to understand?" Miss Langley had a pleasant, if guarded way about her.

"Is there anyone…. placing pressure on you from the outside in any way? Is there an, um, organizer, whom I should know about?

"I am our organizer." Miss Langley answered with a quick smile.

"I am happy to hear that. My friend Mrs. Nesbit and I have been active in the suffrage movement and applaud women-run businesses, what few there are."

"That's what we are. Right, ladies?" Miss Quince and Miss McFee nodded.

Lucille spoke. "Is there any reason we should fear trouble could follow you?"

Miss Langley regarded Lucille directly. "I assure you, no trouble will follow us. We are well acquainted with our gentlemen friends. I have known one in particular since childhood."

"In that case, why not rent an apartment?" Carter asked. "Surely that would give you privacy and discretion you seek. And would cost you far less, I'm sure."

"This suits us better," Miss Langley spoke firmly. "Are you asking us to move on? Or for more money?"

Carter could sense disappointment in Miss Langley's words.

"No and no. You pay what any guests would for the rooms, and your kind gratuity is welcome. As you know, this is a new establishment. I just want to assure myself and Mrs. Nesbit that all is well and well managed. If that should change, we would need to reconsider our relationship."

"I can assure you we are well, and well managed for that matter."

"Miss Quince, you have an exquisite complexion. It's like porcelain," Lucille interjected to break the tension. "And Miss McFee, you have the most arresting red hair. All of you are quite striking. And so smartly dressed. I've been admiring you from afar and don't believe in withholding compliments."

"Thank you," Miss Langley said. "We go by our maiden names here, but please call us by our given names: I'm Elizabeth. This is Helen and Rose."

"And we are Lucille and Carter." *Maiden names?*

"I agree about not withholding compliments," Helen said, her face brightened. "I simply adore my room with all those mirrors on the wall. They bring in the light and water so beautifully. I also love how they reflect candlelight at night."

Carter laughed. "Thank you. See, Lucille? I told you we should place the mirrors like that. Lucille had her doubts."

"I did, but I agree it came out well," Lucille said. To the ladies she added, "We've had such fun decorating the rooms with various odds and ends. Rose, you're in one of my

77

favorites. I love the pale-green wicker bed frame and how it faces the water."

Rose quietly responded, "It's very pretty."

Enjoying this lighthearted banter, Lucille said, "Have any of you met our friend Genevieve Blanc? She's an expert seamstress and is also staying here at the inn."

"Yes," Rose volunteered. "Actually, she helped me with this dress. I've lost weight, and Genevieve offered to tailor it. She did a beautiful job." Rose, with her striking copper hair, had a youthful face, though Lucille sensed sadness behind it.

"Ahh, she certainly did."

"We never met a Frenchwoman before," Helen added. "I could listen to her accent all day long. You don't meet many foreigners in Old Saybrook, where we're from." Helen, a dark brunette with contrasting ivory skin and sky-blue eyes, had an open face and a far more animated manner than Rose.

Elizabeth gave Helen a disapproving stare when she revealed their Connecticut origins.

"Well, I guess we are all transplants here," Lucille said. "Carter is from Des Moines, and I'm from Chicago. Margaret here," who had just returned to the room to refresh their tea, "is from County Cork in Ireland. And now we're all New Yorkers."

Helen and Rose looked to Elizabeth, from whom they were clearly taking their cues.

"We still live in Connecticut," Elizabeth said. "With our children."

"Children?" Carter hoped she suppressed the alarm in her voice.

"And husbands?" Lucille ventured. "You mentioned maiden names."

"We're war widows," Elizabeth explained. "Rose and I have one child each, Helen two."

"Who stays with the children when you're here?" Carter asked.

"My parents watch my babies and Elizabeth's as well," Helen said. "Rose lives with her folks."

Elizabeth seemed relieved, as though a burden had been lifted. She said, "None of us want to do this forever. We just have so few options. We were housewives. We are not educated to be teachers or nurses or work in offices. We could be caretakers of other people's homes or children, but then we'd never see our own. This is the best we can manage. We come here because no one knows us, and well, it's just for a few days a week at most."

Lucille's hand touched her chest. "I'm so sorry for your losses. And then to have to leave your children, if even for a few days."

"So many women have it worse," Elizabeth stated, almost defiantly.

"Still, I can only imagine how difficult this all is. I'm sure they are darlings." Her eyes glided from woman to woman.

It was Elizabeth who answered. "Yes, it is all hard. You don't count on your husband serving his country and not coming home. You don't count on not having means to support your child. The three of us are still waiting to receive the meager widows' pensions we had to apply for from the government. But life presents opportunities in the strangest of ways, and you find yourself, well...." She looked away, blinking away tears before shrugging her shoulders. "You'd do anything for your children."

Carter saw the vulnerability in Elizabeth's eyes and leaned forward and touched her arm. "My mother was on her own, and it wasn't easy. She would have done anything to care for me. Any woman would, Lucille and I included."

Lucille smiled sympathetically.

"All of this said and understood," Carter added,"I just need your word that you are in control of this, and that no harm will come to the inn."

"You have my word," Elizabeth Langley said, looking into Carter's eyes with a firm nod of her head.

Carter was satisfied. As she walked out with Elizabeth and Rose, Lucille and Helen behind them, Carter thought about how life always surprised her. And how random it all was. God forbid Davidson didn't come back, and if she couldn't make a success of the inn, then how would she fare any better than these women, with or without children to support?

After they bade the women goodbye, Carter asked Lucille to wait for her in the foyer for a moment, as she wanted to fetch something from her room. When Carter returned, she motioned to the basement door, located in an alcove next to the inn's front entrance. Carter opened the door and descended the stairs, Lucille closely behind her.

"That was unexpected, wasn't it?" Lucille said to Carter's back.

"What?"

"The ladies, of course. And Helen gave me a bit more information as we were leaving the room."

Carter turned around when they reached the the bottom of the stairs. "You minx, Lucille! How do you get people to confide in you so?"

"It's what I do, Carter. I'm good at it," Lucille said matter-of-factly. "Anyway, it seems Elizabeth was pursued by her previous boyfriend while her husband was at war. The former boyfriend is wealthy, a shipping executive who's now married with two children. He lives in Sag Harbor."

Carter frowned. "Now that's the kind of family I was hoping to attract. Instead, we are the site for trysts with his mistress."

"Let me continue. When he heard Elizabeth's husband died, he pursued her again and pays her money. He charters a boat to bring her to and from Old Saybrook to Ram Island. That is how this all started. She then told him about her good friends Helen and Rose, and well, here we are."

"Let's not ask any more questions," Carter said. "The less we know, the better. Unless there's a problem, of course."

"Agreed. Wait, what are we doing down here?"

"You'll see," Carter said. "Follow me."

Carter turned to the left and made her way along a concrete wall of what looked to be the main storage area, which was lined with boxes, shelves, as well as some spare furnishings. She stopped when they reached a wall of shelves filled with cartons of what seemed to contain canned goods.

"What is this, Carter? Are you building a bomb shelter?"

"Hardly." Carter pushed aside a box that hid a lever that allowed her to slide the shelves aside to reveal a door with a padlock.

"My word!" Lucille exclaimed.

"This leads to the hidden space I told you about," Carter said. She used one of the keys on a chain she always wore around her neck to unlock the door, which opened to a cavernous room with stacked crates and aisles in between.

"I can't believe what I'm looking at," Lucille said, marveling at the bounty as she walked further into the room.

"There's another door to the outside that's hidden by a leafy evergreen bush—only Graham and I know about it. That's how he loads in the goods. I tell you, Davidson thought of everything. I would like you to give you keys to the padlocks for both doors, Lucille. I don't want secrets between us." She produced two keys from her pocket – the items she must have retrieved while Lucille waited. She folded them into Lucille's hands. "Both doors can only be locked and opened from the outside."

"I appreciated not knowing…. Like you said about the ladies: the less we know, the better." Lucille started counting the crates but gave up after a few dozen. "Carter, I thought you said it was a handful of crates – Davidson's and Goodwin's."

"These are neither. We passed those when we first walked in."

"I'm not following."

"These are new ones, all carefully labeled if you look closely. I am getting storage rent from the owners for each."

"Storage   rent?

"Yes. I have become bolder. Goodwin told Graham that this was always Davidson's plan, once he heard that politicians were moving to outlaw the sale of liquor. That is why he built the hidden room. He knew how ideal it would be to hoard spirits in great quantities."

She could see Lucille wasn't grasping the point. "Shelter Island is remote, and Ram Island is even *more* remote. An island off an island off an island – that's three islands away from the island of Manhattan. It's the perfect place to hide what needs to be hidden. That's why the war widows chose our inn to do their business. Probably why the Schnedekers are here too.

Can you see what an opportunity we have here?"

Lucille walked down the aisle, shaking her head. "An opportunity for what? To aid and abet crimes?"

"Look, I need the money—er, the *inn* needs the money. You have no idea the debt I'm in. *I* had no idea the debt I was in...so many things hadn't been paid for. I need to square it all away, and Davidson gave me a way to do that. I'm sure it was what he was planning all along. When he returns—"

"Stop. Just stop," Lucille put up her hand. "You are my dear sister-friend, and we've always been honest with one another. I've told you things I dare not tell Henry. So, I must be frank: this is a dangerous world. How will you get it back to the owners when the ban takes hold? And it's not like you'll be able to serve any of it!" she said, gesturing wildly around the room.

"I believe the plan is to return the crates before the ban, or right thereafter. Insofar as serving our liquor, we won't, not openly anyway. Goodwin told Graham that Davidson foresaw opening a clandestine bar down here."

"I'm not following."

"An underground bar only a few people will know about. Davidson will be back before January, so don't worry."

Lucille shook her head in disbelief. "Carter, what have you gotten yourself into?"

CHAPTER NINE

"WHERE IS MY WIFE? GOD DAMN IT, WHERE IS SHE??"

The screaming woke Carter out of a rare sound sleep. It was so loud, she had no doubt it must have awakened the entire inn. She grabbed her robe and raced downstairs.

There stood a rain-soaked Laurent Blanc next to William, the latter also clearly just stirred out of bed. William had his own house on the island but kept a room on the staff floor for the nights he worked late. Carter was grateful that this was one of those nights.

"Sir, lower your voice," William reprimanded.

"I'm not lowering anything, other than my fist to your face, if you don't get Madame Blanc NOW!"

Gone was the French accent, gone were his impeccably tailored clothes. He looked like a madman, spitting with rage.

Carter stepped in. "Monsieur Blanc, please calm down. There is no reason to shout."

"No? It took me forever to find this godforsaken place. Your receipt only said Rams Head Inn, Shelter Island. I had to find a ferry to take my car – then I got lost when we landed, driving in circles and even when I was steered to the right road, I had to wait for low tide to cross that spit of land."

"Well, you found us," she said with a tight smile. "Please come into the dining room."

He grabbed her arm tightly. "I won't follow you anywhere, you whore. I always wondered how you paid for your clothes."

"How dare you!" Carter shook her head in disgust.

"Oh, I dare alright." Laurent looked like he was about to strike her, but he was stopped by a thick muscled arm belonging to Curtis Schmidt, a local police officer, who must have come down the stairs upon hearing the commotion.

"Take one step further and you'll regret it," Curtis said.

"Who the hell—"

Just at that moment, Genevieve appeared at the top of the stairs in a blue satin robe. She trembled as she made her way down. Her voice was high-pitched and pleading. "Laurent, you must leave now. This will not end well. Please, for all our sakes, including your own, just leave."

"It will end when you leave with me."

"I am not coming with you," Genevieve replied.

"You heard her," Carter said. "I don't even have to call the police, they're here." She gestured toward Curtis. "Meet Officer Schmidt."

Laurent was undeterred and sneered at Curtis. "Nice to meet you, *officer*. I'm here to collect my wife, who has been kidnapped by this one. I fully expect you to help me —unless you are the man staying in my wife's room."

Curtis was unruffled. "The lady said to leave. I suggest you do that. You are disturbing the peace."

"Or maybe you mean interrupting everyone's hanky panky. If you really are an officer, surely your superior would have something to say about you being here."

"Save your breath, buster," Curtis said. "It is well known that I occasionally rent a room here. It's fortunate tonight was one of those nights. Now you either leave on your own, or I will assist you."

Carter had no idea why Curtis was there, but she was grateful he was.

"You can't prevent me from speaking to my wife."

Just then, Lucille came down the stairs, fully dressed and looking very much the society lady she was. She remained on the second to the bottom step, giving her just a bit of height over everyone else in the room.

"Monsieur Blanc," she greeted him serenely as if she had just entered his dress salon. "This is a surprise."

He stood erect, greeting his best customer, and a highly influential one at that. The French accent returned. "Mrs. Nesbit, *bon soir*. The surprise is mine seeing you here in such a place."

"Such a place? I am here with my dear friend Miss Carter, helping with her new establishment. Mr. Nesbit and I plan to spend a great deal of time here in the future. While your urgency to see your wife is understandable, your timing and manner leave much to be desired. Be that as it may, she clearly does not share the sentiment, and I strongly urge you to leave us in peace, and no one need speak of this night again. I am sure your business would appreciate such discretion on my part."

"What business? Madame Blanc left me high and dry — Blanc Couture is at a standstill while she fritters away her time here doing God knows what else..."

"You have a loyal clientele," Lucille cut in. "And I'm sure you are clever and talented enough to find other help."

"It is not so easy to find such a seamstress."

"Nor such a designer, I'd imagine," Carter said.

He glared at the insinuation. "They are all Laurent Blanc designs. Every last one of them."

Lucille regained his attention with her calm voice. "That said, if you wish to speak to Madame Blanc during decent hours, I am sure she will receive you at a suitable place and time, which this is not." She descended that last step and spoke in a low, though pointed voice. "For now, you must leave, or I assure you, your business will *never* recover—nor will your reputation."

Carter widened her eyes at her friend, while Laurent considered Lucille's words, and finally holding up his hands, gesturing innocence.

To Genevieve, he said, "We will be speaking soon, *ma Cherie.*" He spat out the last word, like it was poison on his tongue.

Curtis and William took Monsieur Blanc's arms and led him outside the front door where his rained-soaked Model T awaited him.

"Where will he go this time of night in the rain?" Genevieve asked after he left.

"Wherever he came from," Carter answered. "It is not our problem."

Genevieve's shoulders dropped in relief, realizing he was gone, at least for now. "How can I thank you?"

"Where is Curtis? Is he okay?" The three women looked up to see Margaret in a white slip, her hand clutching the top of it. The dots connected, and now Lucille grimaced with frustration.

"Let us all return to our beds, ladies," she said, pointedly staring at Margaret. "We need our rest, as we have much to sort out in the morning."

The next morning over coffee, Lucille filled in Carter. "Margaret says they are in love," she said, shaking her head while stirring a teaspoon of honey into her cup. "At least, Curtis is not married. He lives with his parents."

"I gather this all still offends you," Carter said.

"It doesn't you?"

"I have never shared your puritanical views."

"And yet you're religious," Lucille stared at Carter in wonder. Lucille always found Carter's faith fascinating, since she was such a modern woman.

"Yes, and God gave us the gift of our bodies to enjoy."

Lucille shook her head. "Margaret is an innocent, and this has happened under my watch. She is nineteen years old, living far away from her family. I plan to meet with Officer Schmidt today and insist he make an honest woman of her as soon as possible."

"You cannot insist on that!"

"Can't I? I will not have him take advantage of her. If they are truly in love then he will happily marry her, and you will have Margaret forever on this Island with you. Meanwhile, I am losing one of the most competent and trustworthy maids I have ever had. And I've had quite a few."

"Boo hoo. How will you ever cope? Surely, she signed an indentured servant agreement for life?"

Lucille hit her friend's arm with the back of her hand. "My life is more complex than you think."

"I'm sure keeping track of all your jewelry is a job in and of itself. Oh, and how will you ever comb your hair – why, you will look a fright!"

"Hush, will you? Mostly I worry for Margaret. She is naïve and sheltered. What if she is with child and he denies all responsibility? Our Isabelle isn't enough for you?"

Carter sighed. "Maybe you are right to speak to him."

"Maybe I am."

"But selfishly speaking, I love that we have a police officer staying under our roof, whether the two marry or not. He could prove quite useful."

"I want them married!"

"And so they shall be, if you have your way of it, which I suspect you will. Now, have you seen Genevieve this morning?"

"No, but her charming friend Mr. Bennett arrives tonight. They seem quite taken with one another. What a complicated world we find ourselves in," Lucille said.

"Let's just hope that Monsieur Blanc took our advice and went back to where he came from."

Just then Carter saw William slip behind the front desk. She caught his eye and waved for him to come over. He looked his groomed and pressed self, despite the late night they all had. A person's appearance says so much about their state of mind.

"I want to thank you for handling the unpleasantness last night," Carter said.

"We all did our part," William said.

"True," Carter smiled. "Queen Lucille here made her displeasure known to all."

Lucille rolled her eyes at Carter's sarcasm.

"Will that be all?" William asked politely.

"Yes. I should also mention how grateful we are for your assuring presence here. Everything runs smoothly, thanks to your direction."

"Indeed," Lucille smiled. "William, I am addicted to your honey. It's truly the best I've ever had. Beekeeping sounds so scary to me, but you don't seem to suffer from stings."

"Honeybees only sting if you threaten them. I give them a wide berth and have nothing to fear."

"I gather you've been at this for a while."

"My father passed it on. It's not for everyone."

"Well, it's definitely for you," Carter said. "And, thankfully, for Rams Head Inn. Your brother uses it quite a lot in his delicious sauces."

"He does." A small smile escaped him. William gave the women a slight bow of his head and went back to the foyer desk. He was an oddly reserved man, Carter noted not the first time. She reminded herself that Davidson trusted him, which was all she needed to know.

MAY 1919

CHAPTER TEN

My Beloved Henry,

I don't have words to express my delight about your most recent letter. My goodness! That is an obscene amount of money, and they are placing it all in your capable hands. They have figured out what I've always known: you are brilliant beyond compare. Moreover, you well represent their legendary company, their unparalleled integrity and now, their limitless future here in America. I wish you were here, and I could hug you like you've never been hugged in your life. I am just SO proud of you!

The extension of your stay abroad is fine with me. But no, I do not wish to join you, much as I love that you want me by your side. It is just not practical, especially if you are traveling throughout Europe. The last thing you need is a wife and her countless trunks trundling behind you, and I would be lonely by myself in London, missing you more than I already am. You have Vance, who is fine company as well as helpful. I am confident this will be the last time we are separated. In the future I will be by your side, whenever you wish. Though I beg of you, please stop telling everyone how beautiful I am. I am only so in your eyes and will feel foolish when I finally meet your new associates.

In the meantime, I am enjoying being with Carter and feeling quite useful. Only five weeks have passed, which means she has another month and a half or so to fully ready Rams Head for the summer. As I have explained, it's not so much the inn itself, which has only seventeen rooms, but more the restaurant business, which is fairly robust thanks to the harbor and locals. You will laugh when you see how much of our house – the things stored in the basement you keep telling me to part with – is here and has been given a new life. I have met so many young women to whom I've been able to give my older dresses. Their enthusiasm pleases me no end.

Isabelle, the teenager who is with child, still refuses to identify her family. We hope she gives the baby up for adoption, but do not want to pressure her, lest she runs away. She is a skittish one.

I will soon be looking for a new maid. Margaret has fallen in love with a local police officer on Shelter Island. He is a marvelous young man, and I bless the union wholeheartedly. We will have the wedding here at Rams Head, where our staff and his family can attend. I have offered to sponsor Margaret's parents and sister's voyage to the States should they wish to attend.

I am so happy for Carter. Everything is coming along swimmingly. She still believes Davidson will appear, despite the odds plummeting with each passing day. Most mornings, she looks for a particular cardinal by the dock, convinced the bird was sent by Davidson. I am serious. Does love makes us all daft? I fear so — goodness knows I started dancing with your recent letter held close to my heart. I even curtsied with it.

You hold my heart — and I cannot wait for you to hold my body again too.
—Your proud and loving Squirrel

P.S. I am excited for you to see Shelter Island. Maybe we should consider building a summer cottage for our future family. The land is reasonably priced, and the vistas are magnificent!

Carter patiently waited for Graham's boat to arrive. The late morning was misty, which brought a rawness to the air. She was glad she wore her thickest shawl, a coral-pink woolen knit. She wasn't needed on the dock this early, as she could easily come down once he arrived. But she loved the peace and quiet this time afforded her. No cardinal today, but that was fine. Carter was back to feeling hopeful. Even the skirmish with Laurent had proved to be a good thing. Rams Head would soon be hosting a policeman's wedding, with all his fellow officers and even the chief of police in attendance. Take that, Shelter Island politics!

Almost every other week, a representative from Shelter Island Town would show up to survey how Rams Head was doing. Fortunately, the inn attracted a more mature crowd. The rabble rousers, usually young crewmen, went to the saloons next to the main dock, which were cheaper and more raucous. And a shorter distance to stumble back to the ship should one become too drunk to man a skiff. Rams Head attracted clientele who appreciated the glorious view, fine food and table service and, of course, Genevieve's piano playing. While Carter didn't fear the occasional inspection, she knew the Town was suspicious of a female proprietor.

Yet the one thing she didn't need was anyone nosing about when Graham arrived. He was bringing more and more crates to her basement, and it was one business she'd rather not have to explain.

When Graham's boat appeared around the bend of the cove, he had another smaller boat in tow, captained by a rugged-looking man in his mid-thirties with angular features and olive-toned skin. He wore a bottle-green cap and clothes that had seen better days. He had a smirk on his face, and as he` tipped his hat toward her in greeting, she sensed trouble. Graham's eyes were wide as he looked at Carter, as if attempting to signal something.

"Miss Carter, this here is Mr. Gabriel Romano," Graham said, as he and Romano jumped onto either side of the dock. "We met him in Sag Harbor as we were delivering a crate to a captain. Says he's never been to Shelter Island and insisted on following us."

"Yes, that's right," Romano smiled, a bit too close for comfort. "I see Graham here has a lot of cargo and wondered if I could help him and the boys bring it to your house."

"Thank you for your kindness," Carter said as pleasantly as she could manage. "But I'm sure we don't need the assistance."

"Really? You have a lot of crates on board here for one household," Romano said.

"Yes, I do. But this is an inn, not a household. We will be hosting a wedding here, in fact. Next Sunday, the island's own Officer Curtis Schmidt is getting married. Do you know him? The whole Shelter Island police force will be in attendance, as well as many officers from Sag Harbor and Easthampton— over 100 people in all."

Mr. Romano looked at her long and hard. "Isn't that interesting."

"It is, yes. You'll be able to watch the festivities by boat. And thank you for your generous offer of help."

Her tone suggested a goodbye, but he didn't make a move to leave. Instead, he held her eyes. Not for the first time, she was grateful for her six-foot height, which towered over him.

"I bid you a good day, Mr. Romano," she said with all the lightness she could put into her voice.

He waited one moment more, before tipping his green cap and slowly turning around. He then jumped onto his boat and commandeered it swiftly from her dock.

Tim, the older of Graham's sons, made a motion. Carter could see he was putting down a pistol he had held behind his back. Her eyes widened.

"No worries – we always have a pistol on board," Graham assured her. "That was some quick thinking on your part, Miss Carter. Lately there have been a bunch of hoodlums on the docks, trying to figure out where large shipments are going. They've always been there, but now they are getting aggressive. I don't think we'll be seeing him again – you handled him well with that talk of the police."

"Well, it's true," Carter said, smiling. "And I couldn't be more grateful to have some built-in police protection. You never know when you'll need it."

"Quiet, someone will see us," Margaret shushed Curtis, who moaned while kissing her. They were up against a tree, not far from Rams Head.

"Let them! A man may kiss his betrothed, can't he?"

"Not like you're kissing me." She moved his hand from under her skirt, which she promptly straightened as she moved away from him. "We're supposed to be taking a walk to see the sand bar. A proper walk."

"'A proper walk,'" he imitated the brogue he told her he loved so much. "There is nothing proper about my feelings toward you, my love. Ever since we've become engaged, we've had one proper meeting after another. With my parents, with my fellow policemen and of course with Miss Carter and Mrs. Nesbit. I'm tired of all this proper stuff. When do I get to be alone with you?"

"After we are *properly* man and wife," Margaret laughed, full of joy. She still could not believe this was happening to her. Not only was Mrs. Nesbit gifting her with the silk and beads for the bridal dress that Genevieve was making, but she was paying to have Margaret's parents and sister join them from Ireland for the wedding, hence the six-week delay.

"Will you still tell me to be quiet when I'm your husband?"

"As long as we live at the inn, yes."

"Then I will find us a house immediately."

"As long as it is big enough to invite my whole family to stay with us for long visits."

"I need to be alone with you first, my love. For a good long while," Curtis looked at her, his rugged handsomeness enhanced by a huge grin under his mustache. "Let's tell Miss Carter we wish to stay at the inn, if she'll have us. At least for the summer."

"Really? She will be so happy. So will Mrs. Nesbit. You make us all feel so safe."

"As long as I make you feel other things too."

Genevieve was outfitting Isabelle in another dress, as she had outgrown the last. The baby due in a little over three months' time, and it was becoming impossible to hide the girl's predicament.

"Isabelle, you must stand still while I pin you," Genevieve insisted. Genevieve wore a white head wrap to keep her dark curls from falling in her face. They stood in Genevieve's room, one that faced the garden as per

Genevieve's request. All the women loved Genevieve's room, as it was filled with flower paintings of every description. Genevieve loved flowers, and always came back with a botanical painting or two from the town center thanks to the weekly outdoor market where locals would sell their wares, be it baked goods, freshly caught fish, used home furnishings or artwork. Today, Isabelle noticed none of the floral paintings. She was too anxious.

"I don't mean to be rude, but can you hurry up or can we take a break? Isabelle asked. "I have two more rooms to finish, and it is only a half hour before check in."

"Hush. They will manage the rooms, no worries. Or they will wait. You are growing by the minute and need a dress that fits correctly."

"No one ever sees me."

"We all see you, *mon amie*! Especially now. You are getting hard to miss!"

"I hope not," Isabelle said. "I would rather not be seen in public, lest anyone recognize me."

"Who would recognize you?" Genevieve asked. When Isabelle did not respond, Genevieve caressed the teenager's face. "You are a beautiful young woman. You are glowing with life. Do not be ashamed. This is part of your story. Do you have plans for the baby once it is born?"

"No plans. But I don't want it."

"I see," Genevieve rubbed Isabelle's arm.

"I just don't want to cause any trouble here," Isabelle went on.

"I am the one who has caused trouble. You heard that night, no?" Genevieve laughed. "I too came here to hide. I was found, and the world did not stop. Use me as an example. Whatever you fear, you are protected here."

"I guess so."

"And I am your friend. So is Mrs. Nesbit and Miss Carter. You have many friends here, and you can trust us." Genevieve put the last pins in place and gingerly lifted the dress over the girl's swollen belly. "Ok now. I will have this ready for you in a few days."

"Thank you, Genevieve."

"Au revoir, ma petite."

After Isabelle left, Genevieve stared at the white peonies she had recently purchased in town and gathered in a water pitcher William had lent her. Laurent hadn't allowed flowers in her sewing room, as he thought it was a waste since only she would see them. (The salon, on the other hand, always had a massive arrangement delivered weekly.) Now her room was never without flowers.

Genevieve hadn't been this content in years. She loved her new life and freedom, not to mention her love affair with Stuart Bennett. He made her laugh, smile, blush, all those expressions she thought her facial muscles had forgotten. She had felt dead for so long. She was like the root of a flower in the winter, long buried but ready to rear its head and blossom with enough warmth and sunlight. Not only was Stuart a sensitive lover, but he was also kind and thoughtful in other ways: he never came without a small and delightful gift and always insisted on paying for her room at the inn, not that Carter had asked for it. He rarely spoke of his wife Rebecca – only to say they married quickly, and she had been unwell for quite some time. When they first met, he had found Rebecca to be a fun-loving, free spirit, having no idea her outrageousness was owed to the fact she was mentally unstable. Rebecca no longer went out in public, except for a daily walk with either him or her caretaker. Stuart knew people still whispered about the fits she'd had in social situations, so he did his best to shelter her from that kind of scrutiny.

Since Stuart was married and they were not free to be together, Genevieve was in no particular rush to meet with Laurent. Yet Lucille and Carter encouraged her to do so. Carter worried he would appear at Rams Head again, as he was clearly agitated, and his business must be suffering. Moreover, Genevieve had possessions she had left behind, including a handful of treasured items that belonged to her. Why not retrieve them, Lucille asked? How could she possibly explain to her friends that he might beat her, or chain her foot to her sewing machine, as he had done before? No, nothing was worth being alone with him, even for a moment.

Isabelle tugged and tucked the bedsheet into neat folds like Cora had taught her. Then came the damask coverlet, which she smoothed over the bed. Lastly, she fluffed and propped up the pillows in an inviting manner, pleased how well the bed turned out. Her mother would laugh if she saw what a capable domestic she had become. But she quickly erased her mother from her mind—her last memory of her was her face contorted in pure rage.

"What have you done?" her mother had shouted. "How could you let a man use you that way? How could you ruin our lives—because that is what you have done."

When Isabelle asked why her mother took the word of Mr. Chandler over her own, her mother slapped her for her impertinence. Mr. Chandler was the husband of her mother's best friend, Mrs. Chandler. Isabelle tried to explain that Mr. Chandler had forced himself on her—that she didn't even understand what he was doing until it was too late. And that it hurt, and she bled for a long time afterward. But her mother wouldn't hear her. "I have seen how you flatter him, how you laugh at his jokes. Men cannot control their baser instincts. You have shamed us. We will all have to suffer for your silly flirtations."

"Hi! Do you need help finishing the room?"

It was dear Cora, always quick to hurry her own work so she could give Isabelle a hand. Isabelle wiped her eyes. "I'm good."

"You have been crying." When Isabelle didn't answer, Cora said, "Iz, it's okay. We are friends, you can talk to me."

"You have enough problems. I know Miss Carter is upset with you for bringing me here in the first place. Probably your mom, too."

"Trust me, my mom is fine, and so is Miss Carter. Besides, she's relaxed now that Mrs. Nesbit is in your corner."

"I think that's overstating it. Mrs. Nesbit keeps asking about my family."

"Well, that secret is safe with me, *Isabelle*. Have no fear."

CHAPTER ELEVEN

Lucille looked up from her reading – *Summer,* the latest Edith Wharton novel — to see Carter, resplendent in a lavender raw silk dress, waving a piece of paper while she ran down the hill. It was an unseasonably warm day for mid-May, so Lucille was with her book, sitting on a blanket close to the water, under one of the umbrella-like oak trees to protect from the sun.

"Goodness, what is it?"

"He's alive – or at least he's not dead. Well, there's no proof he's dead, and good evidence he's alive."

"Slow down, I'm not following."

"Davidson! His friend and shipmate Paul," she waved the letter again. "Paul Winslow!"

"Tell me."

"They think Paul is alive. His wife, my friend Marjorie, received a letter from an American that a man who looks like Paul has been seen on one of the islands. It was in answer to her advertisement. The American said the man they thought was Paul seemed confused. So, Marjorie is soon to head down there and look for this man. I want to go with her."

Lucille clasped her chest. "No, you mustn't act rashly. I fear Marjorie is acting so. The letter writer could well be a fortune seeker."

"But maybe not. I applaud her for being so creative as to take out ads in the local papers. I never thought of that. You would do the same for Henry, you know you would."

Lucille paused, careful how she'd answer. "I don't know the islands, and never would I put myself in danger, chasing a rumor. Henry would not want that, and neither would Davidson. If Marjorie is determined, let her pave the way. Is she going with someone?"

"Yes, with Paul's brother."

"There you have it. Let them go and see what they can find. But do not go with them, I beg of you."

Carter looked off, tears streaming down her face. "I can't stand not knowing what happened to him."

"I know."

"I still believe he's alive. I do. I know you think I'm crazy..."

"That's where you're wrong. Until we hear otherwise, you are entitled to keep the faith. I feel like he's here with us now, don't you?"

"Every minute of every day."

The crates were piling up, bringing the hidden basement to almost full capacity. A dam had burst, which Carter didn't know how to close. The money she was getting was far too good to reverse course now. But the evidence was building up, along with the crates.

One day, a Mr. Samuel Oliver, one of the "storage customers" appeared, wanting to know and, even worse, see where his goods were being held. He seemed a nice enough man. Perhaps in his thirties, with a forgettable face and dark brown hair slicked back under his fedora. Graham had assured her the "customers" were mostly private citizens or restauranteurs, all carefully screened by the mysterious Benjamin Goodwin. It was a reasonable request, Mr. Oliver argued. And it was. But Carter acted like she didn't know what he was talking about. She offered him a complimentary drink in the lounge, with apologies that his trip had been in vain, then sent him on his way.

"You didn't bring him to the basement, did you?" Graham was aghast at the prospect she may have. It was the morning after Mr. Oliver's visit. Graham's sons were rolling up a crate as they spoke.

"No, I didn't. I played dumb about all of it."

"Good. Ben told me to do the same. He said it's imperative we confide in no one."

"And I haven't. But the man's visit made me want to meet this Mr. Benjamin Goodwin. Would he consider visiting us here?"

"I think that's a good idea," Graham said, his lips pursed. "This little operation has grown past what I was told it would be. I'm thinking maybe Benjamin should position someone here to watch out for you. Davidson would have a fit, if he thought I put you in harm's way."

"I am a big girl, Graham, so don't worry about that. But a meeting with Mr. Goodwin still feels necessary. This undertaking is requiring too much of my time. I must focus my efforts on the inn."

"How is that going?"

"Very well. Most of the locals have come to accept us. Some even seem quite invested, telling me which neighbors are troublemakers and which I should get to know better. Mrs. Crosby from down the road called on me with the most delicious blueberry muffins. Well, it turns out the muffins are just the beginning of what she bakes, so I've enlisted her and a few of her friends to supply our bread and cakes."

"Oh, I know Sheila. She's a real nice lady. A widow. Bet she could use the money."

"And I could use her help. Chef Adam was delighted, because his kitchen is inundated preparing lunch and dinner. He has had to hire two assistants."

"Do you have enough guests?"

"Yes, I'm happy to say we do. We have a good number of steady clients, including a couple of captains and senior crewmen who come to Shelter Island on a somewhat regular basis."

"Davidson would be so impressed, Miss Carter."

"It is a lot, I must admit. I need him here. I was supposed to be the hostess, and now I am holding down the fort, as well as hosting an underground business that, well, let's just say I never planned on."

"Not sure many women could do what you have done."

"It helps that I have someone as trustworthy as you at my side," She placed her two hands around his. "Graham, I must meet your wife. Would she ever come spend the night with you here, along with your two boys?"

"If she could bring Petal. Her damn dog," he grimaced. "I swear she's more devoted to it than the rest of us."

Carter laughed. "Come for the wedding weekend, all of you!"

Graham hesitated. "Let me ask her and get back to you."

"Oh, good. I want the wedding to be our grand opening, which means you must be a part of it."

When Graham's boat approached the dock two mornings later, Carter could see an additional man on board. Benjamin Goodwin. It must be him, because Graham's body language was relaxed and familiar; this was no interloper, but a friend – a blond and very tall friend.

The boys tied up the boat, and the men boarded the dock.

"Mr. Goodwin, I presume?"

He tipped his hat. "At your service, Ma'am." He wore an ivory-banded collared shirt with navy linen pants, held up by striped suspenders. A matching jacket was slung over his shoulder, hooked by a finger. The effect was comfortably wrinkled, but not shabby. It reminded her of Davidson.

Propriety be damned, Carter thought. She threw her arms around him and started to sob. She hadn't realized just how much tension she had been holding.

He seemed to sense her relief. "There, there. It's okay. Graham tells me you've been doing a masterful job."

"I apologize about my familiarity. Not many people were close to Davidson, and I know he trusted you."

"He did, and I'm sorry I didn't come sooner. I have been busy with business matters, but I plan to stay on Shelter Island for a time now."

Carter covered her mouth as she sighed. "I am so grateful. Thank you."

Graham gave her an encouraging smile.

Carter straightened, feeling more herself. "Please, come have some lunch. We must get you settled in, Mr. Goodwin."

"Please call me Ben."

"If you call me Carter."

Benjamin Goodwin felt like a godsend. It was as if Davidson saw her frustration and sent Ben to the rescue. He was as tall as Davidson and had the same capable, take-charge manner. How she missed that kind of male confidence. As they sat in the Garden Room after lunch, Ben showed her ledgers of the storage receipts, explaining how he and she were equal partners, splitting the fees after Graham's transport costs. He also explained how he and Davidson had envisioned the basement storage unfolding, though admittedly Ben had taken it further by renting the space to hold others' crates too.

"Would Davidson have wanted to include others?" Carter asked. "It doesn't seem wise."

"Much has changed in Davidson's absence," Ben said. "But no need to worry. We are the only ones who know where the crates are stored."

"Let's hope. Secrets have a way of getting out."

"True, which is why I need your word that you will continue to keep this business between us. Don't tell a soul. As Davidson says, even a small hole can sink a large ship."

He quoted Davidson so many times, she could hear his voice, his colorful expressions. It almost felt like he was in the room.

"You sound just like him," Carter said.

Ben shrugged. "I'll be honest, I was surprised to learn from Graham that Davidson left you title to Rams Head, especially as he hadn't told you anything of the storage below."

"I suppose Davidson wanted to protect me if anything happened to him. He also left me with Mr. William Smythe, whom you met in passing when you first arrived. He is a local, who helped Davidson build the inn. No one knows this place better than he does. He's our general manager."

Ben looked skeptical. "So, he knows about the basement. How well do you trust him?"

She smiled. "A great deal. Yes, Mr. Smythe knows about the hidden room, but has not been in it since we have been using it for storage. He focuses on managing the restaurant and inn, which is more than enough. He's a good and reliable man, and I'm so thankful he is here, another gift from Davidson."

"How considerate of Davidson to look out for you in his absence."

"Davidson is coming back. I just need to manage things while he's away."

Ben looked at her kindly. "But the shipwreck…."

"I know all about it. I also know they have not found him. Until they do, he is alive. I have a good friend on her way to Barbados as we speak. She heard of a possible sighting of her husband who was also on the ship. I wanted to join her, but my friend Mrs. Nesbit, whom you will soon meet, wouldn't hear of it. I still may go…"

"I agree with your friend Mrs. Nesbit. It is not safe for a lady to be unaccompanied in Barbados – or any Caribbean Island, for that matter. I would accompany you if you were so determined."

"Well, let's wait until Mrs. Winslow returns and see what she and her brother-in-law have found."

"A prudent plan, I agree."

Just at that moment, Lucille knocked on the open door. She looked her gracious self in a pale peach drop-waist dress.

Carter waved her into the room, as Ben rose in greeting. "Perfect timing, Lucille. This is Mr. Goodwin, the

113

friend of Davidson's I've been telling you about. Mr. Goodwin, Mrs. Nesbit."

"How do you do," Lucille greeted him pleasantly, if not especially warmly. Lucille was never quick to trust anyone.

Ben nodded in return. "Pleased to meet you. Are you staying here at the inn?"

"Yes, she's here while her husband is abroad on business," Carter explained, before Lucille could answer. "I can't tell you how comforting it has been to have a full-time confidante. Lucille, Mr. Goodwin has come to stay and manage the basement business."

Ben looked wary. "I didn't realize anyone other than Graham knew about our affairs."

"Mr. Goodwin, your secrets are safe with me," Lucille said. "My only interest is my friend's well-being, which is not a small concern. Will you be staying at the inn?"

"Call me Ben, please. And no. I purchased a fishing cottage on Little Ram Island. It was Davidson who encouraged me to do so. However, the cottage, which is more a shack, needs a good deal of work, which I will begin to oversee now that I am here."

"Will you be joined by family?" Carter asked.

He smiled. "No. Like Davidson, the war proved an obstacle to any kind of family life for me."

Carter nodded in understanding. "Well, you're now a part of the Rams Head family, right, Lucille? We have assembled a friendly group of residents as well as regular patrons."

"I look forward to meeting them all, as well as getting to know you better, Carter." Ben smiled, his hazel eyes staring into hers. Carter blushed. Despite missing Davidson, she could not help but note that Ben was a handsome man.

CHAPTER TWELVE

Late the next morning, Lucille crossed the foyer on her way to fetch a book from her room. She stopped at the sight of a young brunette by the reception desk, looking completely lost. She was quite petite, making even her modest valise seem burdensome.

"May I help you?" Lucille asked.

"Yes, I'm here to meet my friends, Miss Langley, Miss Quince and Miss McFee."

"Oh yes," Lucille said. "They are most likely on the veranda. Come, I'll show you to them."

The Connecticut Ladies, as Carter and Lucille had come to think of them, had been at the inn for two days and would no doubt leave the next, which is why this new girl's appearance was curious.

Helen noticed her first. "Mae, you made it! Join us for tea."

Mae half-smiled in answer, her eyes darting all around, before joining the trio.

When Helen later passed the main dining room where Lucille and Carter were sitting, Lucille called her over. "Is your friend all right?"

"She will be. Rose and I were like Mae the first time. James has a friend he'd like her to meet."

Lucille smiled, but inwardly shuddered. It was one thing when the confident and polished Elizabeth came to Rams Head, followed by the poised Rose and outgoing

Helen. But Mae looked like fear personified. She also seemed younger than the others, nineteen at most. Lucille wanted to ask more questions but thought better of it. Yet she didn't like that their operation was growing. She resolved to speak to Carter about it.

Dinner that night was relatively quiet, with few occupied tables. The mannerly Schnedekers were seated at what had become their usual table. Lucille smiled warmly at them, wishing them a good evening. They smiled back and wished her the same. Carter gave them her usual cool greeting, merely nodding her good evening, something Lucille thought silly and even rude given Carter's role as proprietress.

"Honestly, Carter, can't you be more generous? They are simply an unconventional couple." Lucille whispered once Carter joined her at the table.

"Call it what you want. They make people uncomfortable."

"I'm not uncomfortable."

"Henry would be, and you know it." Carter spoke to the menu.

Lucille didn't answer. She couldn't because Carter was probably right.

Ben Goodwin entered the dining room and made a straight line to their table, as he did every evening of his Shelter Island stay thus far.

Lucille eyed the Connecticut Ladies table and couldn't help but notice that Mae wasn't participating in the group's joviality. A man's arm was inappropriately around her chair, and Lucille didn't like the look of him. He was a very large man for starters, and she was a mere slip of a girl. He also seemed 20 years her senior, if not more. Elizabeth followed Lucille's gaze, and Lucille caught her eye, purposefully looking over to Mae. Elizabeth nodded. Lucille could only hope Elizabeth and the other two women would look out for their new young companion.

"Lucille, Carter tells me your husband is in the steel industry, traveling abroad," Ben said, trying to draw her into the conversation. They were now on a first-name basis. "Were you not eager to join him?"

"I don't fare well on ships, as Henry knows too well," she answered politely. "Best I stay here with Carter while he gets his work done. He's in Paris this week, I believe. He is setting up a partnership with a London-based import firm for European expansion."

"You must miss one another."

"Dreadfully so."

"I can imagine," Ben smiled. "He must take great comfort knowing you are here with such a dear friend."

"Henry adores Carter. He feels she is smarter than most men he knows and would love to have her join his company. She knows she has an open invitation to do so."

Carter side-rolled her eyes. "Lucille— "

"Any interest in doing that, Carter?" Ben asked.

"Of course not. I'm rather enjoying this business, even with its unique challenges. Everyday offers a new experience, a new problem to solve."

"You have done an impressive job," Ben said approvingly. "Intelligence like yours is quite disarming in so beautiful a woman."

Lucille noticed Carter's cheeks redden. Maybe this Ben Goodwin was exactly what was needed for Carter to accept Davidson's passing.

After dinner, Ben bade them goodnight and headed back to his cottage. Carter and Lucille hung back to wish a good evening to the stragglers, gently encouraging them to call it a night. This was their usual practice, to keep their establishment from becoming a place for drunken, late-night revelry.

To that point, at the Connecticut Ladies' table, the large newcomer stood up and pushed his chair away from the table. "Why are we lingering?" he asked. "Shouldn't we all be heading upstairs? This is too expensive a night to waste. Come on, little lady." He yanked Mae's arm.

"Charles, lower your voice and sit down," said Mr. James Morton, Elizabeth's regular companion, a balding man with a hefty mustache. "And let go of her. Now."

"Why should I?"

"Because I asked you to, and I won't ask again." He looked to the women at the table. "I apologize, ladies."

"Why are you apologizing to these girls? They know why we're here. Everyone knows why we're here."

119

"Lower your voice, I said." Mr. Morton spoke calmly, yet forcefully.

Carter signaled to William, who was entering the room from the kitchen to prepare the table's check.

The burly man was intoxicated and needed to leave. Mr. Morton gave Carter a nod that he was taking care of it. Helen's gentleman friend took the drunk patron outside, while Mr. Morton settled the bill. He apologized to Carter before leaving with the remaining gentleman. The handful of guests lingering in the dining room visibly relaxed as they left.

Elizabeth rushed over to Carter. "I—"

"Let's talk about this in the morning," Carter said under her breath, smiling at the other patrons, who seemed to be observing them.

Elizabeth bit her lip before gathering her friends for the night.

Lucille was mortified. When Carter returned to the table, Lucille couldn't help but say, "and you thought the Schnedekers made people uncomfortable."

Carter frowned at her friend. "Don't start. I am upset enough."

Carter descended the stairs early the next morning to see several bags by the door. She tightened the red sash on her floral dress, knowing she would have to confront Elizabeth.

Elizabeth spotted Carter first, walked over and spoke softly. "Good morning. I'm glad you're up early. There was no one at the desk to settle our bill."

"I can do that," Carter said as she went behind the counter. "Don't worry about the extra room."

"That is very kind of you," Elizabeth said, avoiding eye contact.

"Elizabeth, look at me. Last night was appalling.... In so many ways," she added. "Fortunately, your friend Mr. Morton handled matters smoothly and quickly. The other gentleman, safe to say, won't be returning."

"Mae won't be returning either."

"I am very glad to hear that. Lucille had been particularly concerned about her. Do I have your word that your business is under control? I do not want more women showing up, nor more men you don't know."

"Agreed," Elizabeth answered without elaboration.

Rose, Helen and Mae came down the stairs together. Carter greeted them with a smile. "Please help yourselves to some coffee," she added, which Isabelle was just now putting up.

Mae looked at Isabelle's stomach. "Did you work here? Is that how..."

"Mae!" Helen quietly admonished her.

Isabelle didn't understand the implication, that maybe she had been a sex worker. "I'm a chambermaid, yes. I know your rooms well — thank you for always tidying up."

Helen laughed. "That's what we do. We're well-trained housewives."

Margaret descended the stairs at that moment and noticed the bags. "This is early for you," she said to the women. Margaret had dinner with Curtis's family the night before and missed the excitement.

"Yes, I asked James to send us an early boat," Elizabeth said. "One cup ladies, and then we depart."

Carter sympathized with the ladies, she did. However, she had to put the inn and its reputation first and therefore couldn't help wishing they would not return of their own accord. But she did not feel that lucky.

CHAPTER THIRTEEN

Later that morning, Carter received a telegram from Bertha Krantz:

> **Sending my good friend Estelle Church to stay at your inn. A fellow suffragist. Arrives tomorrow. You'll adore her. Ask her to sing! Love you,B**

Lucille shook her head when Carter showed her the message. "Bertha is such a bohemian. No wonder you're friends."

"I've always sensed disapproval from you about her."

"She's just so, so...." Lucille paused, "*flamboyant.* Outlandish for the sake of it. That crazy hair, the kimonos and, of course, the long cigarette. Like she has something to prove."

"Maybe she's just unburdened from the norms that bind women."

"It helps to be single and rich. In any event, she makes it clear she thinks me a bore."

"Ha! Then Bertha doesn't know you very well. Whatever else, I adore her. I'm also indebted. She's how I met Davidson, don't forget. He didn't exactly grace many guest lists in fine dining rooms."

Recalling Davidson's rather casual appearance the few times they met, Lucille couldn't argue with that. "Fine. I'm sure her friend will be interesting. But please don't ask her to sing — unless she's a classical performer. This isn't a saloon."

"How many saloons have you been to?"

Lucille squinted her eyes. "Very funny."

Estelle Church arrived the following day on Graham's steamer. From the dock, Carter saw a woman's wide-brimmed hat, and as the boat came closer, she could see that Estelle was colored. Bertha hadn't mentioned that. What if Shelter Island didn't welcome negros – not that Carter had previously given any thought to the matter; she didn't know many colored women herself. Will Estelle's presence be a problem?

Graham nodded to Carter and tied up his boat. He avoided her eyes, and she wondered if he had an issue with having Estelle on his boat.

"You must be Miss Church. I'm Miss Carter."

"*Mrs.* Church," the woman said, her tone wary as she took in Carter and everything around her. Dressed in an olive-green traveling suit, Estelle possessed a natural elegance, tall and slim, her neck long and swanlike. Carter judged her to be around forty. She relaxed at Carter's smile. "Thank you for having me, Miss Carter. Miss Krantz thinks the world of you."

"And I of her. Welcome to Rams Head."

Estelle turned to take her two bags, which Graham had left on the dock. Neither son offered any assistance.

"Let me get you some help with those," Carter said. She turned and widened her eyes at Graham as she looked at the bags. He immediately motioned Tim to take them.

Lucille was already on her way down the hill. "You must be Miss Church."

"*Mrs.* Church," Carter corrected Lucille.

"Hello, I'm Mrs. Lucille Nesbit. I understand you are a fellow suffragist."

"In a manner of speaking. I'm with the Alpha Suffrage Club."

"Ah yes, I'm from Chicago. I'm aware of your organization's important contributions to the cause."

Estelle smiled politely at Lucille. Carter sensed the tension and appreciated the resentment of being pushed out of the larger suffrage movement. The Alpha Club had been founded by Ida B. Wells-Barnett in answer to white women excluding colored women from the greater suffrage movement, even after Illinois women were granted the state vote (the first state east of the Mississippi to do so.) Worse, a vocal and prominent group of white Chicago women fought against colored women and men voting at all and aided in making it difficult to do so. There were many reasons why white suffragist leaders sought to marginalize their colored counterparts, including not wanting to alienate

Southern lawmakers who opposed increasing the colored vote at all.

"So, what brings you to our island," Carter inquired, as the women traversed the hill. "Miss Krantz didn't say."

"I am looking for my grandmother's sister, who was born and worked for a time at an estate called Sylvester Manor. While the rest of the family moved, she stayed on Shelter Island to get married. The family lost touch altogether."

"Have you tried writing her?" Lucille asked.

"I'm not sure where she is. And most likely she doesn't read. I thought it better to look for her in person. I understand the island is quite small."

"That it is," Carter said.

They arrived at the foyer, where Estelle's bags awaited. Originally Carter had planned to place Bertha's friend near her and Lucille's rooms. Instead, Carter took the key to room #17, which was on the far side of the hall where the Connecticut Ladies usually stayed. Carter didn't want to chance alienating white guests with Estelle's presence. Carter was flustered and hated thinking this way, but accommodating coloreds was uncharted territory.

"Let me bring you to your room," Carter said. "Afterwards, Mrs. Nesbit and I would be delighted for you to join us for lunch on the veranda — in a half an hour or so?"

"I would enjoy that, yes." Estelle said, removing her hat and looking around her. "What an enchanting place you have here."

Minutes before lunch, Carter knocked on Lucille's door so they could speak privately. "What do I do?" Carter asked anxiously as she entered the room. "I had no idea she was colored. Perhaps I should have had lunch served in my room."

"No. That would be rude. So typical of Bertha to think the whole world was as progressive as Manhattan. Sadly, it's not." Lucille sighed. "Let's not fret about it now. Mrs. Church seems lovely."

"Everyone seems lovely to you. I'm trying to run a business."

"Well, she's here. As my mother always said, just be a lady whatever the circumstances."

"You quote your mother at the oddest times. Let's head downstairs, shall we?"

Estelle joined them at their table on the end of the veranda, having changed from her olive ensemble into a lighter floral frock.

"My room is most pleasant, thank you," Estelle said. "I appreciate it has its own bathroom. I gather not all the rooms do."

"You gather correctly," Carter said. It was yet another reason she chose #17 – so that Estelle would not be sharing a bathroom with other guests. The room was also next to the back staircase.

Carter poured their iced tea from the pitcher on the table. "Tell us, how did you meet Miss Krantz?"

"Several years ago, she reached out to the Alpha Suffrage Club, wanting to better align forces. She was outraged colored women were sent to the back of the 1913 DC protest and wished to personally apologize to Ida Wells-Barnett, who had pushed her way forward."

"I didn't realize Miss Krantz had done that," Carter said, admiring their mutual friend. Carter had been at that protest – her first in Washington DC – and had not considered how the movement treated colored women.

"Miss Krantz is one of our fiercest allies," Estelle continued. "She disagreed with the suffrage movement's focus on educated women which, let's face it, was designed to sideline colored women. Miss Krantz and I liked each other immediately, and she invited me to visit her in New York."

"I agree we should all be aligned," Lucille concurred. "But why do you assume the call for educated suffragists is directed only at colored women? Many white women aren't educated."

"Perhaps, but it's rarer for a colored woman to have schooling—many have been denied education. Part of Ida's effort has been to encourage women to vote for race-conscious leaders who would help further their rights with protective laws. Right now, a colored woman could be robbed, beaten, or raped with little legal recourse."

Carter couldn't resist responding. "I see what you're saying Mrs. Church, but we must do what it takes to get the vote, which ultimately will benefit *all* women. It's not like any of us were especially happy to support the war effort, but our forceful show of patriotism went a long way." President Wilson initially balked at the suffrage movement but came around after millions of women proved vital to the war's success. Carter was a believer in looking to the greater good when choosing one's battles.

Estelle paused a few moments before speaking. "Surely you know *all* women are not treated the same in this country, whatever the law says. Presently, our men have a hard time voting, as my husband Walter has discovered. Poll taxes and literacy tests are bad enough, but he also faces the real threat of violence every time he goes to vote."

"How dreadful," Lucille said, shaking her head.

"I'm not disagreeing, Estelle," Carter said. "But maybe our leaders didn't want to complicate the bigger movement by adding on racial issues."

"When you lift one injustice, you have the opportunity to lift them all – which is how *our* leaders see it," Estelle answered. She then relented. "I'm sorry, I don't want us to start off on the wrong foot. I believe we're all on the same side."

Carter smiled. "We certainly are."

Cora arrived to serve their lunch, which consisted of a variety of quarter-cut sandwiches and potato salad.

Lucille seized the opportunity to change the subject. "So, you believe your aunt is living at Sylvester Manor?"

"I don't know where she is, though we have no reason to think Aunt Agnes ever left Shelter Island."

"Does your family descend from those who worked the Sylvester plantation many years ago?" Carter asked.

"Yes. That estate had enslaved coloreds for almost two hundred years."

"I had no idea," Carter said.

"We all think of slaves in the South. But Long Island was home to the largest slave populations in the northeast. I'm close with my grandmother who grew up on Sylvester Manor – though she was born free. She hasn't seen her sister since they were young teenagers. At the very least, I'd like to see where my family lived."

"Understandable," Lucille said. "Tell us about your present-day family." Estelle shared that she was married to her childhood sweetheart, an investor, and they had two grown children. It was through the suffrage fight that Estelle began traveling, and she hoped to do more now that she was less needed at home.

"Your husband doesn't mind you traveling?" Carter asked.

"Walter's always supported my outside interests," Estelle said, adding. "I've been blessed that way." Lucille and Carter briefly recounted their lives and how they, like Estelle and Bertha, became friends through the suffrage movement.

After the trio consumed a dessert of caramelized brownies, Estelle patted her mouth with her napkin. "May speak frankly, Miss Carter?"

"Why, of course," Carter said. "But please call me Carter."

"Thank you, and please call me Estelle."

"And you may call me Lucille."

"The way Miss Krantz, Bertha, spoke," Estelle said. "I was expecting a colored person's inn, or at least a mixed inn, which this is clearly not. Even your help is white. I don't want to cause you problems. Nice as this lunch is, I am happy to take meals in my room. In fact, I'd prefer it. I suspect white folks won't welcome my presence here."

Carter exhaled. "I appreciate your candor – and yes, I don't want *you* to feel uncomfortable. We have many seafaring guests here at the bar and for dinner. I can't vouch for their behavior. But Lucille and I would love you to join us if and when you feel comfortable doing so."

"As I said, it's my preference. I *like* being alone. I will let you know if I have a change of heart."

"Please do."

After Estelle left the table, Lucille spoke. "That poor woman. I hope she finds her Aunt Agnes. Wait, what are you doing?" She asked, as Carter was frantically gathering up their plates.

"Lucille, poor *us*! I have no idea how to handle this. What if someone is rude to her? Or refuses to eat or stay here?"

"Calm down. Estelle is only here for a short while. She'll eat in her room and spend her days looking for her great aunt. She has no more interest in mingling with your guests than they will have with her. It'll be fine," Lucille stood and touched Carter's arm. "Leave the dishes for Cora. She has that nice big tray."

Carter put down the plates and took a deep breath. "You're right."

"Exactly. You can't possibly carry them all."

"I mean about Estelle."

"Carter, try not to worry. I am here with you, and if need be, I will tell people she is my friend."

"Even you can't ease this situation, Lucille. I must speak to William and let him know about our newest guest."

CHAPTER FOURTEEN

Since arriving two weeks earlier, Ben Goodwin liked to greet Graham at the Rams Head dock whenever he made his deliveries. There were few, if any, crates as the basement was at full capacity, which made the visits seem more of an excuse to see Carter. At first, Carter missed her quiet mornings looking for the red cardinal, but then she came to look forward to seeing Ben's navy cap atop his messy blond hair. One sunny morning, after they bade goodbye to Graham and his sons, Ben insisted that Carter visit the cottage he was building. It was nearby on Little Ram Island, directly across Coecles Harbor. He took her in his small boat.

"This is an incredible spot," Carter said above the the sawing and hammering.

"Thank you. As you can tell the house was a small fishing cottage, the part where I'm staying. I'm enlarging it to be a year-round home."

"Do you plan to live here full time?"

"That would partly depend on the woman I will marry someday. We would need to keep our city home, of course."

"I love that you speak of her as if you know who she is."

He smiled at her, holding her eyes a moment too long.

Carter broke off eye contact first. "Ben, if I may, what exactly is your business?"

"I'm in importing/exporting."

"Same as Davidson."

"Yes."

"Do you travel much by sea as well?"

"I used to. It's how I've earned my living. But I would like to have a home now, and let others do the shipping. I desire a steadier life."

"I well understand. I too traveled for my work. It wears on you."

"Yes, I remember Davidson saying you were a fellow traveler. You can sense that about someone. They have a broader perspective than most."

"Thank you. Though my travels were mostly contained to New York State. I gather you've traveled more extensively."

"My work took me up and down the coast. And I served as a Merchant Marine for much of last year. Anyway, it's nice to be home. I grew up here in New York."

"You did? Where?" Carter realized she knew so little about him.

"Brooklyn. I later moved to Manhattan — after school."

"You don't have a New York accent," Carter remarked.

"Traveling will do that," he offered. "Listen, I had an ulterior motive in bringing you here."

"Oh?"

"I need some design ideas – from a woman's perspective."

"But I was about to ask you stories about growing up in New York City, where you went to school and how you started your business."

"I'm an open book, Carter; you may ask me anything – over dinner," he said. "But we're here, and I need to make decisions – and soon, my workers tell me."

The next hour, they talked about the layout of the expanded cottage and its grounds: where will the gardens go? Which side gets the most sun, the most wind? Where to position the dock? It was indulgent to imagine someone else's carefree future, as opposed to her own which felt full of unknowns, or worse, a rickety house of cards that could tumble at any moment. How can you know yourself so well one moment and feel so uncertain the next, she wondered? She looked back and Ben and forced a smile.

At one point, Ben excused himself and came out of the cottage with a basket, some pillows, and a blanket.

"So, we agreed this side for the veranda? Let's walk as far as we can from the construction noise." They found a spot by the water. Ben's face broke into his crooked grin as he spread a blanket and then patted a pillow for her to sit on. "Please excuse my poor table service."

Carter was thoroughly charmed by his foresight and thoughtfulness. The fruit, the bread, the sliced salmon, the cured pickles, the various spreads and pastries, and two bottles of wine, one red, one white. More than the delicious lunch, it was glorious to spend time away from Rams Head. She hadn't realized how exhausted she was. It was a relief to hand over the reins to someone as capable as Ben, if even for an afternoon. He caught her staring at him, and she felt her cheeks enflame. Was it the sun she wondered?

She suddenly felt sad and realized why: her first date with Davidson was also a picnic. "I'm sorry," she said. "Much as I'm enjoying myself, I must ask you to take me back. I need to check in with my staff. Also, Lucille will worry, as I didn't tell anyone I was leaving the inn."

"Certainly." He didn't encourage her to stay longer, which she appreciated. Together they gathered the remnants of their lunch into the basket. Ben stood first, offering his hand to Carter. When she stood their faces were inches apart.

"I am not used to looking eye-to-eye with a woman," he marveled.

Flustered, she stepped back. "This was a treat, Ben. All of it. Thank you."

He blinked. "Yes. Let's get you back to Rams Head."

When they arrived back at the inn, William was waiting by the front desk and asked to speak with Ben privately. Ben followed him out to the street side of the inn. Carter sensed friction between the two men but understood that it must be difficult for William to see another man on his turf. She waited in the foyer. When the two men returned, William dashed into the lounge to finish whatever paperwork he had left on the bar.

"Is everything okay, Ben?"

"Oh, yes. William wanted to know if I knew a disagreeable character who showed up while we were gone. A man named Romano."

"I've met him."

"Yes, I thought that was the man you told me about. I instructed William to make sure the man knows he is not welcome here."

"Thank you," Carter said, then stopped him before he left. "Small thing Ben, but William reports to me. Please don't 'instruct' him without letting me know first."

"I apologize. But he was the one who called me outside."

"You're right, but I would appreciate you deferring to me with my staff."

Ben was about to leave but stopped. "Carter, it's not a bad idea for your staff to know I'm here keeping an eye on things. You're a strong woman, no question. I won't assert myself unnecessarily, but Davidson would probably appreciate my watching out for you."

Carter knew he was correct but couldn't bring herself to admit it. Instead, she smiled. "We're all grateful you're here."

Henry, my love,

Time is just flying by – you have been away for almost two months! In that one and only sense, time has not flown at all. I have had you at my side for almost ten years, and I am anxious to have you back.

Much has happened here at Rams Head. Davidson had arranged to store liquor in the basement. At first, we thought it just his liquor, which was fine, but then it turned out he had a partner – a Mr. Benjamin Goodwin – who has 'rented' out space to other liquor owners in advance of the inevitable enforcement which, as you know, will occur nationwide as of January...

Lucille stopped writing. Telling Henry of this liquor operation was risky for many reasons. He might insist that she leave immediately. He might even notify the authorities, God forbid, potentially shutting down Carter's inn altogether.

Carter and Ben would never forgive her if she were responsible for alerting outsiders. Yet Lucille worried about the dangers this kind of hoarding might open them up to – or already had opened them up to. Two nights ago, when Mr. Romano had come with a friend asking Ben where the liquor was kept, she learned was not his first time nosing around the place. Fortunately, Ben and William were able to steer him away – but not before he stormed into the basement, where to everyone's relief, nothing looked suspicious. Ben promised Carter he would call the police should he visit again. This liquor business was not for the faint of heart — and Lucille feared it was only the beginning.

Lucille crumpled her letter and began anew, filling Henry in on the upcoming wedding details, the beautiful garden where Chef Adam was growing the restaurant's produce, the handsome chicken coop William had built, as well has his impressive honey farming, and her secret hopes for Carter and Ben. All true, if somewhat incomplete.

Lucille had tried to talk to Ben about her fears regarding the basement. One afternoon, she pulled him aside for a tete-a-tete. "No harm will come to any of you. You have my word," he said. "The only people – clients - who know about our business are in New York City. Moreover, alcohol is legal as of this date. We are allowed to store it for a price, just as any warehouse owner may store others' wares for a fee."

"Surely this is different, since alcohol is soon to be outlawed."

"Alcohol itself won't be outlawed – manufacturing, transporting or selling it will be outlawed."

"We are splitting hairs, no?"

"Not at all, Lucille, I appreciate your concern, I do, but please just worry about today, not tomorrow. Today, all is well, and this is very much under control. Carter needs the extra money. By January, let's hope she will be self-sufficient with Rams Head's business paying for itself."

Carter was right: Ben's dark blond hair and uneven smile were beguiling. He was easy to trust.

"Ben, may I ask you something else?"

"Of course."

"Do you believe Davidson is coming back?"

"No."

"You answered that quickly. What makes you so sure?"

"I wish I believed otherwise, as Davidson was a close friend, yet given what I know of the shipwreck, there is simply no way he could have survived it. Besides, much time has passed. We would have heard from him or about him by now. I believe Carter will see to reason with time. Sooner than later, I hope."

"As long as we are speaking confidentially, may I ask: how do you feel about Carter?"

He smiled. "You may be the most forthright woman I have ever met – other than Carter, of course."

"Yes, forgive my indiscretion. Still, I would appreciate just as forthright an answer."

Ben waited a moment before letting out a long sigh. "Yes, I do. I care for her. Greatly, if I am honest. Yet I will not approach her while she mourns Davidson."

"I wish she was merely mourning. She truly believes he is alive."

Carter sat in the Garden Room in her favorite leather wingback chair, the beautiful cut lilies from the garden softly perfuming the air. The inn's ledger that William had provided was before her on the round table. There were still a few open construction costs, but the "basement rent" had closed most of that window. She was fortunate William wasn't the type to ask questions and that she had never confided her personal money woes. He must think she had a a sizable nest egg somewhere. Carter then compared the monthly restaurant and bar tallies with her fixed expenses and the numbers were getting closer. This was good news. Of course, the bar was a thriving business; losing it in January would surely affect the bottom line. She had no back up plan, and that worried her most of all. What if this inn didn't work out? What would she do? Where would she go? She had no family, no education, no employable skills to speak of. No, she couldn't think about that. Besides, for now at least, the ledgers looked promising.

"Miss Carter?" A woman in her mid-thirties appeared at the room's entrance. Carter straightened. One look at the woman said she wasn't a local: she was dressed in navy, from the expensive-looking tailored jacket belted over a matching dress to her pearl-buttoned shoes. Her cloche straw hat was also navy. It framed coiffed auburn curls around a fine-featured, tight-lipped face. This was a patrician woman in style and posture. Maybe she was here to book a family summer vacation?

"Yes, I am Miss Carter. May I help you?"

"I hope so." The woman entered the room and spoke softly, almost conspiratorially. "I'm looking for my daughter. Her name is Charlotte Worthington. She is sixteen years old. Curly red hair."

Somehow, Carter knew right away. Isabelle. Could the domestic upstairs be this woman's daughter? But why would the girl hide if she was from a well-off family, as evidenced by Mrs. Worthington's presentation.

"There is a girl here by that description, but she goes by a different name."

"Hmmm. Do you have a young girl here named Cora Smythe working here by chance? Cora worked in my home. I looked up her employment references. She and my daughter were friends, I came to learn."

Carter's stomach plummeted. Cora's friend. Isabelle's fear of revealing her identity. Her refusal to consider going home. Carter was hiding this woman's daughter upstairs. But still, something told Carter there was more to the story.

"The girl I'm thinking of is quite nervous about her family," Carter said. "She seems to believe they don't want her to return."

The woman sat down in the wingback across from Carter. Her shoulders slumped with relief as she let out a sigh. "So, she is here." Carter didn't answer. "She's with child, as you must know."

"Yes."

"I frightened her. Her father only knows she ran away. He doesn't know about her condition."

"You frightened her away?"

"Trust me, if her father knew about her condition, he would have done worse than frighten her. He is a prominent man of the community, and an expectant teenager would mean certain ruination of all he has worked for. How is she?"

Carter tried to keep her face still. Isn't this for the best? For Isabelle to be reunited with her family? "Assuming she is your daughter, she is quite content at Rams Head."

"What does she do here?"

"She's a chambermaid."

Mrs. Worthington rolled her eyes. "Dear God."

"She shares her duties with two other young girls, Cora being one – the three are good friends," Carter found herself babbling. "There are only seventeen rooms, so it's less than a half day's work. She feels productive, and it provides her room and board."

"I see," Mrs. Worthington said, her face etched with disapproval. "I'm now doubting it's Charlotte. My daughter has never made a bed or cleaned a room in her life."

"What if it is your Charlotte? May I ask what you have planned for her?"

"I have not thought that far ahead. Her father doesn't know I am here."

"Would she be safe going home with you?"

"What are you implying?"

Carter knew to avoid antagonizing Mrs. Worthington. "I apologize. We need to establish if this girl and your daughter are one and the same. Allow me to speak to her while you wait here."

"Do not attempt any funny business with her, Miss Carter. I am a mother looking for my child."

"Understood. I'll be right back." Carter gathered the papers she was working on. "Again, please remain here. I will bring the girl down."

Carter found Isabelle quickly, as she was cleaning room 11 next to the main staircase. She cried when Carter asked if she was Charlotte Worthington. Her body shook when she was told her mother was waiting for her downstairs.

"Please, no. Let me hide or run away. My mother is not as nice as she may have appeared to you. Her public demeanor is very different from her private one."

Carter couldn't imagine she had met the 'nice' Mrs. Worthington. "Be that as it may, you need to come downstairs. You are a minor, and I cannot keep you here without your parents' permission."

"I   can't.   I   won't!"

Carter sighed. She wished Lucille were here. She would know how to convince the girl. "Fine. Let us go downstairs and see what she has to say. I will stay in the room, if you want me to."

"Yes, I need you to, Miss Carter." Isabelle was again the scared girl she was when they first met. "You, Mrs. Nesbit, and Madame Blanc are the only adults who have listened to me. My mother cares more about *him* than me." Carter sensed this wasn't the time to ask who "him" was.

"Come," Carter said, holding out her hand. "I will stay with you."

Carter and Isabelle entered the Garden Room. Mrs. Worthington was looking out the window. When she turned around, her eyes were unreadable. She looked at Isabelle, her face first and then her round stomach. She also eyed Carter whose staunch expression made it clear she was not leaving the room.

Mrs. Worthington smiled tightly. "You have put us through such worry." She stepped forward and touched Isabelle's face with one hand. "Your brother, sister and I have missed you terribly."

"Thank you. Has Father noticed my absence?"

"Of course," she said, annoyed. "He just has a different way than the rest of us."

Isabelle did not cry. "I am well and wish to stay here. If I may." She looked to Carter and then to her mother, as if asking permission from both.

"Yes, so I see," Mrs. Worthington said. "I've investigated homes for unwed mothers. There's a highly regarded one upstate in Binghamton."

"But I like it here!" Isabelle said.

"I can't risk you being seen, Charlotte."

"I am hidden from public view."

"But is that foolproof?"

"Mrs. Worthington, it's not in my interest to have an expectant teenager in full view of my guests."

"I should think not."

"I want to stay here," the girl pleaded.

Carter said, "I'm not sure that is a good idea. You should go back with your mother."

"No!" Isabelle shook her head vehemently. "Please," she implored Carter.

"I can't very well have her return with me in any event," Mrs. Worthington said, talking over Isabelle's pleas. "Let her stay here until I come up with a plan. In the meantime, I will pay you, so Charlotte does not have to clean up after others."

"I like earning my keep, Mother."

Mrs. Worthington kept her eyes on Carter. "Charlotte, I would like a moment alone with Miss Carter. Please, wait in the other room."

As Carter closed the Garden Room glass-paned door, Mrs. Worthington felt around in her purse and removed a roll of bills, which she thrust into Carter's hand. "There will be more when I return. I will think of a longer-term solution and how best to transport Charlotte to a home, be it the one in Binghamton or some other place. The election is in November, and this simply cannot interfere. We have told the workers that Charlotte is traveling abroad with her aunt."

"Election?"

"My husband is a New York state congressman from Oyster Bay."

"Oh. Isa— I mean, Charlotte has said nothing about her family. Or of the boy who," she paused, "is the father."

Mrs. Worthington studied Carter's face. "All the better. Charlotte seems well, and I like that she uses another name here. We are indebted to you, Miss Carter."

Before Carter could think of a response, Mrs. Worthington turned and left, her heels clicking out of Rams Head as quickly as possible.

Carter looked at the bills in her hand. Great, she thought. Now we're officially a home for unwed mothers.

CHAPTER FIFTEEN

"She doesn't want to be called Charlotte?" Lucille said. "I wondered where 'Isabelle' came from."

Carter and Lucille sat outside on the Adirondack chairs, wrapped in shawls, enjoying a glass of white wine before dinner. They had invited Genevieve and Stuart to dine with them that night, but Carter wanted to speak with Lucille beforehand about Mrs. Worthington's visit.

"That's what you get out of all this? Her name? Somehow harboring a pregnant teenager feels all the worse, now that we're being paid for it. Like we're some kind of unsavory institution."

"Wouldn't be the first time," Lucille murmured under her breath, while she took a sip of her wine.

"Don't start," said Carter, throwing her a look.

"Listen, her mother sounds ghastly," Lucille said. "I like Isabelle and am glad she's with us. You're getting an extra housekeeper at no cost. In fact, you're now being paid for having a housekeeper."

"Except that she's not supposed to be a housekeeper anymore. Although I don't think I can stop her—she wants to do the work, despite what her mother says. And her mother wants assurances that no one will see her, but I can't keep her locked in her room. Fortunately, the dresses Genevieve has made mask her stomach well."

"She uses the staff staircase to go in and out of the hotel," Lucille said. "There is no reason she can't walk the grounds. People will assume she is a happily married guest."

Carter closed her eyes at Lucille's naivety. "Minus the husband."

"Or a traveling husband who would prefer his wife safe and sound while he's away. Like me."

Lucille's reasoning was beginning to calm Carter.

"Never a dull moment here," Carter said.

Lucille smiled in response and looked towards the water. "Carter, those three singular chairs by the beach look lonely. Someone must have moved them. Let's go group them together."

Carter laughed and stood. "Fine. I bet you've been looking at them this whole time, just itching to move them." The friends walked down to the wayward chairs, Lucille deciding which should be moved. Each took an armrest.

"Why did you choose such cumbersome chairs?" Lucille asked as they moved the first in unison.

"Because they're comfortable. And I couldn't resist the story: an Adirondack man designed them and his friend, who lived near a sanatorium, realized how good they were for opening up one's chest and had them patented. Speaking of friends...."

Cora and Isabelle suddenly appeared and offered to help move the other chair. They accepted Cora's help, but not Isabelle's. "No straining yourself, dear girl," Lucille admonished.

After the chairs were put in place, Cora and Isabelle continued their walk, most likely to Cora's house for dinner.

"They remind me of us," Lucille said, watching them walk away.

"Come," Carter said, taking Lucille's arm. "Genevieve, Stuart and Ben will be waiting for us."

Estelle played with her meatloaf and corn salad. She wished she had some of Grammy's secret sauce to spice it. The food wasn't bad here, it could just use a little something. Still, she was grateful to be at Rams Head, away from Chicago and away from New York and Bertha's generous, but overbearing presence. How many salons can one possibly attend? Or leave when they are hosted in the very house you're staying?

Estelle's husband Walter had died from the Spanish Flu a month ago. She took advantage of Bertha's open invitation to visit her in New York, having no idea what Bertha's lifestyle was like. But Estelle needed time away from her family, her grown children, Walter's friends, as well as his and her fellow workers — all of the well-meaning people in her life.

She was as angry as she was devastated at Walter's passing. Negros were less likely to contract the flu, thanks to being segregated from the larger population. But if and when they did get sick, they were less likely to survive it due to poor health care and crowded conditions. And it was spreading like wildfire; the Chicago papers reported that hundreds of people—colored and white—were dying every day. Despite Walter's social standing, no white hospital would admit him. Provident, the only colored hospital in Chicago, was woefully overwhelmed and understaffed. Estelle hadn't even been allowed to visit him, for fear of it spreading, so he died alone, and from what she could surmise, unattended.

If Walter were white, Estelle was certain he would be alive today. But harping on the unfairness of it with others only made mourning him all the more impossible. So, Estelle came to New York, not even telling Bertha the real reason why she had come. What she was running from. She was desperate to leave behind the shock of it, the pity, the sympathy. She needed to think. To recover enough to go back into the world and face life without her husband.

Rams Head Inn was good for now. Even if it was a white woman's hotel. Carter and Lucille were so busy with the inn's business, they mostly left her to herself. If they only knew how well that served her. And while Carter and Lucille invited her to join them for meals, she was just as happy not to bother with the stares and whispers of other guests, and have meals brought to her room. William always obliged her, bringing her a handwritten menu for breakfast, lunch and dinner. She had only to check the boxes next to her preferences. Carter had sent up a bottle of wine, so she need not even request a glass with dinner. Isabelle, who cleaned her room, was a cheerful presence — and another person who asked no questions. The young girl was clearly had her own troubles, given her belly. She may think that blousy dress hid it, but nothing got past Estelle. No matter. She could keep a secret.

Her search for Aunt Agnes was real. Grammy was now 82 years old and living back in Chicago with Estelle's older brother Michael. As she got on in years, she wanted to know what happened to her older sister, who at 17 years old decided to stay at the Manor to marry her boyfriend John Mason when the rest of the family took off for Greenport and beyond. Estelle only knew Agnes from a very faded and creased drawing that sat framed on the fireplace in Grammy's home. Any revelation about her sister's whereabouts would be a gift to Grammy. And imagine if she actually managed to find her! Now that she was settled in, Estelle would head out to Sylvester Manor. Perhaps there were records of who came and went from the former plantation. Maybe Agnes and John had children – which would mean discovering even more relatives.

Estelle was under no illusions that a colored woman asking questions would be welcomed. But she would persevere. It's what she did.

Carter, Lucille, Ben, Stuart and Genevieve's dinner was a success from the minute they sat down. Ben peppered Stuart with questions about his business, and both agreed it was curious they had never met before, though it seemed Ben did more island transport work than Stuart did. Lucille discovered Stuart was a voracious reader too, so the two got caught up in comparing and discussing various titles. They all lingered at the table, outlasting most other diners.

Afterwards, Stuart and Genevieve retreated to her room. Stuart leaned Genevieve against the closed door and gave her a long, searing kiss. She loved Stuart's kisses. They were slow and sensual, just like his lovemaking. He was never rushed and made it clear he only wanted to please her, however long it took. Laurent's kisses, on the other hand, had been sloppy at best, and she stupidly married him anyway, thinking she could improve him. You cannot, she discovered. A man's kiss tells you everything.

She broke off their kiss for a moment. "It was brave of you to dine with my friends tonight. Especially Lucille."

"Brave? Because of Rebecca? Lucille does not strike me as a gossip."

"No, she is not," Genevieve walked over to the dresser's mirror to remove her earrings. "It was our debut dinner. We felt like a couple."

He grabbed her breasts from behind and kissed a trail across her neck. "Because we are."

She turned around and playfully struck him. "Stop. You know what I mean. It was nice to see you with other people – to be us with other people. Not like a secret. We live our relationship in the shadows."

He sighed. "I know. You deserve better. *I* deserve better." He looked her in the eyes, his hands on her shoulders. "Genevieve, you must know what you mean to me. You keep me sane. My life was a dark shade of gray –

and that was when I wasn't trying to control Rebecca's outbursts, which thankfully the medications seem to do now. I thought it was my lot. Now, well, now you have colored my life with promise. God knows I wasn't looking, but I am so grateful to have found you." He sealed his gentle words with a kiss.

Genevieve's eyes were moist when their kiss finally broke. "My heart repeats your every word, your every emotion," she whispered. She had never felt so loved, so *seen*.

The next morning, Margaret returned from her trip to the town center with two letters for Lucille among other supplies in her bicycle basket. One letter from Henry, the other from her mother-in-law. Lucille proceeded to her favorite chair under a big oak tree and opened Henry's first.

My darling Squirrel —

I love how much you are enjoying your stay at Carter's inn. I love the descriptions of your day and how excited you are about every unfolding detail. Your joy delights me, as my business here is on track. We have signed contracts with major distributors, and Nesbit Industries is about to double in size. When I return there will be much work to be done in preparation, which will entail many a trip to Chicago, maybe another overseas. Should we be fortunate enough for you to be with child after I return, I am heartened to know you have a safe environment to rest in. Unless you would prefer to stay with either of our parents, that is.

"Not likely," she said out loud.

His letter went on about his recent social and cultural activities, including parties, concerts and museum visits. Unlike her, Henry was what she would call a seeker. He always wanted to learn new things, go to museum exhibits, meet new and interesting people. Lucille was more of nester. She loved her four walls – and garden – and loved to read as well as write. Henry felt they were the ideal balance.

"Do you ever wish you were with someone less shy and maybe more adventurous?" She once asked him after a dinner party where he did all the laughing and talking, and she did all the smiling and nodding.

"Only if her name was Lucille Kraft Nesbit, and she was a sensual squirrel," he said with that seductive smile. "You are the woman of my dreams just as you are."

Being at the Rams Head Inn had her rethinking who she was without Henry by her side. She did not have the force of personality Carter had, but she wasn't shy about asking questions or voicing opinions. Last night's dinner was an example – she was doing the laughing and talking. Would that have been the case if Henry was there, or would she have remained quiet? Would he enjoy this outgoing version of herself? She honestly didn't know.

Lucille then opened the other letter, the one from her mother-in-law. She was all too familiar with Mavis's light blue paper emblazoned with their family crest, the even penmanship in rich blue ink. Of course, like all her directives, it was to the point.

Dear Lucille -
I am disappointed in you. You should be with your husband — NOT cavorting with a friend at a resort while Henry works so hard for the family business. You still have time to join him. I suggest you do so immediately.
Yours,
Mother Nesbit

The note was pure Mavis — short, declarative sentences without a hint charm or wit, much less any sensitivity to how her words might land. She spoke in the same manner. Like many privileged women Lucille grew up with, Mavis Nesbit acted in charge wherever she went. Lucille shrank around Mavis, hoping to keep the interaction as polite and brief as possible. Henry was oblivious, of course, and Lucille knew why: Mavis idolized her son. His mother's whole demeanor softened around him, even smiling sometimes. Lucille suspected Mavis was jealous of Lucille for having Henry's rapt attention.

Lucille's decision to not accompany Henry had caused a stir in the family, with her own mother as well, and she had received a similar letter from Mavis shortly after Henry left. With the first letter, Lucille shook after reading it and almost joined him, worried about the impropriety of not doing so. What surprised Lucille about this second letter was how little she cared. She went to crumple it up, but then thought it would be amusing to share with Carter.

Just then Lucille saw a figure walking down the causeway. It was a long way to town, and most people borrowed one of the inn's bicycles if they didn't hire a car. As the person came closer, she saw it was a woman, Estelle in a yellow dress. Did she not know about the bicycles?

"Estelle!" She called out, rising to her feet. She started walking in Estelle's direction. As she got closer, she saw Estelle's dress was torn and caked in mud, her hand covering her face, which was bleeding and she seemed to have a slight limp.

"Hello Lucille," Estelle said, clearly struggling to hold back emotion. "Some boys stole the bicycle. Don't worry, I'll pay for it."

Concerned by Estelle's appearance, Lucille put her hands on Estelle's shoulders and spoke softly. "Forget the bicycle. What happened to you?"

"I'm fine. I hadn't even made it to town when I was knocked to the ground. My face must look a fright, I'm sure. I stupidly tried to reason with those schoolboys."

"How many were there?"

"Three. Maybe thirteen years old, I'm not sure. They pulled me off the bicycle and pushed me to the ground, then they threw rocks at me when I tried to stand up. One of the boys went to grab my dress hem, and that's when had I to get away. I ran, which made them all laugh all the more. I'm just fortunate they didn't follow me."

"Where is your purse?" Lucille asked, swallowing her outrage. "We need to report this."

"No!" Estelle said too quickly. "I left it in the basket. There wasn't much in it. I carry my money on my person." She showed Lucille a pouch tucked in the top of her dress. "I'm fine. I just need to get to my room to clean up."

"The island is small. Our friend Curtis will find them, I assure you. For now, you're right, let's get you to the inn," she said, quickly grabbing her things. They walked a few paces, but then Estelle sunk to the ground, her shoulders rounded, and started sobbing.

"I feel like a fool, Lucille. For so many reasons. What am I doing here?"

Confused, Lucille sat down next to her. "You've come to find your great aunt," Lucille said soothingly.

"Yes, but I also came to find peace," she cried. "What was I thinking? I need to go home."

Lucille moved closer to Estelle to rub her back. "To Chicago?"

"Yes. My children think I've lost my mind, and maybe I have. I thought it would help to be at a place that had nothing to do with Walter. That I wouldn't miss him here." Her weeping continued at full force. Lucille wondered if it was the first time Estelle gave into such emotion.

"Where is Walter?" Lucille asked as gently as she could.

"Gone," Estelle looked at Lucille's questioning face. "He died a month ago from that dreadful flu. He was my world."

"Oh Estelle," Lucille's eyes watered and then she hugged Estelle. At first Estelle resisted, but then turned into Lucille's arms. "I'm so very, very sorry. And then to be assaulted by some mean kids. You shouldn't have been alone."

"I shouldn't be *here*," she said aloud, tears streaming anew.

"Well, you are here," Lucille said. With one arm around Estelle, Lucille reached for a handkerchief in her bag and dried Estelle's face, blotting the blood. "Let's go get you cleaned up, so that cut doesn't get infected." Lucille stood and grabbed her bag. "Here, hold onto my arm."

The two women slowly walked toward the inn, Estelle leaning into Lucille's arm.

"What was I thinking venturing out on my own like that?" Estelle said to herself. "I know better. I always told my kids *walk in groups, so you don't walk into trouble*."

"Well, you won't be alone again. I will go with you to Sylvester Manor. I would love to see that part of the island. You can't leave Shelter Island without at least trying to find your aunt."

"I'll need to rest my leg after today."

"Fine. You tell me when. I am available whenever you're ready. We'll make a day of it!"

Estelle stopped and looked at her for a long moment. "Walter sent you, Lucille. I needed an angel, and here you are."

Lucille was grateful to be a comfort, but she secretly worried what lay in store for Estelle at Sylvester Manor.

CHAPTER SIXTEEN

Carter could smell trouble, and tonight's air reeked of it. Before she could figure out why she felt this way, the Schnedekers called her over to their table.

"You may want to check out the bar at the lounge," Mr. Schnedeker said. "There are some unsavory types drinking quite a bit. Happy to get involved, if you need."

"Thank you. But no, I'll handle it. I apologize if you were disturbed."

"We are fine, dear," Mrs. Schnedeker said. "We just feel protective of you and what you're building here."

Carter took a deep breath and headed to the bar. Romano was there, donning his green cap, in the company of an equally menacing-looking friend. But so was Charles, the burly man who had to be escorted out of the restaurant days earlier. Charles was with a heavily made-up woman in a shiny peacock blue dress with an uncomfortably low décolleté. There was loud laughter between the two groups, though it didn't seem like they had come together. Mr. Manuel, the white-haired bartender, wore his usual unruffled expression, though he threw Carter a pointed look.

Fortunately, Ben walked in the front door just at that moment. She was equally relieved and pleased to see him. Before she could say a word, Ben recognized Romano and headed straight to the bar.

"You were asked not to return to this establishment, and I am politely asking you to leave," Ben said. "We do not want trouble."

"Who wants trouble? We're just sitting here enjoying a drink, right, Bo?" He slapped his friend on the back. "We like this place."

"You have no business here."

"I have no business?" Romano glared at Ben. "Do you?"

"Wise guy," Ben said sharply. "I am asking you to leave."

Charles laughed. He had been openly listening to the exchange from his neighboring bar stool. "Ha! I was kicked out too last week. They thought I was too loud with one of their hookers. This week, I brought my own girl with me." He hit the girl on her rump, and she snorted with laughter.

Ben looked confused. "There are no hookers here."

"Really? I came with a group of guys last week for that one and only purpose."

Ben looked at Carter. "Have you seen this man before?"

"Yes," she said carefully. "He came with a group for dinner. The men in his group found him unruly and escorted him home."

"Liar," Charles sneered. "We came for dinner — *and dessert*. And you know it."

"I know nothing of the kind."

"Well, I already rented me a room here tonight."

"I'll go ahead and cancel that room for you," Carter said.

"Like hell you will." He stood up, his bar stool loudly crashing to the floor.

Ben moved Carter behind him.

"Miss Carter, please tell Mr. Smythe he is needed," Ben's voice was eerily soft. "Then I'd like you to wait for me in the dining room."

Carter summoned William from behind the front desk. On a hunch, she looked for Curtis, who thankfully was in the dining room with Margaret. Carter gave him a discreet point of her hand that he was needed. She smiled at the Schnedekers who were looking at her. She mouthed "thank you" as if to say all was under control.

By the time Carter returned to the lounge, Ben had Charles' arm twisted behind him.

"Let go of my arm," Charles said.

"Gladly. As long as you and your lady friend agree to leave peacefully."

When Curtis arrived, Ben let go of Charles' arm and stepped back, while Charles rubbed his arm, shaking it out. "Officer Schmidt, glad you are here," Curtis said. "This man and his lady friend were just leaving, were you not?"

"Yes, we are," he turned to face Ben. "You will regret this, I promise."

"Just like you will regret the way you threatened Miss Carter." Carter saw just how intimidating Ben could look when called upon. "Do not think to return here."

Romano and his friend threw back their drinks, and Romano left some bills on the bar. "Not a very friendly place you have here. Let's go find somewhere else to eat, Bo."

Upon their departure, Ben turned to Carter, anger in his eyes. "May I have a word, Miss Carter?" he asked, his voice barely civil.

"Of course," Carter answered.

"*Alone,*" he clarified, eyeing William, who was watching them intently. Then quietly to Carter, "This is not a conversation I wish to have with you in public."

"We can talk in the Garden Room," Carter said, heading in that direction. William made a movement to follow them, but Carter put up a hand and said, "thank you, William. I'll be all right."

As soon as Carter shut the doors behind them, Ben launched into her, "Why is that man always butting into our business?"

"Mr. Romano?"

"No, William."

"William? He is just protective of me, especially in Davidson's absence."

"I hope that's all," he said. "However, we can talk about William another day. Carter, why did that man think this is a brothel?"

"I have no idea."

"I think you do."

Carter contemplated her answer. She could tell from the fury in his eyes that he wouldn't stand for silence.

"There are a handful of women – three or four to be precise – who could make someone ignorantly think that. But they are not prostitutes, they are war widows."

His wide eyes insisted she divulge more, so she told him the whole story.

"So, you see," she said, "that disgusting brute was just a bad apple. Everything is under control, and no one has any reason to call this a brothel."

"Do you accept money from these women?"

"Not anymore, no."

"Not *anymore*?"

"No. In the beginning, I was flustered and broke— and quite frankly, I didn't know what they were tipping me for. But once I understood they were supporting their families, well, you'd have to be heartless to take any of their money. They pay only for their rooms, and the men pay for dinners. Besides, our basement business has assuaged my money worries."

"Yes, *our* basement business." Ben closed his eyes before speaking again. "*Our* basement business, as you call it, is the reason why we cannot risk being raided under suspicion of being a brothel. We cannot have anyone think even for a moment that we have any illegal activities going on here. We could be arrested, at the very least."

"I thought you said there was nothing illegal about it."

"Carter, whatever else it is, it is *not* a licensed business. We are *not* paying sales tax, nor registering it in any way."

"So, *your* illegal activities are fine. But a bunch of women—women who, I might add, have very few other options—have their own little business going, suddenly it's a problem?"

"Carter, you're an intelligent woman." She could see that he was trying to control his voice. "There are people who could easily make our lives difficult. They could turn us in, confiscate the crates while putting a gun to our heads."

Carter covered her mouth. She hadn't fully focused on the dangers. She then brightened. "But we have Curtis. And the local police love us, with all the free drinks I give them."

"That's nice, but if I wasn't here tonight, what would you have done?"

There was a knock at the door. "Carter? Is everything alright?" It was Lucille, waving at them through the paned glass doors. Carter went to the door and opened it a crack to speak with her friend.

"Everything's fine, Lucille. Please start without us. We'll be finished here in a moment."

Lucille went away and Carter closed the door again, turning to Ben. She lowered her voice. "I adore you, and I'm so very grateful you're here, but—"

He put up his hand. "I'm moving in. Clear a room for me. Preferably one next door or across the hall from you. Now go and meet Lucille, and I'll join you shortly."

The next morning, Carter and Lucille were clipping from the flower garden to pepper throughout the inn. There was a threat of rain in the air, so they were working quickly.

"I don't mind Ben staying here. I'll sleep better knowing he's here," Lucille shrugged, clipping a pink peony and adding it to her basket.

Carter raised an eyebrow. "Well, I do mind. Ben is butting into business that has nothing to do with him. The nerve. That he thinks he can tell me how to run my inn."

"He does have an edge to him," Lucille remarked.

That got Carter's attention. "What do you mean by that?"

"Well, despite his good manners and wholesome looks, you can tell he's seen more than drawing rooms and fancy schools. He's a gentleman, yes, but I more than suspect it's a studied persona, not a natural one."

"Interesting you should say that. Last night I was glad to see a very intimidating side of him."

"I'm not surprised at all. One senses these things by simply observing. Henry always says my quiet nature comes in handy."

"Well, whatever Ben's story is or is not, this is not his inn, and he is not in charge. I have informed him not to interfere with the Connecticut Ladies or any of those under my employ without speaking to me first. He even asked me about Isabelle – who she was and why she worked here. I told him she was a girl in need. Please do not share her identity with him."

"I wouldn't. I'd rather everyone think what we did – that she is a domestic in trouble."

"Agreed," Carter said. "Benjamin would probably have a fit if he knew her father was a congressman. Much too public and risky."

"He's not wrong. Though I tend to think Congressman Worthington won't be publicizing a place that's hiding his pregnant daughter. He sounds as heartless as his wife – even worse. Imagine putting your career over your child. You are far kinder to Isabelle than her parents have been."

"I certainly didn't plan to be. But yes, their behavior is blasphemous." Carter looked at the ominous sky. "I give it another half hour before it pours."

"While we're on the subject of troublemakers, I need to tell you about what happened to Estelle." She then recounted the story, both of the assault and then discovering Estelle was a grieving widow.

"Oh, no. Do we know who the kids are?"

"No, but I plan to ask Curtis to go after them."

"Please don't, Lucille. The last thing I want is a police officer going after kids for stealing a bike. Their parents will declare war on me."

"Your bike is the least of what those young men did. They attacked Estelle! She has an ugly gash on her face, and she was limping for God's sake."

"I understand, but we need to at least consider the bigger picture."

"There's nothing to consider. I want them found and be forced to apologize to Estelle. We should press charges too."

Carter threw up her hands. "I'm not saying no, just that we should take a breath before doing anything. You'd be putting Curtis in an awkward position, assuming he would even do it. I doubt Estelle would like you to pursue this either. Do you think she wants to see or hear from those boys again? I'm sure their parents would defend them. I beg you, leave it be."

Lucille dropped it for now. She suspected Carter didn't want the inn caught up in the mess. Maybe Estelle would agree with her.

"It's starting to sprinkle," Carter said. "We should hightail it inside."

"One more thing," Lucille said. "I promised Estelle I would accompany her to look for her aunt."

Carter was grateful the sky opened up, which ended their discussion. Anything Lucille did could not help but reflect on the inn. It was all fine and good for Lucille to play the heroine here on Shelter Island, but would she do so in front of Henry's place of business?

CHAPTER SEVENTEEN

Isabelle was cleaning the rooms when Genevieve saw her pass by. "Come in, *ma cherie.* I want you to see the beginning of Margaret's bridal dress."

"Yes, Iz, please join us," Margaret said, her brogue brimming with excitement. "You won't believe what Genevieve has done. I feel like a princess!"

Margaret stood smiling beatifically, fabric draped around her. Genevieve was on her knees pinning away. Isabelle had seen a version of this many times with her mother, but this scene was joyous. With her mother, there was so much sniping, griping and disapproval. Genevieve's flower paintings in the room added to the special, feminine feeling.

"You look out of a fairytale , Margaret," Isabelle said. She fingered the roll of pearl-encrusted lace that sat on the nearby dresser.

Genevieve waved her hand. "Curtis will fall in love with you all over again."

"Oh, I don't know about that," Margaret said. "Men prefer women without their clothes."

"Not always," Genevieve said. "Men like their princesses. I am delighted that I am able to put you in a fine-fitting dress. Your clothes are all too big for your petite frame."

Isabelle looked down and rubbed her protruding belly. "I wonder if I'll ever be someone's princess."

Genevieve looked at Isabelle for a minute, then stood, reached for her hand and led her to the side of the bed, where she patted the mattress for her to sit down. "Of course you will. Great love waits for you."

"I doubt it. Even if I did marry, I can't wear white."

"Poppycock," Margaret said. "You may wear any color you like, right Genevieve?"

"*Absolument.* Do you wish to marry, Isabelle?"

Isabelle shrugged sheepishly. "I am not sure that is even possible. My mother says I'm damaged goods."

"There is nothing damaged about you," Genevieve said, her tone angry. She patted Isabelle's hand and resumed her normal voice. "I fell in love with a bad man and married him. I followed him to a foreign country and did what he told me. I thought I was in prison – my life sentence for being stupid. And one day, I escaped and came here. I started a new life. I met such kind women, and I met a loving man. Do you see what I am saying?"

"Maybe. But how can I ever start a new life?" Isabelle said, crying. "Even my body won't be the same after this – how could it be?"

Margaret sat on the other side of Isabelle, trying hard not to crease the satin or stick herself with pins. "Listen to me. Genevieve is right. This is a just moment in your life – not your entire life.

"I fell in love with a man who broke my heart," Margaret continued. "I too thought I was damaged and almost went home to Ireland. Instead, I came here with Mrs.

171

Nesbit. Now look at me in this white silk. You too have magical moments ahead, I promise."

Carter wore her softest leather shoes as she walked down the well-worn nature trail, yet even they cut into her ankles. She stopped and sat on a tree stump to rub her sore skin. She paused to breathe in the fresh air. Birds were singing and sunlight danced through the leaves. It felt heavenly to be on her own in the serenity of nature. God's real church, as her mother would say.

She just wished her mind would quiet and let her enjoy such peace. She hated that Estelle was attacked the way she was. She also knew there was little to be done about it. She briefly visited Estelle in her room the night of the attack, and, sure enough, she was bruised and shaken. The gash would leave a scar, a permanent reminder of the unprovoked abuse. Estelle hadn't wanted to talk any more about it.

"I've learned to be grateful for what didn't happen," Estelle had said. "I'm fine. I just need to rest and stay off my feet for a while."

Carter knew when she was being dismissed and respected Estelle's wishes. Carter could only imagine the dignity it cost Estelle recounting the story to Lucille in the first place.

Sitting on a fallen tree, Carter resented that owning the inn had made her silent in the face of such injustice. Where was the Carter who stormed the streets screaming for women's rights as full citizens? Carter was now beholden to her future at Rams Head and its surrounding community. She had to make a go of it. Every penny she and Davidson had was now invested in the inn. Still, those boys couldn't get away with this. Surely there was something she could do. She *would* do, she vowed.

There was also the thorny issue of Carter softening towards Ben. Difficult as he could be, she secretly enjoyed having him across the hall. He made a habit of tapping three times on her door to say good morning before leaving for his cottage, and twice on her door to say good night, if they had not headed up the stairs together after dinner. And he was respectful of her ownership. Still, he would step in if a restaurant patron had too much to drink or was too loud. He did it in his pleasant manner, followed by that lopsided grin that assuaged any embarrassment. Endearing was the only word to describe him.

He was also good at negotiating with suppliers, using that same carrot and stick approach, which always got Rams Head the best price. Like everyone else, she was feeling susceptible to his charisma. Only William seemed reserved around him, but that was William's style toward everyone. Yet Lucille was right about Ben: there was a steel edge beneath the amiable smile. When the smile fell, it was like the light left the room and the target of his disappointment or consternation would feel it immediately.

Carter hated admitting it, even to herself, but there was also a physical pull between her and Ben. When he placed his hand on the small of her back to guide her up the stairs, she felt an electric current at their touch. Goodness, what was wrong with her? Maybe she was just missing Davidson.

Through the birds chirping, Carter could make out a faint sob. Then a sniffle. She turned around to see a flash of blue peeking through the trees. Carter made her way toward the blue and soon saw Rose in a blue dress, sitting on a fallen tree. So absorbed in her thoughts, Rose was unaware of Carter's presence until she was standing over her.

"Rose, honey, what happened?" Carter crouched next to her on the log.

"No, no. I'm so sorry. I come out here sometimes," she looked away, embarrassed. "I don't get to be alone very often, here or at home."

Carter didn't know if that was a cue for her to leave, but decided to see if an ear would help. "Is it something you want to talk about?"

Rose's face collapsed. "I wish it was one thing. It's everything."

"Okay. Well, what's at the top of the list?"

"Where to begin? My parents and their stinging looks. My son Aidan, who seems to side with them." She paused, her voice dropping. "It's like he's Herbert, knowing and disapproving of me."

"How old is Aidan?"

"He just turned two."

"All right, so that part you're imagining," Carter smiled softly.

"I'm not so sure. He is the spitting image of Herbert. Same black hair even."

Carter winced. "Aidan's your baby. He loves you."

Rose's tortured face looked at Carter straight on. "And I love Herbert! I haven't had the space or time to fully grieve my husband. But here I am. I hate having relations with men who aren't Herbert. It makes my skin crawl. Smiling, telling them how great they are. It sickens me. James has loved Elizabeth since school, so it's different for her, even if she doesn't love him in return. But me? I'm just a willing woman to bed the men James brings here – it doesn't matter if they're fat, old or smell foul, which most do. How did this happen? Who am I?"

"It's mostly the same men, no?"

"Mostly, but once in a while there's someone new."

"Have you talked with Helen about how she feels, how she copes?"

"Helen loves the physical side of being with a man. Always has. Even if she doesn't like the man, she turns it into an acting session, which she has encouraged me to do as well. But I can't. She loves the freedom and money that comes with being here."

"Surely she misses her husband too."

"Other than their physical compatibility, Helen had a terrible marriage with Edgar. I'm not saying she wished him dead, but the mourning is different. I loved Herbert with all my heart. I don't want to move on."

"Yes, that is very different," Carter admitted. "Do your parents know what your trips here are about?"

"Not entirely. I told them we have jobs here in the hotel, but I think they suspect what we really do. Still, the money is good, and they play along." Rose sobbed, "I hate myself. I hate having to act happy when I am dying inside. Even my rage is leaving me. I just want it all to stop."

"You realize you didn't cause any of this. You are doing the best you can under very trying circumstances."

"Am I? Are my choices worthy of forgiveness in Herbert's eyes? In God's eyes?"

"Are any of our choices perfect? We make them and hope for the best. Be kinder to yourself. Life has been cruel to you, but you don't have to be."

Carter rubbed Rose's back, not knowing what else to do. Underneath the fabric of Rose's dress, Carter felt protruding ribs – Rose was skin and bones.

"Are you eating, Rose? I worry you've lost so much weight, even in the short time I've known you."

"You sound like Elizabeth. I eat plenty."

Carter dropped it. The last thing she wanted was to nag Rose. What she did want to do was assure her there was a long life ahead of her and that love would surely find her again. But who knew what was true or not. Besides, Rose was not looking to her future. Her life had blown up spectacularly and unfairly. Sometimes you just needed to give voice to your feelings and not have someone try to talk you out of them.

"Rose, take as much time as you need," Carter said after a few moments of silence. "I'm heading to the water, which fills me with peace. Would you like to join me?"

"No, thank you. I'll stay here."

As Carter made her way to the water, she could hear Rose resume sobbing behind her. While their circumstances were different, Carter could relate: she simply couldn't fathom Davidson not coming back.

CHAPTER EIGHTEEN

My Beloved Henry,

Great news — I think Carter may have found someone to help her get over the loss of Davidson. Or he may have found her. Either way, Benjamin Goodwin, whom I mentioned in my last letter, moved into the inn, and has proven a worthy addition for so many reasons. First, he brings a sense of security. We are fairly secluded out here on Ram Island, even more so than on the rest of Shelter Island. While we have men on staff, Ben is such a commanding presence, one feels he could handle any kind of problem — not that we have any, rest assured. But as an example, Ben is intolerant of loud drinkers and escorts them out immediately if they don't agree to lower their voices. No one would dare argue, as Ben cuts a tall, imposing figure.

Important as that is, it is his effect on Carter I am most happy about. They have a terrific rapport, almost like siblings, though he clearly fancies Carter. Gentleman that he is, I believe he is waiting until she accepts that Davidson is truly gone.

I am so enjoying the planning of Margaret's wedding. She and her betrothed are both so appreciative to us for bringing her family over and for all the extras we are providing. So many local police officers and many of our new friends will be attending. Margaret feels like a princess, and I love seeing her so euphoric. I wish you could be here for the wedding, though I appreciate you now need more time abroad thanks to your success. Still, a lovesick wife may fantasize...

I miss you more than I can express in a letter. I laughed when you wrote you are always asking yourself "what would Lucille say or do?" I do the same! I try to see my world through your eyes. I also hear your voice — indulging, soothing, defending, admonishing, loving me, especially when I am unsure of myself. You are with me always, my love. Always. Just as I'm with you. I love you so.
Yours forever, Squirrel

Lucille knew her letter left out so much, as did her letters before this one. She didn't want Henry's opinions or judgments at this juncture. She had been having picnic lunches with Estelle and immensely enjoyed her company. Like Lucille, Estelle loved to read. Lucille had been lending her books and they would discuss them at length afterwards.

Moreover, Estelle, a college graduate, was much better informed than Lucille. She was horrified to hear what Estelle had to say about the negro experience in this country. They may have been emancipated dozens of years ago, but they had few rights that were respected or honored. They were paid far less than white people, with no laws in place to prevent it. Lucille knew they couldn't travel in the same cars on trains nor welcomed to eat in the same restaurants as whites. But coloreds could not use the same public toilets or drinking fountains, even if there wasn't a colored accommodation in sight, which there seldom was. Worse, few hospitals would admit them, even on an emergency basis, so many people simply died in want of medical attention.

The assault those ghastly boys perpetrated on Estelle was commonplace, done just for mere sport because they knew no one would punish them for it. Colored people rarely reported crimes committed against them, knowing that the police and the courts would do little, if anything at all. Estelle did not want to pursue those boys. "They could set fire to the inn if they knew I was staying here. For all of our sakes, let it alone."

Lucille had been living with the luxury of not knowing any of this.

Estelle was mostly fortunate, Lucille learned. Walter had earned a great deal investing in the stock market, pooling money from friends and family, and then repaying them with interest from the returns. He was respected in Chicago, and his wealth allowed Estelle to devote herself to the suffrage effort. From what Lucille surmised, they lived comfortably in Lake Forest and had two grown children, Atticus and Angela, who were both doing well. Estelle worried about her future without Walter but was financially stable for now. Lucille sensed that Estelle was in no rush to look for her great aunt, as she was breathing in the comfort of her seclusion – her first in a lifetime, she said.

And Lucille was breathing in the joy of making such a gracious friend.

Did every imminent bride question her sanity, Margaret wondered, as she stared at the water from her third-floor bedroom. Were pre-wedding nerves inevitable? It was six o'clock in the morning and daylight was beginning to wake the harbor in that glorious way it did when a sunny day was on the horizon. Everything was quiet except for a symphony of birds, some nearby, some distant.

She loved Curtis, but did she really know him? Their wedding was a little over a month away, and she was harboring doubts. Was she ready to give up her Irish identity and become an American? Was she going to surrender a well-paying job with the Nesbits, where she had saved a good deal for herself and her family, for a future with a man she'd only known for two months? Would Curtis make a good father – as good as her own father had been? Would Curtis be generous and patient with her once they were married? Did she have a right to question these things? Shouldn't she just be grateful he did not shrink from the idea of marrying her when Mrs. Nesbit confronted him the morning after Genevieve's husband showed up at Rams Head?

The irony was Margaret was not a virgin that needed protecting. She lost her virginity in her small room at the Nesbit house to Vance Broder, Mr. Nesbit's assistant. He was tall, black-haired and had serious way about him she found irresistible. They had exchanged many a glance before they formally met. She would bring a tea tray into Mr. Nesbit's home office and Vance would look up and stare at her intensely as she put it on their shared worktable. This went on for weeks.

One night, when the Nesbits were out for dinner, Vance appeared, ostensibly to deliver some papers for Mr. Nesbit. Margaret heard him downstairs and told Mr. Wiles, the house manager who was buried in a book, she would greet Mr. Broder. The minute she reached the main floor, Vance took her hand, guided her into the office and kissed her as if his life depended on it. A month later, late into the evening, he snuck into her room. Wet from rain and holding a wilted bouquet, he told her he loved her. In her twin bed, they then consummated their love for one another.

Therein started a clandestine romance. She spent her off days in his small apartment and mostly in his bed. He gave her little presents — a poem, a flower, a romantic note he wrote. It felt wildly adventurous. But he drew the line at going public. Vance convinced her they'd both be fired if either of the Nesbits found out. After six months, Margaret broke it off, almost as a dare for him to reveal to the world his love for her. But he didn't. Instead, he went with Mr. Nesbit on a European business trip, making no promises before he departed. That left her heart wide open for Curtis, who was proud to tell the world she was his.

After Vance Broder, Margaret vowed she would never make love with a man again without a commitment. She and Curtis had kissed—*kissed intensely*—with a few other liberties, perhaps, but Margaret knew when to stop. Curtis told her he was in love with her and respected her.

They were in her room for privacy, since it was raining that night. But the die was cast according to Mrs. Nesbit, and that was that. Curtis seemed nothing but happy. He had told Margaret he fully intended to ask for her hand even before that fateful night.

Yet that didn't mean she knew Curtis. She was thrown off by what had happened yesterday afternoon, the way Curtis had spoken to her. She had been shopping for Mrs. Nesbit in town, when she saw a small black and white dog tossed out of a bar onto the street. She picked up the dog and stormed back into the bar, only to see a bunch of drunk men laughing it up.

"Whose dog is this?" she demanded.

"Damned if we know," the hefty bartender said. "It wandered in here looking for food. Can't feed the world, honey."

"So, you throw it out like garbage?"

"It is," one of the men said.

She sneered at him. "You are the garbage for doing such a heartless thing."

"Did you call me garbage?" He walked over in a threatening manner.

"Yes, I did. And if you have an issue with that, take it up with my betrothed, Officer Schmidt."

"Curtis?"

"Yes." She held up her chin defiantly.

"Well, it's only out of my friendship with Curtis that I'll let you out of here without a good spanking – or something worse." The other men laughed. "Tell him Tommy spared you."

Margaret contemplated her next move, which she concluded could only be to leave. She looked each man in the eye before storming out with the dog.

As she walked out, she heard one of the men say, "Let's hope for Curtis she's that feisty in bed!"

When she recounted the story to Curtis later, he was furious. Not at the boorish men, but at her. "What were you thinking walking into a bar? And then to provoke them by name-calling!"

"Your *friend* Tommy threatened to spank me."

Curtis fisted his hand. "I will deal with him, believe me. But you should not have walked into a bar under any circumstances.   You   embarrassed   me."

"Maybe you didn't hear me, Curtis: they threw this little fella out onto the sidewalk. It could have gotten injured. She stroked the dog, who nuzzled into her side. She had already fed him, removed a dozen ticks and bathed him. The dog wasn't going anywhere.

"I have news for you, Margaret. I don't care what happens to the dog, either. It's certainly not staying with us. It shouldn't even be in this room."

It was as if he had slapped her. "Curtis, I love animals. I will always have a pet or two in my home." She said the last sentence with conviction, almost daring him to say otherwise.

"In America, men rule the home," Curtis stated. "A wife may have an opinion, but a husband decides."

"Is that so?"

"Yes, that is so. When I tell you to act in a certain manner, as my wife, you will do so."

"Is that so?"

"Yes, that is so."

Margaret digested his words and then said, "I need you to leave, Curtis."

"Excuse me?"

"You have given me a lot to think about, and none of it good."

"Margaret—"

"Space and silence are good after an argument, I have been told."

"This isn't an argument."

Margaret continued to stroke the dog as she measured her words. "I assure you, it is a very strong disagreement. I am not yet your wife, so you do not make decisions for me. I will ask you again, please leave."

"And the dog stays?"

"The dog stays."

Curtis stared at her, opened his mouth as if to say something, but then turned and left the room. He didn't attempt to come back that evening.

Well, he didn't yell nor threaten to hit me, she reasoned at she stared out the window the next morning.

But would he come back today? What would he say? What would she?

She smiled and reached for the dog, which sat up on its makeshift bed in the corner.

"I bet you are hungry, little fella. Let's take you for a walk and get some breakfast."

Margaret quickly dressed and made a leash out of the curtain sash. She took the staff staircase and headed out onto the road along the side of Rams Head. She wondered if anyone could see them from their window. Despite her bravado with Curtis, she hadn't thought through what to do with the dog. She didn't know if Miss Carter or Mrs. Nesbit would even allow it in the inn. She knew Mrs. Nesbit loved dogs – she had recently lost Sweetie, her cherished Pekingese, but that was a fancy dog. Little Fella wasn't. He was a mongrel — a sad, scrawny mongrel.

After their walk, Margaret snuck into the kitchen and grabbed some leftover meat slices from the previous night's dinner, which Little Fella ate up in seconds. She also set down a bowl of water. Just as she was about to carry him up the staff staircase, Miss Carter walked into the kitchen. Before Margaret could say a word, Miss Carter had Little Fella in her arms and, in a sing song voice asked, "And who is this adorable creature?"

"I've been calling him Little Fella. He doesn't have a home. Curtis forbade me to keep him."

"Hello Fella," Carter kissed the top of his head. "I was thinking we needed a dog around here. I plan to get a

186

border collie to help herd the sheep I want to have some day. But you'll do for now, Fella. Do you mind if I introduce him around?"

"That would be most welcome," Margaret answered, her eyes welling up.

"Margaret, are you all right?" Carter put Fella down.

Margaret sniffed. "I am. Just bridal jitters, I guess." But it was more than that. She hardly knew the man she was marrying, and feared it was too late to do anything about it.

CHAPTER NINETEEN

Genevieve was getting worried. Stuart hadn't shown up in almost two weeks. In his absence, he'd sent her a gift of lavender perfume (her favorite) with a note via Graham's boat:

> *My darling G,*
> *I have some urgent issues to which I must attend. Not sure when I can return to Rams Head. I will explain more fully when I see you. Please keep the faith and know my heart is with you, always.*
> *Yours, S*

Genevieve wished he had elaborated. What could these issues be? His business? His elderly mother? His sister or her family, whom Stuart supported? Rebecca, God forbid?

Not that Genevieve didn't have her own issues. Laurent had served her with legal papers claiming spousal desertion and accusing her of destroying his business. She met with a local lawyer in Sag Harbor who believed the claim had no merit but would still require her to show up in court in Manhattan to defend herself.

Divorces were very rare in America, her attorney said, and women did not fare well in them. Only one in a thousand couples had divorced the previous year in the United States. Did she really want to go that route, he asked? Genevieve felt she had little choice but to counter Laurent with a threat of divorce. She had no intention of returning to him or going back to work for him. He would look like a fraud, never mind a fool, to pursue this further. She asked her lawyer if they could delay or settle his lawsuit in some manner. Maybe Laurent would find another seamstress and leave her alone.

Fortunately, thanks mostly to Carter and Lucille, word had spread among Rams Head customers of her seamstress work, and she had picked up a few projects, which helped Genevieve pay for the lawyer.

Still, Stuart's absence was a hard one to take in stride. She was in love with him. He made her feel wanted, safe and cared for. He was complimentary, always noticing if she wore something new or styled her hair differently. Far more than that, it was his touch she missed. Sex, yes, absolutely. But the small kisses, the gentle caresses when he thought no one was looking. When she played the piano, she would look up and see Stuart watching her intensely with appreciation and heartfelt pride. It was as if the universe was trying to make up for every injustice Laurent ever had inflicted upon her.

Stuart was also helping her build her business. He ordered a sewing machine, one of the newest electric irons and a wooden ironing board. He had asked what she wanted most in life – besides him – a piece of jewelry? Orchids? Her response made him laugh: "The newest Singer model. From what I can tell it all but sews the dress itself!" He added the iron and board after the salesman insisted ironing was vital when you sewed clothes. That was Stuart. Considerate, kind, and generous to a fault.

So where are you, my love? She pushed the fabric through the rapidly moving needle in a precise straight line. *Are you alright? I pray the issue isn't your health.* Oh no, please anything but that.

After completing the second sleeve of the dress she was working on, Genevieve decided to get some fresh air. She threw on a paisley-print housecoat, grabbed Fella, who had quickly become the inn's housedog, and headed down to the harbor. She spotted Lucille on the veranda, looking like her usual put together self, strawberry blond hair sleekly coiffed into a French braid, wearing a blue-and-white toile dress Genevieve remembered making for her. Oh, to have a life like Lucille's, Genevieve thought. Yet, Lucille was too nice to resent.

"Good afternoon, Lucille," she smiled. "Fella and I are going for a walk. Would you like to join us?"

"Why, yes! That sounds most welcoming. Just what I need to turn off my mind." She bent down to pet Fella, who wagged his tail.

"I thought only my mind twisted into knots," Genevieve said with a laugh. "You always seem so knitted together."

"Ha, a good act. I am a terrible worrier. Carter calls me an awful-izer."

"A what?"

"Someone who imagines everything as awful as it can be – or at least worries it to death."

Lucille gathered her book and things into her cream linen tote with a wooden handle, and she, Genevieve and Fella started down the inn's stone steps toward the water.

"I mean no disrespect," Genevieve ventured, "but what could you possibly be worried about? Your life seems rather blissful."

"It is, and I don't take any of my blessings for granted. It is just that, well, I love being here, but it is not my real life. It has awakened me to thoughts of how unsuited I am to my real life, if that makes any sense."

"Of course, it makes sense. Who can judge another person's life?"

"I've also been misrepresenting my life here to Henry. If he had any idea that this is not the idyllic seaside spa he believes it to be, well, I would be packed up and off before sunset. Usually I tell Henry everything."

"Have you lied to him?"

"No, just soft-peddled here and there. I come from a world of strict rules about how a lady should act and with whom she should associate. Even what kind of dog I should have – sorry, Fella," she looked down.

"Yes, that is Stuart's world too. Have you met his wife, Rebecca?"

"Once, at a dinner party, about a year ago. It was only memorable because she had a fit. She accused the hostess of purposely trying to get her sick with bad meat.

Spit it out in front of everyone. Stuart tried to manage her, but the best he could do was escort her out as she screamed obscenities."

"Oh, dear. She really is badly off."

"Yes, though I understand she is no longer seen in public."

"Stuart said she was beautiful and was the most desired debutante the year she came out."

"I'm sure of it. Her beauty is startling, as her hair is jet black and her eyes almost violet. Yet she is clearly not well in the head."

Genevieve nodded. "I worry about Stuart and the toll she must take on him." She paused. "You may have noticed he has not been here in almost two weeks. I have not heard from him since his last note saying he had urgent issues."

"He has not reached out since then?"

"No."

"That is worrisome. He adores you –
it's obvious to all."

Genevieve wiped a tear away. "He does adore me. Though I know he is a gentleman with commitments. With each passing day, I know better those commitments could take him away from me."

"The heart is the strongest commitment of all. You have his heart."

"But not his name or his home. Rebecca has those."

When Genevieve returned to her room, she found a note that Margaret slipped under the door, asking if she could have a word. She climbed the stairs to the staff floor and knocked on the door number Margaret wrote in her note. Margaret welcomed her inside. The room was much smaller than her own, just a twin bed, a nightstand and dresser, but the water view made up for the lack of space.

"My dear. What can I do for you?"

Margaret wrung her hands. "Now that you're here, I feel silly for bothering you."

"Nonsense, what is it?"

"Did you have doubts about Laurent before you married him?"

"I should have, but no. None at all. I thought he was a dream come true." Genevieve shook her head. "I was very wrong." She paused. "Why, do you have doubts about Curtis?" She sat on the bed to indicate she was in no rush.

"No, not really."

"What is it?"

"It's such a small thing. A few days back, Curtis and I had an argument about Fella. I love animals, and Curtis was adamant that I am not allowed any pets once we are married. That he makes all final decisions. I pushed back, and now I haven't heard from him. Here I am fitting a wedding dress and my parents are about to get on a ship to cross the ocean for the wedding. Curtis's silence is worrying, that's all."

Genevieve looked at her thoughtfully. "The dog is one thing, but I do not like him saying he makes all final decisions. That was Laurent. Margaret now is the time to talk things through. The wedding can be called off. Your parents would have a nice stay here with or without a wedding. Your dress could be boxed up for another day. I am not suggesting anything other than that you must be certain of what you want. And that you are going to marry a man who will treat you right."

"This is what I want," Margaret said. "I want a man to want me. To honor me as his wife. I've been in love before, and I didn't get that respect."

"Respect is important," Genevieve agreed. "But it must be on both sides."

"It would be silly to cancel a wedding over a dog. It just threw me. I will reach out to him and make things right."

"Or wait for Curtis to reach out to *you*. He can make this right too."

"I don't think he will," Margaret answered. "Curtis did not like being challenged."

"I see."

Margaret fingered her long braid. "Genevieve, please don't mention this to anyone until I figure it out."

"Never, my dear." Genevieve got up to leave, and then turned around. "Marriage is the biggest decision you make in your life. You only get one chance. Please be certain as possible. I made a bad choice, and my life has been difficult ever since."

The Connecticut Ladies returned on their usual Tuesday afternoon. Carter, who was sitting in the lounge with paperwork, was taken aback to see Mae with them. Elizabeth headed directly over to her, as the other women were seated at their usual table on the veranda for tea.

"May I?" she asked, gesturing to the chair next to Carter's.

Elizabeth sat and leaned in, speaking in a lowered voice. "I promise everything is fine. James has a quiet and shy friend. He says the friend mostly wants someone to talk with, and James assures me there will be no drama whatsoever. Mae has been having a tough time of it and could really use the money."

She continued. "She is my little sister, in case I hadn't said that before. Our husbands were in the same unit, stationed in France, and all were killed just six weeks before the Armistice. Mae too has a baby, a girl named Florence. Her husband's family is helping, but it is not enough, and I don't want her to leave the baby to work for another family. I had a long talk with her, and we agree this is her best option. James is very protective of her – he's known her since she was a child."

Carter was still wary. "Elizabeth, there must be no further incidents whatsoever, otherwise none of you will be welcomed back."

"I can safely promise that."

Carter sighed.

"Good. Mr. Morton takes care of you."

"Yes, he does. Back when we were younger, we went together for a little over two years. Everyone assumed we would marry. He is older than I am, but he wanted to build his business first."

"That seemed wise," Carter said.

"Yes, but I met Leonard while James was traveling." Elizabeth smiled what felt to be her first genuine smile since Carter had met her. "I didn't know it could be that way between a man and a woman. We were so in love and married immediately. When James returned, I was already pregnant with Jeremiah."

"He must have been heartbroken."

"And angry. He married Julia, my best friend, to spite me. They have two children. He does well, very well, and they live on Captain's Row in Sag Harbor."

"I know Captain's Row. He must be doing exceedingly well."

"When James heard about Leonard's passing, he showed up on my doorstep, wanting to help, yes, but to be with me too. James felt safe and familiar, and I could not resist the love and comfort he was offering."

"Are you in love with him?"

"I loved Leonard, who is gone," Elizabeth said. "Now I have a child to worry about. If James were not married, I would marry him. I have many problems, and this arrangement solves most of them, plus James cares for me and is most generous."

"And he helps your friends and your sister," Carter smiled, despite her sadness that Elizabeth was with a man she didn't love.

"At a price, yes. But he is a good man. I trust him."

"And I trust you. My friend Mr. Goodwin is wary of any trouble coming to Rams Head, but he has agreed to trust you because he trusts me."

"Understood."

At dinner that night, it appeared that James's new friend was mesmerized by the doe-like Mae, and the two talked nonstop. After the meal, Mae and the friend retired to the Garden Room to continue their conversation.

"Some people are just looking for someone to talk to," Carter mused to Ben, with relief. "Even if they have to pay for it." Lucille had gone to bed long ago, and it was just Carter and Ben lingering over nightcaps.

"I've never had that need to talk for the sake of talking," Ben said.

"Everyone has that need, Ben. Lucille and I have what we call our 'office meetings' just about every day at breakfast. I depend on those talks."

"Maybe I should join you."

"No. It's women only. But you and I are talking now. Give it a turn, as I'm all ears."

He stared at her for a long moment. "Okay. I'm falling for an infuriatingly strong and independent woman, but I don't think the feeling is mutual. At least not yet."

Carter bit her lip. She had invited this, hadn't she? "Maybe she needs more time."

He covered her hand with his. "She can take it, but I can't wait forever."

"I'm sure she knows that. You are too good a catch."

Ben caressed her hand, looking in her eyes with a smile in his, and a hint of hope. "Well, that's the best thing I've heard all day. Maybe you and I should talk more often."

"Maybe we should," she said softly.

Ben and Carter stood. She looked to Mr. Manuel, the bartender, who should have left by now. But he pointed toward the Garden Room, indicating Mae and her gentleman caller were still in there talking.

Carter and Ben headed up the stairs shortly after that. At her door, he stopped, and cupped her face with both hands. Wordlessly, he leaned in and kissed her goodnight. Carter lingered in his kiss, then eventually pulled away, and they headed into their separate rooms.

Late the next morning, Carter sat by herself, Fella at her feet, folding napkins on the veranda. It was a chore she found most meditative and was all too happy to relieve Isabelle and Cora of napkin duty when possible. Lucille, Margaret, and Isabelle had left for the city, Ben was at his house, and the only person about was William. He was cutting the grass, which had started to grow quite rapidly at this point in the late spring. When he was finished, he approached Carter.

"I am going to fetch an iced tea; may I get you one as well?" he asked.

"That would be most appreciated, thank you. Would you join me for a moment, when you return?"

Two iced teas in hand, William sat across from Carter. "Should I have a notebook?" he asked, always ready to take on new assignments.

"No. I just wanted to chat. First, let me thank you again for how you've been handling everything, both the inn and the restaurant. I never imagined it all would be running this smoothly so soon."

William nodded. "It's a beautiful property."

Carter suppressed smiling at his inability to accept praise. "It is. Next, I have a question: do you have any information about Mr. Goodwin that you wish to share?"

William shifted in his chair. "I hardly know him."

"Well, it's just that I sense some animosity between the two of you. I wonder if there is something I should know." William didn't answer, so she continued. "I also want to assure you, as I have made clear to Ben—Mr. Goodwin— that you are here under my employ, not his. Mr. Goodwin was a friend of Davidson's, and he is just trying to help me sort things here."

"I never heard of Mr. Goodwin before," he said without being asked. "I was here the whole time Davidson was. Never met Mr. Goodwin."

"No?"

"No."

Carter considered this, but then thought of a possible explanation. "They were seafaring buddies. Mr. Goodwin must have bought his house after Davidson had left on his latest voyage."

"That must be it," William said in his usual monotone. "Anything else?"

"No, that will be all, William. Thank you for your honesty—and for all the work you have put into Davidson's dream. I could not have done any of this without you." He nodded, gulped his iced tea, all while expressly avoiding her eyes.

Carter smiled. She was learning to accept William's taciturn demeanor. It was who he was.

CHAPTER TWENTY

Lucille returned to Rams Head brimming with news from her city visit. Carter was descending the main staircase, when Lucille rushed forward, her fine-woven straw hat having fallen off her head and onto the floor. Margaret and Isabelle were trailing behind Lucille along with Graham's boys and the trunks.

"Carter – we did it!!! Women across the country will soon be voting! The House passed the amendment yesterday, May 21st – remember that date!"

"Are you certain?"

"Yes, yes, yes! The senate gets it in two weeks. This is really going to happen!"

Carter eyes welled and sat down on the next to bottom step. "I knew the vote was imminent, but assumed something would get in the way. Again, are you sure?"

"Stop asking me that. I read an article just this morning. I'm absolutely sure!"

"I had my doubts this would ever happen." Carter looked shellshocked.

"We all did," Lucille joined her on the step and hugged her tightly.

"It'll take a while before this sinks in," Carter said. "President Wilson has been softening since New York made it law two years ago, but the whole country?"

"Yes, the country. After it gets through the Senate, it must be ratified by each state, which hopefully will go quickly."

"Nothing ever goes quickly, Lucille, you know that."

Carter felt guilty. She had all but abandoned her suffrage involvement since she had come to Ram Island. She had kept track of the suffrage gains as best she could, reading the newspapers and receiving occasional telegrams from fellow suffragists, but her own work in the movement had been sidelined by her role as proprietress of the inn. She reasoned that now they were heading in the right direction, she was less needed. Even her home state of Iowa was about to fold.

"As soon as it becomes official, we will have a huge party here," Carter declared.

"Yes, we will need to quickly toast while alcohol is legal."

"I'll always be able to serve it privately, just not sell it."

"Right. But you won't be able to replenish it."

"Have you seen our basement?" The two friends laughed. "What crazy times we're living in, Lucille."

"I'm glad to be living through them with you," Lucille's eyes were bright with happiness. "Oooh, we need to tell Estelle. Let's have a celebratory picnic lunch! It's warm enough to do so."

"Let's! I'll get the bottle of champagne and glasses and have a basket packed for three. Should we meet in a half an hour or so?"

Lucille started up the staircase with her bags, then stopped.

"I have other news." Resuming her position at Carter's side, she looked around to make sure Margaret and Isabelle were not nearby. She spoke quietly. "I took Isabelle to Dr. Jenkins. She's well, and the baby should be here in two to three months' time. Moreover, he gave us the name of a Christian adoption network. Isabelle was amenable to the idea. We should probably get written permission from her parents. Powerful people can make trouble for others if they change their mind."

Carter grimaced. "If we ever hear back from her mother. She wrote me a note with some money, saying she would do her best to try and visit soon. But I have my doubts."

"Can you imagine *not* visiting your child in this condition?" Lucille marveled. "Whatever happens, I like Isabelle and am glad we are helping her. Oh, one more thing..." her voice lowered even more. "I saw Stuart."

Carter's eyes widened.

"I practically tripped running across the street calling his name. I'm sure people thought me most forward chasing and screaming after a man."

Carter laughed. "I would have loved seeing you so undignified."

"I suspect he was avoiding me."

"Why would he avoid you?"

"I don't know. In any event, I caught up to him and asked where he has been."

"Yet another forward move on our Mrs. Henry Nesbit's part."

"Yes, but how I could I not ask? Genevieve has been so troubled by his absence."

"So where has he been?"

"He wouldn't say, but promised he would return here tomorrow night."

"That's a relief."

"Perhaps. I hope I am wrong, but I didn't have a good feeling about it. He didn't look well."

"I pray he's not sick."

"He looked more haunted than sick – the hallowed eyes, the distracted attention."

"Whatever it is, we'll find out soon enough. Okay, you get going. I'm looking forward to our picnic lunch. Chef found a shrimp supplier, so he is experimenting on us for lunch."

"Fun."

"And I have some news of my own...about Benjamin Goodwin." She whispered, "We kissed."

"Even more fun! Okay. I will change, fetch Estelle and meet you shortly on the lawn – we have lots to celebrate!"

The three women placed an old floral bedspread on the lawn close to the small bluff that separated the grass from the sand and water. They laughed at how their outfits looked coordinated in shades of blue: Lucille in a Liberty print house dress, Estelle in a powder blue smock style and Carter in a bright teal wrap-waist look. Carter and Lucille kicked off their shoes and sat crossed legged. Estelle used the back of a chair to lean against. Chef Adam had pulled together a lunch of boiled shrimp and a mix of raw garden vegetables, and a right-out-of-the-oven loaf of bread with a small glass jar of William's honey to spread on it. As promised, Carter brought champagne and crystal stemware. The sea breeze only added to the joyous atmosphere.

"To women," Carter said raising her glass after serving Lucille and Estelle. "We still have a long way to go to get true justice for all [she nodded to Estelle] but every step on the road should be celebrated."

"Yes, And we're on the road together!" Lucille said.

"Hear, hear." Estelle smiled. "Thank you for including me in this merry moment."

"Of course," Carter said. "We did this together – along with a few hundred thousand other women. And let's not forget the men who marched with us and those who voted for this. Here's to them too!" She raised her glass once more.

"Can you imagine the party Bertha will be throwing tonight?" Estelle said, now taking a sip. "I wrote her by the way. I told her how grateful I am she sent me here. I'm sure going to miss this place."

"Miss it?" Lucille said. "Why, whatever do you mean?"

"I'm going home," Estelle said. "Back to Chicago. My son Atticus wrote that there has been more than the usual amount of race trouble—a number of protests, some resulting in violence. He's worried about my house being empty, and I'm worried about my kids, even though they are grown. Also, Atticus wants me to move in with him and his family now that Walter is gone."

"How do you feel about leaving your home?" Carter asked. "I assume you raised your kids in that house."

"Yes, I did. I don't know what I feel about anything moving forward. Mostly scared, if I'm honest. Walter was my world. He was my protector, my right hand, my strength. Now Atticus wants to fill that role. I also need to figure out my finances – that was Walter's domain. So, you see, I have decisions to make." Estelle sighed. "I thought Walter would outlive me. He was so healthy. Who would think a pandemic would sweep in and take him without warning."

"I'm so sorry for your loss," Carter said. "Though very different of course, I lost my mother to influenza. I was only 19 and had no one else in the world. Until it happens to you, there's a smugness we all have that bad things happen to other people."

Unless they live in denial that it happened at all, Lucille thought, thinking of Carter about Davidson.

"Agree," Estelle said. "We're all guilty of feeling invincible – until we're not."

"Please don't rush off," Carter said.

"Yes, we've hardly spent time together," Lucille added. "You've turned down every invitation until this one."

"I've needed this time alone to think. I went straight from my parents' house to one with Walter and the kids. Being on my own has been a gift."

"Well, we have a wedding next weekend," Carter said, adding, "I'd love you to be our guest."

Estelle demurred. "How kind. Thank you. Let's see how the week unfolds."

As they were finished with their lunch, Estelle stopped. "Oh, and by the way Carter, room 13 wants more fresh towels." She looked at Carter's puzzled face and added, "People assume I work here. I've gotten used to it and simply pass along their requests to Isabelle when she drops off my meals."

They returned to the inn to hear hammering in the lounge. It seems that Ben had a beautiful mirror made and, with William's help, just finished hanging it over the bar's fireplace. The mahogany-framed mirror was trimmed in gold leaf and crowned at the top with a golden ram motif.

"Ben, where did you get this?" Carter said with wonder, as William and Estelle slipped out of the room.

"I found the mirror a few weeks back in Greenport and then had the gold trim and ram painted on it," he said.

"A gift to our partnership. There's more…" he grabbed a box sitting on the bar. It contained what looked like hundreds of labels, each one stamped with a gold ram — the exact ram motif as on the mirror.

"What are these to be used for?" Lucille asked.

"Whatever we want them to be," he said. "The sign of the Ram."

"Surely not for the alcohol?" Lucille said. "The bottles belong to other people."

"I haven't thought it out. But they just seemed like a useful thing to have."

"Oh, I just love how they look!" Carter hugged Ben. "It's just so clever – no name, but clearly ours."

"I am so happy you view it that way, Carter," Ben smiled.

Lucille's forehead wrinkled. "The gold ram identifies this establishment. We need to be careful what we put it on. It shouldn't go on anything in the basement."

"Let's not worry about that now," Ben said, still smiling at Carter.

Carter nodded. "I agree. We can use the labels for our soaps, maybe perfume bottles. I just love that they match the gorgeous mirror. Oh Ben, what a brilliant idea!"

Lucille noticed there was something different between them. A comfort, yes, but also the hint of a spark. She smiled. *See, Henry, told you so!*

Margaret stared in the mirror longer than usual as she dressed for dinner. She had put extra care into her appearance, wearing a soft lavender dress that Mrs. Nesbit said made her skin glow. She topped it with an ivory woolen sweater her mother had knitted. She wore her light-brown hair a bit looser than usual, and she even spritzed on some of her precious rose water, one of her last gifts from Vance.

Earlier, she had come back from the city to a note on her bed from Curtis:

Meet for supper at RH, 6pm. C.

She stared at the paper all afternoon, looking for clues that did not exist. He had never left her a note before, so she didn't know whether to read into its brevity. Given Curtis's lack of poetry in general, probably nothing. She had enough florid words with Vance for all the good it did her. Curtis was more like her father: succinct and declarative — and true to his word.

She and Curtis hadn't spoken in a week, an eternity in their brief relationship. She did her best to seem normal around Mrs. Nesbit and Isabelle, which was easy to do while they were in the city. Before that, she told everyone Curtis was busy with work. She was as confused about Curtis as ever. Maybe she had rushed into this.

Then again, she thought of how much she adored him and couldn't bear the thought that his heart may have soured on her. Curtis was a good man, that much she knew. He was also handsome and strong, and made her stomach flutter with nerves. Much as she had wanted to approach

Curtis during this absence, she heeded Genevieve's advice to wait. *Absence makes the heart grow fonder,* she told herself. But maybe this was a case of *out of sight, out of mind.* Either way, the note indicated the wait was over. She would see him tonight.

Margaret peeked at herself again in the foyer mirror before heading into the dining room. She pinched her cheeks and bit her lips to heighten their color. Curtis was already there and stood when she entered. Her heart pounded. He looked his usual dashing self – she loved how his broad shoulders appeared in his white shirt and dark jacket. His expression was neutral, but his eyes locked with hers as he pulled out her chair. She was relieved to see the usual spark of hunger for her in his eyes.

"You look beautiful Margaret. I've missed you," he said, reaching for her hand across the table. Still staring into her eyes, he rubbed her hand with the tips of his fingers. "Did you have a nice visit to the city?"

"I did, thank you. Was all well here with you and your family?"

"Yes. Did you miss me?"

"Of course."

"Good." He withdrew his hand and looked at the menu.

"That's it, Curtis? Shouldn't we talk about our disagreement? Or the fact we haven't spoken for a week?"

"As you said, we needed the time, but here we are, back to normal."

"I don't think it's enough."

"What?"

"It's not enough. To just come back and expect everything to be as it was. We have to talk about things, Curtis."

"Is this about the dog?" He spoke with a small measure of impatience.

"No. Yes. I don't know," she said honestly. "You want to make decisions for me."

"That's what husbands do."

"No, they don't. Or they shouldn't."

"Yes. They take care of their wives and children, and that means making decisions. A man must run his household so everyone is safe and loved."

Margaret looked at him and realized he believed it. That making decisions was a form of caring for those you love. Her heart softened.

"I don't want to be 'run.' I want a say in my life. For example, I love animals and would like a pet. Or two."

"Are all Irish girls as stubborn as you?" His tone was flirtatious.

"You need to listen to me."

"I am doing that now, Margaret."

She let out a breath, realizing he was. "Will you always listen, even when we disagree?"

"Of course. You won't let me *not* listen."

She giggled. "That's true."

"I love you, you love me, and we are to be married. We will figure out the rest, I promise. The dog looks happy here, I've seen it running around. So that's no longer an issue. Let's hurry through this dinner so afterwards we can make up for lost time." He gave her one of those devastatingly sexy looks.

"All right, then," she said. And she meant it. No marriage was without its flaws, but they loved each other and would learn. She was certain of it – wasn't she?

CHAPTER TWENTY-ONE

The next evening Genevieve almost stopped playing the piano mid-song when Stuart walked in the room. Lucille said he would come, but until he actually showed up, she had her doubts. Yet there he was, smiling at her, his eyes glassy with emotion. He must have missed her as much as she missed him. She stared at him and smiled as she played. Stuart had already ordered their usual drinks and dinner by the time she joined him.

"How do I not kiss you now?" Genevieve said, straining to contain her joy.

"We'll have time for that later. Eat up."

"I have been so worried. Are you okay?"

"I'm fine. I've had a lot going on. I just want to bask in seeing you again. Indulge me."

So, she did. She also indulged him quietly while they made love back in her room. And she indulged him again in the morning when they made love to wake up to the day together.

But then she couldn't hold back as they lay in one another's arms. "Stuart, are you sick? You've lost weight."

He sat up and, oddly, started putting clothes on.

"Why are you getting dressed?"

"Because you may not want me here after what I have to say."

Genevieve was befuddled as she watched him dress. "I am listening."

"Rebecca is pregnant." He sat on the bed and reached for her hand. She snatched it back, stood up and fished for her robe, which she tied on tightly.

"I do not understand. Did she have relations with one of the household staff? Does she have a lover?"

Stuart couldn't meet her eyes. "It was me, and no, I did not force myself on her."

Genevieve grabbed a pillow and held it against her chest like armor. "Explain."

Then came an avalanche of meaningless words. Rebecca enjoyed their marital relations. It was her only connection to her former self. She was always reaching for him. Always seducing him. He turned her down repeatedly. And sometimes he didn't. Sometimes, he rationalized, it was all he had in this marriage, so why shouldn't he take whatever pleasure he could. But then he met Genevieve, and he knew love again, real love, and that's what he wanted from life.

"You said that part of your marriage was over. That you are husband and wife only in name."

"That was mostly the case, yes, and is certainly true since I met you. Surely you know – no, you must *feel* – my love for you."

"I'm not sure what I know, Stuart. I no longer trust my feelings. I no longer trust your feelings, either. Besides, what does this mean now? Your wife will have your baby. We cannot keep seeing one another."

"Why can't we? I have given this much thought while I was away. Nothing has changed between us. The love is still there."

Genevieve looked at him incredulously. "Everything changes. You will have a child!"

"Yes, with a sick woman whom I do not love."

"A sick woman who is your wife." She dropped the pillow and cut the air with her hand. "Even if I believe there is nothing between you – and I would be a fool to believe that – you will be needed at home."

"You are my joy, Genevieve. I am not giving you up, not without a fight. I was married when I met you. I am still married. Yes, there will be a child. However, I still have my business that causes me to travel here. I still have this life, my life with you."

"Who will take care of your child?"

"My parents. Rebecca's parents. There is a whole family awaiting this child. I will be there as well, of course. And then there will be nannies..."

Genevieve put her hands over her ears to make him stop talking, which he did. He moved to put his arms around her, but she flinched and started hitting him.

"What about *my* feelings?" She screamed at him. "What do I get out of this arrangement? Half a man and Rebecca gets to be a mother and enjoy all the love and fuss that comes with it?"

"You have my heart, Genevieve. I was never going to leave Rebecca. That was never a possibility. Surely you knew that."

She stood quietly for a moment, absorbing the truth of his words. He would never have left a sick woman. She did know that. But Genevieve had been so busy being happy, far away from Laurent, she never thought about anything else. Now she had to think about what her future would look like based on decisions she made today.

"She's gone!" Helen came down to the dining room at breakfast, waving a piece of paper. "Who's gone?" Carter stood up. She was having coffee by herself as Ben was at the dock and Lucille hadn't yet come down.

"Rose! I knocked on her door and there was no answer. I have the key — look!"

Carter scanned the note Helen thrust in her hand. As she was reading, Elizabeth came down the stairs, still buttoning her dress.

Sorry. I tried. I really did. I can't be without Herbert. Aidan will be better off without me.

"Where should we look?" Elizabeth asked Carter.

Carter was at a loss, but then remembered the woods. "I have an idea. Follow me." The three women ran out the door, down the road and then onto a path into the dense woods. Over her shoulder Carter explained, "She told me this is her place of peace."

Sure enough, Carter spotted Rose, sitting on the same fallen tree trunk as last time. In her hand, Carter saw the flash of a knife's blade.

"No!" Rose stood. "Please leave me alone. I know what I'm doing." Her face was one of pure agony, awash with tears. "I need to join Herbert and ask for his forgiveness. Then maybe God will forgive me, too."

Elizabeth ran to Rose and gripped her by the shoulders, causing the knife to slip from her hand. "My dear Rose. There is nothing to forgive. You are a good woman."

"I'm not like you, Elizabeth. I am weak. I cannot see any other way. How can Aidan have a whore for a mother? I'd rather he has little memory of me."

Carter discretely picked up the knife and tucked it into her skirt pocket while Elizabeth spoke softly and firmly to Rose.

"You are not a whore. You are a mother providing for your child. None of us are whores. We are mothers and are still wives in our hearts."

"I am with child."

One could only hear the rustle of the leaves as Elizabeth, Helen and Carter took a moment to absorb the news.

Elizabeth recovered first. "Being pregnant is no reason to leave us, much less your son. You need to put yourself together. We are here to help, whatever it takes. You are not alone."

"But I am. I have been alone in my heart since the telegram saying Herbert wasn't coming back," she sobbed.

"Elizabeth is right," Helen chimed in. "We are here with you. All of us."

Rose looked to Carter, who was standing at a distance, who returned her gaze with a firm nod.

"All of us," Carter confirmed.

Lucille breathed in sharply when Genevieve told her what transpired with Stuart. Fella at her side, Lucille had gone to the dock looking for Carter who wasn't at their usual table waiting for her. Instead, she ran into Genevieve, had just said goodbye to Stuart. Lucille could see his boat in the distance leaving the harbor. Genevieve was openly crying.

"Does he know what he will do about the baby?" Lucille asked as they strolled back to the inn. "Rebecca seems most unsuited to be a mother."

"He said he looked into ending the pregnancy but given her state of mind, there is no safe way."

"Aren't there experienced midwives and doctors who can help Rebecca? Especially in Manhattan."

"It is hard when a woman is mentally unfit to consent."

Lucille nodded. "I've heard of something called 'French pills.' Many people call them female pills. Something to do with a grain called ergot. I cannot swear if they are safe or effective."

"Would you take one?" Genevieve asked.

"Of course not. I am married."

"As are they," Genevieve said bitterly.

"Sorry, I sound heartless," Lucille said. "I'm trying to see a way out of this situation, but I see there is not. And you, dear Genevieve, what are you thinking to do?"

"I do not know. Stuart wants things to stay as they are."

Lucille grimaced. "Of course, he does."

Just then they looked up to see Carter and Elizabeth talking on the veranda. Elizabeth shook her head looking distraught. She glanced at Genevieve and Lucille and quickly excused herself after wishing them both a good day.

Now it was just Lucille, Carter and Genevieve standing on the veranda. Carter motioned the two to walk to the vegetable garden with her. Fella happily followed them, as if he too was concerned.

"Rose is pregnant," Carter said without preamble.

"Oh no!" Lucille said. "Does she know whose baby it is?"

"She has been with more than one man."

"Right. Why must women always bear the burden of scandal?" Lucille asked, inspired by her recent reading of the *House of Mirth*. "Rose will suffer the fall from grace, not any of the men she's been with. It's quite unfair."

"I agree," Carter said. "You realize this is our second pregnancy since we've been here."

"Third," Genevieve corrected. "Rebecca is pregnant."

Carter just stared.

"Yes," Genevieve said dryly. "My gentleman friend has been cheating on me with his wife."

Carter and Lucille exchanged worried glances while Genevieve plucked a carrot from the garden bed and gave it to Fella who ran off with it. After a moment, Genevieve said, "It is remarkable how easily women get pregnant. Unless of course they are trying. I tried with Laurent for years. I am grateful it did not happen. My body rejected him in some way. Or motherhood rejected me." She looked away, trying to blink tears from forming. "Let us turn to Rose. What to do?"

"First, we need to know if she is truly pregnant," Carter said. "Elizabeth has her doubts. Rose hasn't been eating for a long time and is painfully thin. It is like she's starving herself. We've all noticed."

"Yes," Genevieve said. "I keep taking in her dresses. I would have noticed if her breasts were fuller. I sometimes know a woman is with child before she does. Though Rose has been so before."

"True, but it still could be a mistake," Lucille said. "I am not a woman of faith, but I will pray that's what it is."

"We need to get her to a doctor," Carter answered. "The closest doctor I know of is in Sag Harbor. The women are leaving tomorrow morning, so maybe she can go early next week when they return."

Genevieve offered to take her, and Lucille said she'd pay for the doctor as well as their travels. She assumed money was an issue for Rose, so easing her mind there was the least she could do. Genevieve said she would ask the doctor for something to help her sleep.

"Can you ask for a double dose?" Carter asked. "I don't remember my last night's good sleep."

Lucille sighed in sympathy and patted her friend's hand.

"I meant to ask, how is Mae?" Genevieve asked. "I see her in the lounge by my piano. She comes with her friends, always meeting that same man."

"I don't ask, but yes, I've noticed the same thing," Carter responded. "I understand he is single and enjoys her company."

Lucille perked up. "Can I pray that works out? Or is that too many prayers for one day, my religious sister-friend?"

"As if I know. But sure, I'll add that prayer too to my otherwise long list."

JUNE 1919

CHAPTER TWENTY-TWO

Lucille and Estelle set out for Sylvester Manor early on a Monday morning. Lucille sensed Estelle was dreading it, as she kept putting it off with various excuses that felt flimsy: her leg still bothered her, she wanted her face to fully heal, it was too cloudy, she was waiting for a telegram etc. Lucille was scheduled to go to Manhattan the next day and used that as a reason to finally schedule their outing. William helped secure a hired car for the morning and off they went.

"You don't seem excited for this venture," Lucille said during the bumpy ride along dirt roads. "Or even happy about it. Am I wrong?"

"I will be faced with my family's past," Estelle said. "Those poor people who were owned by others. *Owned.* What kind of lives could they have had? It's a difficult thing to take in."

"It's impossible to comprehend, I agree." Lucille said. "But look how far negros have come since then."

"On one hand, yes, things are quite different, but we still have so far to go," Estelle said. "White people seem to fear any success we have. Whether it's getting to vote or getting good work. They're worried that we'll take their jobs. Not to mention the lynchings that go on daily down south. And it's not just in the South—the Klu Klux Klan his migrated to the north as well. Ida was always warning us to keep our guard up wherever we went. There's trouble everywhere, and I can't see that this island is any different."

Lucille nodded in agreement, knowing it wasn't the time or place for any Pollyanna-like sentiments, the optimistic heroine she adored as written by Eleanor Hodgman Porter, the beloved children's author.

Estelle stayed silent as she took in the untouched beauty of the nature that surrounded them. The salty sea breezes, the rolling hills, the verdant trees of every description, the ubiquitous water views. It was breathtaking and unlike any place Estelle had ever been before. She wondered if her long-gone relatives from the West Indies had seen anything beautiful about it. Or if they ever left the estate to have the chance to leisurely take it in.

When they arrived at Sylvester Manor, they found a grand, but not overwhelmingly so, estate. The main house was an appealing yellow, with three-stories built in the Georgian-style. It was surrounded by more acreage than Estelle had ever seen in a private home. The driver pulled up to the front gate, which was locked. "Doesn't look like anyone's home," he said. "It may be too early in the season. Miss Horsford usually only comes for the summer months. Or she could be traveling."

"You know her, Oliver?" Lucille's heart jumped. On the ride over, they discovered their driver was an off-duty policeman, a friend of Curtis's.

"No, not personally."

Estelle spoke up. "Do you know if Miss Horsford has any servants with the last name Mason – Agnes or John Mason, or anyone else with that last name?"

"Doesn't ring a bell, no. In most cases, servants on Shelter Island come and go by the season. Unless they travel with their employers. But that would only be a few at most."

"Drats," Lucille sighed. "We've come all this way and can't even get past the gate."

"I probably shouldn't be doing this," Oliver said, looking to Lucille. "But if it's really important to you, I can let you in. There's an entry the police have access to in case there's a fire or disturbance and the caretaker is nowhere in sight. But you must promise not to tell anyone. It would be our secret."

Estelle was wary about trespassing, but Lucille immediately said yes. After Oliver unlatched the hidden cast iron gate, they walked several minutes on the expansive lawn until they reached the house. Oliver was hired for the morning, so he was happy to wait at the gate as the women walked around. Estelle was mesmerized, her hand to her chest.

"Is this what your grandmother described?" Lucille asked.

"More or less. She had a watercolor drawing of it. The house looked enormous." They peeked in the window to what seemed to be the living room. The furnishings were comfortable and not at all ostentatious, just tasteful. A carved newel post introduced the stairs that led upstairs. Estelle wondered if Grammy spent any time in this room. She doubted it.

"At least you know your Great Aunt Agnes isn't toiling away here as a maid," Lucille said, assuming Estelle was disappointed.

"I guess," she answered. "Truthfully, I didn't expect to find my great aunt. It's been so long. Over 70 years. But my grandmother lived here as a child, and I'm able to tell her I stood on this porch and also on the very lawn. That's worth reporting back."

As they walked about the property, Lucille could sense Estelle was overcome with every kind of emotion, from awe to anger. Lucille purposely didn't speak, allowing her friend to absorb the experience on her own.

They could sense someone approaching. They looked up to see Oliver coming their way. "In case you're wondering," he said to the women, as he pointed to the roof of the building, "many of the slaves slept in the attic, crammed in together. Can you imagine how hot it was up there in the summer months?" Lucille covered her mouth with her hand, while Estelle didn't respond. Oliver, who seemed to enjoy imparting whatever knowledge he had, added, "follow me. I want to make sure you don't miss this."

He led them to a small, gated yard surrounded by white pine trees. Inside was a huge boulder. As the three came closer to it, they saw it was inscribed:

Burial Ground of the Colored People of Sylvester Manor from 1651

Estelle looked at Oliver, her expression questioning.

"It's a mass grave. For all the slaves that worked here, or at least as many as they could fit in this cemetery." He added, "and it wasn't just coloreds – Manhansett Indians, the natives born on Shelter Island, were slaves too. They intermarried, so it was all a big mix. True of all the big estates here."

Oliver had no idea how hard his indelicate words hit Estelle. Lucille felt helpless, feeling her friend's anguish. Then a thought occurred to her.

"Maybe a way to look at this is you are your ancestors' revenge," Lucille whispered to Estelle. "Look how beautiful you are, how well you and Walter live. Why, you're a guest at a white woman's inn down the road. Say your prayers for these souls before us, yes, but know that *you* are the very embodiment of all their prayers."

Lucille turned to Oliver and took his arm to lead him back to the car. She turned to Estelle and said, "Take your time."

A few days later, a huge box arrived at the inn, holding an ornate shimmering chandelier. It was a gift to Carter from Bertha Krantz.

> *"A touch of New York City sparkle is always in order. Hope all is going well with Estelle. Can't wait to visit. Love, B."*

William and Adam hung the chandelier in the foyer, where it looked immediately at home.

"How elegant!" Carter exclaimed when they were done, marveling how the crystal lights elevated one's first impression of Rams Head. "Bertha is right about the sparkle – it's a festive greeting when you walk in the door. I can't wait for Lucille to see it." Lucille was in the city and due back the next day.

Just as Carter spoke, Mrs. Worthington, Isabelle/Charlotte's mother arrived, unexpectedly as usual. She wore a tailored dress in wine-colored silk, with pearls at her throat. There was an underlying tension to her stately demeanor. Perhaps that was her assured manner as a politician's wife. She nodded to William and Adam.

"Good morning, Mrs. Worthington," Carter greeted. "We just finished hanging this gorgeous chandelier, a gift from a friend of mine in the city." Carter wanted Mrs. Worthington to understand that she was held in high enough esteem by important people to be given such a gift.

"Nice," Mrs. Worthington said, barely looking up. "May I speak with you privately?"

"Of course. Come this way." Once they reached the Garden Room, Carter said, "Thank you for the money you've sent. I hesitated to write, well, for obvious reasons."

Mrs. Worthington nodded, done with pleasantries. "My husband knows everything. Like me, he is most grateful Charlotte has found her way to you. We've decided she should remain here."

"I thought you had planned to situate her in a home for girls in her predicament," Carter said not bothering to hide her annoyance.

"This suits us better, and she seems happy." Before Carter could answer, Mrs. Worthington continued. "I would guess the baby is due somewhat soon?"

Carter was taken aback by the woman's rudeness but answered anyway. "The doctor estimates sometime in August."

"Fine. I would like her back at her studies in September. This would make sense of the summer-abroad story."

"Let's hope God and nature comply," Carter said, the sarcasm barely disguised. "But I never agreed for her to stay here to completion."

"Surely you see how settled in she is. Would you have me uproot her now?"

"No, I wouldn't," Carter said. And it was true. She had grown attached to Isabelle/Charlotte and was wary to send her to the care of some faraway "home for girls." Were those places even safe?

Mrs. Worthington went on, "You seem like a kind Christian woman. And my husband and I will make her stay here worth your while."

Carter was confounded by Mrs. Worthington's uncaring nature toward her daughter, as if she were negotiating the boarding of a dog. She thought of her own benevolent mother and felt for Isabelle.

After regaining her composure, Carter asked, "Mrs. Worthington, what do you intend to do with the baby?"

"We can organize a discreet adoption, perhaps through a church. Or just give it to an orphanage. I am hoping this can be part of your care."

Part of my care? The audacity. "Have you spoken to Charlotte about this? Is that what she wants?"

"She's a child. I want her back to her life as soon as possible, like this never happened."

"Let me get her for you. I think it would be helpful for her to know your position – and that your husband is aware of her condition."

"Yes, but he desires no contact until she returns in a suitable state."

Carter nodded, too stunned to speak. "I'll be right back."

Isabelle was calmer than Carter would have imagined. After a perfunctory kiss on the cheek, Isabelle accepted everything her mother said with an obedient smile.

Mrs. Worthington seemed satisfied, though Carter noticed she avoided looking at Isabelle's belly. "We are anxious for this unfortunate business to be finished, Charlotte. Miss Carter and I will stay in contact, and I will return when I am next able."

With that, Mrs. Worthington left. Carter observed Isabelle follow her mother's movements from the window.

When she was out of sight, Isabelle closed her eyes, her shoulders sagging in relief.

Carter found herself putting her arms around Isabelle, who clung tightly in return. Carter rubbed the girl's back, offering what little comfort she could.

Lucille was on the returning afternoon train with Margaret, when she spotted Ben's wavy blond hair peeking out from a newsboy cap. He was deep in conversation with another man in the front of the car. The other man was nodding vigorously at Ben's words, as if taking orders from him. Lucille approached them.

"Mr. Goodwin, I thought that was you!" She said as she drew nearer.

Ben looked startled, but quickly recovered. "Mrs. Nesbit. How delightful! I didn't realize you would be on this train. This isn't your usual hour, is it?"

"No, it is not. Margaret and I were unavoidably detained this morning." She looked to the man with whom Ben had been speaking. "How do you do? I am Mrs. Lucille Nesbit."

"How rude of me," Ben interjected. "This is Mr. Bailey, a business colleague of mine from way back when." Mr. Bailey was shabbily dressed and when he smiled, she noticed a missing front tooth. He did not look like a business associate of any kind. Ben continued, "Mr. Bailey is overseeing the house I am building on Little Ram Island."

231

"Yes, Carter told me about your construction plans. It sounds so promising," Lucille said. "You must invite me to see its progress. I plan to speak to Mr. Nesbit about buying property on Shelter Island to build our summer home."

"Absolutely, let's plan an outing soon," Ben said. "Let me finish my business with Mr. Bailey, and I'll escort you and Margaret off the train when we arrive."

"No need," Lucille responded. "We will see you on Graham's boat."

Mr. Bailey might not be a businessman, she thought, but he didn't quite look like a construction foreman either.

Later that afternoon, after Lucille settled in from her trip, she joined Carter for tea on the veranda. Lucille loved the new chandelier as much as Carter knew she would. Lucille had brought back gifts, too—Carter's favorite perfume as well as hard candy and other trinkets for the women of Rams Head.

"Carter, what is the status of the basement business?" Lucille asked, setting down her cup.

"Everything is the same. Why do you ask?"

"Have you been down there recently?"

"No, Ben has taken that over, thankfully."

"I saw him on a train with a man. He didn't look like someone Ben would associate with. For some reason, it came into my head that he might have something to do with the basement business. Do you know the man I'm speaking of? Ben introduced him as Mr. Bailey. Ben said he was overseeing the building of his house, though my understanding from what Ben has said in the past was most of the workers live here on Shelter Island."

"I don't recall a Mr. Bailey, but I will ask Ben about him."

"Okay, but perhaps we should go down to the basement ourselves and have a look around."

"I thought you trusted Ben?"

"I do. It's just that I trust our eyes even more. We – or you – need to know what's going on under your roof, that's all. It's too easy to leave it in a man's hands."

"You leave everything to Henry."

"I do. But I've known him since school. Though being here has made me want to assert myself there too."

"Watch out, Henry!" Carter laughed. "Okay, let's go downstairs before the daylight fades."

When they arrived at the rear of main basement, they noticed a new padlock on the door behind the shelves. Lucille looked to Carter, who tried her many keys to no avail. Carter bit the inside of her lip.

"Did Ben tell you he was changing locks?" Lucille asked.

"He told me he was planning to do so for security. I will ask him for the key."

"Good. It will be a useful way to remind him that you own this place."

"I feel like we have reversed positions on Ben."

"Not at all. I just don't like you not having access to every room on your property."

"I like this new Lucille," Carter laughed.

The two climbed the stairs only to be greeted by Ben and his associate Mr. Bailey.

"Ben, we were just talking about you," Carter greeted him.

Before he could answer, he smiled and casually handed her a key. "Miss Carter this is Mr. Bailey, Mr. Bailey, Miss Carter. Mrs. Nesbit and Mr. Bailey have already met."

Lucille nodded. Mr. Bailey did the same.

"Mr. Bailey is working on the house I'm building," Ben said. "But I also believe he would be very useful assisting me here on occasion. Our crates are quite heavy to move around." As if to answer Carter's questioning eyes, Ben added, "Mr. Bailey and I go back a long way. I trust him implicitly."

"Then I trust you as well, Mr. Bailey," Carter said.

"Good," Ben said. "Would you two ladies like to come back downstairs with us?"

"I will forgo the invitation," Lucille said. "I am tired from my trip this afternoon. I will see you both shortly at dinner. Good day, Mr. Bailey."

The Schnedekers came to Rams Head on average twice a week for dinner. Lucille liked them very much, and always made a point of saying hello and stopping by their table, as they were early diners.

After witnessing a particularly long and laugh-filled greeting, Carter expressed her exasperation when Lucille finally seated herself next to Carter at their table. "Lucille, why do you persist on being friends with them? I'm not sure it's the best thing for your reputation."

"Phooey on my reputation! They are a lovely couple. Edwina has turned into Genevieve's best customer."

"You're now on a first name basis with *Mrs.* Schnedeker?"

"I am."

"I wonder what Henry would say about that?"

"I don't know and frankly don't care. Like I said, they are a lovely couple."

Just then Ben arrived to claim his customary seat. "Let's ask Ben," Carter said. "He's as sophisticated as they come."

Ben knew the couple well without having to look. "They are good customers. You should leave it at that."

"To paraphrase someone's mother's words of wisdom, 'once you get a reputation, it is sealed forever.'" Carter looked pointedly at Lucille.

Lucille gave her a sarcastic smile, just in time for the Schnedekers to stop at their table on their way out.

"The roast pork is sublime," Alfred said to Carter, Lucille and Ben. "If you haven't yet ordered, I suggest you consider it."

"That sounds delicious," Ben answered, smiling. "I will take you up on the suggestion."

"Any dessert ideas?" Lucille asked.

"We only order Mrs. Crosby's apple pie," Edwina laughed. "It's heaven!"

Carter smiled politely and said, "Then we'll have to make sure we have it every night."

The Schnedekers bade them a good night and took their leave. Lucille winked at Carter and said, "That's more like it. It takes all kinds for this great world to spin, Carter."

Carter took a long sip of her nightcap. "It's not the world I worry about, it's my inn."

CHAPTER TWENTY-THREE

Carter was on her knees weeding the boxwood hedge that wrapped the hotel's front – the side that faced the road. She wore a wide-brimmed cotton hat to protect from the sun. She enjoyed weeding; there was something satisfying about pulling out an interloper by its roots right out of the soil. It was a mindless chore that let her think things through. And everything looked so much cleaner when they were gone. While bending over a particularly wild patch, she heard the sound of young chatter coming up the road. She knew exactly who it would be, as she had asked Curtis to bring them to her straight after school. Two days earlier, Curtis had returned a hotel bike he found at a house on the edge of town which helped to identify the boys who took it. Apparently the three inseparable kids were known troublemakers.

While Carter thought better than to pursue punishment, she felt this was too good of an opportunity to at least confront the boys. Carter promised Curtis she wouldn't involve their parents, much less press charges. She just wanted the boys to come to the inn and apologize. She stood and brushed the dirt off her skirt and waited for them to reach the hotel on the hill. Curtis was walking his police bike.

"Good afternoon, Miss Carter," Curtis said, and then nodded at the boys. "This is Mitch Malone and Rufus and Peter Gaines. You asked to see them about the bike I found."

The three boys looked no older than fourteen and all wore clothes that looked second-hand at best. Mitch, the tallest one with pitch black hair, stepped forward. Like the others, he was dressed in a well-worn shirt, suspenders and pants rolled up at the ankles to reveal tattered shoes. His shirt collar was frayed.

"We apologize," he mumbled. His voice was unusually deep for a boy. "We should have brought your bike here when we found it." The other two nodded. Curtis nudged each on the shoulder, signaling they needed to speak for themselves. Rufus's voice trembled while expressing his regret; Peter's face turned bright red when he said he was sorry.

Carter folded her arms. "There's more to the story than that, isn't there? You all threw rocks at at the woman who was riding it. So that's the lady to whom you should also apologize."

"That darkie?" Mitch snorted. "She was probably the one who stole your bike in the first place. Ain't no way I'm apologizing to her."

Rufus agreed. "My folks would sooner whoop me for making nice to a darkie than taking a bike."

Carter's eyes widened in alarm at the boys' words, while Curtis's widened at Carter, as if she had blindsided him. "Miss Carter, I understood you wanted an apology for the missing bike."

"Yes, but more importantly, they attacked an innocent woman and should apologize to her, not just me."

Curtis ran his hand through his hair. "Boys, go on your way. You're done here." The trio looked at Curtis, who nodded unsmilingly at them. "Go. And don't give me any more reason to come after you." The boys looked at each other and sprinted down the road.

"Why did you tell them they could go? I want them to apologize to Estelle!"

"I'm protecting *you*, Rams Head, and yes, myself to some degree*,*" Curtis scowled with impatience. "Most people around here would not take your side in this. 'Just boys being boys,'they'd say. And I'd never hear the end of it either. It's not my place."

"So, they are allowed to act that way? To attack a defenseless woman? What kind of men will they grow into?"

"That's not our concern," Curtis said. "How you and your inn are regarded among locals is our concern. You're a single woman and *you live here*." He emphasized the last three words.

Carter knew he was right; it was exactly what she had said to Lucille when the bike incident first occurred. "I don't like this, Curtis. Not one bit."

He stared at her for a moment. "I'm sorry you feel that way, but I'm not taking this any further. I can't. I'd advise you not to pursue this either." With that, he jumped on his bike and pedaled away down the hill.

Carter took off her hat, crumpled it with both hands and threw it to the ground. She stomped her foot several times and inhaled. She then grabbed her gardening gear and picked up her now-wrinkled hat and placed it on her head. She sensed someone looking at her. It was Estelle sitting by her open window. She had seen, and no doubt heard, the entire exchange.

Later that week, Genevieve joined Carter and Lucille for a glass of wine after dinner. She had spent the better part of the day accompanying Rose to the doctor in Sag Harbor. The appointment had to wait until the Connecticut Ladies returned.

"Well?" Carter asked, thankful Ben was not at Rams Head tonight, so the women could talk freely. "How is she?"

"Dr. Franken believes she has scurvy. He could tell by her gums and her weakness," Genevieve said. "He sees it with sailors. It is when you do not eat fruits and vegetables. By the time the men get to him, many cannot be saved."

"Rose is not at sea!" Lucille said indignantly.

"But she eats nothing. And she is covered with ugly bruises, another sign of scurvy."

"Bruises?" Carter asked, alarmed. "Did you see them?"

"Yes. I stayed in the room while she undressed. The bruises are everywhere. She insists on no lights when she is with a man."

"Could a man have caused those bruises?" Lucille asked.

"I asked. She said no."

Carter sighed. "This is terrible, but what about her weight loss and not having a flow in a good long while? Is there a possibility she is with child?"

"He cannot say, but he doubts it. Starvation can cause a woman to miss her flow. It is a medical condition." She stopped to retrieve a piece of paper from her purse. "It is called anorexia nervosa. That, along with the scurvy, could shut down her body."

"Did he give her medicine?"

"He told her she must eat and care for herself. He was very firm. He says her monthly flow will resume if she eats properly – though it could take a while."

"Does he know that for certain?" Lucille said.

"He sounded fairly certain." Genevieve said. "We stopped for lunch on the way back and she took a few bites. She said she could not eat more but will try tomorrow. She is upstairs resting – the door is unlocked so I can check on her."

"Still, I worry she'll try something again," Lucille said.

"I am not as worried after today," Genevieve said. "She seems to want to get better and is happy the doctor does not believe she is with child."

"Perhaps we should talk to Elizabeth and Helen," Carter said.

"They are dining with their men. As is Mae," Lucille said. Smiling she added, "I like Mae's gentleman. Maybe he'll ask for her hand. He has a kind face."

"Stuart has a kind face, too," Genevieve said sadly.

"He does, my friend, he does." Carter covered her hand. "Will he be here tomorrow as usual?"

"Yes. I am to tell him if I want to continue our relationship. Despite my concerns, I love him."

Lucille sympathized. "Maybe that is your answer."

"I agree," Carter said. "Don't look for logic in feelings. They just are."

"Speaking of Mae," Lucille whispered, "she and her gentleman friend are heading over to us."

Mae wore a pale blue dress which flattered her dark hair and pale skin. She said hello to the trio in her shy way. "Please don't get up. I just want to introduce you to my friend Mr. Gerald Rogers. He is eager to meet the woman who owns Rams Head. Mr. Rogers, this is Miss Carter and her friends Mrs. Nesbit and Mrs. Blanc."

The three women looked up and nodded their greetings.

"G-G-ood evening, Ladies. Miss C-Carter, I wanted to meet you, as I am so impressed with this inn. W-w-hen Miss Langley said the p-p-proprietor was a woman I almost did not believe her."

"It is true," Carter said, quietly miffed at the suggestion only a man could run a business. "My fiancé built Rams Head, but I have opened and managed it. I am awaiting his return, as he has been detained in his travels."

"I am s-s-sorry to hear that," Mr. Rogers said. "H-h-he will be pleased with what you've done in his absence. Miss Langley and I greatly enjoy our time here."

"Thank you. It is our pleasure to have you."

"P-p-pleased to meet you." He nodded as he and Mae bid their goodnights and headed upstairs.

Lucille spoke first. "Wasn't that nice, if a bit odd? I felt like Mae was seeking our approval, like we were her mothers, or perhaps her aunts."

Genevieve grinned. "In a way, we are. We look out for one another here, don't we?"

"We certainly do," Lucille said.

Carter headed up for bed long after Lucille and Genevieve had retired for the evening. She saw a light coming from under Rose's door. Elizabeth, Helen, and Mae were still with their men, so she knew Rose would be alone. She hesitated, then gently knocked.

"Come in, Genevieve," Rose said.

"It's me, Carter," she offered as she entered, closing the door behind her. "I wanted to see how you were." Rose was sitting up in bed, reading the D.H. Lawrence book Lucille had lent her. She wore an ivory lace-edged slip, her long red hair loose. Her hair looked thinner than Carter remembered, with patches of scalp peeking through the wisps.

"I feel mostly relieved, I suppose. It doesn't appear I am with child. Just a sick woman. Sick in the head."

"You are not sick, at least not in a way you cannot fix."

"I am not so sure. The idea of eating makes me ill."

"Start with a bite. Then another until you can't eat any more. You'll get your appetite back eventually."

"Herbert always loved how slim I was. He wanted me to lose weight after having Aidan, but it was hard. I thought by becoming slim for him, he would return. At first it was a game, but then I just stopped eating waiting for Herbert to appear. I know how crazy it must sound."

"Yes, crazy," Carter agreed. "But I look for the same cardinal to appear every day, convinced it is Davidson. If I see the bird, I am happy; if I don't, well, it ruins my day. We're all a little crazy that way."

"I saw my body today — it's a fright. No man would want me, at least with the lights on."

"Maybe that was your secret goal, unbeknownst even to yourself."

Rose sighed.

"Rose, I wanted to tell you I understand. As much as I am able. Davidson may well be with Herbert in heaven. The odds are great he perished. Yet here I am, moving ahead, having no idea what I'm doing. I am scared and uncertain and cry that my life is not turning out the way he and I had planned. Like you, I have made some decisions I greatly question."

Rose didn't respond, so Carter continued. "Should Davidson be gone, my only regret is that I didn't get to have his child. You have Herbert's. What a gift! God gave you a warning that brought you to a doctor today. An alarm bell to wake you up to this life you wanted to throw away. Herbert is gone, but you are not. And Aidan is not." She put up her hand. "Please don't say he has his grandparents. They do not replace you. He needs his mother."

"He does not need me. I am a mess," Rose said, eyes brimming.

"Oh, you are not. Whether you like your choices or not, they were not easy choices to make. You made them for the right reason — to provide for your son and give him a life as best you could. You can change your mind – nothing is forever. Why don't you go home and stay there? Maybe get a job in a local store. You don't seem suited for this life."

Rose blinked away threatening tears. "I'm not good when I'm home. It's difficult to function. It's easier to go through the motions here. Everyone thinks of me as quiet Rose. If they only knew how I used to be — talkative and happy. Herbert would laugh that I was incapable of *not* talking."

Carter was overwhelmed with the sadness of her story. Rose needed to rest – away from her family and away from this tawdry business in which she didn't belong. "Why don't you stay here for a while—but not to work. Stay for as long as you need to recuperate. I know you can do this. You need time to yourself more than anything."

Rose's face crumbled. "I don't have money to do that."

"Don't worry about paying me. I only ask that you eat."

Rose could no longer control her tears, which flowed down her face. "That is so kind of you. But I can't. For so many reasons. My parents will wonder where I am."

"Write them. Elizabeth will explain that you are here and safe. They will understand. You need to heal. You need to find the beauty of life again. You can do that here."

Carter started to walk away and then thought of something. "Rose, have you seen the colored woman who has been staying down the hall in room 17? She keeps to herself, so you may not have."

"Helen thought she saw her once, but no, I haven't seen her."

"Well, her name is Estelle Church. She is a good friend of my good friend. Estelle recently lost her beloved husband and is here to mourn him, among other reasons. Maybe you would do well to meet her."

Rose looked skeptical.

"She's a woman like yourself, in unbearable pain."

The emotional whirlwind at Rams Head continued unabated. The second-to-last week of June, the post included a letter for Carter from Marjorie Winslow, the woman who had gone to Barbados in hope of finding her husband Paul. The handwritten note was tucked into an announcement of Paul Winslow's memorial service.

Dear Miss Carter,

As the announcement sadly makes clear, I did not find Paul. Instead, I found a fortune hunter, well versed in preying upon the hearts of grieving widows. He was taken aback when I arrived with Joe. When Joe objected to giving him any more money without some kind of proof about Paul, it became apparent he wanted little to do with us.

I did meet someone who was there in the aftermath of the wreck. He believed all the men had perished, I'm sorry to say. With the heaviest of hearts, this time I said goodbye to Paul.

Sincerely, Marjorie Winslow

Carter sat under one of the huge oak trees, staring out at the water. Lucille made her way down to join her.

"You found me," Carter said, dry-eyed, but somber.

"Well, your flamingo pink dress gave you away," Lucille smiled as she sat next to her. "What's wrong?" Carter thrust the letter into Lucille's hands.

Lucille's breath became audible. She caressed her friend's back. "How heartbreaking. For you as well."

"It changes nothing for me."

"It doesn't?"

"No, not a thing. I know in my heart that Davidson is alive."

"But this letter."

"Not all the men's bodies are accounted for. Would they not all have washed up to shore?"

"In time. But you haven't heard anything from or about him. Why hasn't he contacted you?"

Carter leaned forward in a most serious manner. "My dear Lucille, if Davidson were dead, I would know it. Something inside me would have died with him. I am still whole, so I know he must be out there. Please stop insisting otherwise. I know you mean well, but it is difficult enough to keep going every day."

"What about Ben? You seem to have a new fondness for him."

Carter sighed. "Ben has made my life bearable. What he has done with the basement business saved the inn. As a man, he is handsome, smart, and attentive. I enjoy my time with him. Very much so. But he is not Davidson."

"I will stop my naysaying, I promise," Lucille said. After a moment, she added, "I also swore the same thing to Genevieve. She has decided to remain with Stuart, you know."

"Yes, I saw them together last night. He gifted her with a diamond and sapphire broach. Did you see it?"

Lucille smiled. "How could I not? She was showing it to everyone. I worry about such an expensive piece being on the premises."

Carter looked at her friend. "Lucille, do you dream up things to worry about?"

"Now you sound like Henry," Lucille responded.

"Surely you realize we have bigger fish here than an expensive broach."

Even Lucille knew the diamond and sapphire piece paled in value next to all the liquor stacked up in the basement.

CHAPTER TWENTY-FOUR

Carter waited until the inn was quiet and ventured alone down to the basement. She hadn't tried the new key and felt it time to see what, if anything, might be different. She opened the door, and, at first glance, everything looked as she remembered. At second glance, however, the crate's labels had all been stripped and replaced with white ones, stamped with the Rams Head logo. The only information on the labels were initials. She didn't quite understand and planned to ask Ben when she saw him.

There was also a new lock on what had been a small utility closet. Her key didn't work on that one. Ben had already left for the city where he claimed to have business over the next two days. When he returned to the inn, she would insist on a detailed briefing of the basement business, which she probably should not have handed over unquestioningly. She was thankful for the money it brought in, but now was mindful of the danger it brought in too.

Rose stayed at Rams Head for the rest of the week. She wrote her parents that she feared she was sick with a bad cold and was better off keeping a distance from them and Aidan. With the Spanish Flu outbreak, Rose knew the excuse would work. Carter had said she could stay rent-free as long as she ate a little each day. That seemed like a fair proposition—a generous one, at that. Carter also insisted Rose spend her days outside for sunlight and fresh air. Fella kept vigil at her side, and Rose returned the favor by sharing her food.

Rose also introduced herself to Estelle, steeling up her courage to knock on the woman's door one afternoon. After that first day, the two struck up a fast friendship and met outside, almost every day for long walks, often with Fella at their side.

After one such walk, Estelle and Rose sat on the lawn chairs for a rest. Isabelle spotted the two women.

"Hello Miss Rose, Mrs. Church, mind if I join you?"

"Please do," Rose smiled. "We must bore Fella terribly. Mrs Church is wary of him, which he senses, and I can't throw his ball very far."

"Ha! I'm good at that, watch!" Isabelle threw it almost down to the water.

"Impressive," Estelle laughed.

"How are you feeling?" Rose asked, looking at Isabelle's growing tummy in her periwinkle blue summer frock.

"I am well. It's awkward having a stomach in my way, but otherwise fine."

"I loved being pregnant with my son Aidan."

"I didn't like pregnancy at all," Estelle said. "But I loved my babies once they were born."

"This is different," Isabelle explained. "I will never know this baby, as I am giving it up."

Rose frowned. "Your baby doesn't know that. He or she just knows they have a warm and splendid place to grow inside you."

Isabelle bit her fingernail. "I suppose that's right. I am trying to take good care. Being here makes me feel better. I don't cry as much as I used to. Everyone is so nice."

"They are," Rose agreed. "Especially when you are feeling lost." She leaned down to pick up Fella's fetched ball and handed it to Isabelle to throw again.

"It refreshing to be outside with the two of you. It helps to clear the head," Estelle said. "I've spent too much time in my room."

Isabelle tossed the ball again. "Maybe we were sent here by God to figure it all out. Maybe someday we'll look back and realize this wasn't all bad."

"Maybe," Rose smiled wanly at Estelle. "You have a good spirit, Isabelle. Thank you for joining us today."

"You're the only other redhead I know," Isabelle remarked to Rose. "I mean really red. My brother has dark red hair like my mother."

"A blessing and a burden, isn't it?" Rose said. "We stand out."

Isabelle laughed. "That we do. I used to hate it, but I've come to like it."

Rose nodded. "Me, too. My husband Herbert loved my hair. He said he'd recognize me in any crowd."

"I hope I find a man like your Herbert someday," Isabelle said. "A man who loves me and my red hair."

"Oh, you will, I'm certain of it. There's a lid for every pot, my mother says. Right, Estelle?"

"Most certainly."

Isabelle giggled. "Look, here come the Schnedekers. I've heard staff talk about them, but this is the first I've seen them."

The ladies looked up to see the couple making their way toward them. Alfred and Edwin were the same height as one another and had a similar build. The only way one could tell the difference was Alfred wore a white shirt with suspenders and dark pants, while Edwina wore a fetching teal print sundress, her hair tucked into a wide-brimmed hat.

"They're an odd couple, I'll give you that," Rose said. "But gracious. Always saying hello when we see them."

"Good day," Alfred said when they were closer. "I am Alfred Schnedeker and this is my wife, Edwina. May we join you?"

"Of course," Rose said, her hand gesturing to the two empty chairs beside them. "A pleasure to officially meet you. I am Rose, this is Estelle, and this is Isabelle."

"The pleasure is ours,"Estelle said.

"Hi," Isabelle waved to both.

"May I throw your dog's ball?" Edwina asked Isabelle.

"Sure. He's not my dog. He's Fella. He belongs to all of us, though he fancies Miss Margaret and Miss Rose here the most. Fella senses Mrs. Church here doesn't like dogs, so he's trying to win her over."

"I love dogs," Edwina said. "We lost our little dog Scotty a few months back. Mr. Schnedeker promised we would get another one soon."

"And I will keep that promise," Alfred sighed.

"You are my witnesses." Edwina winked, before sitting down.

"May I fetch you ladies some lemonade?" Alfred asked.

"Yes, please!" Rose and Isabelle said in unison.

"Actually, I was just leaving," Estelle said. "But thank you for the kind offer. Nice to meet you both."

"Nice to meet you," Alfred said, with Edwina echoing the sentiment. "I'll walk with you up to the inn."

"Are you sisters?" Edwina asked, turning to Rose and Isabelle. "You're both so beautiful with your red hair."

"No," Rose answered, blushing. "Though I'd be so happy if we were."

"I'm sad your friend didn't stay," Edwina said.

"She keeps to herself," Isabelle explained. "I think she's self-conscious about being a colored woman. But, to me, she seems just like one of us. My parents wouldn't feel the same way, though, I can tell you that."

Alfred returned with their lemonades, and the pleasant chitchat continued for the next hour or so. Suddenly Isabelle realized the time.

"I need to doublecheck the rooms. It's almost check in time." To the Schnedekers she explained, "I'm a chambermaid."

"What about your husband?" Alfred asked, glancing at her stomach. "Does he mind you working here?"

"Alfred!" Edwina admonished.

"Not to worry," Isabelle said. "I am not married. It was this or a home for unwed mothers. This is so much better!"

The Schnedekers both offered her a smile before she ran off.

Rose watched her as well, adding, "Don't be uncomfortable asking questions. As you can likely tell, I am convalescing from my own illness — one of the head." She tapped her brow with a finger.

Edwina patted Rose's nearby hand. "We are all misfits in one way or another, aren't we? You look lovely and whole to me. Everyone here does." Fella barked. "See? He agrees. Animals know the truth."

From her position on the veranda, Carter saw Rose sitting with the Schnedekers. She also saw Estelle and Isabelle sitting with them earlier. She and Isabelle exchanged waves as she scurried into the building.

Not exactly the crowd she had in mind, Carter thought ruefully, then smiled. She assumed things will change the closer they get to summer. City people coming for their yearly holidays or even just weekend escapes. She was told that Shelter Island more than quadruples in summer — at least it did before the war and the pandemic. Just yesterday, a Mr. Walker, the house manager for the Perrys came by this week. Colonel Perry made his fortune in railroads and owned a ton of property west of Little Ram Island. Mr. Walker said the Perrys enjoy dining out at least once or more a week in the summer, usually with their houseguests. He promised to highly recommend they come to Rams Head. Word of mouth – especially from people like the Perrys — meant everything. Carter must keep the faith all will be well.

CHAPTER TWENTY-FIVE

My beloved Squirrel —

How could it be that I miss you more with time? Your letters delight me. Every line radiates energy and excitement. Imagine you spending so much time in the garden with the chef, learning all those herbs. And biking, swimming, and playing croquet most days! I am certain the extra freckles you fret about only make you more beautiful. I miss your face more than I can say — and to think of you smiling broadly, well, that is a level of joy I need to see in person. While I've always loved that you are a lady of letters, I also love this more active, engaged woman you have become. What an asset this "new you," as you put it, will be to building my business and raising our future family.

To that end, I am wondering if Carter would be open to us investing in the Rams Head Inn. Surely there are improvements and additions the two of you would like to make. I am amenable to whatever assures your future happiness. Yes, I will undertake building our summer home on Shelter Island. We will investigate land opportunities when I arrive....

Lucille shook her head. No, Carter would not be open to investment, that she knew for sure. She herself had proposed the idea early on, but Carter shut it down, saying Rams Head was wholly hers and Davidson's and always would be.

On a personal level, Lucille hoped she had not misrepresented her time at the inn more than she should have. There was no way she could tell Henry about some of the goings-on — the Connecticut Ladies, Genevieve and Stuart, the Schnedekers. And of course, the basement business.

It was true Lucille took up swimming, and even purchased one of those new rubberized Jantzen bathing costumes the last time she was in the city. She and Carter had been taking refreshing late morning swims further down the harbor where they wouldn't run into guests. She also occasionally rode bicycles into town with Margaret. Oh, and yes croquet – it had become a hotel favorite, though not particularly *her* favorite. And she did spend some time in Chef Adam's garden, culling herbs and picking flowers for the dining tables. If she were being honest, however, she exaggerated a number of items on the agenda, highlighting those activities of which she knew Henry would approve.

Yet she had not overstated her joy at this new life she was creating. Even helping Genevieve establish her new business was fulfilling, writing up pamphlets and then distributing them in town as well as at the other hotels. Genevieve rented a small storefront in town. Isabelle, Cora and Margaret were also pitching in with cleaning and painting. Margaret had asked Curtis helped to build shelves across one of the walls. It was work, but also fun. Genevieve named the shop "*Atelier* Genevieve," and her business card showed a silhouette drawing of a woman in a slim dress and one of the new small-brimmed hats seen all over Paris. She was awaiting delivery of those very hats.

Lucille helped Estelle write a letter to Miss Cornelia Hortsford and other prominent families like the Nicolls and Havens, inquiring if they knew what became of Agnes and John Mason. Estelle and Lucille discovered there was a mass exodus of coloreds from Shelter Island after the turn of the century. With the grand hotels burning down and families only there seasonally, full-time service positions were low in demand. The majority went to the boroughs of New York City for odd jobs, many to Eastville, Sag Harbor and became whalers, while others still went to Greenport, which had an established fishing community. The Great War complicated matters further, as many colored men enlisted, and their fates were unknown. Estelle wrote letters as well to the all-colored churches in Easthampton, Sag Harbor, and Greenport. Lucille felt vital in their efforts to find out anything they could.

Oh, and Rose! Dear, sweet Rose was returning to herself right before their eyes. While she clearly had a way to go, she seemed livelier lately. Just last night, she joined the Connecticut Ladies and their men for dinner. Rose didn't have a date — thank goodness — but there she was laughing and drinking with the group. It was heartwarming to see her smile again.

My darling Henry. You are returning to a happier, more energized wife. But will you really like whom I've become and the friends I've come to adore?

Carter was irate, hands on her hips. She was in the basement with Ben, having confronted him about the locked utility closet.

"There should not be one inch of this building for which I do not have access." He had already explained the new white labels on the crates were to unify and organize the storage system.

"The locked closet is for safety reasons – your safety," Ben assured her in his irritatingly calm voice, which bordered on patronizing.

"I will worry about my own safety, thank you very much. Now open that closet before I start screaming, which I assure you I won't hesitate to do."

Ben stared at her, contemplating his next move. He advanced slowly toward the closet but paused before opening it. "There are guns in here, Carter. More than one. I am happy to show you them, but I do not feel you should have access to them at will."

"Ben, I am from Iowa, for heaven's sake. Do you not think I know how to use a gun? The bigger question is why do you have guns here?"

"Maybe because we have a basement full of valuable spirits. And once the law takes effect, that expensive alcohol will only rise in value. We are vulnerable out here and can hardly call the police, should there be an incident."

"I thought you planned to return the crates."

"Not all at once, no. That's what the fee is for – to hold the liquor until the owners run out of their own supplies."

Carter's eyes widened. "So, there will be a constant flow of liquor in and out of this inn?"

"Please don't worry. It's all under control."

She tried to suppress her doubts. "Open the closet, Ben."

He did. Sure enough, there were three guns that she could see – two pistols and a rifle. There was also a binder of loose papers.

Carter reached for the binder and began flipping through it. It seemed to be an inventory of the liquor in the various crates.

"Does anyone other than you have access to this closet?" she asked.

He produced a key. "Only you now. But I want your word you will not open this closet without me or Bailey with you."

"Mr. Bailey? That man you introduced us to last week? You said he was working on your house. What does he have to do with," she gestured around her. "All this?"

"He is a man I would trust with my life – and yours. But no, he does not have a key for himself."

Carter wanted to believe him, but the whole episode gave her a queasy feeling. She contemplated telling Lucille but thought of her friend's propensity for worry and opted against it. Ben wasn't wrong—Rams Head needed protection.

Given Rose's pregnancy scare, it was rather ironic that Elizabeth turned out to be the woman with child. She, Lucille and Elizabeth were sitting outside, on chairs down by the water. Elizabeth had asked to meet with them privately. This was as private as they could find, even more so than the Garden Room.

The baby was James's, of course. Elizabeth told Carter and Lucille that James was happy, no thrilled, about it. So thrilled, in fact, he wanted to build a house on Shelter Island for them and her children — the one on the way and Jeremiah, the son she had with Leonard.

"But he's married," Carter's words escaped her mouth before she could hold them back.

"Yes, he is. He has some ridiculous notion about balancing his two families."

"Elizabeth, what do you wish to do?" Carter asked.

She let out a bitter laugh. "Besides turn back the clock and have my beloved Leonard come home from the war and resume our lives?" She rubbed her eyes. "I don't have many options, do I? I have a wealthy man who has loved me since childhood and would like to provide a home for me and my children. James will finally have his wish come true – complete possession of me in a gilded cage built to his specifications."

"You make him sound calculating, Elizabeth, when he seems so loving," Carter said.

"If he was loving, he would have simply given me money to get by instead of making me pretend to love him to get it. The sad part is, I have been saving money and believed Jeremiah and I could make a go of it on our own, maybe with Mae and baby Florence." She blinked back tears. "But with two children…. I don't have family money, and Leonard's mother does what she can, but a child by another man would not be well received."

"Maybe James would help support you?" Lucille ventured.

"Never. Not if I left him. James hasn't truly forgiven me for marrying Leonard those years ago."

"For what it's worth, my father carried on a second life with his mistress," Lucille said quietly. "She fared better than my mother in many ways."

"Lucille," Carter turned to her. "I had no idea."

"He had another family a few towns over, with whom he spent much of his time. My mother was hurt, but clung to her respectability — the big house, his name — telling herself no one knew." Lucille's voice quivered as she spoke. "As a child, I always assumed he liked his other family better. I imagined them having fun, getting the best of him. Of course, who knows if that was true or not."

"How sad for you, Lucille," Elizabeth said.

"I'm fine. I didn't mean to make this about me," Lucille said. "Life is so complicated — I suspect James's wife believes you are getting the best of him, which maybe you are."

"Julia despises me. She was relieved when I married Leonard, leaving the path clear for her to claim James for herself. And now, well, once again I have his heart and attention."

"Does she know about your rendezvouses here?"

"I have no idea. Though yes, probably."

"So what will you do?" Carter asked.

"James suggested I move into Rams Head with Jeremiah during my pregnancy, while the house is being built. He would pay, of course. I don't know what your policy is regarding children."

Another unwed mother, Carter couldn't help think. "We don't have a policy, per se. But would you be comfortable here? I have no idea what the school situation is on Shelter Island."

"James will hire someone to help me, I'm sure. I would put off the move for as long as possible. I like things as they are. We are an extended family in Connecticut and all support one another. And I'm not quite ready for Jeremiah to know James and to try to explain to my son who he is. James assures me he will treat Jeremiah as one of his own — or at least as much as he can. We will want for nothing."

"Well, you and Jeremiah and the baby are welcome here, Elizabeth," Carter said. "Just tell us what you need and when you need it."

"Thank you." Elizabeth smiled briefly. "Needs are so different from wants, aren't they? And they always must come first. I'm so grateful to you both."

After Elizabeth left, Carter looked at Lucille. "The drama never stops here, does it?"

"No, it doesn't."

"You never told me about your parents."

"It's not the kind of thing one shares casually," Lucille said. "Elizabeth gave me a reason. Lives are so often more involved than they seem."

"Yet your own marriage is a happy one, so devoted."

"I couldn't have it any other way. My biggest fear was becoming my mother, a woman so closed she can't love, not really, not even her own daughter," Lucille said. "I work hard not to worry about propriety the way my mother does. And not to judge other people. But sometimes, it's difficult to get her voice out of my head. It's easy to lose myself in there."

"You seem to blame your mother, but it was your father who strayed. That can't have been easy for her."

Lucille flicked away a bug on the chair's arm. "You're right. I don't really know what happened in their marriage. Perhaps my father was always in love with Daphne, a woman beneath his social station, and instead married my mother, who was his social equal. I never knew his side, just my mother's. He passed four years ago, so I'll never know his thoughts on the matter. How foolish I never thought to ask him."

"Did you ever meet Daphne or your half-siblings?"

"I saw them once from afar when I was around twelve. There was a little boy and a girl. I blamed them for my mother's unhappiness as well as my own, unfair as that sounds. I should meet them now. I will try to do so when Henry and I next visit Chicago."

"Why now?"

"Being here, I've learned life is not as black and white as I once thought it was, and neither are the emotions or people in it. If I am honest, my childhood is why I've resisted having children. I feared I would fail – myself, Henry, and whatever children we had. That I wouldn't be confident or loving enough. Perhaps it's time to face these ghosts."

A part of Carter had always resented Lucille's easy life. She was sheltered, protected, and had money to spare. Carter now appreciated no one had a free ride. *Be nice to every traveler you meet,* her mother would say. *You never know what baggage they carry.*

CHAPTER TWENTY-SIX

Screaming awakened the inn at early dawn. Blood-curdling shrieks. Carter and Lucille, each in their nightgowns, nearly collided as they ran down the hall toward a light coming from Rose's room. There stood Elizabeth, Helen, and Mae. Helen was still screaming. Off to the side, Carter could see Margaret, Genevieve, Estelle, and Isabelle too. Isabelle's face was buried in Estelle's bosom.

"She did it. Rose. She did it," Elizabeth whispered, her face a puddle of anguish. Carter pushed her way into the room. There in the bathtub was Rose's lifeless body, awash in bloody water.

Carter checked Rose's pulse and then covered her mouth. "Oh Rose, no...."

Ben and William appeared within seconds of each other, and quickly absorbed the situation. Genevieve barged her way into the bathroom and came out. Lucille guided Carter away from the tub and closed the bathroom door behind them to protect Rose's modesty.

"NO! She was better," Genevieve sobbed. "We spoke every day."

"I know." Carter rubbed her arm.

Still holding Isabelle at her side, Estelle stepped forward, shaking her head. "She was struggling. Sometimes it's hard to see past the face people want you to see."

There was a long silence among those gathered. Some quietly wept, others made the sign of the cross. Ben led Carter and William out of the room to the red velvet settee at the top of the landing.

"We need to come up with a plan," he said to the two of them. "We need to get her back to her family, her town. She can't be found here."

"Not now, Ben," Carter said. "This just happened. Let's say our prayers and try to comfort one another. I'm going back to the women. We'll take her out of the bath and wrap her in blankets. We have time to plan beyond that."

With the help of William's connections, they reached out to the local coroner, who came right away to determine the cause of death and issue a death certificate. He, in turn, contacted the island's only funeral home, whose undertaker arrived later that morning with two men. James Morton managed to get on the earliest ferry of the day to help in any way needed. He paid for the coffin and arranged for it to be transported by a private boat to Old Saybrook, accompanied by Rose's friends. An Old Saybrook funeral home was contacted, and a hearse would be waiting for their arrival on the other side. James generously tipped where necessary for discretion. The transport and connections, however, could not happen until the following day.

"Ladies, I need to get back to Sag Harbor," James said, a few hours after he arrived. "Telegraph my office with anything else. I can return if needed." He addressed the last line to Elizabeth, who hadn't said much since Rose was found that morning. She absently thanked him, her mind elsewhere.

Carter and Lucille walked him to the door. "Thank you for coming, Mr. Morton," Lucille said. "I know Rose was a friend of yours too. I'm sorry for your loss."

"Thank you, Mrs. Nesbit. This is unspeakable. I am worried about Elizabeth. Please keep a close eye on her for me."

"Of course."

Lucille liked James and felt his grief, despite his efficient manner. Through the whole ordeal, he was considerate, gentle, and attentive toward Elizabeth, as well as to the other women. Was it guilt? Surely, he could have seen Rose was not suited to this lifestyle he had promoted, or at least enabled. Everything he did was for Elizabeth, that much was obvious, including coming up with an income stream for Helen, Rose, and even Mae.

Lucille sighed deeply as she closed the door behind him. Carter took Lucille's arm. "Carter, I really thought we got Rose through the worst of it. She seemed so much better. I don't understand this."

"There's nothing to understand, Lucille," Carter said. "Let's go and join the others. Grief is something best shared."

It was as if a black veil had been draped over Rams Head. That night the group wordlessly ate dinner in the back of the dining room, away from the other patrons. Carter wanted to close the restaurant but realized that would cause inconvenience for those who had already made arrangements to dine there. Estelle had asked Isabelle to join her in her room for dinner, not wanting the young girl to be alone on this mournful night.

Helen broke the silence at the table. "I will always hate myself for encouraging her to join us for dinner two nights ago. She looked so good, so refreshed. I was certain she was our old Rose."

"We all thought so," Elizabeth said. "She seemed fine. Who knows what was actually going through her head. I just hope she didn't resent me for, well, all of this."

"I'm sure she didn't, Elizabeth," Carter said. "She missed Herbert. Try to leave it there."

Elizabeth didn't answer, so Carter continued. "When tragedy occurs, we want to retrace our steps to see how we might have prevented it. Or we blame ourselves. Had I not wanted a house apart from the inn, I doubt Davidson would have gone on that last voyage. I think about that all the time, then force myself not to."

"I imagine everyone here has at least one such regret that eats away at them," Lucille said. "And yet what's done is done. We can't change it however much we beat ourselves up."

The next morning, Elizabeth, Helen, and Mae left for their private boat, which would pick up Rose's casket along the way. They didn't know if or when they'd be back. Carter didn't ask; she just told them they were always welcome.

Isabelle was heartbroken. She had felt bonded to Rose, with their matching red hair. Carter kept a close eye on her, asking for help with all sorts of mundane chores, just to keep her busy. Today they were polishing the silver together in the Garden Room.

"Thank you for helping me. It's not anyone's favorite task, I know."

Isabelle smiled politely.

"Do you want to talk?" Carter asked her gently.

Isabelle stopped polishing for a moment, pausing on a fork she was buffing. Then she said, quietly, "She left me a note. She told me not to take this personally. That I was the sister she never had. But if that was true, then why would she leave me? She knew how much I needed her." Her face dissolved into tears.

Carter looked at the young girl beside her, a girl she had initially wanted to see gone from the inn as much as Isabelle's mother wanted her gone from her home. Rose saw the girl, not the problem – maybe because Rose herself was beset with problems, none of her own making.

To Isabelle, Carter said, "Rose was right. It had nothing to do with you—it was about her and she wanted you to know that. Her own pain, that nothing could help. I know that is no answer, but it's the truth. Rose's own son couldn't prevent her from leaving."

Carter paused. "But I understand your anger. When my mother died, she was the only person I had in this world. I thought God had it in for me, that he was going to test me over and over while giving other girls these charmed, easy lives. It took me a while to realize that my mother lived inside of me, and I needed to honor her by being strong."

"Well God certainly has it in for me," Isabelle said now scrubbing a serving spoon with undue force. "I've done everything asked of me: obeyed His commandments, obeyed my parents and my teachers, didn't talk back, never mind fight back, even when I should have….and yet I find myself with child, cleaning silverware and making beds."

"You know you don't have to do any chores," Carter said. "Your parents are providing for your care, even if you do nothing but throw Fella's ball all day."

The two continued their polishing. Then Isabelle spoke, her brows knitted. "I will do what you did."

"What, open an inn on an island somewhere, having no idea what you're doing?" Carter laughed.

"I will honor Rose by being strong," Isabelle vowed.

Carter looked at the girl beside her. "Honor her by being yourself. She adored you, just as you are. Rose was right. You're a special girl, Isabelle. You've already reinvented yourself, starting with your name. I have no doubt you will continue to be your own person going forward."

They worked in silence, Isabelle's completed silver pile grew far more quickly than Carter's. The young girl seemed lost in thought.

Carter decided to broach the subject never discussed between them. "Isabelle, I know you've spoken with your mother, but I'm wondering if there is any part of you that wishes to keep your baby."

"No, absolutely not," Isabelle said emphatically. "I need to go to school and get on with my life. I want to travel and then work with animals. Maybe be a veterinarian."

"Oh, I love that. But does the father of your baby know of your plans, or even that you're pregnant?"

"There is no father of this baby." She glanced at Carter. "It was not a love affair, if that's what you're thinking."

Carter nodded. "I see. Do you have any wishes as to the type of people who will adopt your baby?"

Isabelle put down spoon she was holding, her eyes watering. It took her a moment to speak. "Just kind people. Loving people. Fun people." She turned her body to Carter. "I want this baby to be happy, despite…." She shook her head, swallowing the rest of the sentence.

Tears fell from Carter. She went to cup Isabelle's face, but realized her hands were grimy with polish and dropped them. "Oh Isabelle, that's what I want for *you.* To go off to school, pursue whatever you want. I love that you have a direction, even if changes. Most of all, I want you to be happy. And have fun, yes! You know what would be fun now? For us to wash our hands, quietly raid Chef's kitchen and have some of his fancy chocolate pudding he makes with chocolate mint from the garden. You game?"

Isabelle giggled like the 16-year-old she was. "Yes!"

CHAPTER TWENTY-SEVEN

A few nights later, Mr. Walker, the Perrys' house manager, telegraphed to say the Perrys and their two children would be dining at Rams Head at 6 pm. Carter spent the afternoon reviewing every detail. Deciding which table she would seat them, who would wait on them, and what was on Chef's menu, something that she normally didn't oversee.

"I've never seen you fuss so over the restaurant," Lucille said in the cutting garden as Carter snipped jasmine flowers and small lavender whorls to be table centerpieces.

"It's the *Perrys*, Lucille. Colonel Perry. They are Shelter Island royalty."

"Nonsense. America doesn't have royalty."

"I just want them to have a wonderful evening, so they recommend us to their friends."

"Let's meet them first," Lucille said.

"Think of how the likes of the Perrys could elevate this place." Carter stood up, a fragrant bouquet in hand. "Catering to a crowd like that would guarantee our success."

"I'm stunned to hear you say that. I've always admired how little status means to you."

"You wouldn't understand, Lucille."

"Try me."

Carter sighed. "I didn't grow up in genteel society. Or even an educated one. Yes, my father was a lawyer, but he died when I was young. I had to work odd jobs to help my mother make ends meet."

"Which is where your fortitude comes from..." Lucille's forehead crinkled as if she was waiting for the follow up.

"I always felt less than when I met the Perrys of the world. As if there was an exclusive club that I wasn't invited to join."

"Carter, that doesn't sound like you. You didn't try to marry money or hold yourself out as anything other than who you are."

"I know." They walked into the dining room where Carter had all the small vases lined up on a table.

"I'm still not understanding," Lucille said. "You're confident — fearless, I'd say. What does status matter when you have that?"

"You couldn't understand Lucille. The world's doors have always been open to you. Women want you at their luncheons. You and Henry are invited to all the important galas. Status is power."

"It can be handcuffs too," Lucille said. "I dread those evenings. I've had to befriend many a person I didn't want to. Yet there is no such pressure on you. I'm confounded that you would put that pressure on yourself." She sat and helped Carter arrange the white and purple flowers.

Carter shrugged. She appreciated that status was like money or health; you only notice its absence. You can't explain what it feels like not to have it, nor can you expect someone who has it to fully to understand your feelings. A fish doesn't know that it's wet until taken out of water.

Despite her own complicated history with money and prestige, what Carter really needed was for Rams Head to be a success. And that meant building a reputation among the crème de la crème—trendsetting always came from the top. What they did and said, others would follow. And for Carter that meant one thing: more business.

At 6:30 pm, the Perrys walked in the main door. The wife, a middle-aged, thick-waisted brunette, held up her nose as if smelling something unpleasant. The Colonel, a rather portly gentleman with an oversized mustache, nodded at Carter as she introduced herself. The wife just kept looking about, as if she didn't hear Carter speak.

"Will your children be joining you, as Mr. Walker's telegram suggested?" Carter asked the Colonel.

"No."

When they reached their table, the waiter George greeted them with two glasses of the inn's finest champagne on a silver tray. The wife shook her head, still not speaking a word. Carter instructed George to remove two of the table settings.

"Welcome to Rams Head," Carter said as warmly as she could to the couple. "I hope you enjoy your dinner."

When she returned to Lucille, who awaited them at their usual table, Carter murmured under her breath, "Not the friendliest people."

"I could see the frost in the air from here," Lucille smiled. "No matter, we don't need more friends."

"Just customers," Carter said. "Do you want to go over and ask if the husband knows Henry?"

"No, I don't. Then I would have to engage with them."

The Perrys ate their dinner and left in short order; all in less than an hour. As instructed, George came to Carter and reported what they ordered, though said the husband ate both meals and drank both glasses of champagne too.

"Did they seem content?"

"I guess so. He asked to open an account, which means they'll be back."

"Oh, that's great news, George. Thank you."

Lucille smirked. "Rich people always open accounts. Let's hope they pay that account before the summer is over and done."

"Lucille!" Carter admonished.

"What? I said let's hope," Lucille said.

The Connecticut Ladies returned ten days later. Lucille greeted them as they walked up the lawn from the dock, throwing her arms around each one. "Thank you for your telegram, Elizabeth. We didn't know when, or even if, we would see you again," Lucille said, her voice cracking.

"It has been a hard week, as you can imagine," Helen said.

"Go settle in, and let's meet in the Garden Room in half an hour for tea. I'll fetch Carter, Estelle and Genevieve, and you can tell us all about it."

When the women met up, Elizabeth, Helen, and Mae all remarked on the beautiful flowers the Schnedekers left in each of their rooms. "What a kind gesture," Helen remarked.

"Indeed," Carter said. "Now please tell us about your week. Our hearts were with you."

The telling was simple. There was no hiding that at 22 years old, Rose had taken her own life. Rose's parents accepted that she wished to join Herbert. Their small town had seen so much heartbreak because of the war, it was well versed in funerals and mourning. Elizabeth described watching Rose's coffin being lowered in the ground next to where Herbert's may be one day. "I was shaking with sobs, knowing I'll never see our sweet Rose again, and yet there was something comforting, knowing that she may be reunited with Herbert again."

None of the bodies of the women's husbands had been returned, and there was a question if they ever would be. Having lost nearly 117,000 American soldiers in Europe, bringing back the bodies was an expensive and logistically complicated undertaking. Many of them had been buried in temporary grave sites that would need to be exhumed. Still, thousands of mourning families were demanding the government bring their men home. The widows had no idea if and when it would happen, but they held out hope. So, Rose was buried in the reserved plot she had recently purchased for the two of them.

"How is Aidan doing?" Lucille asked.

"I'm not sure he fully understands," Helen said. "Which is a blessing. His grandparents adore him, and he's spent so much time with them."

Elizabeth nodded. "Rose's parents are loving people. They will do a fine job with Aidan."

Genevieve dabbed her eyes. "She seems so alive. I cannot accept that her story is over. I cannot accept Aidan will not grow up to know how beautiful she was, her smile."

"We ask that all the time about our own children and their fathers," Elizabeth said.

Carter leaned forward. "I never knew my dad, but I know that he loved me. My mother told me that all the time, that he chose my name."

"He chose Carter?" Genevieve asked, her eyebrows raised.

"No, he chose Priscilla."

Elizabeth suppressed her reaction, but Helen laughed out loud. "I'm sorry, you are *not* a Priscilla."

"He thought it was feminine and that it rolled off the tongue like a piece of music," Carter mused. "But I wear his last name with enormous pride."

Mae piped up. "I think Carter suits you."

"Thank you." Carter turned to address the group, "Let us know what we can do. We've been feeling so helpless. And then there's Isabelle, who is bereft. She and Rose spent a great deal of time together in the last couple of weeks. Estelle as well." She nodded at Estelle.

"Yes," Estelle said. "I only knew Rose a short time, but we had a unique understanding between us. Our talks were so comforting. I'm grateful to have known her."

"I wonder if Rose realized how many lives she touched," Lucille said. "I wonder if any of us do. We just blithely say hello, wile the day away with one another and move on. I want you all to know how I too am grateful to have known Rose. I'm grateful you're all here, that we've had a chance to meet and be together this way."

Elizabeth touched her chest in answer to Estelle and Lucille's words. "That's why we wanted to return. We feel most ourselves here, especially now, strange as that may sound."

"And I thought it was just me who felt that way," Lucille smiled.

After Rose's death, Estelle was now in no rush to leave the inn. She told Lucille she was determined to give herself more time on her own. Also, Margaret had asked her to stay for the wedding, the two women having become closer in the wake of the tragedy. In fact, most all of the women at the inn bonded together, as if there was strength in numbers. Perhaps their was.

One early morning at daybreak, Carter looked out the window to see Ben and Bailey hoisting a crate up the lawn. She threw on a dress and shoes, tying back her hair as she ran down the stairs toward them.

Bailey tipped his head in greeting as she caught up to them. "What's going on, Ben? Where did that crate come from at this hour in the morning?"

"My house," he nodded toward his skiff tied up to the dock. The two men kept walking toward the inn.

"So, keep it there. You said we were at capacity here."

He spoke quietly. "My house is too open at this point. You saw it. It's not safe to store anything there. I will find space for it below."

"No, I won't have it, Ben. This crate is immense."

"Let's get it into the basement and we will discuss it there, Carter." He spoke quietly and sharply, which took her aback.

Following the men down the stairs, Carter slid open the shelves to the hidden chamber. Ben signaled Bailey to set down the crate, and Ben went in first on his own. Bailey avoided eye contact with Carter.

"There is no room in there," Carter said when Ben returned.

"I just found some," Ben answered tersely. "Bailey." They picked up the crate and took it to the end of an aisle.

"But you can't walk around there," Carter said. "You said we needed access around the crates."

"I was wrong." He nodded to Bailey. "I'll meet you at the dock."

Bailey tipped his hat to Carter and exited. Ben turned to her. He was sweaty from carrying the crate, his

281

expression one of exasperation. "This was delivered to my house. I can't have it there or it will be stolen. Or invite problems. This is the safest place."

"You gave me your word that no more crates would be coming here."

Ben gave her that crooked grin. "Don't you trust me, Carter?"

"I want to. But then this happens...."

"It's just one crate," he spoke softly. "It arrived with construction materials. Bailey panicked and woke me up. I agreed we should move it before the crew came, and we did. Not a big deal. You and I can't afford to doubt each other at this point. We're partners."

Carter nodded, though unconvinced. She looked around the storage room. She was in too deep to start asking questions. Besides, who would she turn to if she didn't like the answers? She couldn't call the police—it was her own basement filled with soon-to-be-illegal alcohol. Ben had her over a barrel, and he knew it.

CHAPTER TWENTY-EIGHT

Over a hundred guests would be attending Margaret and Curtis's wedding. Many were police officers, their wives and children, and still others were Shelter Island neighbors. The Connecticut Ladies were coming, of course, and Lucille had invited her five servants from Manhattan, all of whom Margaret worked with and considered close friends. The challenge was how best to house all those traveling from far away, including Margaret's family. It created an opportunity for Carter and Lucille to meet the other hoteliers on the island. Lucille secured a block of rooms at The Mayfair and a few at The Empire House. Lucille was happy to pay for the rooms for her invited staff, knowing what a treat it would be. She also gifted the honeymoon suite at The Mayfair for Margaret and Curtis.

Given the great distance Margaret's parents and sister Gerty were traveling, they were hoping to spend at least a couple of weeks on Shelter Island. Fortunately, Curtis knew of a family who would rent their summer house during that time. The O'Reilly clan would be arriving in two weeks.

"It's almost going too well," Lucille said to Carter, as they mapped out where the tables and chairs would go, contingent on the weather.

"Lucille, why must you always look for trouble?"

"I'm not looking for trouble," she answered. "I'm just superstitious about anything that comes this easily."

"Speak to Chef Adam. He doesn't think feeding over a hundred people is so easy."

"You know what I mean. Or maybe you don't. It just seems like a lot of people, no? Even William looked stressed when I asked if we had enough glassware."

"You're projecting. You can't help it, you're an awful-izer."

"I'm worried about Henry, if I'm honest. He promised he would be here, and I almost wish he was delayed. Does that make me a terrible wife?"

"No, just an honest one. It will all be fine, I promise. He will love that you are so engaged and productive here."

"I hope so."

"All right, we need a helping of good news. Isabelle seems in better spirits. Genevieve's dress shop is bustling from what she says. The restaurant is doing well, thanks to the summer crowd that's been rolling in. Our dock has been expanded and improved upon. No miscreants at the bar in recent days. Even our gardens are thriving, just in time for this glorious wedding."

Lucille brightened. "You're right. Sister-friend, I need to take lessons from you. Maybe it's all the bright colors you wear. I worry too much."

"Worrying is a luxury I don't have at the moment," Carter said, her expression turning serious. "I need to keep moving forward until Davidson returns."

Lucille nodded, wondering sadly when reality would set in for her friend.

A week and a half later, the two women received a formal dinner invitation written in elaborate calligraphy. It was from the Schnedekers. Lucille urged that they answer affirmatively to which Carter reluctantly agreed.

"I keep trying to tell you, I have nothing against them personally," Carter insisted. "It's my patrons I worry about."

"I don't know why. Edwina is Alfred's *wife,*" Lucille said. "Who is anyone to question otherwise?"

"Oh please, Lucille," Carter said. "You know as well as I do that they are not husband and wife, and no one could believe they are."

"Well, it's good business to know your community. And I'm curious to see their house. I bet it's beautiful."

The night arrived and the two friends consulted on their clothes. If the invitation was anything to go by, it would be an elegant evening.

"Isn't this exciting?" Lucille said to Carter as they headed toward the dock and into the Rams Head skiff. "I love that we have a date."

"I'm glad it's a windless night," Carter replied as the two climbed into the small boat, which Carter would command. Taking the skiff seemed easier than worrying about the causeway and tides. "At least we'll be dry when we arrive."

The Schnedekers had drawn a map to identify their dock. They promised it would easy to find. Other than an occasional lunch together in town, this was Carter and

Lucille's first real social outing since they arrived three months ago. They were relieved to simply have a night off.

They found the Schnedeker dock. A white-jacketed man awaited them and helped them climb out and tie up the skiff. "I am Frank," the man introduced himself. "I'm here to escort you."

The property was one big garden, colorful blooms of every variety amidst trellises and hedges. An elaborate pergola covered in wisteria crowned white iron scrolled chairs facing the sea. So, so pretty, Lucille said to Carter, who smiled in agreement. The three traversed the stone path leading to the house. The Schnedekers' home was much grander than either woman anticipated. It was white with many Victorian details, including intricate lattice work and a spacious porch that wrapped almost completely around. They climbed the stairs and Frank firmly tapped the brass ram knocker against the wooden double doors to signal their arrival before opening the doors himself. Edwina quickly descended the circular staircase with its sculpted mahogany railing. She wore a beautiful aqua-blue silk dress, her chin length hair tucked behind her ears. She was stunningly stylish and had a smile that swept you in.

"Thank you, Frank," she said. "Carter, Lucille, we are honored to have you here. And on such a lovely night."

"Indeed, it is lovely," Carter agreed, presenting her with a basket of small jars of spices from the inn's garden. "A little something from our house to yours."

"How sweet. Alfred is finishing up some business and will join us shortly."

"Your house is divine," Lucille said, glancing into the living room and dining room beyond it.

"Thank you. It took us almost four years to complete, but we couldn't be happier," Edwina said. She gave them a brief tour of the downstairs, which was generous in scale, yet decidedly welcoming with its botanical colors and many windows that afforded views of the splendid outdoors. Edwina said, "Come, we're all set up on the back porch."

She guided them to the covered veranda behind of the house overlooking the bay. Dinner for four was set with exquisite stemware, gleaming silver and a crystal chandelier overhead.

"This is extraordinary," Lucille exclaimed, admiring the view. "Just magical, Edwina. My husband Henry will be joining us in a week, and we're planning to build a house here. At the risk of being presumptuous, may I bring him around to see what you've done?"

"But of course, dear, anytime you'd like."

Just then, Alfred appeared, apologizing for his tardiness. "Please let's all sit."

Wine was served and the four toasted the beautiful evening together.

"Tell us, how are the ladies faring?" Edwina asked. "We were very fond of Miss Rose, the little we knew her. Fond of all the women, actually." Frank and another man wearing white gloves ladled creamy clam chowder into their porcelain bowls.

"As you would expect," Carter answered. "She is missed very much by her friends. Miss Rose was devastated at losing her husband and never quite recovered. She's with him now."

"Yes, that is the one consoling fact, I suppose," Alfred said. "Still, she was far too young to leave us."

"No doubt," Lucille said, eyes watering and needing to change the subject. "Edwina, I love what you're wearing. A Genevieve design?"

"Yes!" Edwina answered, her eyes lighting up. "Isn't it divine? I just love that we have someone as sophisticated as Genevieve on the island. Moreover, she's open to collaboration. Many dressmakers are not."

Alfred laughed at how seriously his wife took the design process, clearly reveling in her enjoyment. Apparently the two had been together for eleven years, and the warmth between them was palpable. They met in Norway, they explained, where Alfred lived, and Edwina had traveled after college. Holding hands now, the two agreed it was love at first sight. Alfred, a Norwegian novelist, had family means and was all too glad to follow Edwina to New York, her adopted hometown. They loved the lively and diverse culture of the city and still maintained their apartment alongside Washington Square Park. But they desired a full-time home, away from the crowds and noise.

"Edwina wanted a garden," Alfred said. "And she certainly created a magnificent one here."

"Yes, you did," Lucille said to Edwina. "It is just remarkable — with so many species in a rainbow of color. Genevieve must have swooned when she saw it."

"She did," Edwina nodded, clearly basking in the compliment.

Carter said to Alfred. "It must have been difficult to leave your family in Norway."

"To some degree, yes," Alfred said. "But they didn't accept Edwina, so it was easier to come and live here. I try to return every other year, usually on my own. Fortunately, my family all love to write, so we exchange long letters. They are happy for me, though I suspect also grateful that I live in the States. It's less complicated this way."

Edwina's story was shorter, though sadder; her family disowned her when she returned from her travels abroad. She added that she had returned a new woman, and her parents would have none of it. She did not elaborate on her transformation. "Alfred is my family now," she said simply.

Carter was moved. She knew what it was like to have no family other than the man you loved. At least Carter's parents never rejected her. How painful it must be for Edwina knowing her family wants no part of her, or Alfred either, for that matter.

After the main course of chicken Kiev was cleared and the lemon chiffon cake served, Alfred leaned forward, his face suddenly taking on a more serious expression.

"Carter, Lucille, we wanted to talk to you about Isabelle."

"I didn't realize you knew her," Carter said. "She doesn't work the evening shift when we see you."

"We've met her on your grounds in the afternoon on a number of occasions, often with dear Miss Rose and once with Mrs. Church. Isabelle is an enchanting girl. Let me not mince words. She is with child, and we gather neither she nor her family have an intention of keeping the baby. Edwina and I would like to adopt the child when the time comes."

Lucille and Carter looked at each other "You haven't spoken to her about this, have you?" Carter asked.

"Of course not. She suggested that you were taking responsibility for what happens with the child," Alfred said.

Edwina jumped in. "All Alfred and I have ever wanted was to be parents, but sadly we are unable to have our own. We have so much love to share. A beautiful home. We could give the child a wonderful life, starting with a devoted mother and father. Nothing would be spared in terms of education."

Lucille glanced at Carter, who appeared dumbstruck. So, she asked, "Have you tried to adopt before?"

"We have been disappointed in the past," Alfred said. "That's why this is a perfect opportunity. You know us, maybe not as well as you might, but we can further avail ourselves if you wish. We can also help Isabelle with money...."

Carter finally spoke. "Surely you can appreciate you are a most unusual couple and how that might pose difficulty for a child."

Lucille gave Carter a hard look.

"Unusual," Alfred paused on the word as if tasting it. "We've been called that before – and worse. Yes, we appreciate a child would have to deal with such name calling. Hopefully we would give him or her the kind of love and example how to answer such silliness."

"Silliness? Children get bullied for far less," Carter said. "It's fine and good that you know how to navigate such hostility, but why put that on an innocent child? It's unnecessary and, well, unkind."

"I feared this would be your reaction," Alfred said. "I thought your suffragist experience would help you see past such close-mindedness."

"Close-mindedness — I beg your pardon? What you are asking has little in common with women having the right to vote."

Alfred fisted his hand on the table. "What about our right to be parents?"

Carter blinked, at a loss for words.

Lucille knew it was time to leave. "Let's refrain from getting heated. You've given us a lot to think about. This would be a good time to say goodnight." She stood and Carter followed suit.

The Schnedekers stood as well. Edwina spoke softly. "Very well. We see where you stand this moment. I may not be a traditional mother in many senses of the word, but I would be a far superior mother than most. My child would know a mother's love without fear, judgment or reservation. That's more than I can say for Isabelle's mother who doesn't appear to be there for her daughter in her time of need."

The words hung in the air as the women thanked them for dinner and bid one another goodnight.

JULY 1919

CHAPTER TWENTY-NINE

Ben had not been spending much time at the inn as of late, explaining that he had business in the city. In fact, he offered up his room for the wedding week if needed, though he promised to attend the wedding itself. Carter was relieved. For one, perhaps with him gone, this business with Bailey and the basement would abate somewhat. Furthermore, she worried she had been misleading him in her affections. Yes, they had shared a few kisses, but there was no question Davidson had her heart.

So, when Ben invited her for dinner at The Empire House when he was on the island for a brief visit, she was unnerved. They took his Model T, thanks to the nice weather and low tide. Carter wore a new Genevieve dress – a magenta silk tiered number, her hair fashionably pinned in a style that resembled a bob. Ben wore a fine suit, one she had not seen before, and she noted to herself that he looked especially handsome. His hair was cut, his beard neatly trimmed.

"We want the competition to think we're high-born," he grinned. "Of course, with your beauty and stature, no one would ever doubt that."

Fortunately, Carter and Lucille had visited The Empire House just a few weeks earlier, so Carter knew to dress formally for the establishment. They were seated at an exceptionally private table, lit by a single candle, in the far corner of the main dining room. The waiters wore jackets. Ben ordered for the two of them, having first confirmed Carter's approval of his choices before nodding to the waiter. He also requested a bottle of champagne. He seemed nervous. Which made Carter nervous.

To mask her agitation, Carter chatted on and on—about the upcoming wedding, improvements on the inn, the expanding gardens, the weather. Anything to keep them from falling into silence. Meanwhile the waiter uncorked the bottle and poured their champagne. When he left, Ben lifted his glass. "To us and the success of the Rams Head Inn. We have proven to be a great team."

Carter raised her glass and and clinked it against his. Although she felt she was toasting the wrong man—it was Davidson who ought to be her partner here—she couldn't deny that Ben was right. It was his management of the basement business that infused the needed cash for the inn to survive.

"I can't thank you enough Ben," she said. "You came in just the nick of time."

"It's only the beginning, Carter. Of everything." He reached across the table and took her hand. "We have so much ahead of us. This upcoming wedding will showcase to all the majesty of Rams Head Inn."

"I agree. What a fantastic celebration, in more ways than one. Adam has planned a delicious menu, and Mrs. Crosby from down the road is baking the most remarkable three-layer cake, together with an assortment of pastries. Plus, we have plenty of wine to serve, thanks to you."

"Thanks to *us.*"

As they were eating their appetizers – herring in cream for him, chicken consommé for her – Carter asked Ben something that had been nagging at her. "Ben, when did you buy your house?"

"I came out for the first time in December, and that was that. I fell in love with the place and went straight to the listings in the general store. Davidson inspired the location."

"Yet you weren't at the inn. William said he hadn't met you before."

Ben tore off a piece of bread. "William," he groused. "Figures he would try to seed suspicion. I knew where the inn was, but no, I was not here while it was being built. Tell me, do you trust William?"

"Very much so, why do you ask?"

"I have an uneasy feeling about him."

"Well, I've known him a lot longer than you have — and indeed longer than I've known you," she said too quickly. She softened. "William's a quiet man, so he's easy to misread. Yet please know he's simply being protective."

"That must be it. Two men looking out for you. Men are always suspicious of one another when a beautiful woman is about." He smiled as if to apologize.

Dinner was served, and good as it was, Carter and Ben agreed it didn't have anything over Chef Adam's food. In fact, the heavily seasoned French sauces drowned the meat, which made them hope it wasn't disguising anything.

"I'd hate to be up all night, expelling this expensive meal," Carter groaned. "Ooh, that was unladylike of me, wasn't it?"

"I love that about you, Carter. You're the most direct woman I know. The strongest, too."

"Thank you. I've had to be."

"I'd like to ease that burden."

"You have, trust me."

"No, I mean officially. I'd like to be your husband, the man legally responsible for protecting you. True partners in every sense of the word," he stopped. "Forgive me, that came out all wrong." He suddenly knelt on the floor and reached for something in his pocket before producing a small red leather Cartier box. Opening it, he said, "I have loved you, Carter, from the moment I laid eyes on you. Would you do me the honor of becoming my wife?"

Carter looked at the sparkling ring and hoped her alarm didn't register. "But I am promised to another man, Ben."

Ben laid the box on the table and took his seat. He took a deep breath. "Surely, you know by now that Davidson is not coming back."

"I don't know that," she said quietly.

"I do. So does everyone else familiar with the shipwreck."

Carter didn't respond, so he kept talking. "I can't compete with a ghost. I would be foolish to try. I want you to know my intentions. I am in this for the long term. You are a woman out here alone. I have never felt it was safe, especially with what's going on in the basement. When the ban is enforced, liquor of every variety will be become contraband and open season for criminals. As your husband, I can ensure you are not part of any of that. I can keep you safe."

Ben looked so sincere. She was starting to feel guilty about rejecting him so abruptly the way she had.

"Thank you, Ben. I am genuinely flattered. And you must know that I am attracted to you as well. Were I a free woman, things would be quite different." As the words came out of her mouth, Carter wondered if they were true. "Even if Davidson were not to return, it is simply too soon for me to give my heart over as fully and completely as you deserve." Ben started to interrupt, but she put her hand up. "You *do* keep me safe. You keep us *all* safe. Insofar as the basement business, maybe there is another way to look at it. As a woman, I'm less likely to be suspected of anything untoward. So, in that way, I keep *you* safe."

Ben chewed on that for a moment and then smiled mischievously. "If there is one thing, I am certain about, it's this: you are the ideal woman for me, Carter. I will wait until your heart knows it as well."

Margaret's family arrived to much fanfare at the train station in Sag Harbor, where Graham, Curtis and Margaret greeted them. Curtis shook their hands heartily, his broad smile both respectful and friendly.

"You're as handsome a lad as my daughter said you were," Mrs. O'Reilly said. A stout woman with graying brown hair, she had a twinkle in her eye that belied her drab clothes.

"Mother," Gerty reprimanded. She was a younger version of Margaret.

"But he is, my sweet. Look at that face."

Curtis laughed. "And I can see from where my future wife gets her beauty and direct manner. It's wonderful to finally meet you all."

Mr. O'Reilly, a bear of man, patted Curtis on the back. "Likewise, son. Any man who can handle my Margaret is a pleasure to meet."

"Stop it, Father," Margaret said grinning. "Or Curtis will get the wrong idea."

"Better he knows now what trouble lies ahead," Mr. O'Reilly said with a wink.

The O'Reillys enjoyed the short boat ride to Shelter Island, though they couldn't wait to spend time on solid earth after such a long voyage. Anticipating that they would need to unwind, Curtis and Margaret took them straight to their rental house, which Carter had sent Isabelle and Cora to freshen with clean sheets and equip with groceries. The family's late morning arrival gave them time to settle in and rest up before heading over to Rams Head for a welcome dinner with the Schmidts.

Carter and Lucille agreed to jointly host the dinner. Ben had business in the city, so he wasn't able to join them.

The two girlfriends stood at the fireplace by the front door, greeting the families as they arrived for dinner and directed them to the Garden Room, where champagne-filled flutes on silver trays awaited them. The room was lit with candles, the table lined with crystal vases that held small clusters of roses – Margaret's favorite flower.

When it was time to be seated, Lucille and Carter sat at the ends of a long table, situated in the middle of the room, with the bride and groom's families flanking them on either side. In all they were a party of fifteen people.

To begin the meal, Lucille stood, glass of champagne in hand, and offered a toast. "Carter and I tossed a coin as to who would speak, and well, here I am. First, let me welcome all of you to the start of a joyous week full of love and celebration. When my dear friend founded this beautiful inn, Margaret and I came along for moral support and a bit of adventure. We have been here for over three months and, I must say, they have been among the best months of my life. My guess is Margaret and Curtis would say the same – or they had better!" She took in the room's laughter. "To the Schmidts and to the O'Reillys, we are honored to have you here at the Rams Head Inn, which has become such a special place to so many of us. Let the festivities begin!"

After everyone clinked glasses, Carter laughed and said to the room, "By the way, it was a trick coin, look!" Sure enough, she produced a coin with heads on both sides. "You did well, my sister-friend."

Dinner was a lively affair with lots of laughter and toasting. It was as if the families had known each other forever. They were not dissimilar; Margaret's family were sheep farmers and Curtis's father was a commercial fisherman. Both knew hard work and both were proud of their children and were excited for the first wedding in their families.

The petite and winsome Ellen Schmidt, Curtis's mother told the table she had taken to Margaret right away when they met many weeks earlier. A mother of three sons, she was elated she would soon have another woman in the family. The sentiment was shared by the rugged Shamus O'Reilly, Margaret's dad, who only had girls on his side.

"We were meant to join families, if you ask me," he said, jovially. "Even if we had to travel halfway around the world to meet up!"

At one point, the glass door opened partway, and Mr. Romano dipped his head in, his eyes darting all about the room. He wore that ratty green cap. Carter immediately went and crowded him out of the door and into the barroom.

"What are you doing here?" Carter said in a harsh whisper.

"I'm looking for Ben. We have business."

"Mr. Goodwin is not here tonight. But Officer Schmidt and his brothers are. Would you like to speak with one of them?"

"Given your business below this establishment, I wouldn't go threatening me with the police."

"I'm not threatening anyone. We have a private dinner going on that the Schmidts happen to be attending. I suggest you return after the weekend for whatever business you have with Mr. Goodwin."

He looked at her long and hard. "Fine. Tell Ben to expect me on Monday."

Carter frowned at his familiarity, then returned to the dinner party. Minutes later, William appeared asking to speak to Carter.

"The Perrys are here for dinner," he said.

"Goodness. Mr. Walker didn't alert us," Carter said. "Let me go greet them." She headed toward the dining room.

"Wait, there's an issue."

"An issue? Are there no available tables?"

"The Perrys saw the Schnedekers and refuse to enter the dining room."

"Oh dear," Carter said. By then she was in the foyer, where the Perrys awaited.

"Good evening, Colonel and Mrs. Perry," Carter said. Mrs. Perry did not acknowledge Carter.

"Glad you are here, young lady," the Colonel said. "You're new on the island, I know. Perhaps you are unaware of what is sitting in your dining room. Those, people. They are a disgrace to the island, and to polite society."

"I can seat you in another part of the room from the Schnedekers, if you'd like."

"We don't wish to occupy the same room as them at all. Please have them removed." He said it in a commanding voice, as if issuing her an order.

Carter flinched. Then anger swelled inside her. This was *her* inn—how dare he talk to her that way, despite whatever fleet he had been colonel of. Out of the corner of her eye, she saw Alfred Schnedeker motioning her to their table.

"Excuse me," Carter said to the Perrys.

"Good evening," Alfred said, when Carter reached their table. "I see Colonel Perry is here, no doubt asking for our removal. He has done this before. If you could have a piece of apple pie wrapped up picnic-style for Edwina, we will finish our dinner on the lawn chairs."

"He's done this before?"

"Yes. We are not welcome at The Empire House."

Appalled, Carter said firmly, "Please finish your meal *here* at your leisure. This is *my* dining room. *I* decide who stays."

She turned swiftly and headed over to Colonel Perry. "I'm sorry if you and your wife are uncomfortable in this room. The Schnedekers are our guests, however. You are welcome to dine in our lounge to the left, if you prefer."

The Colonel looked at her for a moment. "We are the kind of people you should have in your main dining room. Surely even a novice innkeeper knows that."

Carter bristled at being called a novice, even if she was one. "As I said, you are welcome to dine in the main room."

"Not with those people ruining our dinner." His impatience was obvious.

"I may be a novice, but I recognize bad manners when I see them. If you don't wish to dine with us at the Rams Head Inn tonight, I bid you a good evening."

The Perrys each harrumphed in their own way – she with a silent side-roll of the eyes, and the Colonel said haughtily, "You won't be seeing us again, nor any of our friends, young lady. What a foolish position to take for a new business."

Carter clasped her hands to steady her shaking as they left the building.

She returned to the Schnedekers. "My apologies. I'm aghast at their behavior," Carter said. "You are always welcome here. Whatever our differing views on adoption, we consider you friends of the house. Others might have stayed away after our last encounter."

Edwina spoke. "We adore you and Lucille. We were not entirely surprised at your reaction to our adoption request. You were being protective. I appreciate your strength, Carter. Too many women confuse femininity with being soft."

Carter was touched. She also had a new admiration for the couple, who were comfortable in who they were, despite the judgement of those around them. They did not put on airs, nor bother to fight with those who did, like the Perrys. "I know this is last minute, but we are hosting a wedding on Sunday – Margaret O'Reilly, who was Lucille's maid, and Curtis Schmidt, a local police officer. I'm sure you've seen them here. I would be honored if you would come as my guests."

Alfred looked at Edwina who nodded. "Thank you. We would love that."

"Fabulous. I need to get back to the dinner in the Garden Room we are hosting for the bride and groom's families." On her way out, she stopped George, the waiter, who was smiling at her. "Please offer everyone in the room a glass of sherry on the house."

Carter couldn't sleep. What have I done, she wondered. How would Davidson have handled it? Ha! I bet with his usual directness. He didn't suffer fools nor snobs. She remembered a time they went to the acclaimed Delmonico's in Manhattan. The maitre d' didn't like Davidson's jacket because it wasn't part of a suit. Davidson said, "a jacket is a jacket, and I'm wearing one." No discussion, no apology, just daring him to disagree. The maitre d' sat them straight away. *I'm learning, my love, I'm learning.*

CHAPTER THIRTY

The following evening, the dining room was as crowded as it had ever been. Not only were Margaret and Curtis's family in attendance, but so were many of the summer people. Carter suspected the wrath of the Perrys had not yet spread across the island. The main room looked especially beautiful with multi-colored floral arrangements bright against the white tablecloths. Wine glasses sparkled in the candlelight, and the well-buffed silverware shone. The staff, including the few recent hires, all wore aprons with the new gold Ram insignia applied by Genevieve. Maybe it was the upcoming wedding or maybe it was just a general feeling of summer having truly arrived, but excitement permeated the air.

Halfway through the dinner hour, Estelle walked in the room and stood by Genevieve at the piano. Estelle looked elegant in a simple white silk sheath. Her hair was styled to partly conceal the cut healing on her face. For a moment, heads turned to her, and there was a collective hush. Estelle nodded to Genevieve, who smiled back and played a few notes before pausing.

With no introduction, Estelle said to the crowd, "I sing for three women. Miss Carter, Mrs. Nesbit, and our dear Miss Rose McFee." And then she began. Her voice was astonishing: sweet and soulful, as if an angel were delivering a message to the room.

Why should I feel discouraged, why should the shadows come, Why should my heart be lonely, and long for heaven and home, When Jesus is my portion? My constant friend is He: His eye is on the sparrow, and I know He watches me; His eye is on the sparrow, and I know He watches me.

One man got up, threw his napkin on the table, and glared at his wife, who quickly gathered up her purse and shawl and followed him, as he stormed out of the room. Another man stood as well, demanding, "*Who authorized this intrusion?*" But then sat, arms folded, looking around the room for support, which he didn't receive. The two men were lone dissenters, as many of the diners were visibly annoyed at the men's disruption. Estelle kept singing.

I sing because I'm happy,
I sing because I'm free,
For His eye is on the sparrow,
And I know He watches me.

"Let not your heart be troubled," His tender word I hear,
And resting on His goodness, I lose my doubts and fears;
Though by the path He leadeth, but one step I may see;
His eye is on the sparrow, and I know He watches me;
His eye is on the sparrow, and I know He watches me.

I sing because I'm happy,
I sing because I'm free,

RAMS HEAD

For His eye is on the sparrow,
And I know He watches me.

Whenever I am tempted, whenever clouds arise,
When songs give place to sighing, when hope within me
dies,
I draw the closer to Him, from care He sets me free;
His eye is on the sparrow, and I know He watches me;
His eye is on the sparrow, and I know He watches me.

The diners, thoroughly mesmerized, broke out in applause when she finished. A gray-haired man called out, "more, more!"

Smiling, Estelle bowed her head and mouthed, "Thank you."

Carter approached Estelle with tears trailing down her face. She placed her hands on her heart and bowed to Estelle. One man tried to get Estelle to join his table for dinner, but she graciously declined and joined Carter, Lucille, and Ben at their table.

Estelle looked to Carter and said, "Miss Genevieve assured me you would not mind an impromptu song."

"That was sensational," Carter said, still wiping her eyes. "And brave."

Lucille asked Estelle, "Where did you learn to sing like that?"

"In church. From the time I was a little girl," Estelle said. "I didn't know how better to thank you. I'm leaving tomorrow. As I told Margaret, while I appreciate the offer, I'm not going to stay for the wedding. It's time for me to return to my life."

Carter's eyes welled up again. "Estelle, no. Please, you've been on your own here for too long. Please stay as my guest. You must be part of the wedding. While you were singing, I realized just how much the wedding will be a celebration of all we've done here. I beg of you, stay."

Estelle cast an eye around the room. People were still looking at her direction and smiling. Gloria O'Reilly silently clapped when Estelle made eye contact, as did her husband, shaking his head enthusiastically. Estelle nodded in return. She looked back at Carter. "Let me think about it."

Henry Nesbit arrived two days later with his assistant Vance Broder. Lucille hadn't counted on Henry bringing Vance but, in retrospect, she should have figured he would; Henry seldom went anywhere without him. Sighing, she waved as Graham brought them to the dock.

Henry's wide smile made her heart skip a beat, as it always did. He looked his usual handsome self — that dark hair, those white teeth, that strong build. He jumped off the boat before it fully docked and ran toward her. He swung her in the air and then held her so tight, she thought she would burst. He kissed her – too long and improperly, given they had an audience.

"My god, I've missed you my gorgeous Squirrel," he said his face just inches away, adoring hers. "Look at your freckles! And your hair, it's so light. Even if you hadn't told me, I would have known you were in the sun."

"You've grown a beard," she said, caressing it.

"Do you like it?"

"I'm not sure. It covers up too much of your handsome face. But I like the way it feels."

"Then I must kiss you again." Which he did, not caring who was nearby.

Vance stood discreetly in the background with their luggage, which Graham had piled onto the dolly. Lucille broke their kiss, turned and extended her hand. "Mr. Broder, such a pleasure to see you. Your European adventures sounded marvelous!" Vance, too, looked just as she remembered — tall, wiry with shiny unruly, but short black hair. He had a friendly, if controlled way about him.

"They were indeed, Mrs. Nesbit."

Just then Margaret came barreling down the hill, Fella in tow. She stopped when she saw Vance Broder, her mouth open.

"Look, Margaret, they've just arrived!" said Lucille, not taking her eyes of her husband, as if she couldn't drink in enough of him.

Quickly regaining her composure, Margaret said, "Hello Mr. Nesbit, Mr. Broder. I came to see if Graham had anything for me." She felt self-conscious, over-explaining, but was embarrassed by her unladylike run down the hill.

Graham saw her and immediately came out with a package. "Yep, here's the one for our little bride-to-be. It's rather big. Wait for one of my boys to take it for you."

"I'll carry it," Vance volunteered.

"How kind, thank you," Margaret said, avoiding his eyes. "I didn't realize you would be joining us Mr. Broder."

Mr. Nesbit laughed as the four started up the hill. "Lately there are few places I go without Mr. Broder, right Vance?" Vance nodded with a slight smile.

"Well, we have all been eagerly awaiting your arrival, Mr. Nesbit," Margaret said.

"As have I," he smiled broadly. "Mrs. Nesbit's letters made me feel part of all the happenings here. I look forward to meeting your Officer Schmidt."

Lucille was grateful for Henry's warmth. She feared he would be his more patrician self. He was accustomed to being lord of the manor at home.

Graham's boys returned from wheeling the luggage trolley to the inn's front desk. Vance discreetly tipped them.

"Graham, we look forward to seeing you and your family on Saturday," Lucille said. "And I understand you will have your dog with you."

"Yep, wife won't go anywhere without Petal," Graham said as he petted Fella on the head. "We all have a soft spot for these creatures."

"Fella will no doubt attend the wedding," Lucille mused. "Come on, boy, better keep up." Margaret had already headed up the hill with Vance carrying her package.

Lucille linked her arm in Henry's, hopeful all would be well. The beard, she silently plotted, would have to go.

Vance Broder was as handsome as ever, and Margaret found herself lost for conversation. That long front curl of dark hair still fell on his forehead when he spoke, and she remembered all times she'd brushed it back when they were alone, her fingers lingering on his face. She was glad they were walking side by side without a chance of looking at him head on. His pale grey eyes had a way of piercing right through her. As it was, she could hardly breathe.

"You're getting married this weekend," he stated.

"Yes, I am. To Curtis Schmidt. He's a policeman."

"I look forward to meeting the man who stole you from me."

"You can't steal what isn't yours, Vance."

"Surely we were more than a passing fancy," he answered. "At least it felt that way to me."

What a mean thing to say Margaret thought, as if she would have given her virginity on a mere whim. She refused to engage him. "Well, at least you no longer have to worried about being fired."

"Margaret, we could have worked that out with time. After this trip, I feel far more comfortable with Mr. Nesbit. I'm sure you feel so with Mrs. Nesbit."

They had reached the inn. "Here we are," Margaret said. "You can put the box down by the fireplace. Thank you." Vance did as she asked, and Margaret excused herself to go see about their rooms—they'd have to find an accommodation for Vance, as he wasn't expected as part of the party.

Henry could not stop touching Lucille as they entered the inn, giving her those intense looks she loved so much. She knew they would make love at the first opportunity. She counted on it.

Vance awaited them at the front desk. "Margaret went to find a man named William to search a room for me to stay in."

"Oh yes," Lucille said. "I apologize. I wasn't certain you were coming. Which way did Margaret go?" He pointed toward the kitchen. "Okay, I'll try the Garden Room." She sent Henry and Vance to the bar while she looked for William.

The best she, William and Margaret could do to accommodate Vance was essentially a closet on the third floor, with the idea that he would check into one of the reserved rooms at The Empire House the next morning. Vance was quite gracious about the closet, but it barely fit his trunk and he would have to share a hall bathroom. Lucille asked Margaret if Vance could put his trunk in her room, to which she said yes. Lucille left the two and went to join Henry.

There Henry stood at the bar, amicably chatting with the bartender who had served him a refreshment. She could see Henry's strong jaw was laughing at something Mr.

313

Manuel had said. Lucille loved Henry's easy manner with others, but she was anxious to be alone with him.

"Henry?"

"Ah, there she is." He faced beamed with joy when he turned to her.

When they finally reached her room and closed the door behind them, he kissed her soundly with a promise of what was to come. It was only when he came up for air, the warmth cooled a bit as he looked around.

"This is our room?"

"Yes, my home away from home," Lucille said with pride. "Look at that view."

But she could tell from his face that he was not impressed. It wasn't a large room, and certainly somewhat cramped for two people. He didn't seem to appreciate the sumptuous drapes, the line of her favorite books on each windowsill, the two plush chairs with the table between them, nor the painting of Benny, her childhood horse, which hung at the head of the four-poster mahogany bed. He opened the room's one and only small closet.

"I'm not understanding how you lived in such a small accommodation," he said. "Where are your clothes? Where will mine go?" His trunk was wedged between the bed and the dresser.

"Yes, it's a bit rough compared to the Ritz in Paris," Lucille said, "But it's meant to be quaint and human scaled. Such is the architecture of these old houses on the coast. I have no doubt you will adjust as I have. I suppose I should tell you now that we share a bathroom with Carter."

"We do?" His eyes bulged.

"Yes, this is what is referred to as a Jack and Jill room – two separate but adjoining rooms with a shared bath. Carter and I were fine to share."

"Perhaps, but now your Jack has arrived."

"Yes, he has," she snaked her arms around his waist. "And he's a gracious Jack who appreciates that a seventeen-room inn can't spare two rooms for a married couple on a weekend when it is hosting a wedding. As it is, Carter and I had to reserve rooms at another hotel."

"Fine, let's stay at the other hotel." He kissed her neck.

"Henry!" She stepped back. "You are being a snob, and I will not have it."

"Snob? I just want us to be comfortable. Surely you can't think this room is adequate now that I'm here."

"I love this room. What would it say to others if I left? That the Rams Head is not good enough for us?"

"I have no problem explaining to anyone who is interested."

"Do not think to embarrass me among my friends."

"Embarrass you?"

"Yes, when you talk about a room not being good enough for us, the grand Nesbits, you embarrass me. Surely you can see how settled and content I am here."

"Yes, but I am not."

"You just arrived!"

Henry was flummoxed. "Where is my soft, accommodating wife, Lucille, the one I have longed for these many months?" There was a challenge in his voice.

"Standing right in front of you, Henry," Lucille said, hands on her hips. "I thought our reunion would be more celebratory than this."

"As did I." She let out a long breath and looked out the window to the water, a sight she always found soothing.

She turned and looked at Henry. "You've pointed out what's wrong with the room but let me point out what's right: I'm in it." With that, she began to unbutton the top of her dress. "Unless you'd rather look elsewhere."

Henry's chest visibly expanded as she worked her way down her way down the bodice. He grabbed with with delicious force. "You've always had a way of making me see to reason, my little vixen."

Carter was having lunch with Ben, when Lucille appeared, looking quite well, albeit a little flushed, and took one of the two remaining seats at the table.

"I was just asking Ben about Romano's visit to us a few nights ago," Carter explained to Lucille.

"And I told her not to worry," Ben said. "I'll take care of him when he shows up next."

"I don't like him, and I don't like how he keeps turning up out of the blue. What does he want, anyway?"

"Like I said, I'll handle it," Ben said. Lucille noticed that Ben didn't answer Carter's question, but they would have to ply him for more details later. Henry would be joining them at any moment. He wanted to change into casual clothes before he came down.

"When Henry joins us, which he is expected to do at any moment, can we please table all this basement talk? He's already been thrown by not not having his own closet and sharing a bath. The downstairs business will surely put him over the edge."

"I hope you found some way to calm his nerves," Carter said, cracking a knowing smile.

"That's enough out of you," Lucille scolded with a mischievous wink.

With that, Carter laughed out loud. "Poor Henry. Ben, we indeed will pick up this discussion later. But for now, please handle that dreadful Romano. He has little on us. I would rather sit with the chief of police and tell him about our side business and risk losing it all, than be blackmailed by a petty scoundrel."

"I agree with that," Lucille said.

"What do you agree with, my beautiful one?" Henry placed his hands on Lucille's shoulders as he appeared at the table. Ben stood, while Carter threw her arms around Henry in greeting,

"Henry!" she exclaimed. "Finally, you're here. I can't tell you how much Lucille has missed you. We all have missed you. Please have a seat."

"Warm congratulations to you Carter. This place is impressive, such an accomplishment." He looked to Ben, extending a hand. "Henry Nesbit."

"Benjamin Goodwin." The men shook hands.

"My wife speaks highly of you—Ben, if I may. Your presence here has been a great comfort."

During the course of their chicken pot-pie lunch, Carter and Lucille updated the men on the family dinner they had missed and the many plans ahead for the weekend. Ben graciously offered Henry his room, but Carter interrupted and said it was already spoken for after tomorrow night.

"Many guests are not local," she offered by way of explanation.

"Of course," Henry said. "I've been without my wife for over three months, so close quarters are most welcome." He took her hand under the table and squeezed it.

She smiled at him. "Henry, would you like to join me for a walk to survey the grounds? The gardens are bursting right now. I'd also love to show you the path to the sandbar, which isn't far from here."

"I would enjoy that, my love," he kissed her sweetly.

Lucille was grateful Henry was proving amenable to the Rams Head way of life – at least to what he knew of it so far.

CHAPTER THIRTY-ONE

Curtis was not keen on Vance, as he was instructed to call him. He told Margaret he found the young businessman to be full of himself and condescending, deliberately speaking of matters Curtis knew little to nothing about, like international trade, shipping regulations, and taxation. Curtis liked him even less when Vance mentioned he and Margaret had been close friends in the Nesbit household. To make matters worse, Fella wouldn't leave his side.

"Please be understanding, Curtis," Margaret implored, when he grumbled all this to her, as they took Fella for a walk later that night. "I'm the only one he knows here."

No one regretted Vance's presence more than Margaret. Earlier, when Mrs. Nesbit left Margaret and Vance together, he was flirtatious and seemed to enjoy her discomfort at being asked to keep his trunk in her room. She tried not to notice his sensuous lips or recall how many times those lips kissed her and where. At one point, however, he asked her if she was marrying as a way to get back at him or over him. The nerve. In truth, she had asked herself that very question but had concluded it wasn't the reason. She loved Curtis. He respected her. She would not give him reason to be jealous. Margaret had told Curtis she had lost her virginity in Ireland, a white lie, but it was something he had taken fairly in stride. Knowing it had been Vance would be an entirely different matter.

Curtis now smiled at her mischievously. "The Connecticut Ladies return tomorrow – maybe you can introduce Vance to one of them. Or maybe he can make an honest woman of Isabelle."

"That's mean."

"Which suggestion?"

"Last I heard, I'm marrying *you* in short order. My family is here. Jealousy has no place in our relationship, especially at this point."

"I don't like Vance, and I don't want you being so friendly to him."

"Curtis, you're trying to provoke me, and you are succeeding. Fella will escort me back to the inn. Good night."

"Do not turn your back on me Margaret Mary." He learned her full name from her mother the night before.

"Back turned. Good night."

He grabbed her and kissed her hard and long on the back of the neck until she melted and moaned. She turned to kiss his lips.

Foreheads touching, he whispered. "I will kiss you like that in front of Vance and the world if you do not behave. Do not try me."

She pushed him away, her eyes wide. "You even bully me with your kisses."

"Oh, for God's sake, Margaret." He threw his hands in the air. "Do we have to argue these few nights before our wedding too?"

"I am worried, Curtis. I will not be the complacent wife you imagined."

"Don't I know it," he said with resignation. "You invited a negro to our wedding, despite me repeatedly saying it won't go over well with the boys. My parents aren't exactly comfortable with it either."

"You want to open that up again?" Margaret said, angrily. "*Both* our families heard Estelle sing and saw what a special woman she is. It is an honor to have her bless our wedding."

"So you keep telling me," Curtis said.

Margaret grabbed both his hands. "We don't have to get married. There is still time. I can put away my dress and my parents can have an enjoyable stay in America without a wedding." She echoed Genevieve's words, telling herself it had nothing to do with seeing Vance again.

Curtis's eyes narrowed in disbelief. "We are getting married. You are my woman, and I am your man. We love each other."

"Then you need to listen to me, to consider my feelings. My friends. You don't like Estelle, you don't like Vance, don't like dogs, you don't like—"

"I like *you*," he hugged her tenderly.

"Then be open to the things and people that I like. We need to fit into each other's worlds."

"You are my world," he whispered as he caressed her face. "Let's call a truce and chalk this up to wedding nerves."

Still uneasy, Margaret looked into his eyes and nodded in agreement.

Genevieve had been so busy at her shop with dresses for the wedding, she forgot it was Stuart's usual night and had not secured him a table. Unfortunately, every table was taken, so she asked Carter if he may join her group this evening while she played the piano. Carter readily agreed, and when Stuart arrived, she waved him over to her table. "Mr Bennett! You'll be dining with my group tonight, if that suits you."

"Why, of course it does, Carter. I am a lucky man for such company."

Just then, Henry and Lucille entered the dining room.

"Mr. Bennett?" Henry exclaimed. In all their reconnecting, Lucille hadn't thought to share anything about Stuart and Genevieve. She and Henry had made love again after their afternoon walk, hence their late arrival. She had also shaved his beard, which was easy to do since she offered to do it naked, which led to more lovemaking. Now, she sent Carter a desperate plea for help with her eyes, but there was nothing to be done at this point.

"Mr. Nesbit, good to see you. But please, let's use first names." Stuart stood, and the two men shook hands. "Welcome home. Your charming wife told me you would be here for the wedding. So glad you made it. I trust your travels were productive." Stuart seemed nonplussed by Henry's arrival, most likely assuming Lucille had filled him in.

"Yes, all that and more. I take it you have been well?" Henry responded. The two men sat down, Henry nodding to Carter and Ben in the process.

"Very well indeed," Stuart said. "This beautiful inn and its lovely ladies have made my summer most memorable. This has become my home away from home when my ships leave or come in."

"Indeed. And how is Mrs. Bennett?"

"Well. Thank you for asking." Fortunately, he didn't have time to elaborate, as the Schnedekers approached their table. Henry, Ben and Stuart all stood.

"Please sit down," Alfred said to the men. "We had an early dinner but wished to say hello before we left."

Carter extended her hand. "Hello. This is Mr. and Mrs. Schnedeker. Mr. Goodwin, you know. Perhaps you've seen Mr. Bennett here."

"Yes, you are the gentleman friend of the talented pianist. Delighted to meet you," Edwina said. Lucille knew better than to look at Henry.

"And this is my husband, Henry Nesbit," Lucille said. "He arrived in time for the wedding."

"How fortuitous," Alfred said. "Let's plan a lunch at our house so we may take Mr. Nesbit around and show him the island. Lucille mentioned you might be interested in real estate here." Henry looked like he was struggling not to stare at Edwina.

"Yes, we are. How gracious of you to invite us, thank you. Will you be at the wedding?"

"We wouldn't miss it for the world," Edwina clasped her hands. "A wedding on Shelter Island is a grand event—especially this early in the season." To Stuart, she added. "Your Miss Genevieve is making me a stunning dress for the occasion. We had our fitting today."

"I hope to have a sneak peek."

"Will you be here on Sunday?"

"I am trying to arrange it," Stuart said in the most affable tone.

After the Schnedekers left, Stuart leaned forward, "Now that is a most interesting couple."

"A quite wonderful one, I assure you," Carter smiled, realizing how protective she felt of them. "Lucille and I had a splendid dinner at their house on Friday."

"You did?" Ben and Henry spoke in unison.

"We did," Lucille said with an edge to her voice. Turning to Henry, "How kind of them to invite us to lunch."

"I look forward to it," Henry said with his ever-polite smile.

Genevieve appeared and gently caressed Stuart's face as way of a greeting. She looked at the one person she did not recognize. "You must be Mr. Nesbit, I feel like I know you, because for many years I have dressed your beautiful wife."

Henry looked confused. "She wears mostly Blanc Couture."

"My husband's name, yes, but the designs were mine," Genevieve said. "That is a long story. Why spoil such this lovely evening by telling it?"

"Indeed," Lucille said, her smile now as fragile as her spirit, feeling the simmering tension from Henry beside her. She reached for her wine and took a long sip, wondering what it would take, to get her through this evening.

The next morning, Lucille peeked into the Garden Room to find Henry and Vance at a corner table at work with various folders, ledgers and endless lists of goodness knew what. Henry did not see her, or if he did, he did not look up. It was just as well, Lucille thought. After last night, she feared the greeting would be far from pleasant.

Carter was seated in the main dining room, also busy with papers. Lucille presumed they belonged to the wedding, or perhaps supplier invoices. Yet still she looked up at her friend with a warm smile.

"Good morning, sister-friend."

"Good morning to you. Let me get the embarrassing part over with. I'm sure you could not help but hear Henry and me quarreling. I apologize."

"I did not, honestly. Maybe some murmuring, but not actual words."

"Oh Carter," Lucille sat down. "I knew he'd be upset with me, but I had no idea how much."

"Upset with you? Why?"

"Well, I haven't been as forthright about certain things as I should have been. He was upset to find out about Stuart and Genevieve, and that I knew about them. He still has no idea Stuart's wife Rebecca is expecting. And then Genevieve so blithely mentioning her husband, almost as an afterthought."

"All of this has nothing to do with you," Carter pointed out.

"But it does in Henry's book. You are judged by the company you keep."

"He must think I'm a doozy."

"Not at all. But he thinks the Schnedekers are doozies. Don't worry, I defended them to high heaven, but Henry forbade me to remain friends with them. As if I would obey such a command."

"In the past you may have."

"I've never tested Henry before, and last night I refused to back down, which infuriated him all the more. To listen to him, you would believe I will single-handedly bring down Nesbit Industries with my wayward friends."

It was then Carter that saw Lucille's tear-stained face and knew better than to make a joke. "Did you tell him about the Connecticut Ladies or the downstairs business?"

"No. Those were confidences I promised to keep— to you and to Elizabeth. May he never learn about them from someone else, because that would surely be the end of us." She looked up to the sky as if in prayer.

CHAPTER THIRTY-TWO

Gloria O'Reilly, Margaret's mother, was worried she had nothing suitable to wear to the wedding. She had packed two church dresses, but they were ruined during the voyage overseas by some apples she had stashed in her trunk. Genevieve did not have the time nor help to take on another dress. Mary O'Reilly was a short, stout woman, so borrowing a formal dress was proving difficult. Carter had an idea— to take one of her belted and pleated silk dresses, drop the belt and cut a foot and a half off the hemline. Problem solved.

A huge crate of glassware and dishes fell off the dolly as Graham's boys were bringing it up from the dock, breaking all of its contents. Mr. Manuel saved the day, as he had a friend who managed the American Hotel in Sag Harbor and was able to donate a few dozen sets of surplus glass and tableware. Of course, each piece was inscribed with The American Hotel. "Free advertising for free tableware," Carter joked, just relieved the items appeared in time for the wedding.

Perhaps the biggest godsend was both families were of the same religious denomination. Everyone would attend an early morning service at Shelter Island's only Catholic Church, Our Lady of the Isle in Shelter Island Heights, which was a good distance from Ram Island. They and the priest would then return together to Rams Head and the wedding ceremony would commence at noon, late enough to give off-island guests time to arrive and early enough to give them time to return while there was still evening light. Fortunately, it stayed light until nearly nine o'clock this time of year. Graham had made arrangements with a couple of local captains to bring people either to Sag Harbor on the South Fork or Greenport on the North Fork, depending on which direction they were traveling.

"I feel like a baseball batter," Carter joked at breakfast, "just batting these problems away one by one."

"I well know that feeling, don't you, Henry?" Ben said.

"In more ways than one, yes."

He and Lucille were barely speaking. Fortunately, the coolness wasn't obvious, as there was a melee of activities and people around the wedding. The wedding was two days away, and Margaret preferred to stay at the inn though she spent her days with her family; Vance was about to leave for his hotel, so both were at the breakfast table with the group. Lucille wondered if Henry found it inappropriate that they were dining with her former maid and his assistant; what was once "proper" now seemed stupidly snobby to Lucille.

The three Connecticut Ladies arrived at that moment. They were expected to stay through the weekend. Checking in at the front desk, they waved to Carter and Lucille. Vance sat up, clearly interested in the group of beautiful young women.

"Who are those women?" Henry asked.

"They are war widows," Carter said. "Their husbands were all in the same ill-fated unit in France toward the end of the war."

"How tragic," Henry said.

"Yes, indeed," Lucille agreed. "Their sadness is compounded by a more recent death— another war widow who often traveled here with them. I am grateful they have returned, given such memories."

"How did she die?"

"She took her own life."

"My goodness. Is there anything we can do?" Henry asked.

"Focus on this weekend. Those three women are lovely and supportive of one another. You are certain to meet them over the next few days."

"I look forward to it, and I'm sure Mr. Broder here does as well," Henry said. "In fact, Vance, you and I had a very productive morning. I would love to spend more time with my wife, and I am certain you could use an afternoon at leisure once you've checked into your hotel."

"That would be grand, sir. Thank you. Margaret, may I ask you to show the way to my hotel?"

"I apologize, but I cannot. I promised my family I would take them to Diering Harbor."

"Perhaps then you can speak to the driver I have summoned?"

"The Empire House is known by all on Shelter Island.

I'm certain he will know the way. But yes, I will walk you out to make sure he does."

After they left, Lucille said, "I believe Vance fancied Margaret at one time. I hope he has gotten over that."

Henry scoffed. "He is a college man, as is his father. Vance was never going to marry a maid."

In the past, Lucille might have concurred. Instead, she answered, "I'm glad I wasn't a maid then."

He gave her an admonishing look.

She returned it.

Carter and Ben spoke quietly between themselves.

Henry was right: Vance wanted to know more about the Connecticut Ladies. Specifically, Mae had caught his eye as he and Margaret were leaving the inn. The women had given Margaret a warm hug. She introduced them to Vance, one by one, and it was Helen who was most curious, asking almost too many questions about his occupation and why he was at Rams Head and would he be attending the wedding. He explained his connection to the Nesbits, while the other women strained their necks to get a peek at Henry, whose back was turned to them.

"Come, Vance," Margaret urged. "I have little time."

"An honor to meet all of you," he said, though his eyes were trained on Mae. "I look forward to seeing more of you this weekend."

"You seem to know them well," Vance said to Margaret outside the inn.

"Yes, they come once a week for a couple or few days."

"Isn't that curious."

"I don't ask questions. They have children, babies. I believe they live in Connecticut."

"Mae as well?"

"All of them, yes."

"They are young."

"Most war widows are."

"Since you've moved on from me with your police officer, perhaps I should seek Mae out at your wedding for a dance."

Margaret felt he was goading her. "I believe she has a gentleman friend. But do what you'd like. I am marrying Curtis in two days' time."

"So you are," Vance's mouth was a grim line. "He's not the man I would have chosen for you. Not that I would have chosen anyone but myself, of course."

Margaret paused, unsure of what to say. She didn't know if he was serious or mocking her. Fortunately, Vance's hired car appeared.

"Someone has an admirer!" Helen teased Mae after Vance and Margaret left the inn. "Maybe he can replace James's dreary friend."

"He's not dreary," Mae said.

Elizabeth gave both a look to silence them. Fortunately, no one was around to overhear. The women knew better than to refer to their trysts to anyone but themselves.

Despite Helen's teasing, Mae was especially cheerful. Gerald was her one and only *date* and he was single at that. He had a terrible stutter, yet with Mae he somehow spoke fluidly, something Mae took as a sign of his comfort and affection with her.

After breakfast, on their way out for a morning walk, Henry and Lucille too ran into the Connecticut ladies who, having deposited their valises into their rooms, were heading to the veranda to have tea. Lucille made the introductions. Henry was his usual affable self, making small talk about the upcoming wedding. Lucille tugged on his arm, hinting the women wanted to get on with their day, as should they.

"I wanted to offer my condolences about their friend, but thought the first hello should simply be cordial," Henry said as he and Lucille trailed a path in the woods as walked down toward the water. "How nice they come to this little island, of all places, to mourn their losses together. I bet it does them well. They seem lovely."

"They *are* lovely," Lucille said.

"Why do you have an edge to your voice?"

"Because I worry you will judge them. Henry, they come here to date."

"Date?"

"Yes, date men."

"Why would I judge that?" Henry slowed his pace. "Ah, you mean more than that."

"Whatever they do or do not do, they are extremely discreet. They need the money to support their children."

Henry was eerily silent for a spell. She could hear the birds in the trees above. "Are you telling me that Rams Head Inn, the place where you've been residing for over three months, is a brothel?"

"No! It is *not* a brothel. Far from it. They are just a few guests who have a particular routine here. And with very gentlemanly men. Well, usually."

"Lucille, I will shock you. I do not care about those women. Fine, everyone makes choices. Desperate ones in some cases. But I do care about you, my wife, and our reputation."

"All are intact, exactly how you left them, I assure you."

"It does not appear so. You have become quite bold with your menagerie of interesting friends and in your defense of them."

"If you mean I no longer see the world simply, you are correct." She exhaled and softened her tone, resting her hand on his arm. "Henry, our lives are extremely sheltered. We cannot possibly Imagine, much less judge what others have gone through – or are going through. We have money. We have status. We have choices. And most importantly, we have each other. I know this is much for you to take in all at once, but I am asking that you try. Early on, I had a terrible row with Carter and left for a few days to rethink my life here. I even wrote you about my confusion, if you remember."

"You wrote about a teenager who is with child."

"Yes, that was one of my examples. The Connecticut Ladies are another. They feel safe here because it is *not* a brothel. Their gentlemen are discreet. Look at Stuart Bennett and Genevieve. As Carter once said to me, judge the men, if you will, not the women."

"This change in you, it's Carter, isn't it?"

"There is no change in me. I just feel more open, that is all."

Henry exhaled and looked into her eyes. "I love you with all my heart, Squirrel. I always have and always will. I agree we are sheltered, you even more than me, given my travels. This world, the one we live in, is a sheltered and judgmental one, and we can't pretend it's not."

"I understand." She caressed his handsome face, the face she knew and loved for so many years. "If we remain open to one another, we will be all right. I believe in goodness, Henry. I know you do too. I would never do anything to embarrass you. Your mother maybe...." She smiled, and so did he.

"My mother embarrasses easily, I agree." He kissed her. "Very well, no more surprises then." He started to continue their walk.

"I've made friends with a colored woman," she blurted. "Estelle Church. A fellow suffragist. She came here in search of her great aunt, who Estelle thought worked on a nearby plantation, but we couldn't find her. Like me, she loves to read books. Like us, Estelle is from near Chicago. Lake Forest in her case..." The sentences were just that, random sentences, as if she wanted to get it all out on the table at once.

Henry stopped and stared at her, his hands on his belt, a movement which bunched up his jacket. "Why haven't I met this *friend?*"

"You will. She will be at the wedding. That's the only reason she has stayed on." Not knowing how to read Henry's placid expression, she leaned forward and touched his chest. "I hadn't mentioned her before because I didn't know what you would think, and she is the most wonderful of women."

"She wasn't at dinner."

"No, she does not feel comfortable mingling with the other guests. She takes most meals in her room. Estelle's husband passed from the Spanish Flu a month or so ago, so she has been in mourning."

Henry turned his back to Lucille and took a step, his hand pushed up against a tree trunk, as if he were trying to steady himself.

"I know you're not a prejudiced man, Henry," she said brightly to his back. "You have many colored men who work in your foundry. I've seen them."

He pivoted to face her. "You are not that naïve, my love. It's hardly the same thing. They have separate toilets and eating areas and separate *friendships*."

"I understand, more than you think I do. My friendship with Estelle just happened. She will be returning to Chicago right after the wedding."

"Chicago. Where our parents live."

"I promise not to bring her to their dinners." She knew better than to giggle, though she was sorely tempted at the thought of bringing Estelle to either household.

He looked at her for a moment longer before saying in his calmest voice, "Anything else you wish to tell me?"

Lucille thought of the basement business, but quickly pushed it out of her mind. It wasn't illegal—yet—and it had nothing to do with her. Besides, she and Henry would be going back to Manhattan soon to resume their lives.

"No more surprises, Henry, I promise." She then looked at him flirtatiously. "Except maybe in the bedroom…," she looked around, "or in the woods, as the case may be."

"I know what you're trying to do, Lucille, and it won't work. Not this time."

With that, Lucille wrapped her arms around Henry, kissing his neck with her tongue.

"Well," he admitted. "Maybe it will."

CHAPTER THIRTY-THREE

After breakfast, Carter was in the kitchen reviewing the next few days' menus with Chef Adam, when Miriam peeked in to tell Carter she had a visitor in the Garden Room. To her dismay, it was Mrs. Worthington, looking, as always, impatient and annoyed. Carter wanted to scream, as this was the last thing she needed right now.

Mrs. Worthington cut to the chase. "You wrote asking to see me. I worried something was wrong with Charlotte."

"I wrote that there was no rush, and that Charlotte was fine."

"Yes, but I feared you were not being forthright with me. In any event, I just saw Charlotte, and she is indeed fine. She has no idea why you asked for me."

"No, she wouldn't. After your last visit when you requested I to see to the baby's future, I made some inquiries. Apparently, there is a legal paper that would be most helpful if you were to sign as it releases any future claim you might have on the child."

"I would never sign any such document."

Carter was startled. "Have you changed your mind?"

"Not in the least. But if I were to sign such an agreement, our identity would be revealed. We don't want this baby to find us. Or anyone else for that matter."

"But the paper would be sealed. No one would have access to it."

"Everything is found out eventually."

"But we need to find the baby a home. And such paperwork would be necessary for any proper adoption."

"Drop it off somewhere. Anonymously. It must happen all the time."

Carter was stunned but kept her emotion in check. "What if you – or more importantly, Charlotte - change your minds?"

"If we don't know where the baby ends up, all the better. We won't have the ability to change our minds, will we?" Mrs. Worthington gave her an exasperated look, as if she were speaking to a dim child. "Listen, we want nothing to do with this baby. I don't want to know where it lives or who raises it. I want my daughter back, like this never happened."

"But it did happen."

"No, it didn't. Not to us. If you have an issue with that, I can take Charlotte and her baby to people who would not."

Carter managed a smile. "Actually, I am in complete agreement with you. I just wanted to make sure we understood one another. This is not a time for misinterpretation, wouldn't you agree?"

Mrs. Worthington exhaled, her ramrod posture softened with relief. "Yes, I agree. We are crystal clear. Thank you. I'm sure you can appreciate the stress this has put on me, having to lie to our family and friends. We are all anxious to have Charlotte return from her *travels abroad.*" She emphasized the last two words.

"One last request," Carter said. "Would you have this discussion with Charlotte, so she fully appreciates how final this is?"

"I have. She's clear. I have promised her an actual trip abroad when this business is concluded. She is delighted at the prospect." Mrs. Worthington stood. "But to your point Miss Carter, Charlotte must never know where this baby ends up. I want this over and done with forever."

After Mrs. Worthington left, Carter remained in the Garden Room. Would life with the Schnedeckers be so bad? Growing up in that beautiful house, with two loving parents? It would be far from awful, but why impose their eccentricities on child? Then again, Mrs. Worthington was a terror of a mother. Anyone would make a better one.

The Schnedeckers have the confidence to be different, something that Carter admired. She had long worried about having the "right kind" of people come to Rams Head. People like who? Mrs. Worthington and the Perrys? She was hard pressed to find anything right about them. Isabelle asked only that Carter find "kind" people to raise her child. The Schnedeckers were nothing if not kind. Still. Carter held her head — how was she in this position?

That night, Henry insisted on taking Lucille to The Empire House for dinner. He heard from Vance it was a special restaurant, and Henry told Lucille he wanted her all to himself. Lucille wore one of Henry's favorite dresses— a navy silk ruched style that draped across the bodice.

They arrived at the stately hotel and Lucille found herself immersed in front of the gift cabinet, full of trinkets and other souvenirs. She heard a fellow diner approached Henry.

"My goodness, is that really you dear chap?"

"Randall!" Henry answered. "How extraordinary running into you on Shelter Island of all places." Lucille looked over her shoulder to see that the two men had grabbed one another's elbows affectionately, though she could only see the back of the stranger.

"Not so extraordinary on my end," the man who was not Henry said. "I own property and a summer cottage here."

"What a coincidence. My wife and I are looking to do the same. May I introduce you to Lucille?"

Lucille stopped looking in the cabinet and walked over to Henry. The portly man looked familiar, but she couldn't place him.

"Lucille, this is Colonel Randall Perry, whom I've told you about. He has been building railroads all over the East Coast. Randall, this is my Lucille." Henry beamed with pride, the way he always did when introducing her to someone.

Perry? *Perry!* Lucille realized with horror – the same man who tried to evict the Schnedekers from the Rams Head dining room. Carter had been distraught in the retelling of the episode, feeling she had sealed the inn's fate by standing up to this ogre.

"A pleasure to meet you, Lucille. I am dining in the barroom with a gentleman friend as my wife Violet is not feeling well this evening."

Lucille smiled politely, if briefly. "I'm sorry to hear that."

"I'm sure the two of you will get along famously," he said. "Perhaps we can arrange a dinner for you here and introduce you two around."

"We'd be honored, thank you," Henry said.

"Yes, thank you." Lucille mustered a smile and a nod.

Henry took no notice of Lucille's discomfort. "Lucille has been staying at the Rams Head Inn, a new venture her friend Miss Carter has bravely taken on. I have just joined my wife following my European business travels."

"Yes, I've been to that establishment." Colonel Perry's face and voice soured as he continued speaking directly to Henry. "This is the place you want to be. Rams Head attracts a rather questionable clientele." To Lucille he said, "sometimes you must turn away business in order to build the right *kind* of business. Your friend should heed that advice."

"I'll pass it on, thank you," Lucille said with a tight smile. She tugged on Henry's arm, who bade Colonel Perry a good evening after the two men made plans to meet in the city.

"Do you want to explain yourself?" Henry said when they were seated.

"That man is a pompous fool and asked to have the Schnedekers removed from the Rams Head dining room in order not to 'ruin' his and his wife's meal."

"The Schnedekers *are* a rather odd couple, you must admit."

"I would take a dozen Schnedekers any day over insufferable snobs like the Perrys."

Henry looked at Lucille exasperated. "Randall is an important client. I can't tell you how many tons of steel his firm has purchased from us. I fully expect we'll be spending an evening or more with he and his wife Violet at some point."

"Ahh. So, he's a powerful, pompous fool."

"Lucille," Henry said, the warning in his voice. "Let's enjoy our dinner without disagreement. Try to act like you missed me."

Her shoulders dropped. "I did, horribly so. Never question that," she said, reaching for his hand. There was so much to question, but her love for him wasn't one. She hoped he felt the same way, whatever challenges lay ahead.

CHAPTER THIRTY-FOUR

Genevieve hosted a women's lunch the day before the wedding. Isabelle and Cora, who were also guests, helped set up the long table on the veranda. Once again, Carter and Lucille sat at either end, "like parents," Carter joked. Margaret was placed in the middle, the water view before her, with her sister Gerty and mother on either side, and Genevieve and Ellen Schmidt opposite her. Then there were the Connecticut Ladies, Cora's mother Miriam Smythe and sister Dorothy, and Graham's wife Elaine, who had just arrived. There was also Edwina, whom Carter invited at the last minute, but purposely sat away from Isabelle, who was seated with Estelle, next to Carter at the far end. Originally, Estelle had declined to join them, but Carter insisted, assuring Estelle she'd be seated next to herself and Isabelle.

Carter had Mr. Manuel create a special pink cocktail for the ladies that was a combination of cranberry juice, vodka, and orange juice, with a dash lime. "A party in a glass!" Lucille proclaimed as it was set before her.

"Served in the fancy 'Lucille Glass,'" Carter said, affectionately referring to Lucille's donation of the cut crystal coupe stemware.

"In the middle of the day?" Gloria said, her brogue tinged with disapproval.

"Oh, let's drink and be merry, Mother," Margaret said. "It's not like we do this every day."

"Hear, hear," Cora said.

"Shush," Miriam admonished. "You're a teenager and lucky to have even that small taste in front of you."

Genevieve rose from her chair, holding her drink. "My toast is simple. I believe in women. I believe in love. I believe we all find our soulmates. I am happy that Margaret has found hers. Here's to Margaret!"

Clinks could be heard throughout the veranda. Lucille thought about Rose, who was now with Herbert, her soulmate. She thought about Henry and all their lovemaking since their truce last night. She felt flush from the memories.

"Dreams can come true, can't they?" The baritone voice that interrupted her reverie could only be Edwina, who was seated next to her.

"Yes, they do, Edwina," Lucille smiled. "I hope every woman at this table has a fairytale ending like yours and mine."

"Looks like I may get one," Mae whispered. She was seated next to Lucille and across from Edwina.

"Do tell, my dear," Edwina said conspiratorially.

"Mr. Rogers—Gerald— the gentleman I have been meeting here," she said by way of explanation. "I suspect he will ask me to marry him. It is just a feeling. He will be coming to the party tonight and staying for the wedding tomorrow. He said he wants to spend more time together. He even wants me to meet his parents."

"How splendid!" Lucille said.

"This will be the first weekend we will be together," Mae said, her face glowing.

"Ah," Edwina patted her hand. "Call me old fashioned, but is that wise?"

"He knows Miss Langley is a lady who has a baby at home," Lucille said, in answer to the question.

"Perhaps. But men can be small-minded, placing women into categories," Edwina said.

"Not Mr. Rogers. He said he loves me."

Lucille nodded, wanting to believe the best. "That's because you are lovable, Mae."

"Exactly," Edwina said. She tapped her glass with a fork as she stood and faced the table. "Ladies, I just want to add to Miss Genevieve's toast. Yes, we believe in love. Very much so." She paused before continuing. "I am not your typical woman, I know. I have been ridiculed since I was a child. I learned it is essential to love and respect yourself. Every woman here is loving and lovable. Thank you all for including me in that love."

A chorus of hear-hears followed, and the word love could be made out in the chatter.

Carter stood. "Thank you, Mrs. Schnedeker. Thank you all for making Rams Head Inn a true home. When I came here without Davidson, I had my doubts the inn would succeed, but here we are. To us, dear ladies."

"To us!"

Lucille looked around the table, her eyes glistening. She had never felt so whole and grateful in her life. She and Carter locked eyes and held up their glasses to one another.

The pink drink had gone to Lucille's head, so it took her a while to make out what Henry was saying. He was furious. As the ladies' lunch was breaking up, he approached the table, smiled curtly at the women, and took Lucille's elbow to shoo her up the stairs and into their room. His voice was soft but shaking with anger.

"I trusted you, Lucille. You promised no more surprises. You gave me your word."

"To what are you referring?

"The alcohol piled to the ceiling in the basement! Tell me you didn't know about it."

She waved her hand. "Of course, I knew about it. But it has nothing to do with me."

"You have been living under a roof with large quantities of illicit alcohol and you say it has nothing to do with you? Why, I can smell it on your breath as we speak."

Henry was outraged. Lucille blinked, trying to sober up enough to think and speak rationally. She sat on the bed to steady herself.

"Why is it illicit?"

"Do not insult me."

"The law has not gone into effect. Not until January from what I understand. Who will care if they have some spirits gathered?"

"Maybe the criminal who was shaking down Ben for money when I walked into the inn just a short while ago. Or maybe Ben is the criminal, shaking down the other one. I have no idea and neither do you." He threw up his hands. "I cannot believe we are having this conversation!"

"I bet it was that lowlife Romano." The words slipped out before she could stop them.

"You know him?" He said, stunned. "Who are you, Lucille?" His eyes were black with rage and his arms were flailing.

"Henry, it is not anything like you're thinking. Please sit down." Her head was spinning from the drink, and she couldn't deal with his outburst.

"I am not sitting down. We need to leave immediately."

"The wedding is tomorrow, Henry. A wedding we are co-hosting. I would never embarrass Carter, never mind Margaret, by not attending."

"I am your husband and I say we must leave. Where is your loyalty?"

"To myself." She shocked herself with her words, but they only seemed to embolden her further. Or maybe it was the alcohol. She stood and faced him. "I must think for myself and follow what I know to be true. I have been here for over three months, you for three days. I dare say I have a far better understanding of this place than you do." She took a deep breath. "I will stay here, and I am asking, no, I am *begging* you, Henry, to do the same."

He stared at the floor. "Allowing you to come here was the biggest mistake of my life. I hardly recognize you anymore."

"I have never been more myself."

Henry observed her for what seemed an eternity. "Fine. You stay. I am leaving. I will join Vance at The Empire House. When the alcohol wears off, I pray that you come to your senses and join me."

"I will not, Henry. I have begged you to stay. It is you who must come to your senses." She stared at him defiantly, her expression unchanged as he grabbed the handle of his cumbersome trunk and left the room.

Carter and Ben were having their own parting of ways out on the lawn, where Ben had steered her to discuss the latest basement developments.

"No, Ben. No. I will not allow it."

"It is done, and you must understand why."

"You paid him?"

"I did."

"How could you? You knew how strongly I felt. I told you I would rather go to the police than deal with that shady character."

"I had no choice."

"Apparently I didn't either." Her hands flew to her hips. "We are being blackmailed. My inn is under attack, and you've allowed it."

"We are not being blackmailed. We are buying his silence and protection."

"And what's the difference, exactly?"

"Listen, Carter. If I didn't pay him, who knows who else will show up here?"

"And what will prevent him from raising his 'silence and protection fee'?"

"I haven't figured this all out," he said. "Let's enjoy the wedding, and I will come up with a plan afterward."

"Why wait? Chief Jim McNab is coming to the wedding. Let's speak with him."

"Two reasons we should not do that. First, you don't invite someone to a wedding and then unload your problems on him. It's rude. Second, we need to figure out exactly what we're asking. Do we want him to see what we're hiding?"

Carter digested his words. "Fine. Please know I am not happy. This is not how I would have handled the Romano problem had I been given a chance to weigh in."

"I appreciate that, and I apologize. I just wanted him out of here as soon as possible, given all the guests wandering around."

Carter didn't respond. She tried to think how Davidson would have handled it.

"One more thing," Ben said. "Henry witnessed part of my exchange with Romano. Our voices had raised, and Henry came down to see what was going on."

"Oh no! And what did he see?"

"Much of it, as the storage door was open. I tried to explain, but he preferred not to know the details. Nevertheless, I'm sure he got the gist of it."

"Poor Lucille!" Carter's hands braced her face. "And poor Margaret! This is a disaster. Henry will insist they leave at once."

"I can try to talk to him."

"You've done enough. Let me handle this."

Carter found Lucille in her room, weeping on the bed. Through her tears, she explained what happened with Henry. And Carter filled Lucille in on Ben's betrayal, how angry she was.

"So, what now?" Lucille asked.

"Now, we put on a wedding."

"First, let's get more of that pink drink," Lucille said.

Mr. Rogers was at the bottom of the stairs when Lucille and Carter came down. The lounge next to the staircase was busy being prepared for the wedding eve dance party, which would commence in two hours.

"Mr. Rogers!" Carter greeted him. "You're here early. Let me go find Miss Mae for you."

"P-please don't. I-I-I can't stay," he said. "C-c can you give this to her?" It was a thick envelope.

"Why don't you wait and give it to herself yourself," Lucille chimed in. "Oh look, here she is now."

Mae walked down the stairs, wearing the same floral dress she wore at lunch. "Gerald, you're early for the dance. You're welcome to come upstairs while I get ready. Or we can go for a walk, as it's still light out."

"I-I-I am needed back home," Mr. Rogers said. "I c-c-came to give you this." He thrust the envelope in her hands.

"I don't understand. Aren't you staying for the wedding weekend?"

Carter went to the bar to retrieve some more pink drink, leaving Lucille hovering by the front desk in earshot of Mae and Mr. Rogers.

"I am not coming to the wedding, Mae. I had no idea it was to be such a huge affair. I cannot be seen socializing with you in such a public way."

"We socialize here regularly." She said it as half-question, half-statement.

"Yes, but not with the whole of Sag Harbor and Shelter Island about. When I come here, I have the cover of being with men I work with." Lucille noticed his stuttering was gone.

"You're a nice girl, but you're not someone I can be associated with in public."

"You said you loved me. You wanted me to meet your parents."

He put his hat on and turned toward the door. "I am sorry if you misunderstood." He gave her a chaste kiss on the cheek and turned abruptly.

"But wait," Mae said to his back as he opened the door and dashed off.

Lucille's heart fell. Carter had just returned with a drink tray, and Lucille put her finger to her lips for silence.

Mae grabbed onto the newel post, almost in a stupor. The envelope fell to the floor, bills spilling out of it.

The night before her wedding, Margaret paced back and forth in her room at the inn. Her parents wanted her to stay at their rented house, but she told them it would be better if she remained at Rams Head so she could help set up in the morning. That was true, but what she really needed was alone time to think. Curtis was out with his brothers and fellow police officers – his last night as a single man, he said. He had been thoughtful enough to ask whether she minded him going out the night before their wedding, and she genuinely didn't.

How could she still be so full of doubts? Curtis had been especially loving these last few days, agreeable in everything, kind and warm with her family. But was it all an act to keep the peace? Would he change the minute she was pronounced his bride? And what about Vance? Did she still have feelings for him? Well, she knew she did – but did they *matter*?

Just then, there was a soft knock at her door. "Who's there?" she whispered, her ear to the door. No answer, so she opened it slightly. Vance stood there, holding two glasses and a bottle of some kind of liquor. He wedged one foot into the entrance,

"Vance! What are you doing here?"

"Let me in before someone sees," he said.

"Are you drunk?"

"Not quite, but soon." He nudged past her and entered the room, setting down the glasses on the dresser. Then he opened the bottle with a corkscrew he retrieved from his pocket.

"Stop, Vance. You must leave. I am getting married tomorrow."

"I know that. I also know you will be living here on the island. This may be our last chance." He took a step toward her, his arm reaching out.

She stepped away. "Last chance for what?"

"For you and me. We are so good together, Margaret. I've been living on memories of being with you, your body, for the past three months. And I know you haven't forgotten me – I can feel it. Let's end the torture."

In one moment, it became clear that the Vance of her dreams— the man she had hoped would someday see her as his wife, the mother of his future children—simply saw her as a sexual favor, someone to be spoiled the night before her wedding.

"What a fool I was," she said under her breath.

"You weren't a fool," he said, having heard her. "We could have worked things out — eventually. Instead, you took this rash step to show me. Let me be your last memory as a single girl."

He all but lunged at her. She pushed him away with two hands as hard as she could. "How dare you. Get out now before I scream and the Nesbits will see just how vile a man you are. And if they don't see it, I'll tell them myself. *I have no fear of being fired.*"

Vance seemed to sober up at the mention of the Nesbit name. "Fine. I'll leave. But you're wrong Margaret. I cared for you deeply."

Margaret shook her head and pointed to the door. "Just go." He looked at her one last time before slipping out.

She sat on the bed and held her head. Curtis more than 'cared for her deeply.' He loved her. He wanted her for his wife. He introduced her to his family, his friends. Vance treated her like a secret. A dirty secret. How many times did he pull her into the pantry for a passionate kiss? Then not even look at her when either of the Nesbits were in the same room? Tonight proved what she was to him. He wasn't openly declaring his love and trying to stop the wedding. Even if a small part of her wanted him to do exactly that, to give meaning to what they once had, he didn't. He never would.

She remembered at the rehearsal dinner when her father was telling Curtis a boring story about his sheep. How a neighbor threatened to kill any animals who wandered onto his land and the threat caused her father to fortify his current pen at great expense and aggravation…. Curtis listened attentively and even asked questions, prompting her father to expand on what was already a soul-deadening tale. That was love. That was the man she was going to marry.

Margaret slipped into her old nightgown and readied for bed, pin-curling her long hair so it would have some wave on her big day. Her mother used to fix Margaret's hair just like this for the holidays. She smiled. She looked in the mirror at her head full of bobby pins and saw that she looked like the carefree girl of her childhood in Ireland. Minutes later, she was in bed, reading Wordsworth's love sonnets, a bridal gift from Mrs. Nesbit. She was determined to understand this impossible language.

Margaret dozed off, book in hand. She was was awakened by a knock at the door. Good lord, what time was it?

Figuring it was Vance, maybe drunker and more insistent, she shouted to the door, "Please go away. I'm sleeping."

"It's me."

Curtis? She opened it to find him, holding Fella, who was licking Curtis's face. He stepped in and closed the door behind him.

"What are you doing here?" Her hand flew to her head of pin curls. "Why do you have Fella? I stopped allowing him in my room."

"I wanted you to wake up to your wedding present from me," he said, handing over Fella.

"He belongs to Rams Head now," she answered resentfully, as Fella licked her face, his wagging tail pounding her stomach.

"I spoke with Miss Carter, who agreed we could have him. She has her heart set on getting a border collie to round up sheep." He shrugged.

"Really?" Pin-curls forgotten, her face broke into a huge smile. "We can keep him?"

"He seems to love you as much as I do. He'll protect you when I work late. I have his word on it."

"Are you sure it's not the drink talking?"

His eyes never left hers. "It's my love talking. If Fella makes you happy, he makes me happy," he shrugged again.

Margaret gently put Fella down and not so gently kissed Curtis. When their lips broke, Curtis laughed, "Your hair…"

"This is your future Mr. Schmidt."

"God, you're beautiful."

Over Curtis's shoulder she saw Vance's two glasses and bottle. "Someone dropped off a gift. We should enjoy it."

My darling Davidson. Ours was supposed to be the first wedding here at Rams Head. I can't admit how sad I am that it isn't. Even to Lucille. You never cared about such hoopla, I know. You were content to elope at City Hall. But I had this storybook idea about wearing white and seeing you at the end of the aisle. My mother wanted that for me. She even saved from what little money we had for my wedding. She would have loved you. And you would have loved her. How could I not have either of you at my side? Thank goodness I have Lucille. She keeps congratulating me for having done all this on my own, and maybe I have — though God knows not by choice. I fear for you, Davidson. I have no idea what has become of you. I had the worst dream. It felt so real. I'm no longer sure as I once was that you're alive. In my heart, always, but actually alive? Maybe this is my moment of acceptance. But I fear I'm not ready. Please send your cardinal to me today. I desperately need a sign.

"Well, the weather is cooperating," Lucille said to Carter as they descended the stairs early the morning of the wedding. The friends had each passed the night without sleep. Lucille missed Henry, and Carter had nightmares of Romano holding Davidson at gunpoint. It didn't help that both women were hung over from the pink drinks. They desperately needed coffee to get started on the day. Fortunately, the silver service was already set up on the tray near the fireplace. They each poured a cup and headed to their usual seats.

"Soon we will have to snap into action," Carter sighed.

"Yes, but let's enjoy this quiet moment before the storm. It's only 6 o'clock. Everyone who slept is still sleeping. Did you hear the noise last night?"

"Yes! Lots of dancing and laughing. I checked in at one point, but all was under control."

"I'm glad Henry wasn't here to hear it," Lucille grimaced. "I still can't believe he left and, even worse, hasn't returned."

"Vance Broder was here dancing with the Connecticut Ladies last night." Carter lifted her eyebrows as she sipped her coffee.

"Really?"

"Yes. It was quite a party. Elizabeth was with James, of course. Though he's not coming to the wedding."

"I didn't think so. My father always spent Sundays with my mother and me," Lucille said. "I must say, I'm just sick about Mae. I could kill that bum. How dare he tell her she isn't the kind of woman he can be seen with. She's a lovely young girl with a baby whose husband died honorably defending this nation."

"I agree. I think the circumstance under which they met sealed their fate."

"Maybe she and William can fall in love."

"Don't count on William. I know nothing about his private life, but it's clear he wants to keep it that way."

"William is a quiet one, isn't he? Do we know anything about Curtis's brothers? Or any of his fellow police officers? Surely there's someone we're not thinking about for Mae."

"Why do women always need rescuing?" Carter wondered. "Why must they be defined by the men in their life?"

"We're conditioned," Lucille answered. "Unless the woman is as strong as you."

"Or you," Carter countered. "Although you have a man. As for me, I'm not so strong. Nor am I sure of myself. I barely sleep most nights, reviewing all the things I've done wrong and what horrors could lie ahead. Making plans, checking off lists, trying to hold off one disaster or another. But I insist on taking charge of it all. If someone is going to mess it up, let it be me. Women aren't taught to do that, are we? Or perhaps we aren't allowed to. I keep hoping the vote will start to change things."

"It will make us feel like we have a voice," Lucille said. "But it won't change our lives. Not for a long time. Politics are like that. Though I suppose we can vote in leaders who agree with us. That's a lot of power right there. Look at what the Temperance people have accomplished."

Carter shuddered. She was all too aware of what the Temperance Movement had accomplished. In six months, even the transportation of liquor would be criminal. She thought about the powder-keg under their very feet. Surely, it was bound to bring problems. Major problems. It was getting harder to justify this mess of her own making. Or think of a way out of it.

She shook her head and stood. "Sister-friend, we have a wedding to prepare for."

CHAPTER THIRTY-FIVE

The Rams Head Inn property looked especially beautiful on this bright early July morning. The sky was crisp blue, the water sparkled below, and the lush green lawn was speckled with the white Adirondack chairs, like sailboats on a verdant sea. William and his team must have been up all night. Chairs were lined up like church pews in front of the recently completed gazebo down by the shore. Given the glorious weather, the tables were set outside in long rows. Cora and Isabelle had arranged sweet clusters of field flowers in canning jars running along the center of each table, adding color to the white tablecloths. The eclectic dishes and glassware looked homey and welcoming.

As the guests arrived shortly before 1 pm, everything and everyone seemed to be smiling, including Fella, who excitedly took on the role as host, greeting each person who appeared.

Ben arrived in a stylish cream linen suit and headed over to join Carter and Lucille on the lawn. "You two are a vision, I must say." Carter wore a bold pink and white striped silk dress that accentuated her curves. Lucille wore a luminous sea green chiffon dress with a v-neck edged in white lace.

"Don't look too closely," Carter said to him. "We both have circles under our eyes."

"As if anything could mar your beauty." He kissed her on her cheek.

Ben turned to Lucille. "Where is Henry?"

"I'm not entirely sure. He had business to attend to, so I don't know if he'll be coming today." Lucille hated not knowing her husband's whereabouts.

Ben leaned in and whispered, "I apologize for what he witnessed yesterday. The timing was most unfortunate."

She nodded in acknowledgment of Ben's words as she blinked away a threatening tear. Her sleepless night had left her full of doubts. She just needed to get through the day.

Curtis interrupted them as he brought over a tall white-haired gentleman and his petite, birdlike wife. "Miss Carter, Mrs. Nesbit and Mr. Goodwin, allow me to introduce Chief McNab and his wife, Mrs. McNab." After perfunctory hellos to the group, Chief McNab fixed his gaze on Carter.

"A pleasure to meet you," Carter said, extending her hand.

"Yes," he nodded. "I met the man who built this place. Davidson was his name. I heard he was lost at sea."

Deciding this wasn't the time to correct him about Davidson being missing but not definitively lost, Carter said, "Yes, my fiancée. He gave me the inn as a pre-wedding gift."

"I'm sorry for your loss," Mrs. McNab said. "How wonderful you have this place to remember him by."

Chief McNab looked at Carter sympathetically. "I'm sure he'd be pleased about how well things are going here."

"Thank you. We're still figuring it all out."

"Can't be easy for a woman on her own." Before Carter could answer him, he took his wife's elbow. "Mrs. McNab and I are going to have a look around."

"Please do."

Curtis introduced Carter and Lucille to several other policemen and their families. Apparently, Curtis was quite popular on the force, being the star second baseman on the police baseball team. Lucille made a point of making conversation with the wives and complimenting their dresses and bending down to ask the children's names, who were all gussied up in their Sunday best. Oliver, the driver who had taken Lucille and Estelle to Sylvester Manor, was there with his wife Sally and baby Oliver Jr.

The three Connecticut Ladies were conversing with one another on the lawn, each one looking more stunning than the next. Isabelle and Estelle were with them, laughing at something Elizabeth had just shared with the group. Miriam and young Dorothy were mingling, clearly familiar with several of the local families. Cora was talking with Graham's son Tim. Now that would make an excellent match, Lucille thought. Then she noticed the Schnedekers' arrival and watched them join the group with the Connecticut Ladies, who heartily welcomed them with smiles. Estelle seemed at ease with the group, though Lucille appreciated it couldn't be easy to to be the only colored person here today. Yet she was here, out in the open, looking her serene and beautiful self.

Lucille observed Isabelle throw her arms around each of the Schnedekers like they were old friends, even family. And they could be a family, she thought. Just not the kind anyone would have imagined or endorsed. But Lucille was beginning to understand that what made a family was more than shared blood—or a diamond ring.

She shook her head. It all seemed so obvious to her now. People are people, just in different wrappings and often not of their own choosing. Who is anyone to judge? Isabelle saw Lucille looking at her and waved, as did the Schnedekers and Estelle. Lucille enthusiastically waved back.

It was a joyful crowd, and Rams Head felt alive with love and goodwill. Lucille looked around for Henry or Vance, but they were nowhere in sight. How she missed Henry. She wanted him to finally meet Estelle. She was desperate for him to see this new family she and Carter had created. Surely, he could get past his apprehensions if he were here. Henry would only need to witness this beautiful gathering.

Lucille strolled over to join the Connecticut Ladies. Elizabeth looked her elegant self in a buttercup yellow dress with a matching hat. Helen was animatedly talking to Estelle. One look at Mae's quiet, drawn face, however, made Lucille want to weep. After saying hello to each woman, as well as to the Schnedekers, she approached Mae.

"Did you get any rest last night?"

"A little."

Lucille could tell she was trying to stay composed. "I understand your disappointment. He was not the man you hoped he'd be. He had us all fooled."

Mae's lip quivered. Lucille hugged her small frame. "The one thing I know," Lucille whispered, "You are not alone – love comes in many forms. Look around and try to draw strength from the love that is here and the love that awaits you at home."

Mae nodded. "I know. I just fear for the future. What will become of me and Florence?"

"Good things. Life is funny that way – we live in fear of bad surprises but forget good can surprise us too. Try to enjoy today. Would you like to join me? I'm going to go talk to the children."

"No thank you, but please go. I'm fine."

Lucille found the children with Carter in the garden. Carter had promised they could help gather Margaret's bouquet. Each child pointed to a flower of their choice, which Carter promptly clipped and handed to a small dark-haired girl named Prudence — maybe eight years old — to place in a nearby jar with water. So far, they had collected two pink roses, a yellow Black-Eyed Susan, three zinnias, and a sprig of mint. Watching Carter with the children, Lucille found herself having stirrings she never had before. Again, she longed for Henry.

Carter bent down to whisper in the girl's ear, "Prudence, go ask your mother if you may go upstairs with Mrs. Nesbit to give Miss Margaret her bouquet." Prudence, in a pink floral dress a size or two too small for her, lit up, ran to her mother, and returned less than a minute later with a huge grin. Lucille, holding the jar of flowers, took the girl's hand, and the two headed up to Margaret's room.

"When we return, our bride will be behind us," Lucille said to Carter and her group, "so flower girls line up!" The girls all giggled with excitement.

Fifteen minutes later, Lucille returned with Prudence and nodded to Carter, who had already summoned the guests to their seats and the priest to the gazebo.

Estelle stepped up onto the gazebo, and began to sing *Ave Maria*, the traditional prayer to the Virgin Mary. Lucille's eyes welled up hearing Estelle's voice. Prudence ran over to her parents, while Lucille headed to her seat on the right, the bride's side. As she made her way down the aisle, she saw Vance seated next to Mae, Helen, and Elizabeth in the third from last row. He smiled at her. Lucille's heart sank. Henry wasn't with him.

Then she looked up. There was Henry, standing and waiting by her seat in the second row. She inhaled. He looked his handsome best in a pale blue seersucker suit, a small field flower placed in the lapel by one of the flower girls. His eyes gleamed when they met Lucille's, and he grinned widely. She took her place beside him and squeezed his hand. He drew her lace-covered hand to his mouth and kissed it. His tongue found the keyhole near the wrist of her glove, and she smiled.

She then exhaled the breath she'd been holding. Her chest filled with a warm sensation she could only describe as peace. Soulmates were like that, Lucille knew. They could argue, they could vehemently disagree, but they were connected by some gravitational force that would never let them separate. Not really. At least not for long.

Carter slipped into the seat next to Lucille. It was then Lucille noticed the empty chair next to Carter, but assumed Ben was manning the door for latecomers. As Estelle's voice continued to grace the air, two little girls scattered flower petals down the grassy aisle. Curtis's brother Clarence and Margaret's sister Gerty, were the first to walk down the aisle, followed by Curtis's parents.

Then it was Margaret's turn. Escorted by her parents on either side, she looked resplendent in her simple Genevieve lace and pearl-studded tulle dress with its scooped neckline and bell sleeves. Under her veil you could see a waterfall of honey-chocolate ringlets. Angelic was the only word for her beauty, Lucille thought. Curtis stood to one side in the gazebo with the priest in the center. Curtis's chest seemed to expand, his expression intense as he stared at his bride. Fella broke away from Isabelle's grasp and the crowd laughed as Margaret kneeled to take his leash so he could walk beside her.

Estelle finished singing and stepped off the gazebo. Lucille saw her slip into a seat saved by the Schnedekers. The ceremony commenced. It was brief and to the point, for which the family members were thankful since most had attended a full Catholic service that morning. The guests broke out in a whooping cheer when they were pronounced man and wife.

"You did it," Henry whispered into Lucille's ear. They watched the couple walk up the aisle hand in hand, absorbing congratulatory kisses, handshakes and pats on the back. Lucille looked up at Henry, her eyes questioning. He continued, "As you keep telling me, you and Carter created a family here at Rams Head, and I'm honored to be part of it – assuming you'll have me."

Forgetting decorum, Lucille threw her arms around Henry. "*You* are the beating heart of any family I am part of."

CHAPTER THIRTY-SIX

No one noticed Carter slip away right after the ceremony. Something felt wrong – or maybe right — she wasn't sure which. But her intuition told her to head back inside the inn. Was it Ben's absence? Where was he? Her heart slammed against her rib cage. She had read about premonitions, people who saw or felt things before they happened, but she never had such an experience. She almost stopped herself and turned around to rejoin Lucille. But Carter was now shaking.

Fortunately, everyone was milling about outside, enjoying the post-wedding drinks and canapés being served down by the water, so no one could see her nerves unraveling for no apparent reason. She entered the building and peeked into the lounge. Nothing. She then entered the Garden Room, where a lone mother was breastfeeding her baby. She smiled at the woman and left the room. Maybe all the stress was catching up to her.

As Carter approached the foyer, she could make out the silhouette of a tall man standing in the shadow of the front door frame.

Ben? No.

Davidson!

She must be hallucinating. This man was far slimmer than Davidson. And his hair was slicked back, and he had a long beard starting just below his high cheek bones. She walked slowly toward him, not trusting what her eyes. Could she trust her heart? It must be her imagination run wild from all the strain. No, it wasn't that. A result of her hangover from the night before? But that wore off hours ago. Her heart hammered as she approached this phantom of a man.

"You're seeing right, darling, it's me."

He pulled her into the alcove behind the door. She did not throw herself into his arms instead, she touched his face, framing his eyes with her fingertips, then his bearded cheeks, his nose, his lips. She trailed his neck and onto his shoulders.

"Holy smokes. It really is you." Tears slipped down her cheeks. "You're back." She kissed him gently on his lips, as if testing to see if he would vanish into the air. "You're so thin," she said as she began to trace her hands along his ribs. "I'm scared to ask where..."

"A Barbadian prison. But that's for later. What's going on outside?"

"A wedding."

"I'm not up for that."

She looked at him, bedraggled and in need of a bath. "Of course not. Let me bring you to my room where you can clean up."

"Rams Head. You..." He looked around, at a loss for words.

"Not now, not yet. This is a lot to take in, I know. I did it, but I had a lot of help. How did you get here?"

"My little boat Spinnaker. Amazingly, she was still in the harbor, waiting for me."

"I know, I've been paying her mooring fee. I knew you'd need her to get to me. I just knew."

He looked into her eyes and gave her a long kiss. "I didn't tie her to our dock. It was full. Someone was loading a crate onto a boat."

"Hmmm. I'll find out who or what it was." She suspected Romano, or maybe Bailey, but she couldn't investigate this moment.

"I wanted to ask but saw the crowd. Bring me to your room and go back to your guests. We have all the time in the world. I'm not going anywhere, not again."

"Do you have any bags?" Carter appreciated the sooner she got him up to her room the better – otherwise they'd be inundated with people asking all kinds of questions – questions to which she herself wanted answers, but not in front of all these strangers.

"Just this." He grabbed a small, tattered canvas sack. "I'll need to get some decent clothes."

"Consider it done." Her smile dropped when she saw he walked with a pronounced limp. "What happened?"

"What didn't happen," he shrugged. He clutched the railing for balance. "I'll be fine. I just need some time."

When they reached the upstairs landing, he smiled at the red velvet settee, framed by matching wallpaper with twin gilded mirrors and brass sconces, as well as the red rug runners going down the hallways on either side. "I was wondering where my girl's love of color was. This place, what you've done…." Again, he grasped to express himself, the pride evident in his face.

"We have so much to catch up on. I'm staying with you. I just need to tell Lucille…."

They entered her room. "No, don't. Please don't tell anyone I'm here. Not until I'm ready."

"I don't have to tell Lucille about you, I just can just say I'm not feeling well and come back."

"No, go be with your guests. I'll be okay."

"Shall I bring up some food?"

"Maybe later. I just don't want to see anyone."

Carter was torn. She wanted to forget everything going on downstairs and simply lie down beside him. But there was a crowd on the lawn, and she had already been gone a while. So, she made sure the water pitcher was filled and kissed him. And kissed him again and again.

"I will be back to check on you, and I'll bring some food. Just rest up if that's what you need," she said, her eyes welling up. "You're home, you're safe. That's all I need to know. I'll be back as soon as I can. I will spend all my days caring for you."

Davidson grabbed her, kissing her soundly before she left. Leaving him alone in her room, even for a short time, felt like the hardest thing she had every done.

As she flew down the stairs, Ben appeared in the foyer, his face questioning. "I've been looking for you."

"Just freshening up." Carter struggled to compose herself. She wanted to tell Ben about Davidson but heeded his request for secrecy. She grabbed Ben's hand. "Let's go join our guests."

As they walked toward the water, she asked, "Where were you during the ceremony?"

"I was in the back. I was running a bit late and didn't want to disrupt the nuptials by coming forward. But I saw the whole thing."

"What were you running late from? You were here when the guests were arriving."

"I had some business that needed attending."

"On a Sunday?"

"A small thing. It's taken care of."

"Was it Romano again? Is he here?"

"No. I told you, it was a small thing. But I saw the entire ceremony."

"Did you see someone loading crates at our dock while you were standing in the back?"

He paused. "No, did you?"

"I didn't, no. One of the servers asked if we were getting a delivery. But Graham is here, so I told her she must have been mistaken."

"She must have been. I would have known if someone was at the dock."

Something about his explanation for his absence didn't add up. Carter would have seen him standing in the back. But if he was doing something at the dock, wouldn't he have told her?

"Beautiful ceremony, right? Especially when Fella wouldn't stop barking at the end," she laughed.

"I know. Who says dogs don't have a sense of timing?"

But Fella hadn't barked. That was a test. Suddenly Carter didn't know what to think about Ben, his disappearance and feeble explanation, the activity at the dock, any of it. She again reached for Ben's hand. Whatever else, she was not letting him out of her sight. She hoped Davidson didn't see her holding Ben's hand. Though that seemed the least of her problems right now.

Ben suddenly turned to Carter. "Speaking of absences, where is William? I don't see him in the crowd. In fact, I haven't seen him since I arrived earlier. Is he here?"

"William is carrying so much of today's load. He must be in the kitchen helping his brother. Why, are you looking for him?"

"No. But I would expect to see a great deal of him at this event. Usually, he's everywhere."

Now that she thought about it, she hadn't seen William since early that morning when they were setting up. Ben had always been suspicious of William. Now she didn't know what to believe about either of them.

She led Ben toward Lucille and Henry, who were speaking with the McNabs. After a few moments, Carter caught Lucille's attention in a way that only close friends can. Lucille immediately picked up on the cue, "Carter, is this a good time for us to notify Chef Adam and Mr. Manuel to ready the tables?"

"Oh, you're probably right. Ben and Henry, would you mind things here until we return?"

"Wouldn't it be better if we went, so you and Lucille could stay here?" Ben asked.

"It really should be us," Lucille responded. "There are some details we must confirm. Don't worry, we will return in short order."

Henry looked at Ben. "I'm anxious to speak to you about Little Ram Island. I'm hearing that's where I should purchase land." Lucille was relieved Henry wasn't holding a grudge about the conversation he overheard in the basement between Ben and Romano. Maybe Henry came to see it had nothing to do with him or Lucille. Or maybe he wanted this day to be as pleasant as possible.

The two women walked away, each holding their skirts as they climbed the hill toward the inn. Carter smiled until they were safely out of the men's view. "Lucille, I need you to keep a close eye on Ben."

"Why? You looked so cozy holding his hand."

"I have little time to explain, but something is going on with him. Also, have you seen William?"

Lucille thought for a moment. "I'm not sure. His team was bringing chairs from the gazebo up to the tables, but I didn't see him. What's going on Carter? You look like you've seen a ghost."

"Well, you may think I have. Davidson is here."

Lucille halted. "*What*?"

"Keep walking and don't look at me like that. Yes. He's in my room and won't come out while people are here. But I'm also concerned about Ben. He left the ceremony and lied about it. Moreover, Davidson saw something going on at our dock during the ceremony. Something to do with crates. On a Sunday, and Graham is *here*. And William is not. Something, Lucille, is amiss."

"I'll stick close enough to Ben to make Henry jealous," Lucille said in jest. "I'll also keep my eye out for William, if you're worried about him."

"I care mostly because Ben asked," Carter said. "I'm doubting myself. I'm usually good at judging character…." They reached the veranda. She shook her head as if to clear it. "What are we giving Chef Adam and Mr. Manuel notice of exactly?"

"We're not. It was just something I came up with to get us away from Ben for a few minutes."

Carter smirked. "You're good. I don't give you half the credit you deserve."

"Glad you acknowledge that. Now let's both get going on our assigned missions. I'll return to Henry and keep Ben at our side. You do whatever you need to do."

"Thanks, partner."

Lucille had her doubts about Davidson having returned. It was just too fantastical to believe. And today of all days.

Could the stress of the wedding be getting to Carter? But it was not the time to question her dear friend. If Carter had concerns about Ben, that was enough for Lucille to be on her guard. She didn't know what to think about William.

She returned near the gazebo to find that Henry and Ben had been joined by Stuart Bennett and the Schnedekers. She was happy for Genevieve. Lucille assumed he'd spend Sunday with his family, but here he was. She was glad to see the Schnedekers were also part of this group. As Lucille greeted everyone, Ben went to make his exit. Lucille quickly took his arm. "Carter told me to keep my eye on you. She wants to make sure you are seated with us at the luncheon."

"Of course. I thought I would find Carter and accompany her myself."

"No need. She was with Curtis's brother Clarence last I saw. He promised to escort her to the table." Henry looked at her quizzically and she gave a slow nod.

Picking up her signal, Henry said, "Actually, Ben, stay. I want your opinion on this. Alfred, do you really think the Tuthills would sell so many acres? Maybe we can then parcel them off to prospective homeowners, like my good friend Stuart here. Stuart, you would be interested, right — especially if I arranged and oversaw the construction of the houses?"

"Henry, I'd be interested in anything you invested in. I'd love to build Genevieve a home here."

Lucille wondered what Carter was up to, but knew it was more important to keep her eye on Ben. She looked around and saw that everyone seemed to be having a great time. Mae and Vance were quietly sitting by themselves off to the side. Wouldn't it be grand if something worked out there? Lucille just wanted fairytale endings for everyone but knew how silly and impossible that was.

What caused such good fortune for some and bad fortune for others? Yes, much had to do with the circumstances you were born into. She was white and born into a family of means. Estelle was educated and had Walter's financial comfort, but she had few advantages beyond that. Her life would have many struggles, as would those of her children. And the Schedeckers had faced adversity because of their own choices, choosing authenticity over the privileges their status and class would have otherwise afforded them. The cost of staying true to their own happiness sometimes courted hatred from others. And the Connecticut Ladies were all from respectable, hard-working families and one wartime blast had changed their fates forever. Isabelle was from one of the finest families in the Northeast, for all the good it did her. Genevieve had talent and drive, so she made her own fortune, difficult as her path had been. But even there, should she stay with Stuart, she would have to share his affection and attention with his legal family. Elizabeth, with all her beauty, would face a similar fate, or even worse, since she would be completely dependent on James, a married man she didn't even love. The one thing Lucille knew about Carter, even if Davidson was home, she would never be dependent on him – at least no more than he would depend on her.

And Margaret and Curtis? Who knew what fate had in store for them. You enter into marriage so blindly, never really knowing how you, never mind your spouse, will evolve. You could only hope you would grow together. Or that the other would give you the space needed to expand. Henry seemed to be doing that, at least trying to — or so she hoped. This afternoon he had been as warm and personable with Estelle as he was with everyone else. She also saw he spent a great deal of time greeting their Manhattan staff, making them feel welcome and included. And Lucille would have to give him leeway as his business and responsibilities continued to grow, even if it meant entertaining insufferable snobs like the Perrys.

Lucille looked over at Henry who was talking with Ben. She knew every line of Henry's face as sure as she knew her own – even more so. He was a part of her and she of him. Henry sensed her stare, glanced over at her, his smile beguiling as ever. She was so fortunate to have this man. The Schnedekers had that same kind of devotion, she could tell.

Shaken from her thoughts, she saw that people were starting to make their way to the tables. Lucille placed her hands on both Henry and Ben's arms. "Come, let's find our seats, shall we?"

Just as they reached their table, Carter appeared, slightly out of breath. There were five long tables in all – one for the bride and groom and their families. Another was for the officers and their wives. The third was for Carter, Lucille, and the rest of the Rams Head crowd. The fourth was for invited staff, from the inn as well as Lucille's home. A smaller table was alongside for the children.

Lucille knew where they were seated, having placed the cards herself. She and Henry sat across from Carter and Ben. Something told her to switch Carter and Ben to face the water, as opposed to the hotel, a move Carter appreciated. Something was up with Ben, Lucille agreed, as his eyes were darting everywhere.

Carter stood and, clinking her champagne glass with a spoon, welcomed everyone to Rams Head, especially those guests who had traveled a great distance to join the celebration.

"I'm biased, but the Rams Head Inn was born of a great love and great loves keep coming here, whether new ones, old ones, families, friends, partners, or comrades in arms. She smiled at the officers. "It is a beautiful day and love is everywhere. Please join me in toasting today's great love, the marriage of Mr. and Mrs. Schmidt!" Cheers and clinked glasses followed as Margaret and Curtis kissed.

Carter spoke again when the cheers died down. "One more toast before we turn it over to the best man, Officer Durkin. As many of you know, this wedding is being hosted by myself and my dear friends, Lucille and Henry Nesbit. Mr. Nesbit has asked to say a few words."

Lucille had no idea Henry wanted to speak and looked at him questioningly. Henry placed a hand on Lucille's shoulder and stood.

"Good day. If we haven't yet met, my name is Henry Nesbit. I want to welcome everyone and add a few words to Miss Carter's beautiful toast. Margaret, who is the sweetest, most kind-hearted of girls, has been with my wife and me for as long as she has been in America. It has been a great pleasure to meet her family. To know Margaret is to adore her, and I can see the same must be true of Curtis, given how many friends and colleagues have made the not-so-easy journey to be here." He nodded toward the table of officers, many of whom held up their glasses in acknowledgement.

"Much has been written about love. My favorite description, however, isn't especially poetic. I once heard love compared to mittens connected by a string, laced through one's coat sleeves. The string may be invisible to the casual observer, but it makes sure one mitten never loses the other.

"Margaret and Curtis," He picked up his glass and turned to the couple. "As we celebrate your new love, we also celebrate that your love will deepen and strengthen. Just keep checking that string. Reinforce it as needed. And be sure to hold hands whenever you get the chance. That will keep you moving in the same direction." He grabbed Lucille's hand and raised it to the crowd.

Ben grabbed Carter's hand and kissed it. Then he excused himself to go to the men's room.

More toasts, endless toasts. There was much love and joy all around. Lucille thought she'd burst with tears. While the guests were toasting, Chef Adam and his team set up the food on the long narrow table behind them. Carter stood and invited everyone to help themselves and thanked Chef Adam for creating the delicious food they were about enjoy. A shy man, he nodded and quickly left while people started coming up to the tables, plates in hand.

William! Lucille remembered she hadn't seen him since Carter asked her to look out for him. She motioned Carter to the huge oak tree to the side of the tables and headed toward it.

"What's up?" Carter asked.

"I'm not sure. But something is wrong, and I haven't seen William since you first asked about him. Maybe we've been keeping our eyes on the wrong man."

"You're right. Oh, and Ben hasn't returned yet either. You stay, I'll go investigate."

Before Carter could leave, the wedding cake was carried out by two waiters on an enormous silver tray. Everyone marveled at the white, three-tiered confection. Margaret and Curtis cut the cake and fed each other a bite. As their sugar-coated faces kissed, everyone cheered and clapped. When Lucille looked back in Ben's direction. He was still not in his chair. He wasn't anywhere in sight. Lucille interrupted Carter, who had been waylaid by Alfred Schnedeker, and motioned toward Ben's still empty seat.

"Lucille is reminding me of something I need to tend to," Carter said to Alfred. "Please make sure you and Edwina try some cake. It looks delicious."

Carter nearly tripped up on the stone steps as she rushed into the building.

CHAPTER THIRTY-SEVEN

Carter instinctively ran to her room. The door was unlocked, but no Davidson. She began to panic. She glanced at his sack on the floor; she hadn't imagined his presence. But where would he go? There was only one place she could think of. She grabbed the basement keys and flew down the steps two at a time, holding onto the railing for dear life.

"Carter, slow down. You'll hurt yourself!" Gloria O'Reilly admonished her. She was exiting the ladies room.

"Oh goodness, how clumsy of me. It's just that I'm anxious to get back. I need to get a few supplies from the basement."

"I can get whatever you need, Miss Carter," Cora said. Carter hadn't seen her closing the foyer coat closet.

"Thank you, Cora, but no, I'll get it. It's something I need to give Ben, which I put in a secure place. Please carry on. I'll be right back." She hoped her smile looked genuine. The last thing she wanted was anyone following her. Then she stopped. "Cora, have you seen William? Mrs. Nesbit was looking for him."

"I'm here," William said, entering the foyer, one hand holding a basket full of bottles, another with glassware, his clipboard tucked under his arm. "Is there anything you or Mrs. Nesbit need? I just finished helping set up the band by the dance floor – it took longer than we thought it would to get everything in the gazebo. I was about to bring them this basket of refreshments."

Carter looked toward the water and, sure enough, the band was in the gazebo, getting ready to play. She felt foolish for letting Ben make her doubt William.

"Um, no. We just wanted to say thank you, William. For being on top of everything," Carter improvised. "The day is running so smoothly. Thanks for thinking of the beverages for the band. It's the small things that make the difference."

He nodded in his officious way and proceeded out the door toward the gazebo. Carter started down to the basement. Fearful someone might come from behind, she locked the door at the top of the basement stairs.

"Thanks for locking the door, Carter." Ben looked up at her from the bottom of the stairs. "I neglected to do that."

"Ben, what's going on?" She tried to sound matter of fact.

"I think you know."

"Know what?"

"You know that Davidson has returned to spoil everything."

Stay calm, Carter. Stay calm. "Yes, I know he came back, but why do you think he'll spoil everything? Spoil what? Aren't you happy to see him? You are friends after all."

"Then why didn't you tell me he came back?"

"Because there is a wedding going on, and he didn't want to be the cause of any needless drama."

"I agree, which is why I brought Davidson down here." He glanced in the direction of the hidden door.

"What have you done with him?"

"He agreed to stay hidden until after the wedding breaks up."

"He *was* hidden. In my room. So, I repeat, what have you done with him and why?"

"He is in the back. What did he tell you?"

"Just that he's returned. He was in my room to rest up and stay out of sight. What's going on, Ben?" She made her way to the door behind the shelves and fumbled for her key.

"Your key won't work. It's a new lock. I couldn't take the chance."

She turned to face him. "You're frightening me, Ben. I thought you and I were partners."

"We were until Davidson got back. I thought I had finally found the woman of my dreams. Come," he said, handling her roughly by the arm. "Let's go back to the wedding before people start looking for us."

"I am not going anywhere until I see Davidson."

He walked quickly toward her. "Use your common sense. He is locked up with all the alcohol. Call attention to him and you call attention to *your* illegal business. Yes, your name and the inn are on the line, not me."

"Show me that he is safe, and I'll return to the wedding with you."

"No. You'll return to the wedding because you *don't* know that he's safe."

She absorbed his words and considered her options, which admittedly weren't great. "All right. Let's go back upstairs. I don't want to ruin Margaret and Curtis's day."

Carter headed up the stairs, Ben right behind her. Just as she neared the top, Lucille knocked on the other side of the locked door. "Carter?"

"Open it," Ben whispered.

Carter inhaled as she reached for the doorknob but thought better of it. She was not going to leave Davidson alone here — or involve Lucille in whatever was happening with Ben.

"Lucille, I'm with Ben. We'll be out in a few minutes. Please keep everyone occupied." Then, with her hands against the door, she kicked Ben in the groin with her back right heel. He went flying down the stairs.

"What was that crash?" Lucille asked. "Are you sure you don't need me?"

"A crate fell. No worries. We're fine. Please go hostess – we'll be out in a minute."

As Ben writhed in pain on the basement floor, Carter reached for his key ring and found an unfamiliar one. She ran to the hidden door and opened it. Just as she was about to enter, Ben rushed from behind and pushed her into the secret chamber. The next thing she heard was the click of the door locking from the outside. Now she was locked in the room with no way out.

Because the lights could only be switched on from the outside, she was surrounded in total darkness. Suddenly, she felt two hands gripping her waist. Before she was able to let out a scream, she realized it was Davidson. She turned and hugged him tightly.

"How did he get you down here?" she asked.

"Someone came to your room and said you urgently needed me in the basement."

"Who?"

"A young woman. She knew my name, so I had no reason to doubt you'd sent for me. Ben must have directed her. I rushed down and called your name which is when I noticed the hidden door was open. As I walked toward it, Ben jumped out and pushed me inside. I cannot believe Ben Goodwin is on Ram Island. Or maybe I can."

"I thought Ben was your friend. Your business partner."

"Is that what he told you? No, he was the first mate on my ship to Barbados. Came highly recommended. We became friends, drinking buddies. I confided too much. Way too much. Of that I'm guilty."

"That's how he knew about Rams Head?"

"Yes. But that was just a bonus. He had already planned the shipwreck for after we picked up our cargo. He must have assumed I died with the rest of the crew. When they found me, the Barbadian authorities held me responsible for the wreck as the captain of the ship. I was locked up."

"How does one plan a shipwreck?

"Happens more often than you think. After the cargo is loaded and the ship heads off to sea, they steer it onto shoals with decoy navigation lights. Then they have men in smaller boats lying in wait. After they take what they want, they leave the crew to drown from the crashing waves."

"How did you survive?"

"Dumb luck. I managed to cling to a piece of a wreckage wedged between two rocks."

"And then Ben, assuming you were dead, came here and told me you were partners. I was so trusting."

"I was too. I should never have mentioned the inn and what I had planned, including this hidden room," Davidson said. "But enough talk. We have to get out of here."

The wedding guests were laughing, drinking, and dancing joyously. Margaret's parents were demonstrating a classic Irish jig, which several revelers were game to learn. Lucille mingled with some of the officers' wives, wondering why it was taking Carter so long to return to the festivities. She looked up to see Ben talking to Stuart and Genevieve. Relieved, she headed toward them.

She quickly said hello to the trio and turned to Ben. "Where is Carter? She has been gone for long while."

He excused himself to Stuart and Genevieve and pulled Lucille out of their hearing range. "She's not feeling well and went to her room to rest."

"Poor dear. I should go see to her."

"No, please don't. She expressly said she needed to rest – alone."

Lucille and Ben looked at one at one another for a moment. He was either telling the truth, which meant Carter went to visit Davidson, hence the "alone" instruction, or there was a problem. Not wanting to take a chance, Lucille said, "You're right, I'll let her rest."

Lucille found Henry and quietly excused herself to go freshen up.

"Of course, Squirrel. Want me to walk with you?"

"No, please engage Ben if you can. I don't want him to see I'm heading up to the inn."

"What's with all this cloak and dagger swirling about?" Henry asked half-jokingly.

"I'll be right back and explain it all, I promise." Dutifully, Henry headed over to Ben, Stuart, and Genevieve.

Lucille looked at Ben to make sure he wasn't facing her direction as she climbed the hill. She headed straight to Carter's room. Lucille clutched the doorframe when she saw the room was empty. She then ran to her own room, grabbed the two basement keys, and darted down the stairs.

Carter and Davidson were still trying to figure out how to escape the basement when a crack of light suddenly shot into the dark room, almost blinding them. It was the back door that only Carter, Lucille, and Graham knew about.

"Carter?" Lucille called out.

"Yes, we're over here!"

But before Lucille could take a step toward them, Ben appeared directly behind Lucille. "You two stupid women will be the death of me." At once, he grabbed Lucille from behind, drew a knife from his coat pocket, and held it to Lucille's throat. Lucille froze, her foot remaining wedged between the door and its frame.

As their eyes adjusted to the light, Carter said, "Ben, put it down. Let's work this out together."

"There is no 'together,' Carter. Not anymore."

"Ben, you're a smart man," Davidson said. "Drop the knife. We can finish talking without it."

"I wasn't smart enough to make certain *you* were dead. I won't assume anything this time."

Carter found herself eerily calm. "What are you going to do? Kill us all? Surely you know you won't get away with it."

He sneered, his lopsided grin now one of pure menace. "Why not? Davidson is the stranger here, appearing out of nowhere, hiding in the shadows. Look at him. He'd be the first person anyone would suspect. The story will be he returned from Barbados, saw you with me and, in a jealous rage, killed you and Lucille, who was in the

390

wrong place at the wrong time. I managed to kill Davidson when I heard the commotion but was too late to save the two of you."

"I don't believe you're a killer." Carter said in a low voice.

"You don't know who you're dealing with," Davidson said. "He's already killed an entire ship's crew."

"Don't I?" asked Carter, removing a pistol from the back sash of her dress. "Since you gave me a key to the gun closet, Ben, I retrieved this earlier when I began to feel uncertain about you."

"You'll have gunshots go off in the middle of a wedding celebration?" Ben sneered. "I don't think you have it in you to use that gun. Besides, any shot in my direction is more likely to kill Lucille than me. And if anything happens to me, you'll have to answer to Romano and Bailey. Put down the gun now or I'll slash your friend's throat in front of you."

Carter started walking slowly toward him. "So, you are working with Romano?"

"Of course. Did you think I was a one-man operation?"

"Why not tell me you were working with him?"

"Because I needed your trust. And you would never trust Romano. Besides, I wanted to keep this place squeaky clean, which Romano is not."

Davidson spoke. "Was that the guy removing a crate by the dock?"

"What do you mean?"

"I saw some guy in a green cap loading a crate onto a boat."

"You're making that up."

"How could I? I don't even know this Romano or what he looks like."

Ben blinked for a moment. He clearly didn't know Romano was removing a crate from the Rams Head dock.

"That's right, Ben," Davidson said. "Your own people betray you. Like Phil Johnson in Barbados. He turned on you too. There are wanted posters with your mug everywhere on the island."

"You're lying."

"I have no reason to lie."

Lucille whimpered, which caused Carter to strengthen her resolve.

"Henry!" Carter yelled, pretending to look behind Ben. Ben briefly turned away, providing just enough space between himself and Lucille. Without warning, Carter aimed the gun directly at Ben and pulled the trigger. The shot pierced the side of his head. Ben turned enough to stare at Carter in wonder as he fell to the ground, his knife jabbing Lucille's shoulder on his way down.

In less than a minute, two police officers who had been drinking at the bar, filled the basement passageway. After quickly surveying the scene, one left to get Chief McNab. Henry showed up seconds behind the officers, and pushed his way toward Lucille whose dress sleeve was speckled with blood. Then Chief McNab appeared. He began to clear everyone away from Ben's body. Shaking, Carter handed him the gun as Davidson's arms wrapped around her.

CHAPTER THIRTY-EIGHT

Ben was dead. Carter could not stop shaking. She tried to assure everyone she was fine. Chief McNab ordered the body to be covered and not touched. The Chief also directed that no one breathe a word of this to the guests until after the wedding festivities. "I don't want unnecessary hysteria here tonight," he told his two men. Fortunately, most of the wedding guests had long since migrated to the dance floor down by the water when the gunshot went off.

McNab brought Carter, Davidson, Lucille, and Henry to the Garden Room for questioning. He was satisfied enough with the initial briefing to let the party continue. The four of them agreed to report to the police station the next day at noon to give official statements.

"I'm taking Carter back to our room," Davidson said.

"I'm fine," Carter insisted. "People will wonder where I am. Just give me a moment to pull myself together."

"No, Carter. Davidson is right," Lucille said. "You've been gone for a while anyway. We'll explain that you're not feeling well. Henry and I will say our goodnights to the guests."

"What makes you think you're in any better shape than Carter?" Henry said, stunned at his wife's ease. "You had a knife to your throat, for God's sake."

"Maybe the shock hasn't hit me yet," she answered. "Carter, Davidson, go. We will handle this."

William walked into the Garden Room, as if sensing something was amiss. His eyes widened at seeing Davidson but didn't ask any questions.

"William, I need to get Carter to her room without being seen."

He nodded and helped clear the path, making sure no one was near the public space as Carter and Davidson headed to the staircase. He walked behind to insure no one followed them. As they arrived at Carter's door and Carter slipped inside, Davidson turned to William and quickly explained that Ben was a bad actor but now he was gone.

William nodded, absorbing the news.

Davidson patted William on both shoulders. "The whole time I was away I took comfort knowing you were minding the inn."

"I only regret not acting on my suspicions about Ben Goodwin," William said, avoiding Davidson's eyes. "But there was nothing solid to go on."

"Don't blame yourself," Davidson said, his hand still on one of William's shoulders. "We were all taken in. You were my right-hand man before the inn opened and clearly Carter's right-hand man afterwards. I am in your debt. Thank you."

"Yes, well. You should get some rest," William said, turning to walk down the hallway. Davidson knew praise made William uncomfortable.

"See you in the morning."

"Yes, sir."

Lucille had Henry tie a cloth napkin on her wound, assuring him it didn't hurt and wasn't all that deep. She then covered herself in a cashmere shawl that matched her dress. She re-applied her lipstick and looked untouched by the incident. She and Henry bade goodnight to the departing families. Other guests sat on the veranda or strolled down to the water to enjoy the sunset. Two of the policemen were assigned to stay the night to insure there would be no more trouble.

"What a surreal evening," Lucille said as she and Henry made their way to their room. Henry nodded. Once inside, he said nothing as he inspected, cleaned, and better dressed Lucille's wound. Henry was not one for silence, so this made Lucille nervous. She noticed his trunk had returned and was relieved. She hoped he wouldn't have it sent back to The Empire House after the events of the day. She climbed into bed, heartened by the music below. At least the inn was still alive with joviality.

After Henry joined her, she broke the silence. "Henry, are you ever going to speak to me again? I can only imagine how angry you are. Please yell or maybe hit a pillow. Something."

"You think I'm angry at you?" He turned to her, bewilderment in his voice.

"Well, you haven't said a word."

"Yes, I am angry, Squirrel, but not at you, never at you." He pulled her close, his hand caressing her cheek. "I'm angry you were in harm's way, and I wasn't there to protect you. I'm angry at not seeing through Ben from the start. I'm angry for not learning more about the alcohol business when I first discovered it. I'm angry I let you leave my side for even a moment tonight. I'm overcome with fear that you could have died." He was shaking.

"But I didn't."

"Only through the greatest of good fortune. I could have lost you," he whispered, his eyes moist.

"But you didn't. I'm here, alive and quite well. Shouldn't we be grateful for that? Or that Davidson returned, and Ben was stopped? I was unsure about Ben from the start but thought myself overly protective of Carter. I'm free to go home now, knowing Carter is safe from harm."

Even with just the glow of the moon lighting his face she could tell he thought she had lost her mind. "A man is dead. There's a basement filled with liquor. Carter and Davidson could wind up in jail. And you think all is well?"

"No, they won't. Of that I'm certain. Carter shot Ben to save my life. Davidson had no part in any of Ben's shenanigans. He wasn't even here."

"What about Carter? She's the owner of an inn that stows dozens of crates of stolen liquor in its basement. She might have a hard time convincing the authorities of her innocence."

"I'm telling you, everything will be fine."

"I worry about you, dear wife. Sometimes I think your rose-colored glasses blind you to reality."

"But all's well, my love. I've had the most delightful summer, and now here you are in my bed. You were the only thing missing from my complete and utter happiness."

"There you go with your sunniness. For a woman who worries about everything big and small, you have this other side that inexplicably assumes the best. That is your strength — and maybe your weakness."

"I can be sunny because you look out for the clouds. See how compatible we are?"

He laughed and cupped her face. "Do you have any idea how much I love you? How much I need you at my side?"

"No, show me."

In the neighboring room, Carter was still insisting she was alright. Davidson just held her, his strength both calming and infuriating.

"You're treating me like a porcelain doll," she said. "I'm truly fine. He was threatening to kill Lucille. *Lucille!*"

He stared at her. "He was. Just like he left me and my crew to die. Nevertheless, I'm sure fatally shooting someone wasn't on your dance card for the evening."

"Neither was seeing you." And then she startled them both by kissing him fiercely and tugging at his pants. "Let's welcome you home."

He looked at her questioningly, then he succumbed to her desire and took over.

They made love urgently, while practically still dressed. It was as if Carter was releasing all her pent-up tension and fear. Then, as they peeled off their clothes, they made love again slowly and mindfully.

Afterwards, they lay spent, exhausted. Carter curled around Davidson, tracing her fingers over scars she hadn't seen before. Asking him about each one.

"It doesn't matter," he told her. "They have all healed. And now I am back here with you – and your freezing feet."

She chuckled and pushed her feet deeper under his calves for warmth. "Today was the first time I thought maybe you weren't returning after all. I asked you to send a sign," she laughed. "Boy, did you ever."

"We have a lot to sort out. You'll need to educate me about this place. You seemed to have filled it with just the kind of people you wanted."

"No, I haven't. You'll see. They're like us. Flawed, unusual, but kind – kinder than I have been to many of them."

After lying quietly in each other's arms for several minutes, Davidson broke the silence. "We both need to get some sleep. It's been quite a day with another ahead of us."

But Carter had a hard time falling asleep. There was so much she wanted to share with Davidson. She wanted to introduce him to Genevieve, sweet Isabelle, Estelle, the Schnedekers, the Connecticut Ladies too — all the eclectic and wonderful inhabitants of their inn. She wanted him to see the care with which she and Lucille had decorated. She wanted him to meet the fine staff. She wanted him to show him the bountiful vegetable and cutting gardens from which they sourced their produce and decorated their tables. She wanted him to hear his aunt's beautiful piano elegantly played by Genevieve during the dinner hour.

She wanted, she wanted, she wanted.... but there would be time for all of that. He was here, back at the inn, back in her bed. He would soon see how Rams Head unfolded under her guardianship. And he would inevitably want to add his own stamp, and she would have to learn the art of compromise – a first for her. But most important was the comfort of having someone to bounce off ideas, and to share the worries and rewards of this enormous undertaking.

Of course, her thoughts kept returning to Ben. She thought about the many ways he'd helped her. Ben gave her confidence and strength about the inn's future. He gave the inn financial solvency, albeit from illegal sources. He kept out the riffraff in a way she wouldn't have been able to on her own. She had been physically attracted to him, and yet he lied about everything. What did that say about her and her judgement of others?

Lying was the least of his offenses. Planning a shipwreck and leaving the entire crew, including Davidson, to die is pure evil. How can people seem so good yet be so bad? Does such darkness inevitably come to light? What if Davidson had perished along with the rest of the crew?

Would she have blindly believed the best of Ben? Is that all he would have presented to her and all she would have seen? Is that all we ever see in others – what we want to see?

Conversely, would Rams Head have become a criminal enterprise in the months ahead? Would she have been so invested as to have no power to escape it? Would Ben have skipped out of town if the authorities found out about the basement, letting her take the fall, as blithely as he did the sailors after confiscating their cargo? Davidson was right, Ben deserved to be punished. But did it have to be by her hand? Now she would have to live with that final image, and the guilt – or at least the horrific knowledge that she took a life.

A few hours later, Carter was awakened by her own shivering, followed by uncontrollable sobs. Davidson held her, caressing her face softly. "You're okay. I'm right here."

CHAPTER THIRTY-NINE

The next morning when Lucille and Henry descended the stairs for breakfast, she observed the Connecticut Ladies at their usual table and Vance there with them. That could be either a good or a bad sign, Lucille thought as she and Henry made their way across the dining room. She wanted Vance to consider Mae the proper lady she was.

"Good morning," she and Henry greeted Vance and the Connecticut Ladies on the way to their table.

Vance stood in greeting, bowing his head toward Lucille as he addressed Henry. "Mr. Nesbit, I checked out of The Empire House this morning. I assume I will be staying here now that rooms are available."

"Thank you, Vance. Yes, it's safe to say we'll be here for the remainder of our stay on Shelter Island."

While Lucille chatted with the ladies about the wedding, she heard Henry say, "For planning purposes, Vance, I will be here another week. If you have personal affairs you need to attend to, please feel free to return to the city."

Lucille strained to hear Vance's response, but Genevieve and Stuart appeared at that moment and enthusiastically joined in the wedding chitchat. Estelle then entered the room, and the small group gave her a round of applause.

Henry extended his hand to Estelle, who took it. He held it as he spoke. "My wife speaks so highly of you. I regret we haven't had more time to get to know one another."

Lucille noticed Estelle was wearing the same olive-hued traveling outfit she wore on the day she arrived. "You're leaving" she asked, the words catching in her throat.

"It's time," Estelle said to Lucille. Then to Henry, "Mrs. Nesbit has been most gracious during my stay, and I'm sorry I didn't have the opportunity to better get to know you as well, Mr. Nesbit." She then took the seat Elizabeth had been saving for her.

The wedding chatter resumed. No one asked about Carter, the gunshot, or any of the police activity of the night before. Could they possibly have missed it while enjoying the festivities?

Rather than wonder, Lucille leaned over to Genevieve and asked, "Did you hear the loud bang yesterday?"

"Yes," Genevieve said. "We thought it was a Sunday hunter, no?"

"I think so."

"Have you seen Carter and Ben?" Genevieve asked. "We wonder if they were inspired by the wedding and eloped."

Lucille groaned at the very notion. "I don't think so. I'm sure Carter will fill you in when she comes down."

"Yes, I'm sure she will," Henry added. "Lucille, let's take a table and enjoy breakfast before our morning walk."

Lucille stopped and squeezed Estelle's shoulders. She leaned down and whispered, "I'm terrible at goodbyes, so I won't say it. We'll just continue our talks in letters." Estelle nodded and patted Lucille's hands.

Lucille and Henry nodded good morning to the other guests and made their way to a table for two. "I wonder who will come down first," Henry whispered to Lucille. "Margaret and Curtis or Carter and Davidson? They will all have to eat at some point."

Lucille grinned. "We gave Margaret and Curtis a suite at the Mayfair as a honeymoon present, so therein lies the answer to your question."

"I'm not sure I was aware of that. Part of the wedding expenses?"

"Indeed. We may not see Carter and Davidson. She will probably serve herself, as there is a back staircase for the staff leading straight into the kitchen."

"Ahhh. Why didn't we use that?"

"Because someone had to greet the guests this morning."

"I see my Squirrel has turned into quite the hostess while I was away. You even seem to enjoy it. That will come in handy, as we will be hosting many business dinners when we return home."

"A glass of wine always helps."

"Let's be sure to acquire a crate or two from the basement," Henry said. "By the way, who exactly owns all those crates?"

"To be honest, I'm not sure."

Who owned the liquor was one question. A more pressing concern was what they would do with it now that the police were aware of its existence. It was 2 pm and the two couples sat with Chief McNab in his office. They had already given statements about the shooting and the events leading up to it. McNab assured them that no charges would be pressed, in light of the circumstances as sworn by all that it was self-defense. Unfortunately, no one knew anything about Ben's background and family, or whom to notify of his passing.

"Assuming that's even his real name," Davidson said. "You will probably want to send word to the Barbadian law enforcement, as they have an open case against him for a shipwreck he planned and executed. Eleven men died."

McNab nodded and made notes. "Onto the liquor he stored at Rams Head. Do we know where it came from, any documentation of any kind?"

Carter searched her memory. "He showed me a ledger early on, but I never saw it again. I suspect it was fake. There is an inventory binder from the utility closet, but that only lists the type of liquor in each crate, nothing identifying the owners."

"I'd like to see that binder," McNab said.

"Of course," Carter agreed.

Because Ben had relabeled the crates, there was no tracing them back to whomever or wherever he got them, unless such identification was inside the crates, which was doubtful. The books Carter had been keeping were bogus, just busywork created by Ben to create a patina of legitimacy and to insure she wouldn't ask any questions about the operation. Given Ben had money in the beginning, maybe he did collect fees for hiding the liquor, but never told the owners where he was bringing it and had no intention of giving it back. Carter honestly didn't know.

"A man once visited Rams Head claiming to be an owner of some crates," Carter recalled, "maybe he was legitimate or maybe he was sent by Ben to test whether I would let him in the basement, which I didn't. Did you search Ben's cottage on Little Ram? Maybe something there will shed light on the source of the alcohol."

"We went there early this morning. Nothing." McNab sighed, throwing up his hands.

"He had a worker named Bailey who seemed to know him well – perhaps you could find him? Also, Ben used to travel to the city regularly. Maybe he has an address there or even more storage there?" Carter offered.

"I'm not going down any rabbit holes for this," the Chief said. "I'll contact the New York Police Department and let them check into this if they want. Insofar as the liquor, tell no one. It's stolen goods, and we have no idea who it's stolen from. You and I can work together to figure this out, Davidson."

There was something about the way McNab said it that made Carter suspect there was more to that statement than the words suggested. Would McNab want to be partners with Davidson? Perhaps offer protection in return for access of some sort? She was speculating, of course.

"Some of the alcohol is legitimately mine," Davidson noted. "He stole crates from the ship I captained, the one he steered onto the rocks. I should be able to identify those crates at the very least. I sat in a Barbadian hellhole for what he did."

"How did you get out?" McNab asked.

"One of his Barbadian cohorts, a Phil Johnson, was arrested for armed robbery," Davidson said, "and he spilled the beans about the shipwreck — and Goodwin – in order to save his own hide. That's when they released me."

McNab decided their business was finished for the day. He had a number of queries to make on his end and would notify the group of anything he found out. "Please keep all of this to yourselves as much as possible. This is an open investigation."

"May I tell Graham?" Carter asked. "He introduced me to Ben, though I'm sure he had nothing to do with Ben's chicanery."

"I grew up with Graham, he's a good guy," McNab nodded. "Tell him the bare minimum, for now. I won't be telling anyone what happened in your basement yesterday, and neither will my men. The less others know, the better for you, Miss Carter."

"Thank you," Carter said.

The foursome stood to leave. Henry stopped, "Ben clearly left some interested parties in his wake, like this Bailey or that Romano fellow. This is far from over."

"We'll deal with them," Davidson said. "I'll be waiting for whoever shows up."

"So will our department," McNab added. "Maybe we can smoke them out. Can you give me a room in your inn to station a man?"

"As long as he's single and handsome," Lucille said, adding, "we have some single ladies I'm thinking about."

"Lucille, do you ever stop being you?" Carter asked incredulously.

"No, never," she answered, while Henry shook his head beside her.

Henry and Davidson had met only a few times before Davidson's return, and the two didn't have much in common. But Henry appreciated Davidson's openness about Ben and the alcohol. He wasn't trying to hide anything from anyone — at least not until prohibition took effect. And Davidson appreciated Henry was willing to take a back seat in all of this – something he gathered Henry was not accustomed to doing.

On the way back to the inn, Henry asked Davidson, "what if the actual owners want their liquor back?"

"Nothing is labeled, and my guess is the owners don't even know where the crates ended up."

"Do you intend to keep them?"

"Haven't figured that out, but there's no one to return them to. I doubt this Romano guy will tell me who or where the crates came from, and I'm not about to turn anything over to him." Davidson rubbed his forehead. "I've been back for 24 hours. My head is exploding from all of this. I'm famished and would love some lunch, how about the rest of you?"

"Yes. Besides, we need to get some weight on you," Carter said.

"Why thank you, darling," he said.

"I'll never lie to you Davidson."

"I wouldn't have it any other way." He kissed her hand.

"It's the lies of omission you have to look out for," Henry said with a tight smile.

"Now, now, Henry," Lucille interjected, trying to lighten the mood. "You and I have no more secrets between us. That is unless you have something to share about Vance's interest in Mae."

"I know nothing about that. Gentlemen don't talk about such things," Henry said.

"True. Men don't ask the right questions," Lucille answered. "Leave it to Carter and me."

CHAPTER FORTY

When they arrived back at Rams Head, it was past the lunch service, so Carter and Lucille instructed the men to fetch some wine from the bar and pick a table on the veranda while the two women searched the pantry for food – either leftovers from the wedding or anything else they could forage. It soon became apparent that Lucille was helpless in the kitchen, so Carter told her to gather plates, utensils and napkins instead.

"Sure, where are they kept?"

"You'd make a lousy detective, Lucille. Look about, will you?"

After rummaging through countless cabinets drawers, Lucille finally located the needed dinnerware and set it on a tray she found in vertical slots by the door.

"Carter, before I forget, I need to tell you about seeing Isabelle with the Schnedekers."

"Oh no, what?" Carter stopped to look at her.

"Nothing bad. I just saw them hug one another yesterday. Isabelle seems to have warm feelings toward them. Maybe they are the right parents for this baby after all."

Carter leaned against the butcher block counter, having already found leftover Beef Wellington and bread. "Lucille, we are two halves of the same brain. I too have given this a lot of thought. If we give the baby to a church or a Christian network of some sort, we will have no idea what became of him or her. I've heard stories of farmers adopting children to work the fields. And that's far from the worst scenario. Whereas we know the Schnedekers are loving and, by all appearances, have the means to provide the child with a wonderful home."

"My thoughts as well," Lucille agreed. "They might not be the world's idea of a perfect family, but neither was mine."

"Nor anyone's for that matter. I worry about giving a child to a couple that are not legally married, even if they are married in God's eyes, which I've come to believe they are."

"I admire how you've come around on that. My only fear is that some authority will hear of two men raising a child and try to have the child removed. Or what happens if Isabelle comes to visit us down the road and sees the Schnedekers with a red-headed child?"

"Oh Lucille, your worries never end, do they?"

"Worry is another word for love," Lucille said as if stating a fact.

Carter looked at her for a moment and finally understood her dear friend. "It is indeed. But let's not let fear get in the way of love. We'll figure it out if and when something happens, I promise." She smiled. "The men are waiting, though I like they are getting to know each another. Is this enough of a lunch?"

"I hope so. If not, dinner is a short time away."

As they were finishing their dessert of leftover wedding cake, Lucille spotted the Schnedekers walking up the lawn heading toward the veranda.

"Edwina, Alfred, hello!" Lucille called out. She and Carter exchanged glances, given they had just spoken about them.

The couple arrived at the table and motioned for Henry and Davidson to sit down. "Don't let us disturb you," Alfred said. "We've come for cocktails and dinner at our favorite place." They looked at Davidson quizzically.

"Goodness, of course, you haven't met," Carter said. "Mr. and Mrs. Schnedeker, this is my fiancé Davidson Surrey. You may remember that he was, umm, detained at sea."

"So that's how we're describing it," Davidson said with that twinkle in his eye, shaking their hands. "Pleased to meet you both."

"The pleasure is all ours. We were certain you'd return, weren't we, Alfred? Life has a way of righting itself."

"Thank you," Davidson said.

"We look forward to your wedding," Alfred added. "This place certainly knows how to host them."

"Fireworks and all," Edwina added mischievously.

Lucille opened her mouth to speak and quickly closed it.

"We'll be at our favorite outdoor table," Alfred said.

The foursome smiled at the couple as they walked away. "We have much explaining to do," Carter said. "I don't like secrets. Ben quoted you as saying a small hole can sink a large ship."

"I never said that," Davidson said, forehead wrinkling. "But it's true in this case. We won't volunteer the information, but we won't conceal it either. Let's see what and how it comes out. For now, it's an open investigation and our secrecy is required, as the Chief said."

They all nodded.

Davidson smiled. "By the way, I noticed the ram mirror I ordered. It looks great. Did the shop deliver it?"

Lucille and Carter looked at each other. "Yes darling," Carter said. "It was delivered. Such a fitting gift to the inn. William helped to hang it."

Margaret and Curtis received many gifts the day of the wedding, but some were still arriving days later. So, when a box marked "fragile" arrived for Carter, she assumed it was a gift for them. But because her name was clearly written on the label, Carter proceeded to open the brown shipping carton to discover a large turquoise box. Her name was on the envelope tucked under the white silk ribbon. Just then Lucille joined Carter in the Garden Room.

"Ooooh Tiffany!" Lucille squealed. "My engagement ring is from Tiffany. Is that a gift for Margaret and Curtis?"

"No, look." She held up the envelope and quickly opened it to read the card inside.

Just so we're crystal clear.
Thank you. RW

Inside the Tiffany box was a large lead crystal bowl, beautifully carved, its many facets refracting the light of the room. Lucille read the note and looked up, her eyes questioning.

Carter explained, "Isabelle's mother, Regina Worthington. Not that she ever used her first name with me. But she must have used the phrase 'crystal clear' a dozen times to drum into my head that she didn't want to know anything about her daughter's baby."

"What an impressive - and expensive! — way of reinforcing that dreadful message."

"What am I supposed to do with such a thing? Who do I say it came from? Mrs. Worthington wants no association with us."

Lucille considered the question. "Say it's from me. I'll make a fuss that it finally arrived. My congratulations on the opening of the inn."

Carter then stared at the bowl and sighed. "It's beautiful, yes, but it's also sad, even ugly, when you think of the intention behind it. As I've said, I don't like secrets."

"Maybe someday we won't have to keep the secret, if an older Isabelle ever returns here. But there's joy in that bowl too — just think of the Schnedekers reaction when they find out they have a baby on the way."

"Let us wait to tell them until after it is born."

"But they will need time to make preparations."

"Lucille, surely you can see this is a delicate transaction."

Lucille made a face. "Very well, but I need to be here to help organize a baby shower."

"After the baby is born and Isabelle goes home, perhaps."

"Right, Isabelle. Giving up a baby would be traumatic at any age. Goodness, must there always be some melancholy behind happiness?"

"Maybe it won't be as sad for her," Carter said, remembering their chat while polishing silver.

"I'm hoping that is also true for Elizabeth. She'll have a new home, and we'll all be here for her. Then we have your wedding coming up! And who knows, maybe Mae and Vance — though Mae confided to me she is reluctant to date anyone, including Vance. Though he seems hellbent on pursuing her, so we shall see. In any event, this is how one builds a community."

"You make me laugh with your cheerful visions. Maybe Romano will marry Cora."

"That's terrible," Lucille scowled. "How could you even joke about such a thing? Besides, Graham's son Tim has that one all lined up, I could tell."

"On a serious subject—"

"It's *all* serious, Carter—"

"You and Henry will build a house here, promise?"

"Of course, we will. And so will Stuart for Genevieve. And I'm hoping Estelle will return. She can stay at my house."

As the two women left the Garden Room, atop a mahogany credenza, beneath Lucille's gilded mirror sat Carter's crystal bowl and all its fractured dreams.

THE END

POSTSCRIPT

- Estelle returned to a city torn by racial strife. Part of what became known nationally as Red Summer of 1919, the Chicago Race Riot, July 27–August 3, was particularly brutal: 38 people died, 537 were injured, and between 1000 and 2000 people lost their homes, most of them Black families.

- The Volstead Act, passed in October 1919, provided for the enforcement of the 18th Amendment prohibiting the manufacture, sale or transport of alcohol. It became effective on January 17, 1920. The 18th Amendment was repealed by the 21st Amendment in December 1933 — the only amendment ever repealed by another.

- The 19th Amendment, which gave all women the right to vote, was enacted in August 1920 when Tennessee became the 36th state to ratify it. Alice Paul, an outspoken suffragist leader, said the amendment passed "because it became more expedient for those in control of the Government to aid suffrage than to oppose it."

- During Prohibition, Shelter Island was an active bootlegging/rumrunning mecca, valued for its accessible ports and proximity to New York City.

Prohibition brought crime to the island, and many policemen turned a blind eye as they profited from the illicit trade.

- Sylvester Manor is now an educational farm and research center. A visitor can view the historical gardens, the attic where enslaved people slept, and their burial place marked by its engraved memorial rock.

- Rams Head Inn continues to welcome guests to Ram Island. Looking much as it did 100 years ago, the restaurant/inn is now wholly owned and operated by another woman, Aandrea Carter.

ACKNOWLEDGMENTS

"It takes a village" applies to many things, including writing a novel. Especially an historic one. I have countless people who have helped with ideas, critical reading and encouragement. I'm indebted to each person listed for different reasons, including for their time, love and patience: Michael Boyes, Cathy Bezozo, Susan Jaques, Patricia Laudati, Steve Sumser, Paul Donaher, Francesca Hayslett, Hilary Leff, Nancy Alderman, Linda Eisenberg, Stella Sands, Richard Schnexneider, Benjamin Weil, Marilyn Carter, David Currie, Lenore and Sharon Neier.

I want to thank my friend Esther Newberg, the legendary literary agent, for believing in this story and working with her associate Estie Berkowitz to spread the word. To have Esther in your corner is all the validation a writer needs. A special thank you to Michael Engler – a dear friend and executive productive and director of Downtown Abbey and The Gilded Age. He inspired so many moments in this story and kept them true to the era. I'm forever Indebted. And a huge thanks to Andra Miller for her considered and constructive editing.

Aandrea Carter, the current proprietress of the Rams Head Inn, was the inspiration and passion behind this story. I have never met a stronger woman or a more loving friend. Every day, she teaches me anything is possible and the value of believing in oneself. Everyone should have such a friend.

And of course, my husband Hal Neier. There is no greater support than a spouse who loves you. He read every word more times than he'd probably care to remember. I love you.

KATHLEEN BOYES is a New York-based fashion and beauty writer.
She collaborated with Calvin Klein on his book *Calvin* and co-Authored Donna Karan's memoir, *My Journey,* for which Boyes recited the audiobook.
Other books Boyes co-authored include Trish McEvoy's *The Power of Makeup, Fete: The Wedding Experience, Tommy Hilfiger's New England* as well as *Cindy Crawford's Basic Face.* Boyes began her writing career as a fashion editor for Women's Wear Daily and W.